Sin Against the Blood

Artur Dinter

Sin Against the Blood

by

Artur Dinter

Translated from the 1921 German edition
by Mildred Grau

Edited by
Thomas Dalton, PhD

Clemens & Blair, LLC
— 2023 —

CLEMENS & BLAIR, LLC

Clemens & Blair, LLC, is a non-profit educational publisher.
www.clemensandblair.com

Library of Congress Cataloging-in-Publication Data

Dinter, Artur (1876-1948)
Sin Against the Blood
German original: *Die Sünde wider das Blut* (1917/1921)

p. cm.
Includes bibliographical references

ISBN 978-8987-7263-34
(pbk.: alk. paper)

Fiction

Printing number: 9 8 7 6 5 4 3 2 1

Printed in the United States of America on acid-free paper.

Acknowledgment

The editor would like to acknowledge the assistance of Ms. Mildred Grau in the translation of this text from the German original. She has provided invaluable assistance for this project. Of course, the editor assumes full responsibility for the final edits and the final text.

From the original German edition.

CONTENTS

Sin Against the Blood

INTRODUCTION

THOMAS DALTON

It is not often that a fictional work—let alone a novel—is able to capture the public's imagination even as it promotes a striking and controversial worldview. And it is even rarer when it becomes a popular success. But such was Artur Dinter's 1917 novel *Die Sünde wider das Blut—Sin Against the Blood*. He managed to combine a compelling fictional story with a largely factual account of the Jewish assault on the German nation, and he did it in such a way as to achieve a true literary success; his book had sold an astonishing 250,000 copies by the time Hitler came to power in 1933.

Before reviewing some of the main themes, let me offer a few details of Dinter's life. He was born in Mulhouse, Germany (now, France) in 1876, and raised a strict Catholic; his Christian views would play a prominent part throughout his life. He attended university at both Munich and Strasbourg, studying chemistry and philosophy—an odd combination, but one that indicates the breadth of his thinking. Dinter earned his doctorate in chemistry in 1903, at the age of 27. But his humanistic side never left him, and he continued to write literature, including the prize-winning play *The Smugglers* in 1906.

From 1903 onward, he took a variety of jobs, including work at a botanical garden, as a teacher, and as a theater manager. He soon became director of theaters in Rostock and Berlin. When World War One began in 1914, Dinter (age 38) enlisted, fought at the front, was injured, contracted cholera, and ultimately received the Iron Cross.

It is unclear when Dinter had his first negative experiences with Jews, but it was likely around 1910, during his time as theater director; Jews dominated the entertainment sector in Germany at that time, and they surely provided Dinter with a practical schooling in malicious Jewish activities. During the war years, he apparently also read much by Houston Stewart Chamberlain—a prolific writer and a man who was not fainthearted in his critiques of Jews. And Dinter could not have missed the strong Jewish hand in WWI, and especially in Germany's defeat and in the subsequent rise of the pro-Jewish Weimar regime.[1] Adolf Hitler—a man 13 years Dinter's junior—was equally disgusted, and would soon form a German nationalist party, the NSDAP.

---

[1] For details, see my book *The Jewish Hand in the World Wars* (2019).

A Budding Novelist

Sometime during the war years, probably as he was recovering from injury and illness in 1916, Dinter evidently began writing. He was concerned with the presence and activities of Jews in Germany, which was a well-established and popular issue at that time. As early as 1850, the composer Richard Wagner (working under a pseudonym) began to warn the Germans of the adverse effects of Jews in their midst. By 1875, Frederick Millingen was writing about "the conquest of the world by the Jews," and in 1879, German journalist Wilhelm Marr could speak of "the victory of Jewry over Germandom." In 1887, a man who would later work with Dinter, Theodor Fritsch, released the initial edition of his wildly popular *Anti-Semitic Catechism* (later, *The Handbook on the Jewish Question*).[2] So there was a widely-known body of work critiquing the Jews, well before Dinter began his writing.

Apart from the usual concerns about finances and political corruption, Dinter was especially worried about the Jews' detrimental 'biological' influence. Jews, for him, were a racial group above all; religion was secondary. As such, they embodied certain intrinsic qualities that were objectively harmful to the noble (and largely innocent) German people. There was not yet a science of genetics, but as a doctoral scientist himself, Dinter understood that there was a physical, biological essence—something in "the blood," as they said then—that marked Jews as an inferior and dangerous element. Worst of all, this Jewish blood could contaminate noble German blood through sexual intercourse. Both the German woman and any offspring were permanently and irrevocably damaged by sexual relations with a Jew.

But rather than writing a typical anti-Semitic prose text, Dinter elected to put his creative writing skills to work and construct a novel that would illuminate these themes by casting them in a way that might reach a mass audience. Thus emerged the story of a brilliant young chemist, Hermann Kämpfer—literally, a 'fighter,' in German—who would learn the hard way about the deleterious effects of Jews in German society. Through his research and his personal relations, he would come face-to-face with the consequences of a Jewish presence in his life.

The broader concern is what is called miscegenation—literally, a mixing (*miscere*) of race or genes (*genus*). The Germans called it 'racial

---

[2] For reproductions of all these works, see *Classic Essays on the Jewish Question: 1850 to 1945* (T. Dalton, ed.; 2022).

defilement,' meaning, the debasing or contamination of the Germanic / Nordic gene pool. I will return to this topic momentarily.

In any case, Dinter completed his novel in late 1916 and published it in 1917, well before the end of the war. Clearly, the 'sin against the blood' was the primary theme, but Dinter was also concerned to articulate Jewish corruption of (as he saw it) true Christianity. In some way not fully explained, Jews had manipulated and rewritten an originally Gentile Old Testament, and the life of an 'Aryan Jesus,' and turned them into something inherently Jewish. For Dinter, God is not the Jewish God; the prophets are not Jewish prophets; and Jesus is not a Jewish rabbi—despite all appearances to the contrary. This provides us with a fascinating side-theme to his novel; again, I will elaborate further below.

Life Postwar

In the immediate aftermath of the war, Dinter got in touch with leading anti-Semite Theodor Fritsch, and they and others established a new group: the German Peoples' Protection and Defiance League (*Deutschvölkischer Schutz- und Trutzbund*), designed to protect the German people from the pernicious Jewish influence. The League lasted only a few years but was very influential, especially on Hitler and his emerging nationalist movement.

Into the 1920s, Dinter formed his own small nationalist party, but it quickly got subsumed by the flamboyant power of Hitler's nascent movement. Dinter soon openly sided with the NSDAP, even through their ill-fated Beer Hall Putsch of 1923, which landed Hitler in prison for a year. In late 1924, Hitler named Dinter as party leader of the state of Thuringia; in 1925, he was elevated to *Gauleiter*.

Unfortunately, Dinter's fervent Christianity soon got him into trouble with Hitler, who preferred a relatively neutral stance on religion. Dinter believed that the NSDAP ('Nazi') party should lead a religious revival, one that would fully de-Judaize Christianity; but he got little support. Hitler relieved Dinter of his position in 1927 and had him ousted from the party in 1928—all of which caused him to become openly critical of Hitler and the NS movement. Thus he spent all of the 1930s and the years of World War Two in a kind of 'opposition' role, without much influence. He was arrested after the war and given a minor fine for his 'anti-Semitic' writings. Dinter died in 1948 at the age of 71.

Racial Defilement

Despite his falling-out with the National Socialists, Dinter remained a well-known writer throughout his life, and his books remained influential. In 1937, a writer and teacher named Fritz Fink wrote a small pamphlet entitled "The Jewish Question in Education," which was designed as a short guide for teachers on the Jewish racial issue, so that they might adequately prepare and warn German girls of the dangers. The pamphlet was endorsed and widely promoted by Julius Streicher in his weekly paper *Der Stürmer*. Fink's pamphlet gives a very concise explanation of the issue and cites Dinter's *Sin Against the Blood* as essential reading on the topic. I quote it below at length.

The pamphlet begins with a statement that "the poison of Jewish blood entered our people's bloodstream thousands upon thousands of times," via sexual relations with German women and girls. Fink notes that the Nuremberg Laws prohibit marriage and sexual relations between Germans and Jews, which he views as a positive starting point. But a clearer understanding is required. Fink elaborates:

> We recall the knowledge gained earlier in the sciences; we extend it. We learn from the animal breeder; we study the offspring of his animals. He tells us that he breeds only pairs of the same race. Only that ensures that the valuable characteristics of the various races remain intact and improve. Each animal breeder can affirm that crossing the races always results in a bastard, and that such a degenerate animal is worthless. That is clear from thousands of examples.
>
> We then turn to people. Why should they be exempt from these laws? We use pictures as an aid: pictures of children of German-blooded parents, pictures of Jewish children, both of whose parents are full-blooded Jews, and pictures of children who are a mixture of Jew and German. We make the comparisons. We are most interested in the last group of children, those of mixed race. We look to see from which race most of the characteristics come. We see the Jew in his face, his body, his appearance and manner, his thinking, feeling and behavior. We do not need to investigate deeply. Everything about him speaks of the Jew, of discord, of degenerate blood. The person of mixed race is a lamentable creature, tossed back and forth by the blood of his two races. We hold

that the bastard is a burden to a people. He weakens it. His offspring carry on the racial degeneration.

I urge each teacher to encourage the reading of Dr. Dinter's book *The Sin Against the Blood*. It speaks in a stronger way to our more mature girls than the sweet stuff that one still finds here and there. In schools where girls are trained to be teachers, I think that introducing the racial and Jewish Question in this way is the most important task. I know from experience how helpless, inexperienced, and ignorant some young female teachers are about this problem.

The sin against the blood passes its curse not only to the mixed-race offspring, but rather the curse also sticks to the defiled mother, never leaving her for the rest of her life. Racial defilement is racial death. Racial defilement is bloodless murder. A woman defiled by the Jew can never rid her body of the foreign poison she has absorbed. She is lost to her people. What we have learned from animal breeders is just as true here. Our ancestors knew this; we forgot it.

Fink then explains that, ironically, the Jews themselves know this law well, and they respect it religiously. "Only one person guarded it through the millennia as a valuable treasure: the Jew!" We need only recall the basics of Jewish history:

At a time during the Babylonian Captivity [597-538 BC] when the Jews took Gentile wives and Jewish blood threatened to decay and decline, Ezra entered the scene—the savior of the Jews. He gave the people that law of blood to which Jewry today owes its existence. He forbade marriage with non-Jewesses. He forced the Jews to drive their Gentile wives into the wilderness. Ezra's laws are holy to the Jews to this day.

The Jew thus recognizes the significance of keeping blood pure. But he persuades other people of the opposite. He preaches racial mixing to other peoples, bastardization. "Why does he do this?" the girls will ask. Because he sees in racial mixing the surest way to break the life force of the nations, to drive them into the depth of destruction. His goal is to contribute to this process of bastardization wherever he is able. The defilement and deracination of Gentile women by the Jews is not the result of a blood-driven Jewish sexual drive. It is far more the result of devilish planning and calculation.

Fink then explains that such acts of devilry are not just a result of some rogue actors but rather are built into the structure of Judaism itself. As documented in the Talmud, all Jews are directed to defile Gentile women:

> This gives us once again the opportunity to speak to our female youth of the Talmud and to discover that the Talmud not only permits the defilement of Gentile women, it makes it a duty. Once again, we encounter the great Jewish hatred, the great Jewish desire for annihilation, when we read what the Talmud says about Gentile women:
>
> "The Jew may abuse Gentile women." (Maimonides: *Jad Chasakah* 2,2.)
>
> "All Gentile women are whores." (*Shulchan Aruch*: Even Ha'ezer 6,8.)
>
> "A Gentile girl who is three years and a day old may be defiled." (Talmud: Avodah Zarah 37a,1.)
>
> "A man [Jew] may do everything with a woman that he is able to do. He may treat her like a piece of meat that comes from the butcher. He may eat it raw, grilled, cooked, or smoked." (Talmud: Nedarim 20b,4.)
>
> "It is forbidden for Jews to commit adultery with the wife of a Jew. Adultery with the wife of a Gentile is permitted." (Talmud: Sanhedrin 52b,22.)

I have confirmed all the above statements; they are indeed documented in the Talmud and in the shorter abridgement, the *Shulchan Aruch*.[3]

But it is an interesting thesis: that a woman is somehow permanently damaged by sexual intercourse with a Jew—or presumably with any lesser

---

[3] For a good study of this latter work, see E. Bischoff, *The Book of the Shulchan Aruch* (T. Dalton, ed.; 2023).

race or ethnicity. It's hard to see how this would play out in a modern, scientific, biological sense; but perhaps there is another kind of damage—psychological, moral, or spiritual. Presumably there is equal, or greater, damage from intercourse with blacks; but what about Latinos, or Asians? And is it possible to permanently *enhance* one's being via intercourse with more elevated races, such as pure Nordics? And what exactly is the evidence from the science of animal husbandry, that Dinter refers to? Lots of interesting questions to pursue.

Aryan Jesus?

As I noted above, Dinter is a committed and unabashed Christian; he believes in Jesus, and he believes that Christ came to bring "the message of his father" to humanity, and to be "a powerful example" to us. (What exactly that message is, and what specific behaviors we are supposed to emulate, remain unclear.) But Dinter is also a committed racialist: committed to the view that the Aryan peoples are the best and brightest of humanity. He is further utterly convinced that the Jews are the literal "sons of the devil" and represent a grave threat to Aryan wellbeing. This odd mixture of commitments puts Dinter into a terrible fix because, God forbid, his Jesus seems to have been a Jew! Now he has a lot of explaining—and explaining away—to do.

And explain away he does. His Chapter 16 is a remarkable deviation from the first 15 chapters; here, he engages in a lengthy and scholarly attempt—including copious notes—to prove that Jesus was an Aryan, that his disciples were Aryans, that his message was Aryan, and that the Jewish milieu in which he lived caused his true message to get distorted. Dinter thus patches together an impressive array of data in an attempt to make his case. Perhaps his arguments were persuasive in 1910 and 1920, but today, they fall far short of the mark.

Consider what we know today. Everything we know, or think we know, about Jesus comes from the letters of Paul and the four Gospels; there simply is no other source. (The "lost Gospels" are a possible source, but those are highly contentious on many grounds, so I will pass them over here.) No one else wrote about Jesus: *no one* during his lifetime (say, 0 to 30 AD), *no one* (save Paul) for two decades after his crucifixion, and *no one* (save the anonymous Gospel writers) for four decades after that. We have a few words from the Jew Josephus circa 93 AD, a few words from Tacitus, Suetonius, and Pliny circa 110 AD, but otherwise nothing at all. This alone is remarkably telling, given that the Son of God—or perhaps

God himself—had allegedly just come to Earth to save humanity. If he was so unimpressive that no one but a few ragtag Jews wrote about him, then perhaps he was not the miracle man that many claim.

In any case, let's take the New Testament at face value for a moment. There, we learn a vital fact: Jesus, by all accounts, was both a religious and ethnic (racial) Jew. Start with his mother, the "virgin" Mary; she clearly was a Jewess. Mary was a blood relative of Elizabeth, of the tribe of Levi (Luke 1:5, 1:36). When Jesus was born, she, along with Joseph, "performed everything according to the [Jewish] law of the Lord" (Luke 2:39). And she and Joseph attended Passover services in Jerusalem "every year" (Luke 2:41). Since Mary was a Jew, this alone makes Jesus a Jew, on the orthodox reading, because Jewishness is matrilineal, being passed along by the mother; if you are born of a Jewess, you are a Jew.

What about Jesus' father? Let's set aside the nonsense about God being his father, which is nothing more than regurgitated Homeric mythology about demi-gods on Earth. Joseph was of the "House of David," as Luke (1:27) informs us. And as noted above, Joseph rigorously followed Jewish law and attended Passover annually. He was clearly an observant Jew, and (presumably) the biological father of Jesus.

Paul obviously thought Jesus was a Jew. In the early Galatians (4:4) he says that Jesus was "born under the [Jewish] law," and in Romans (9:5), he declares his own Jewishness ("my kinsmen by race...are Israelites"), adding that "of their race, according to the flesh, is the Christ." That is, *a racial Jew*.

Likewise, the Gospel writers clearly viewed their Savior as a Jew. Jesus is repeatedly called 'rabbi'.[4] He was circumcised (Luke 2:21) and celebrated Passover (John 2:13). The Gospel of Matthew opens with these words: "The book of the genealogy of Jesus Christ, son of David, son of Abraham." Even the non-gospel Hebrews remarks that "it is evident that our Lord was descended from Judah" (7:14). Jesus regularly attended the local synagogue (Luke 4:16). He himself told the people that he came "to fulfill the [Jewish] law and the [Jewish] prophets" (Matt 5:17). And of course, everyone thought of him as "king of the Jews" (Matt 2:2; John 19:3).

It could hardly be clearer: both by genetic heritage and according to his evident beliefs and practices, Jesus was a Jew. He was a biological Jew—surely embodying all those wonderful Jewish phenotypical characteristics—and he was a religious Jew.

---

[4] Mark 9:5, 11:21, 14:45; Matt 26:25; John 1:38, 1:49; 3:2.

Dinter, though, will have none of this. "Rather an eagle might hatch from a clutch of crow's eggs, or a hyena give birth to a lion!" The "irreconcilable spiritual contrast" between Jesus and the Jews proves the point, as do Jesus' thundering attacks on the Jews themselves ("brood of snakes," "sons of the devil," etc.). Jesus emphasized the inner kingdom, whereas Jews are all about the exterior, material world of money, gold, and power. Jesus' God is kind and loving, whereas Yahweh is cruel and vindictive, a godly dealmaker. Jesus was from Galilee, notes Dinter, and Galilee was a Gentile stronghold, he claims; "Aryan blood was repeatedly transplanted to northern Galilee." "Jesus could not possibly have been a Jew"; rather, says Dinter, he was an Amorite—the people of present-day Syria and Iraq, who were "tall, blond, blue-eyed, people of fair complexion." In sum: "To consider Jesus a Jew, and the Jews as the founders of our Christian religion, is one of the greatest and most fatal failures of world history!"

Unfortunately, Dinter takes many dubious points as unchallenged assumptions, and he fails to consider some rather obvious conclusions. First, modern scholarship shows that Galilee was far from the "Gentile stronghold" that has been portrayed. Working at about the same time as Dinter, E. W. Masterson wrote of a "Jewish Galilee," one that was "hemmed in on all sides by hostile [Gentile] neighbors".[5] More recently, we now have such works as *The Myth of a Gentile Galilee* (2002) by Mark Chancey, who acknowledges the stubborn idea but notes "how little data there is to support such a claim [of a Gentile Galilee]." Archeological evidence from Nazareth is scarce, but what we do have shows "evidence for Jewish inhabitants at several sites, [but] very little evidence for Gentiles." Of the major, nearby town of Sepphoris, evidence of Gentiles is "extremely limited" during Jesus' life; by contrast, says Chancey, there is "ample evidence" of Jews there at that time. In sum, while not denying that some Gentiles lived there, evidence for them is "practically invisible"; and as a confirmation, Chancey notes that Gentiles "are not prominent in literary discussions of Galilee either".[6]

But there are more fundamental problems. Given the utter lack of contemporary documentation on Jesus, and the general understanding that Biblical-scale 'miracles' are fantasy-fiction, we can say with certainty that a miracle-working Son of God never existed. Rather, Jesus—if he existed at all—was an ordinary, mortal Rabbi, likely a preacher for the poor, who agitated against Roman rule and got himself crucified as a result.

---

[5] "Galilee in the time of Christ," *Biblical World* 32(6).
[6] Such as by Josephus.

A few years later, an elite Jew named Saul of Tarsus had a brilliant insight: he could use Jesus' story in altered form, turning him into a divine being who died to save humanity. Saul—now 'Paul'—created a bogus story, a hoax, which he then propagated among the Gentile masses in order to turn them against Rome, toward the Jews, and to generally foist a defective and detrimental morality on them. Jesus the mortal Rabbi became Jesus the savior of all humanity—a story that ran counter to many orthodox Jewish beliefs, thus turning many Jews against Paul and his constructed Jesus.

After Paul died around the year 70, his Jewish followers elaborated on the Jesus hoax by constructing a 'Jesus biography', Jesus 'miracles,' and Jesus 'sayings'—none of which existed for Paul. These became the four Gospels, appearing for the first time long after the crucifixion: Mark (70 AD), Luke (85), Matthew (85), and John (95), according to current consensus.

Dinter knew little of this. The state of archeology in 1920 simply did not support such conclusions. If he had, he might have reconsidered his views. He might, in fact, have adopted an even *harsher* stance against the Jews. He might have seen Paul and the Gospel writers as masterful liars who pushed a bogus story on the innocent masses simply for the benefit of Jews and Israel.

And in any case, Dinter's claim about an Aryan Jesus is implausible on its face. Would the Jews really adopt a tall, blond Gentile as their "king"? Jews have never been known to bow down to Gentiles. And then, what about all that Biblical evidence of Jesus as a racial Jew? Were they lying? Perhaps they were! If so, then how much of the New Testament can we even accept at all? The story simply does not hold together.

But fortunately for Dinter—and for us—the debate about an Aryan Jesus is not central to his story. Even if we allow that he was flat-out wrong on this point, all of his other critiques of Jews, the Jewish mindset, and Jewish literature are valid. In fact, as I suggested above, they become even *more* valid than Dinter might have suspected. His story becomes stronger, not weaker, once we abandon the Aryan Jesus myth.

But now, lest I give away too much of the plot, I must turn things over to our author and his fascinating story—a compelling mixture of fiction and truth, all designed to impart a profound moral lesson to the reader. Whether he succeeds or not shall be for the reader to decide.

Sin Against the Blood

Sin Against the Blood

—1—

Do not believe every spirit, but test the
spirits to see whether they are of God.
1 John 4:1

In the large room of the chemistry laboratory of the University, a fire was
still burning at midnight. On the workbench of assistant and private lecturer Dr. Hermann Kämpfer, all variety of chemical equipment was in operation. In the corner of the hall, behind the strong glass walls of a fume closet
built into the wall, a cloudy liquid boiled in a powerful glass flask resting
on a high iron tripod. Under the unstoppable blasts of flame, the molecules
raged and howled in confusion. Chased by unspeakable pain, they tore
themselves free from the coherence of the boiling flux and escaped through
the neck of the flask into the charcoal burner, only to be purged by such
vile agony and pain and to waft into the receiver as crystal-clear, silent
drops. The bumping and pounding of the piston and the thudding and whizzing of the water pump filled the wide, reverberant hall with a loud, consistent
noise of such intensity that one felt as though one were in a factory.

In the middle of the worktable, the young researcher, a blond man
about 30 years old, sat on a wooden bench. He had just made a clearing
about the width of his chest in the tangled undergrowth of glasses, flasks,
pistons, and tubes that proliferated on the worktable. He covered the area
he created with a fresh sheet of shiny white paper, which glared imperiously at the surrounding bottles and vials, stretching their slender necks in
curiosity. He bent over the work space thus secured. His pale face showed
feverish excitement. Between the thumb and forefinger of his left hand he
held a small crystal bowl containing a bright syrupy substance, which he
eagerly, even greedily, examined with a magnifying glass. He directed the
entire flood of light from his electric spotlight onto the crystal dish, so that
it sparkled and threw lightning bolts like a giant diamond.

He could hardly believe his eyes. There really were crystals in the
syrup! Indeed, infinitely tiny flakes, hardly visible to the unaided eye, but
undoubtedly crystals. There, for the chemist, was a certain awareness that
the product contained an identifiable compound.

Would he succeed this time? For almost ten years now, he had already struggled with an iron will and tenacious perseverance. After months of highly involved operations and reactions, which he changed and improved again and again on the basis of his newly gained experiences, instead of the hoped-for crystalline body, he had always obtained this accursed syrup, with which nothing could be done analytically. Again and again, he repeated the thoroughly well thought out and well calculated experiments with infinite patience, he, the impatient one, but always with the same failure. This time he had been content to use lower temperatures and pressures in a more favorable stage of the experiment, but had also had to wait three months longer for the chemical conversion to be achieved. And lo and behold, this time the final product differed from the earlier one by its lighter color, and now even tiny crystals had separated out! So far he had anguished about the success of his work, on which he had built his entire future, and now it seemed to have succeeded.

How though, if he was wrong after all, the work was once again in vain and the utter agony of doubt about himself and his research career would emerge anew? The thought seared down his back. But a mistake was no longer possible! In his hands he held the crystal, a whole starry sky was sparkling out of his beaker! If he succeeded in grasping the numerous tiny starlets of this microcosm and bringing together only a few thousandths of a gram, so that a determination of the basic substance was possible, then he would have final certainty! Then it was only a question of improving the method of rendering in such a way that a sufficient yield of the raw material was possible, leading to the determination of the chemical and physical properties of the new compound. Then he was certain—he beamed at the thought—of immortality! For all times, as long as there were people, his name would be mentioned among the first of the natural scientists of the world as the discoverer of the method to assemble the egg, the carrier of all earthly life, from the basic inorganic elements. He had uncovered it, the original mystery of nature, the riddle of all riddles, the becoming of life from lifeless material. From the synthesis of the simple protein body, in which he had succeeded, to the production of the living egg in the living cell, was still infinitely long way! But he had found it! And he would find it! What a tremendous discovery, the consequences of which cannot be foreseen!

Shaking with excitement, he held back his breath as he carefully put down the beaker with his hand that held the entire creation. And in a puzzling association of thoughts to his present activities; the hour that had shattered his sunny youthful happiness in one fell swoop suddenly came before his soul. His father owned a small estate, which he had acquired himself morning after morning in the sweat of his own brow. He had started out as an ordinary farm hand. With the savings from his wages as a manual laborer, he had bought the cheap stone field on the mountain slope, and with the work of his own hands had made it arable. With the stones he collected, he had built single-handedly the hut in which he lived for years. Then his father had married his mother, who brought him some fertile fields in marriage, and from then on, his possessions slowly but steadily increased. But how he worked! He was a quiet, withdrawn, but intellectually active person, constantly striving to improve his farming methods.

After work, he studied the weekly agricultural bulletins. He was particularly interested in the new agricultural machines. But he refused to purchase them, despite favorable payment conditions, because he calculated that they were not worthwhile for the small business that he had. He turned all the more eagerly to the new chemical and biological methods. He carefully tested them on a small experimental field, and then, if they proved successful, applied them to his entire farm. Thus he was the first farmer in the area to work with artificial phosphate fertilizers. The neighbors marveled at his successes, but did not attribute them to the "newfangled gimmickry", but rather said, he had just been very lucky since he had married the lovely girl with the windswept fields. Even the Lord God was in love with her, and that's how everything turned out for him. But the new era knocked in vain at their sluggish minds, and they came back more and more the further Amand Kämpfer got. In fact, they enjoyed it when he bought one field after the other from them for good money. They needed to work less, and when they could no longer do so, they simply moved to the city, where there was ample opportunity to find livelihood and accommodation. Why toil in the fields from dawn to dusk?

Hermann, who attended the grammar school in the neighboring country town, took the liveliest part in his father's studies. His father's pride was limitless when the boy brought light and clarity to his chemical formulas. Amand Kämpfer's mind was made up. Hermann, the eldest of his five children, was to become a trained agriculturalist. Together with him, he would then manage the estate. Then they would earn so much and save so much that the three younger brothers could also become competent and the youngest, Grethel, could be sure of a respectable dowry. Thus the prosperity of the family, its reputation and prestige increased from year to year.

One Easter Sunday, as Amand Kämpfer and his wife and children were coming out of church, the broker Levisohn appeared unexpectedly at the little manor. With stirring words and moving hands, he explained to father how foolish it was of him to agonize up so slowly, step by step. Such a small farm as he had now was nothing for a serious farmer. Now there is an opportunity, which will never come again, to double the size of the farm. Then it would be worthwhile to buy the new machines and he would be able to farm to the full. The farmer Roggenkamp, whose estate bordered on Kammer's fields, was on the verge of collapse, as he himself knew. He has not been able to pay the mortgage interest for three years. He had already agreed with him to buy the property from him at the mortgage value. If Kämpfer would take over the outstanding mortgage interest, Levisohn would be willing to leave the mortgages, to settle for a smaller down payment and to register the rest of the purchase price as a new mortgage on the property, now doubled in size. If the payment of the mortgage interest should cause him difficulties, he stated in advance, he would be happy to help him. He had great confidence in the ability of Kämpfer, who would find it easy to get out of the debts he was taking on in just a few years. Thus, in ten or fifteen years, he would be the owner of the property, while by his present path he would not be able to reach the same goal in his entire life. If he should need cash capital for the better utilization of the thus enlarged property, he would gladly be prepared to advance it to him in exchange for the registration of a double mortgage.

The father listened with bright eyes. The down payment that Levisohn demanded devoured the last penny of his previous cash savings, but he was electrified by the possibility of purchasing machinery and operating on a larger scale. However, he did not commit yet. He said he should to come back in two weeks, so that he could consider the matter at his leisure. With such a favorable offer, Levisohn replied that there was no time to think about it, especially since the matter with Roggenkamp would be notarized tomorrow and he had enough interested parties for Roggenkamp's property. However, since he was particularly fond of Kämpfer, he was willing to wait, not for fourteen days, but only four. Finally, they agreed on a period of eight days for consideration.

Right after lunch, the father hitched up and drove across over to Roggenkamp. Hermann was allowed to accompany him. The farmer vigorously persuaded his father to accept his favorable offer. He was the right man to bring the estate back to prosperity and he was lucky in everything he did. He himself was very unhappy with the farming industry, which was no longer profitable according to the old method, and he cannot get used to the new-fangled industrial techniques. He would move to the city to open a tavern. Levisohn, who was a very humane man and who had by no means been oppressive with the interest payments, would advance him the necessary money in exchange for a pledge on the tavern equipment.

Together with Roggenkamp, father and son now walked through the stables. They were in a bad condition and the cattle already, stick for stick, belonged to the Jew. Then a round trip was made through the fields and the soil was found to be excellent.

Day by day, the father did the math. The calculation did not go smoothly, if he used the most unfavorable figures of return, as he had always done with his previous acquisitions. But with the help of the machines and the agricultural chemistry that Hermann was supposed to study, he would make it. Hermann, who was 13 years old, understood nothing of the matter. However, his confidence in his father and in himself was so boundless that he saw the future sky full of violins. The mother, who in spirit already saw her son as the owner of the manor, did not stop trying to persuade her husband, and when Levisohn appeared again the next Sunday, the deal was closed.

But the Jew had brought disaster into the house. It was as if from that point forward the devil had his hand in the game. Despite good years, new capital always had to be raised. The expensive machines did not pay off as the father had calculated. In addition, the estate was still too small. The debts grew endlessly. The new farm building burned down two days before the fire insurance took effect, because the father did not have the cash on hand to pay the insurance premium in time. And when Hermann, who in the meantime had graduated from high school, had satisfied his military duty and had also moved to the university, came home for the second time for the Easter vacations, he found his father in an excited exchange of words with Levisohn, who had come to collect the mortgage interest, which had only been deferred, but had now become due for payment. Father asked that he wait at least until the fall. But to no avail.

And when the sickly mother threw herself at Levisohn's feet, crying and begging for a postponement, he agreed only on the condition that Kämpfer would promise him the grain on the stalk, since all the cattle had already been pledged. But then the father rebelled. He felt as if he suddenly saw through the trickery of the exploitative Jew. With a cry of rage, the otherwise prudent man jumped at his neck, choked him, and threw him head over heels out of the house, down the high stone staircase, so that he lay at the bottom for dead and was driven from the courtyard. He suffered internal injuries from the fall and died after a few days.

The father was sentenced to prison. But the heirs of the Jew were relentless. The estate went under the hammer, the mother died of grief and sorrow, and when the father learned of her death in prison, he hanged himself on the window cross. The three younger brothers were scattered all over the world. The youngest, however, the beautiful blonde sixteen-year-old Grethel, the image of her mother, went to the city to look for a job as a servant. When she gave her life to a child, and her seducer, who had promised her marriage, abandoned her, she threw herself into the river.

The dreadful fate of his family threatened to overwhelm Hermann's sensitive mind. Nineteen years old, he stood homeless and penniless in the world. But the tenacious peasant strength in him, the precious heritage of his ancestors, could not be broken down. It was not their way to leave unfinished what they had begun. He made the indomitable decision to continue his studies and complete them with an examination. Through private tutoring and all kinds of scientific writing, he acquired the means to do so. He now plowed through the entire field of natural science with all the thoroughness and resolve he had inherited from his father. Chemistry, however, seemed to him to be the queen of the natural sciences. Of the sciences, it alone could solve the riddle of life. He wanted to dedicate himself to it. Often it seemed to him as if Providence, in which he deeply believed, had only brought all the terrible misfortune upon his family, so that he could freely and uninhibitedly serve the science to which he felt called in his innermost being. He was twenty-one years old when he passed his doctoral examination in chemistry summa cum laude with a dissertation in the field of protein chemistry and shortly thereafter his state examination in natural sciences. A chemical factory then made him a glittering offer, but he turned it down. He wanted to remain true to his science.

He applied for a vacant assistant position at the Chemistry Institute of the university where he was studying, and was offered it. He had a monthly salary of one hundred marks and free accommodation, that was all he needed.

After four years he habilitated as a private lecturer. He read exhaustively in his concentration, protein chemistry. He had set himself no lesser task in life than to discover the secret of the living egg and to attempt its synthesis. And now he had succeeded in taking the first step! But meanwhile he had become thirty years old! He had sacrificed his entire youth to his scholarship, because he had to work day and night. The daytime hours belonged to his duties as an assistant, and the professor demanded much of him. Only the night hours and vacations belonged to him, and two afternoons a week from four o'clock onwards, when he gave his lectures. But even this drudgery would now came to an end! A full professorship was certain to be granted to him for his discovery! Soon he would have his own assistants! Now real life would begin! The previous life had been only a precursory struggle!

Carefully, he picked up the beaker again.

What was it? O miracle! The crystals multiplied increasingly! An entire assemblage of stars had formed in one place. Innumerable small suns were clustered around a larger central sun, which seemed to form them. And the whole container seemed to be pregnant with such oscillations. Everywhere they shot out of nothing as if caused by the will of the creator.

He couldn't get enough of the radiant miracle. So spellbound was he that he did not even notice the laboratory attendant entering, whose steps faded away under the loud noise with which the apparatus working under the fume hood filled the room. Only when the servant, standing close behind him, wished him good evening, did he turn to look at him.

It took quite a while before his spirit returned from the starry realm to this earthly world. Then he said, pointing at the beaker to the servant:

"Look here, Brunner! What is this?"

"I think, Doctor, we'll call it a day. Midnight is already past, and I have to turn off the gas," was the somewhat reproachful answer.

"Gosh. Brunner, you old scold, this is where you're supposed to look! What's that?"

The old experienced servant, who belonged to the laboratory's inventory for ages, straightened his glasses and carefully took the container in his hand.

"What do you see?! Now you'll talk!"

"These are crystals," the servant said dryly.

"Yes, they are crystals! But what kind of crystals! Man, if you had any idea!"

"Can I have the magnifying glass?" the servant asked. As he did so, he blinked over his glasses at the young researcher in a superior manner. "Here, Mr. Privy Councilor! Here is the magnifying glass!" The older man looked at the contents critically from all sides. "Well, what do you see?" laughed Kämpfer, amused at the old servant's expert demeanor.

"It seems to me…"

"What do you think?"

"I don't want to say anything, Doctor, but these things, sitting here in the syrup, they look like… they look like barite crystals."

A shock ran through Kämpfer's limbs.

"Brunner, you're crazy!' he said after a moment.

"Not completely, Doctor," replied the old servant in a calm tone. "But I don't want to be a chemist if it's not barite crystals."

"Give it here!" he barked at the servant.

He looked penetratingly at the contents in the glass. At a certain stage of the experiment, he had treated the product with barium hydroxide, but later removed it again quantitatively. In the presence of the manifold organic substances, however, a residue could very well have remained in the solution, which now, when the mass was constricted, crystallized out. That Brunner was right was not so impossible.

Without a word, he took a tiny platinum spatula from a drawer, carefully rinsed it with diluted acid and water, and dried it in the Bunsen flame. Then he took a single tiny flake of the disputed crystals from the dish, transferred it to a sample bag, dissolved it in water, added a drop of a diluted acid and another reagent. If he added a single drop of this now into the clear solution and a milky precipitate formed, then Brunner was right, and he stood once more at the precipice.

With restrained breath, he raised the sample bottle, carefully held the end of the reagent bag over it, and let a drop of its contents fall into it. In an instant, a milky precipitate was formed.

"I'm telling you," Brunner said dryly, "barite!" At the same time, he took the sample bag in his hand and shook it, whereby the precipitation increased still, and repeated: "Barite!"

Kämpfer slumped off the stool and completely collapsed. On the verge of fainting, he put his face in his hands.

"Doctor, what is it?"

Worried, the servant shook him. Then he came to himself again and stared straight ahead.

"You are overworked, Doctor! Yes, it is no wonder! Day and night on your legs through the entire semester and the entire vacation! If I were in your place, I would leave this poison box and find the fresh air!"

"Turn the gas off," replied Kämpfer tonelessly, "and go to bed."

"Yes indeed, Doctor! But you too, if you please! And no more crouching over the damn books, until tomorrow. And when the Christmas holiday comes next week, then be done with this pollution and get out of the noxious closet and go into the mountains! 14 days with a backpack!"

"All right, dear Brunner! And now good night!"

"Good night, Doctor! And no offense about the barite!"

Hermann Kämpfer had a sleepless night. The deep sense of defeat that had followed the joyful feeling of finally having reached his goal had soon given way to a dark brooding. The tough farmer's blood that flowed in his veins probably stalled temporarily, but it could not stand still. Incessantly, heart and pulse worked the inert mass, pounding the tangles, dissolving the deposits, and soon it flowed again with brisk force through the crimson pathways, animating and fertilizing his weary brain.

Again and again, the young researcher climbed through the long chain of thoughts that formed the basis of his experiment. There were countless possibilities to change them, to insert intermediate links, to take others out. Just like a brilliant chess player, after he has made his first move, lets the others follow according to a guiding ideal, and constantly adapts according to the moves of his opponent and the respective situation, and so, despite all constraints and obstacles, surprises, and setbacks, finally advances to victory, so Hermann also always revived the guiding idea and did not give up his will to succeed.

But was he the brilliant chess player, who alone could triumph, since nature itself, the greatest genius, was his opponent? How, if he was mistaken in his abilities and was only a fool, who put his life and strength into something that exceeded his abilities? Had not the laboratory attendant, who understood only the most elementary aspects of all his science, clearly shown him today his amateurish incompetence? Had he not made such a gross error of observation that a student in the first semester was not allowed to make? Yes, was he not the clear-thinking, objective observer that he was taken for by colleagues and students? Or was he not instead a dreamer and fantasist, who confused desire and reality, and who thought that will could be substituted for just such ability? And was he not still standing today where he had stood ten years ago, even though he had thought dozens of times that he already held victory in his hands?

Was the task he had set for himself solvable at all? Or was it such that even the greatest genius had to surrender before it?

"And what nature does not want to reveal, you won't force out of her with levers and screws."

Yes, Goethe was right! "Worship the inscrutable!" But what had he taken for granted! He wanted to fathom the secret of all secrets! He wanted to solve the riddle of life! With a bold grip, he wanted to lift the veil that Providence, in its inexplicable wisdom, had spread over it! He had dared to wrestle with God himself! How senseless, how insane, indeed how criminal his undertaking suddenly seemed to him!

And in doing so, he had missed life itself, the glorious life of which he had once expected so much, but which he had never dared to live, for fear that he might neglect his science by doing so! Only when he had come further with his work, when he had achieved a first tangible result, only then did he want to begin to live, to enjoy life!

But did it make sense at all to sacrifice his own life to this all-consuming science, even if the goal he had set for himself was attainable? What could this exalted science achieve at best? Even if it succeeded in dismantling the last little stone and stalk and bug into its basic atoms and putting them back together again, even if it succeeded in researching all the laws of nature and reducing them to a single, ultimate formula, even if it were possible to discover all the suns and stars at one's fingertips, even if we were able to physically walk through all the Milky Ways and Orions, we would not have escaped from the rigid fetters of matter that surrounds us, and we would not have come closer by a hair's breadth to that which stands *behind* things! Yes, even if we succeeded in the most unbelievable thing, to produce the living cell in a retort, what would we have achieved for our knowledge of life itself? Nothing, but what we already know, namely that the phenomenon which we call life occurs as soon as the atoms and molecules of certain elements enter into very definite bearing and relationship to each other. But why and how life arises under these conditions, and what life actually is and for what objective and purpose it appears, in order to chase its bearers through desire and torment and all heaven and hell, this question of all questions, it would still remain unanswered. Without the presupposition of God, freedom, and immortality a solution could not be found here.

But everything that pointed to a world *beyond* appearances, had not been answered. The researchers of milligrams and millimeters abandoned it, because they could not break it down into its elemental components and weigh and measure them! For what one could not see and hear and weigh and measure, that did not exist! The realm of the only true science was restricted on all sides with barriers, and whoever cared about what lay beyond, was considered a blatant fool!

And *was* he not such a fool? So what was he doing in the realm of this so-called science, this science that calls itself *presuppositionless,* without noticing that it is built itself on one-sided presuppositions? For does it not completely arbitrarily set aside, and even deny, the facts of our inner world, which are no less real and tangible than the facts of the outside world? Truly, this is a beautiful science, which closes its eyes to inconvenient facts and stops searching for knowledge, there where it should begin! Yes, if he had only duly satisfied himself with what this science was capable of doing: the practical-technical! But that glittering appeal, which had been made to him after his doctoral examination and which had opened up to him a whole world of practical activity, a realm in which he could have been king, which he had rejected in hopeless blindness! Now ten precious years of his life had been wasted without result! Was it still even worthwhile to continue such a botched life or must he start over from the beginning?

Hermann Kämpfer was racking his brain with such thoughts when the alarm clock suddenly startled him out of his brooding. It was 7 o'clock in the morning. The night was still heavy and black over the snow-covered university park, overlooked by the windows of his two-room office apartment. At 8 a.m., his duty in the laboratory began. He dressed and was on the spot as usual.

But only a few students showed up. The Christmas holidays, which were just around the corner, were already demanding their due. He had time enough to get back to his work, but any interest in it had dwindled in him. He was not even tempted by the possibility, which suddenly crossed his mind, that the mysterious crystals could not be barite hydrates at all, but the barium compound of the desired protein. He took the beaker again mechanically and examined it in daylight. The crystalline separation had increased. But he put it back under the bell of the desiccator apathetically and locked it away in his work cabinet. When the Christmas vacation arrived, following Brunner's advice, he strapped on his backpack, shod his snowshoes, and set off for the mountains.

In the mountain town, at the end point of the railroad, from where he started his hike, Hermann Kämpfer bought the requisite maps and secured for himself the necessary provisions. Then he stayed the night at the inn, "The Golden Grape Cluster". At dawn the following day he set out.

He liked best to wander cross-country, setting himself some goal, to which he then strove towards over all obstacles in as straight a line as possible. Or he strolled haphazardly in the countryside, pondering and dreaming, leaving himself to chance, in order to find his way again according to map and compass, sun and stars. Already as a child he had made his journeys of discovery alone or with the eldest of his younger brothers, and brought home as spoils stones and plants, butterflies and bugs, and all kinds of creeping and crawling animals. He would have liked now to follow this happy childlike way again, but the high snow prevented him, and with the snowshoes it was impossible to advance through forest and wood and over boulders. So he stuck to the roads and forest paths, mainly using the latter.

The last houses of the small town, which was slowly awakening from its sleep, were soon behind him. The village that blocked the entrance to the mountain valley was also soon passed. In the dance of snowflakes, he wandered gradually uphill. On the way yet stood individual huts with tiny windows, the last offshoots of the village. From their chimneys curled thick blue smoke, into which, fading into a puff, the swirling snowflakes greedily plunged. From a half-opened doorway, which led directly into a kitchen, came the aromatic scent of coffee. A young woman in a red petticoat and wooden overshoes was working at the stove. Heavy braids fell over her shoulders and the white sleeping jacket on her half-exposed chest. With one arm she held a child, a second one played at her feet. When Hermann stopped to look in enchantment, the young mother hurriedly closed the door. For a long time, this lovely image accompanied him, a melancholy longing in him awakened. This was the life he missed!

Spryly he stepped uphill now. Soon the mountain stream joined him. Under the thin, mostly broken ice cover, the water flitted along like an endless pack of black mice. A steel-blue kingfisher flying from stream to stream along the shore accompanied him for quite a distance. On a high alder, a slender magpie sat bobbing its tail. When he stopped to watch it, it flew away silently. His soul drank in deeply this primordial life.

The frozen forest slopes of the mountains were getting closer and closer to the valley road. When the path made a bend, above the edge of the valley, the hilltop was unveiled, which still had to be climbed today. The path became steeper and the snow more plentiful. Now it was time to strap on his snowshoes.

With sweeping movements, his body springing slightly forward at the knees, Hermann Kämpfer glided forward. He moved past snow-covered sawmills with low roofs covered in icicles and frozen paddle wheels, past waterfalls that had solidified into crystal palaces. With a loud hi and a hoot, lumberjacks drove a mighty horse-drawn raft down the valley. The giant tree trunks, held together by iron clamps, were crunching under their own weight, plowing deep furrows into the snow, so that the reddish-brown earth burst to the surface at individual stumps. A heavy iron chain dragged rattling behind them.

The snow-filled clouds descended lower and lower. Wedged between the increasingly narrow walls of the mountain, they rolled down the upper valley. The large, fluffy snowflakes became smaller and smaller. Eventually they turned into a fine granular grit, and before he knew it, he was surrounded by a pervasive snowy mist. It stung his face sharply and got into his hair and clothes. Hermann Kämpfer pushed on harder. Soon sweat was beading off his forehead despite the frost.

Then the fog began to swirl and turn in circles. A sharp wind drove between them and quickly grew into a storm. Loads of fine snowfall were hurled continually into the hiker's face and against his struggling body. Up to the knees, soon up to the hips, he stood in the blowing snow and could no longer go forwards or backwards. When a second snowdrift now came upon the first, he was lost. With a clear mind, Hermann braced himself for death. A peculiar, almost scientific interest filled him, what would come next? Now he would finally have certainty, and all his doubts and striving, torment and suffering would be over. He stood there comfortably, held on all sides by soft arms. A pleasant warmth flowed through him. He had never been so content in his whole life. A sweet languor came upon him, and a desire to sleep followed.

Then a mighty gust of wind started up again. As if pushed by invisible forces, the mass of snow that held Hermann captive moved from the spot. And with that he stirred. But he lagged behind the rush, and suddenly he was standing there free except for foot and ankle.

Astonished, almost unwillingly, he perceived it. Instinctively he began to shift his feet, he stomped back and forth a few times with the snowshoes, cleared himself completely and continued his way higher, offering his forehead and chest to the tempest. Heavy as lead, he dragged himself along at first. But soon the old strength and the old vitality was in him again.

Painstakingly, Hermann Kämpfer worked his way up through the heavy weather to the crest of the mountain. For hours on end, he wrestled with the raging elements. But he was victorious. The drizzling snow gradually lifted. The thick fog became lighter and lighter. Then suddenly, still veiled, the sun emerged from behind a mountain peak. Its arrows of light bored holes through the mist, sparkling bolts of luminescence jumped in behind and tore the clouds to shreds, and soon the Queen of the World shone down in unrestrained splendor from the bluest noonday sky. Far below a sea of haze billowed, on the back of which this unearthly world seemed to float.

Hermann stopped at a rocky outcrop overlooking the ridge, unbuckled his snowshoes and climbed up to the cliff. Like an eagle resting from its soaring flight, he perched up there. Breathing deeply, he opened his shirt. Then Hermann Kämpfer's struggling soul was lifted from the heaviness of the earth and soared rejoicing through the sun-drenched sky.

He rested for about an hour. Afterward he ate a snack and determined his position and the day's goals on the basis of his maps. He examined the rock and gave himself an account of the geology of the area. He always had his geological tools with him. With a hammer he chipped off a piece and examined it with his magnifying glass and acid. Then he climbed down from the cliff, strapped on his snowshoes again and continued his way over the ridge, lined with hardwoods and conifers.

Silently, the lonely wanderer glided through the peaceful winter splendor. Millions and millions of crystals sparkled in the sunlight from all the trees and bushes, a whole carpet of stars lay shimmering and glittering at his feet. He floated over them, like a god over the starry world. How paltry in comparison seemed to him the tinsel that he kept locked under a glass bell jar in his laboratory cupboard!

Now he entered the high forest. The slender fir trees beckoned to him like enchanted princesses. Each one of them had wrapped itself in a shimmering mantle of stars. Under the weight of the heavy snow, hemmed in by the most delicate lace and brocade, the branches hung down almost vertically, as if they wanted to hold their arms tightly around the mantle that protected their virginal bodies from the eyes of the hiker. A mighty beech had stretched a snow-laden branch like a triumphal arch above the path. In long chains the white blossoms dangled close to the path. Carefully avoiding contact, the hiker slipped between them. But he touched them by accident and the finest glittering shower of stars dusted down on him in the sunlight, getting caught in his hair and eyelashes, becoming dew and mist on his coat.

He passed a woodcutter's hut covered in deep snow. Was it a woodcutter's hut? No! It was the gingerbread house from the fairy tale! When he looked back, he clearly saw the old witch's pointed face peering out from her white hood at him.

A fox timidly crossed his path from afar. A fox? It was the wolf, that the evil witch had sent to lie in wait for Little Red Riding Hood. But she was snuggled safe at home with her little mother and was looking forward with her little brother and sister to the holy Christ Child, because today was Christmas Eve!

Christmas!

As if by a stroke of magic, Hermann saw himself transported back to his childhood. The brilliance of the Christmas tree and the sound of ringing bells! The jubilation of the children and the joy of their parents!

The mysterious time began with St. Nicholas Day. Posthaste the children hurried home in the afternoon from school. They ate their evening bread and did their schoolwork more hurriedly, but nevertheless more carefully than usual, because there was no way of knowing whether St. Nicholas would not look at them again, as he did so unexpectedly last year. Then they sat in the darkened parlor around the purring green tiled stove and baked their apples until they puffed and hissed and danced around on the hot plate. Old Lux, a black Dobermann Pinscher, sat there and blinked steadily into the fire. To this the song was sung:

> "Tomorrow, children,
> there will be something,
> Tomorrow, we will rejoice!
> What a joy, what a life,
> Shall be in our house!
> Right when we wake up,
> Heissa, then it's St. Nicholas day!"

During the song, the mother entered. Immediately the song fell silent. All five children jumped towards and up to her.

"Mother, mother, when is holy St. Nicholas coming?"

"Always just pretty well-behaved! When the time comes, holy St. Nicholas will come. And now show me your schoolwork."

With these words, the mother lit the large oil lamp above the table. Then, as she did every evening, she looked through the schoolwork, which the children showed her with boisterous enthusiasm. Hermann hurriedly erased another large blot in his copybook, while his mother went through the arithmetic problems with Hans and Jürgen. Grethel sat with her mother on the desk and watched the scholarly work, while Fritz, who also did not yet go to school, sat on the floor and examined the contents of his burst puppet, which he then stuffed into Grethel's doll's mouth and eyes. After Hermann's workbook had been checked, which now had a big hole in it instead of the blob, mother turned off the lamp and sat down with the children around the stove, in front of which old Lux still sat and blinked into the fire.

The glow of the fire in the stove filled the living room with a cozy flickering light. The cuckoo in the carved Black Forest clock called the sixth hour.

"Now he is coming soon! Last year he came at half past six."

"Yes. Be good and calm," the mother reassured the impatient children, "and say your words again, so that you don't get stuck."

"Where is father really?" shouted Jürgen in the middle of the repetition of the speeches.

His mother's serious look kept him silent. After they finished reciting the speeches, with some tutoring from the mother, she said:

"Father has gone by the train into town to run errands."

Jürgen made a highly incredulous face, but he did not dare to contradict his mother.

At that moment, the sound of a sleigh was heard in the courtyard. The children rushed to the window, but nothing could be seen. At the same time, a loud rumbling sound was heard in the hallway. Lux started barking. Fearfully, the children fled to their mother by the stove. They listened intently to the hallway.

Three powerful knocks struck against the door. Lux barked louder. The door burst open, and in its frame stood St. Nicholas in the flesh, with a long white beard, a short monk's cowl, and high powerful boots. His hood was pulled down deeply over his face. On his back he carried a quarter-full potato sack and under his arm a rod tied together with a red ribbon. On the rope wound around his body dangled several puppets drawn on cardboard with movable limbs and a doll with real hair and real wide-open eyes.

Lux stopped barking, sniffed carefully at the saint, and then suddenly jumped up wagging his tail at him. Quickly, he was cuffed with the rod, so that he went howling behind the stove. Little Grethel shrieked loudly and clung to her mother crying. "Praised be Jesus Christ!" greeted St. Nicholas in a deep bass voice.

"Do I find good children here?"

"Yes, dear St. Nicholas!" they echoed back unanimously.

"Only Jürgen," mother added, "was quite naughty again."

"Step forward!" St. Nicholas commanded with a thunderous voice. Now, Jürgen, who had been trying to get a good look under the hood of the saint, became really worried about the matter. He crept timidly behind his

mother. But she pushed him with both hands right up in front of the hood-
ed man.

"Pray!" St. Nicholas instructed him.

Jürgen sank to his knees, but he couldn't get a word out of his mouth.

"Well?" mother encouraged him. "Can't you pray?" She gently
grabbed his shoulders from behind and whispered to him in his ear the beginning of the Lord's Prayer. Anxiously, the little sinner recited the prayer
and then cast a hopeful look at the potato sack.

"Now recite your poem!" his mother ordered him.

Jürgen stammered:

> "I am a little fellow,
> who can pray well.
> I always want to be hard-working,
> and follow dear little mother,
> and also father — father—."

At this he paused, and looked searchingly in the face of St. Nicholas, who
made a strange noise and turned around. Immediately, however, he remembered his saintly dignity and reached towards the rod. Then Jürgen
quickly completed his verse:

> "And I also gladly follow father,
> and Jesus, our dear Lord."

Satisfied, St. Nicholas reached into the big sack and gave the good-natured
young man a handful of nuts and apples and a small toy. Jürgen quickly
carried the loot to safety, because last year he had to return the hard-won
treasure because he had laughed cheekily in St. Nicholas' face when re-
ceiving it.

Now it was Grethelchen's turn. Crying, held by the mother, she
whimpered:

> "I am small,
> my heart is pure.
> No one may enter but you,
> my dear little Jesus."

St. Nicholas reached deep into the sack and threw two or three handfuls of
apples and nuts at little Grethel's feet. Like a hunting dog, Jürgen was

there and grabbed the fruits that were tumbling to the ground. But in quick succession, he suffered two strokes of the rod over the uppermost part of his back. Enriched by the lesson, he crawled behind the stove to join Lux. Little Grethel, however, received from St. Nicholas a doll with genuine hair and real eyes that could even sleep properly.

Now Fritz, and Hans, and finally Hermann recited their poems, and they also received their treats and trifles. Next St. Nicholas solemnly handed mother the rod with a meaningful look. She received it with a reverential curtsy and put it behind the mirror. Then she sang the song of thanksgiving, which the children joined in with a sigh of relief:

> "We thank holy St. Nicholas,
> for all the nice gifts,
> which we have received from him,
> in our dear parent's house.
> We will always be good,
> and make our parents happy,
> then the holy Christ Child
> will bring us many beautiful things."

No sooner had the last verse, which testified to a practical view of life, faded away, when holy St. Nicholas emptied the sack into the parlor with a mighty swing, and apples and nuts, whole and broken gingerbread men, and all kinds of sweetmeats hailed down on to the floorboard. With the words "Holy Christ will soon bring you rich gifts!" he left the room and slammed the door shut behind him.

While the children and Lux were fighting over the precious treasures lying on the ground, the sound of the sleigh was heard again in the courtyard. But none of the boys, not even Jürgen, showed any interest. They were busy picking up the apples and nuts that had rolled under the sofa and the chest of drawers. Only little Grethel ran to the window, stood on her tiptoes, and peered out into the darkness. Now mother lit the big hanging lamp again and the house girl set the table and brought in the supper.

A short time later, father came back from the city. Jubilantly, the children told him that St. Nicholas had been there. Jürgen looked at him with a deliberate smile. But when his father, whose mouth was twitching strangely, looked him sharply in the face and asked whether St. Nicholas had also brought a rod, he became very meek and grabbed nervously at his trousers.

Weeks of mysterious suspicions and joyous expectations followed, because from now on the dear holy Christ child was present in the home.

The school work was now done with renewed diligence. Even Jürgen showed a commendable daily zeal. Otherwise nothing would become of the skates that he wanted for Christmas. These were at the top of his wish list. Carefully, he had written the price of 3.50 marks next to it, which was indicated in a shop window in the city. Mother was entrusted by the Christ Child to look through the wish lists. It was up to her to make the final decision as to whether a wish was "necessary" or "unnecessary," i.e., was allowed to remain on the note. He knew from experience that 3.50 marks was just about the limit of what the holy Christ Child was willing to pay for wishes that were not "necessary." His mother had once recommended that he get a new suit, instead of a *Laterna magica*. He did not agree, but got the new suit anyway. So why spoil his credit with the dear holy Christ Child! And besides, he was not at all interested in a new suit. On the contrary, it only increased his opportunity to get acquainted with the new rod, because, if he got a hole in it, mother would not disregard his error. On the other hand, she was not so particular about the old suit.

Hermann had asked for a collection box with a glass lid for his butterflies, and in later years an experiment book and all kinds of chemistry and physics equipment. He made electrical elements and a spark inductor himself, but the material for them and the little Geissler tubes had to be brought by the Christ Child. Since mother did not have expertise for this request, the Christ Child asked father to decide about it. Rarely was there a refusal, for father himself had the keenest interest in these things.

So each of the children wrote his or her wish list. These were put neatly, one for each of them, in an envelope and labeled "To the dear holy Christ Child in heaven". The letters were placed in front of the window in the evening and the Christ Child picked them up at night. In place of the letter, the next morning, a piece of candy was there on the windowsill. If, however, one of the letters was not picked up, one could be sure that it was still burdened with a wish that could not be fulfilled. With mother's help, the note was then put in order. However, a letter that was delivered late due to one's own obtuseness usually occurred without the receipt of candy. This had already happened twice to Jürgen, so he was eager to make sure that the letter of request from the outset met the blessed requirements. Once his letter had not been picked up for three nights in a row. Despite his mother's advice, he had written down an "unnecessary" wish, and at the same time was guilty of attempting to bribe the dear holy Christ Child. In addition to his wish for a pair of "real boots with real spurs on them," he had added his weekly pocket money in the amount of ten pfennigs, in the hope that the Christ child would be persuaded to grant his wish after all. However, the letter was not picked up until the wish was cancelled and the filthy mammon removed.

Once he had also been plagued by curiosity as to what would happen if he did not place the letter in front of the window, as was the heavenly rule, but put it instead in the post box. How astonished he was when the letter lay on his coffee cup at breakfast the next day! Now he was cured of his revolutionary spirit and was never again guilty of a violation of the supernatural order.

The closer the feast came, the more noticeable the nearness of the dear holy Christ child became. When he had gone through the closed door of the parlor, a golden hair had stuck to the handle. When the children woke up in the morning, they often found traces of golden hair on their beds. Then, there was even a sweet tidbit hidden somewhere in the bedroom. It also happened that a delightful treat was found in their school satchels or in some other unexpected place. Sometimes, when the children sat around the green tiled stove in the twilight hour and sang a Christmas carol, one could still hear a fine, soft singing echoing in the adjoining parlor, or the door would open softly and sweets and gilded nuts would be thrown among the children by an invisible hand.

On the last two or three days before the holiday, the scent of fir trees drifted through the house. One could clearly discern that it had its origins in the living room. Once when Jürgen looked through the keyhole, he could even see the Christmas tree. Some of it was already decorated and all sorts of packages and mysteriously objects were lying around the room. After showing Hermann his discovery under the seal of secrecy, all the splendor had somehow disappeared, and one could only see into a dark hole. There was great fear that the disappearance would be permanent, and the children looked forward to Christmas Eve with beating hearts.

The day they received their report cards, of course, brought more uncomfortable lessons. Hermann had nothing to fear, because up until then he had always held first place in his class. Jürgen, on the other hand, had an extended lease on the 31st place among the 32 places in his class. But once, contrary to all the laws of nature, he had advanced to the thirtieth, and saw his rights violated to such an extent that he beat up the comrade, who had contested his ancestral seat.

One day, however, Hermann brought home second place on his Christmas report card instead of first. Isidor Rosenbaum was the name of his rival. He was better than him at calculating percentages. Hermann never forgot his mother's eyes when he showed his report card to her. It was enough to bring tears to his eyes. His father, on the other hand, made no secret of his displeasure. Hermann spent the holiday joylessly. When it was over, however, he sat down and achieved such mastery in the tedious calculation of percentages that by Easter he had already regained his first place in the class.

However, Jürgen, who had nothing at all to do with the story, saw his family honor as aggrieved by Isidor Rosenbaum. Without saying anything to anyone, he presented him with a challenge to a duel. Isidor Rosenbaum, however, rejected the request. Now, on the second holiday, Jürgen ambushed him and thrashed him in such a way that Isidor was not fit for school again after the end of the Christmas holidays. But old Rosenbaum reported the matter to the school director and the young instigator got a beating from his father. But he didn't let this restrain him, and promptly passed it on to Isidor Rosenbaum as soon as he returned. As a result, the father received a registered letter threatening Jürgen's expulsion from school. This time, at his mother's urgent request, he contented himself with a warning, and since Isidor Rosenbaum was never again guilty of violating Jürgen's family honor, the matter was settled.

Christmas Eve was finally here. On this day, the children were often banned from the living room, since the good room had only one entrance through the living room. The cheeky Jürgen, however, lay in wait somewhere, and informed his brothers and sister of his respective observations and discoveries. Once, for example, he noticed that the horns of the toboggan he had wanted were sticking out of the large package that father was carrying into the living room for the Christ Child. But he was very disappointment when the toboggan was not to be found among the presents when the presents were handed out. It was not until Christmas Eve that it was carried in unexpectedly by unseen hands and placed under the Christmas tree.

After six o'clock they put on their Sunday clothes, and at seven the cuckoo in the Black Forest clock finally called everyone to the table. The presents were only given out after supper. Together, initiated by the father, the table prayer was said:

> "O Father, childlike we pray
> to you for our daily bread.
> Give to your children, whom you love,
> and bless what you graciously give. Amen!"

The second and third words of the prayer were thereby pronounced as one "O father-childlike". Every year there was beer-battered carp with boiled potatoes and sauerkraut to eat. For the three youngest, who didn't yet know how to handle the fish bones, there was a large pot with sweet semolina porridge. The two oldest, Hermann and Jürgen, received as much of that as they liked, as soon as they had eaten their piece of carp.

The children and their mother had long since finished their meal, while father was still painstakingly dissecting the heads of the two carp, his favorite dish. He didn't finish for ages. Five pairs of impatient children's eyes followed every bite he brought to his mouth. He accepted it with a smile, without allowing his cruel patience to be disturbed. Even mother regarded it as too long, and with a pleading "Man, get on with it!", she urged him to end the torture game.

Finally, he was ready too. With a smile he wiped his mouth and mustache and said grace:

> "Lord, we thank you for your gifts,
> which we have well enjoyed. Amen."

Now the table was cleared. All the children helped, because no presents were given out before the dishes were washed. Meanwhile, father disappeared at a suitable moment into the living room to help the Christ Child light the tree.

Gradually, mother and children gathered again in the living room, and the farmhands were also there again. Mother sat down on the sofa with Grethel on her lap, the other children around her. The servants stood a little further away.

Now mother began to sing the song "Her children are coming", Herman accompanied her on the piano. Jürgen unconsciously expressed his own view of life by saying instead of the last two verses:

> "And see what joy on this most holy night,
> the Father in heaven gives you!"

he gave the version:

> "And see what joy on this most holy night,
> the father in heaven gives himself!"

Then the song followed:

"What is that sweet child
that is found there in the manger?
Oh such a sweet child,
that must surely be from heaven!

And she who kneels there to the side
and looks blissfully at the child,
that is Mary pious and pure,
she must be quite comfortable in her heart!

And he who stands there to the side
and silently pleads up to heaven,
that must be pious Joseph,
may he be quite pleased with the little child.

And what lies there in the corner
to look happily after the child,
a little ox and a little donkey.
They must be good little animals.

And what makes the stable so bright,
and who sings so sweetly and laughs,
those are the bright little angels,
they look in at the door and window.

And they come there pious and good,
with long staff and round hat,
that is the shepherds' pious flock,
they offer their gifts.

And those who come from far away
and faithfully look at the star,
these are the three holy kings
with frankincense, gold and myrrh.

And above the little hut is a star,
it shines near and shines far,
it shines also into our time,
and will shine until eternity!

After the song had faded away, everyone listened expectantly to the living room. From there, a crackling sound full of promise could already be heard, and a bright glow came through the cracks in the door.

Next mother sang the song "Silent Night, Holy Night", and then "O Christmas Tree!" No sooner had the last verse faded away than a fine silver bell rang and the door opened. With loud cheers the children rushed in.

There stood the magnificent tree in a blaze of glory! It reached from the floor to the ceiling, covered over with colored wax lights, and under each hung a colored glass ball, which with its weight gave the little light its vertical position. Gilded and silver-plated apples and nuts hung between them, as well as juicy oranges in red and green nets, and all kinds of lollipops and chocolates. At the very top of the whorl, barely accessible to the outstretched arm, hung the most delicious pieces, the insides filled with sweet syrups. If you broke one while picking, the sweet contents ran from the cracks over your fingers. Fine gold and silver hair stretched from branch to branch. At the top of the tree, however, a beautiful silver star sparkled. Despite all the abundance, the tree, which was always a noble fir and never a spruce, did not seem overloaded. Nothing unattractive and unnatural hung on it. Everything was well-designed and well-distributed. It was the most magnificent of all Christmas trees that existed in the whole world.

The gifts were placed on long, narrow, white-covered tables, along the walls of the room. Jürgen had found out that the tables, whose linen tablecloth reached down to the floor, were made of ironing boards and noodle boards, and that under one of them was a large box of gingerbread. He had taken gingerbread from it during Christmas week, secretly replenished the supply of gingerbread cakes on his plate from time to time. Two large gingerbread men stood like sentinels in front of each offering place, their faces and hands painted with white sugar strokes and their bodies decorated with all kinds of white and red sugar squiggles. The gifts for the servants were set up at a special side table.

While the children frolicked among their presents, finding new surprises over and over again, father and mother stood under the Christmas tree and watched the merry goings-on. Father had put his arm around mother, and Hermann saw how he pulled her to him and kissed her. Then father led mother to a special gift corner, whose structure was covered with a large white cloth, and likewise mother surprised father.

In the meantime, Marie, the old faithful maid, who had served in the house since Hermann's birth, had set the table in the living room again and laid apples and nuts and baked goods consisting of all kinds of animals, stars, and curls. The center of the table was dominated by a mighty Christmas Striezel. It was already cut and the big black eyes of the raisins peeped out of the deliciously fragrant, golden yellow slices. Next to it stood the large punch bowl made of colorfully painted frosted glass, filled to the brim with a sweet drink, whole orange slices floating in it. A glass scoop was used to pour the contents into glasses. The scoop was so clumsily built that some of it always flowed over one's fingers. Only mother knew how to fill the glasses without spilling anything.

She met father's arms and gave him her gift, while father was looking for a large raisin in the Striezel. Indignantly, mother slapped him on the fingers.

Today, the children were allowed to stay up until midnight. Then they were gently put to bed. But they still took their favorite gifts with them into the bedroom. Here mother said evening prayers with them. Then she gave them each a blessing and a kiss on the forehead. Still they could not fall asleep for long. Only Grethelchen fell asleep quite soon, the doll that St. Nicholas had brought her in one arm, and in the other, an even larger and more beautiful one that the dear holy Christ Child had given her.

During the whole Christmas week, the Christmas tree was lit every evening after supper. Around the middle of the week, the candles were renewed again, with Hermann being allowed to help his father. On New Year's Eve, the tree burned out. Tears invariably shimmered in mother's blue eyes, and little Grethel kissed her more intimately than usual. The following day the tree was left for the children to plunder, after the father had collected the inedible ornaments and carefully saved them for the next year. Then Hermann sawed a small fir tree out of the big one and the children played "Christmas" with it for the rest of the Christmas vacations. The small tree was decorated anew, and the dolls and puppets were given regular presents. Finally, this second Christmas tree happiness came to an end. The fir tree, however, stood for a long time in a corner of the yard, until it was dry and withered and completely dead. Finally, it was cut up, father carved cake whisks from the whorled branches, and the rest was chopped up and used as firewood. A little pile of ashes was the end of all the Christmas tree glory.

Guided by such sweet childhood memories, Hermann moved almost silently through the winter forest. Dusk had fallen. He didn't care. The memory of his golden, innocent childhood was the only thing that cruel life had left him. Until now he had still had his science, but this too was now lost to him. When he moved to the university, he had had to promise his mother to spend every Christmas at home, as long as one of his parents was still alive. Joyfully he had vowed to do so. But only once could he keep the vow. His good mother, the tireless, faithful carer, already by the first Christmas after the misfortune that affected the family, lay in the ground, lonely and abandoned, because the father had not been laid with her. He, too, lay lonely and abandoned in unconsecrated ground, far from the cemetery. The brothers were scattered to the four winds and the youngest, the sweet little sister, the blonde Grethel…he shuddered.

In the meantime, it had become completely dark. But it was not until the path emerged from the forest into a clearing that Hermann awoke from his youthful dreams. It was a starry night. The mountains stood out against the horizon in sharp lines. Orion was rising in the eastern sky. He was already standing above the mountain, up on his shining girdle, staring fixedly at the eternally beautiful Cassiopeia, who was combing her shimmering starry hair.

"Are there sinners and mortals high above?
There also the friend becomes the enemy,
And the friend must part in death?"

With the unfathomable starry sky high above him and a profound sorrow deep in his chest, Hermann Kämpfer moved through the winter night. The sparkling snow spray crackled around the bow of the slender gliding tree trunks, like the ocean tide parting at the breast of a swift ship, leaving behind it a path that shone far and wide.

He stopped at a fork in the road. He took out the map and oriented himself by the light of an electric pocket lantern. It was still eleven to twelve kilometers to the international winter sports ground where he planned to spend the night. The path soon led back into the forest and downhill in many twists and turns, promising a quick journey.

As he was studying the map, a buck, followed by two does, emerged from the forest edge. They approached him curiously, lured and blinded by the glare of the lantern. When Hermann moved, they took off in full flight.

With powerful thrusts now he took off, the burning lantern in front of his chest, its strong light threw a sharp cone into the night. Soon he was shooting downhill as fast as an arrow, reducing his speed at the bends in the path with powerful counter-pushing. A cloud of whirling snow dust trailed behind him.

Just around a sudden bend, a mighty fir tree, uprooted by the storm, lay across the path. With tremendous momentum, he threw himself to the side, but he still crashed into the branches with his back.

He lay stunned for a while. Then he stirred his limbs. Nothing of importance had happened to him. Even the lantern was still burning. He had absorbed the entire impact with his back. But the front end of one of his skis, which had hit a branch in the fall, had broken off.

He laboriously worked his way out of the tangle of branches. He had only a slight cut over his right cheek, as if he had just come from a duel. With the help of some pads of cotton infused with ferric chloride from the pharmacy, the blood was soon stanched.

Restoring the broken ski was more complicated. From his backpack he located his repair bag, pulled out an iron yoke clamp, squeezed the broken wooden ends together and secured them with strong screws. Soon he was on his way again. Slowly, cautiously surveying the path in the cone of electric light, he glided down to the valley at moderate speed.

Like a star that comes from the farthest reaches of the heavens, and nearing the earth, strays from the course prescribed by eternal laws, and moves now with inhibited motion in a swaying curve through the cosmos, so Hermann Kämpfer traveled on a winding path through the starry night towards a new incomprehensible fate.

But man is a heavenly being. From eternity he comes down to earth, and to eternity he must return in order to become pure, strengthened by suffering and hardened by agony, ready for his higher destiny, which he only suspects on earth, and which God, in his inscrutable wisdom, sets out for man for mysterious reasons. Hermann did not yet suspect that today was a model of his earthly turmoils.

The magnificent ballroom of the Grand Hotel, the social center of the winter sports resort, was bustling with life. Hundreds of people, in a large social gathering, swarmed around each other. The small tables, at which they had dined, were tightly packed. They were now covered with champagne buckets, wine bottles, fruit and pastry bowls and formed a kind of bivouac for their owners, who, pushing their way through the crowd, visited acquaintances in the grand hall or the adjoining dance halls, only to return again and again to their place at the table.

The center of the hall, flooded with light and music, was dominated by a giant Christmas tree, which wore electric light bulbs, instead of wax candles. Its branches and twigs were covered with layers of white asbestos, and colorful paper garlands formed its only artless and chintzy decorations. Attached to its whorl was a bundle of small flags, composed of the flags of every nation. English and American colors predominated, German ones were hardly to be found among them, despite the fact that the tree stood in the heart of Germany.

An international society celebrated Christmas here, in an international way. Paper streamers flew through the air, which was heavy with cigar smoke and all kinds of conflicting perfumes. Champagne corks popped, confetti was thrown, paper caps and bonnets made of Christmas crackers, worn by men and women as headdresses, completed the impression that it was not Christmas, but that a fool's festival was being celebrated here.

Attracted by the torrent that reached the road, Hermann had stopped, his snowshoes under his arm. He had already taken them off, since it was impossible to get up the steep village street covered with black ice on the wooden ones.

That was life in there! That could drive away the gloomy thoughts that were silencing his soul! Without a second thought, he entered the vestibule, handed his snow gear to a servant and arranged for a room.

The head waiter examined him with critical eyes as he walked across the hallway in his outdoor attire toward the open banquet hall. Remembering his clothing, he avoided entering. He strode along the columned banister that separated the hallway from the banqueting hall, which was slightly lower and open on this side. Only a few guests, who had withdrawn somewhat from the hustle and bustle, were seated here. The front part of this room was illuminated by the light emanating from the hall, further back there was a pleasant twilight. Here Hermann took a seat at a small table. He had a comfortable view of the festivities and the dance hall. He ordered something to eat and a bottle of wine.

Greedily, Hermann sucked in the flood of images. This was the great life he had longed for so often, but to which he had not yet dared to devote himself out of love for his science. How it glistened and shone and gleamed and glowed! The elegant, precious garments of the ladies, which stood out so colorfully against the black background of the festive men's clothing! Those slender, supple girlish figures, laughing and lively, moving down there and turning gracefully in the arms of the dancers on the reflective floor with their delightful, daintily shod little feet! What a contrast to the petty bourgeois sociability of his university town! A powerful desire drew him to immerse himself there. And he could have already had all that! If he had accepted the offer of the chemical factory ten years before, this shining world would have previously been his! What fool he was, that he had missed out on life, life, glorious life because of his science, and had sacrificed his precious youth for it! But it was not too late! He was only thirty years old and real life lay ahead of him still!

Hastily, he finished a glass of wine and ordered a bottle of champagne. Then he moved the table and chair close to the railing to be even closer to the world he now wanted to conquer. Then he caught sight of the monstrosity of a Christmas tree, which until now had been hidden from him by a pillar. A strange feeling took possession of him. How very different was the Christmas tree and Christmas at home and the world from which he came! A deep sadness came over him and with gloomy eyes he stared into the ferment. The waiter brought the champagne, uncorked it and poured a goblet full. He paid no attention to it.

For a long time, leaning over the railing, he had gazed into the ballroom. Close below him, a strikingly beautiful blonde passed by surrounded by several gentlemen. She might have been about twenty-two years old. The splendid symmetry of her figure enfolded by a gown of light blue silk. Girded up in the Empire style, it clung tightly to her noble form, leaving the upper part of her marvelous chest and splendidly rounded shoulders free. Her delightful head, crowned by a wealth of golden blond hair, rose like a blossom on a slender, dazzling white neck. Around her neck she wore precious diamonds and correspondingly sparkling crystals in her fine, almost transparent ears. As if by chance, she looked up at Hermann, whose serious, sad eyes met hers. For a small, barely perceptible moment she stopped, looking at him, then she went on joking with the gentlemen. After three steps, however, she turned around and threw a paper streamer at Hermann, who had been following her dreamily with his eyes. The ribbon wrapped itself around his neck, and laughing, the beautiful girl pulled carefully on the thin strip, as if she wanted to pull the enfettered man down to her. The paper tore. Hermann, unable to move, remained silent and stiff. Then she went on with a mocking smile. One of her companions looked back at Hermann through his monocle with a challenging glance. He paid no attention. Spellbound, his eyes followed the beautiful girl.

Boiling hot, the impression shot down Hermann's spine. The whole room suddenly seemed to revolve around him. He had to sit down, covering up his eyes with his hands. Suddenly he got up again to look at the apparition, which seemed heavenly to him. But she had disappeared into the crowd without a trace.

A feverish restlessness now came over him. Briskly he emptied his champagne glass and immediately poured it full again.

Hermann had never touched a girl in his life, and the feeling of love was foreign to him. All the high and holy feelings of this kind that he harbored within him, he had given to his beloved mother and only sister. After losing them both, his science was mother and sister and lover to him all at the same time. There were times when he felt a nameless longing to hold something in his arms and kiss it. He had looked around then for a companion among the daughters of the little university town, with whom he met at the usual social gatherings. But no stronger emotion had stirred in his heart, and his unspoiled nature prevented him from settling for a love that was not born of the depths of the soul, or even from making a so-called good match.

The only female he met outside society was Röschen Brunner, the lovely late-born daughter of the old laboratory servant. She cleaned his rooms, brought in his breakfast, and put fresh flowers on his desk. For ten years he had known her. She was still a child when he moved into his official apartment. In the meantime, she had turned 18. When she walked through the room with her golden-brown braids and a shy look from her brown eyes sometimes met him, he often felt that he wanted to run after her and press her young body against him. But he had always suppressed the impulse again, because he saw no possibility to honorably call her his. Then he must have gone through agonizing hours and sleepless nights, and had only with difficulty found reassurance in his science. But he had always remained his own master and his iron will had always conquered his rebellious senses.

How very different were the sensations that surged through his chest at that moment! It was not the desire for physical possession that the sight of this young blooming woman had awakened in him. The unique look, which struck him from the eye of the beautiful girl, had ignited in his heart and set the deepest depths of his soul on fire. He wanted to cried out. A veil of twilight seemed to come between him and the throng of people, so that he saw it only small and tiny, as if from far away. His heart beat in his throat and involuntarily he reached for it, as if an arrow were stuck there and had struck him dead. Then again, he wanted to jump up, to run after her, throw himself at her feet, and offer the last fiber of his being to her. He knew that if he was denied the opportunity to lay all his life and striving, his poetry and thinking, all his tireless struggle with himself and the world at the feet of this unearthly being, then life no longer had any sense and purpose for him.

Midnight had long since passed, the hall was already beginning to empty, but Hermann did not move from his seat and did not give up his hope that she might come by a second time. A fruitless effort. Then he took heart and walked through the hall, heedless of his unfestive attire, unconcerned about the startled and mocking looks of the elegant company. Only after he was convinced that she, with whose soul his own had melted, was no longer there, he settled his account and wandered out into the open to bathe his hot chest and glowing forehead in the starry night.

Restlessly Hermann wandered through the winter night. Then he climbed an observation tower and watched the clockwork of the stars for a long time. Orion and Sirius had already dipped below the horizon, and Procyon was already leaping across the Milky Way behind them as he made his way back to the hotel. Dreamlessly he slept then until daybreak. Only the loud bang of the gong, calling the guests to lunch, woke him up.

At the lunch table, he searched in vain for the object of his longing. Even the head waiter was unable to give him any information. For three days he searched the large hotels and sports fields of the town, but nowhere did he find a trace of his beloved.

Who was she? A sudden shock ran through him at the thought that she could be of such high origin that there was no possibility of approaching her, even the thought of possessing her was madness. But she had approached him so graciously and singled him out, the mirthless one, among the hundreds of festive guests! Or was this only the play of a whim, long forgotten by herself, while he presumptuously dared to build his whole life on it? Who were the gentlemen in her company? He had not looked at them more closely, for he saw only her. Perhaps she was a prince's daughter, who followed the idea of cavorting unrecognized among ordinary mortals under the protection of her surroundings? Perhaps it amused her that he had the tactlessness to be the only non-celebrant to force himself on the party? Who did she think he was? The cut that still burned on his cheek from yesterday's accident probably made him appear as a student who had nothing more urgent to do than to boastfully display his first trophy of the fencing hall. She had made fun of that! And what was he but a student, an eternally unfinished one, always searching and never finishing himself? Now it seemed to him as if only mockery and scorn had spoken from her look, which before seemed to promise him paradise. Of course it was like that, and he was and remained the fool and the fantasist, who always confused desire and reality in life as well as in science!

But he wanted to see her at least one more time, to make sure, even if he trembled at the thought that she might no longer recognize him at all or might even reject him with polite coolness! And then again, suddenly, hope carried him up over all the abysses of doubt and despair to those bright heights of certainty that are so close to the supernatural regions from which we come, and an intuition of immeasurable future happiness filled him.

In such a wavering mood, Hermann now went on snowshoes to the neighboring health resorts, as if he had to meet her somewhere unexpectedly. He proceeded in an almost scientific manner. He also had his formal suit, the only one he owned, sent to him by Röschen Brunner, so that he could participate in the social gatherings that took place every evening in a different hotel. He also had money sent to him from the bank where he kept his savings. But New Year's Day was already over and the Christmas holidays were coming to an end, without his inquiries yielding the slightest result.

One day he had an experience that brought him closer to his goal in an unexpected way. On his restless trips, the iron clamp that held his broken ski together had loosened without him noticing. On a steep descent, which he particularly loved and which he recently undertook more often and more daringly than usual, it came off completely. In a sudden fall he rolled over and sprained his right ankle. With difficulty he dragged himself onto the road. An elderly gentleman, who came along in a distinguished sleigh, gave him a lift. The stranger, who aroused little affection in him, introduced himself, returning his name, as Councilor of Commerce Burghamer. His face, framed by a large fur cap and the turned-up collar of the fur coat, had something diabolical about it. Under thick black, slightly graying brows lurked a pair of deep dark, beady eyes. An unattractive, sluggishly curved nose let gray undergrowth protrude from its openings. The unkempt, heavily graying, black mustache fell in long, slender tresses over the bulging mouth, whose thick lower lip hung down. Gray-black stubble covered the cheeks and chin.

Attentively, with almost guarded sidelong glances, the gentleman eyed his passenger as he asked him about the nature and circumstances of his accident. The young gentleman's open nature seemed to please him, he continued his questions, and it was not long before he was informed about Hermann's background, profession, and life circumstances. Hermann also made no secret of the fact that he intended to exchange science for practice. The only thing he said nothing about was the goal of his searching and longing, which had preoccupied him since Christmas Eve. That was his very own secret.

The Councilor offered to drive his guest to his hotel. Hermann gratefully accepted the offer. When he took his leave after about an hour's journey together, the stranger invited him with friendly words to visit him as soon as his foot would allow. He was staying at the villa and would be here for another eight to ten days. He was always at home between 3 and 4 o'clock in the afternoon. Hermann politely accepted without being pleased about the invitation.

Thanks to poultices of acetic clay and the regimen of massages he prescribed for himself, Hermann was restored to the point where he could
walk with a cane after a few days. At the same time, he hesitated to visit
the Councilor. An inner voice, nourished by the deep dislike he felt for the
stranger from the first moment, held him back. In the end, however, he did
not want to be ungrateful and, above all, he wanted to keep his promise. So
one day he went to see him.

To his surprise, he discovered that he was already familiar with the
villa. He had often walked along this street in search of the beautiful
stranger and had stopped in front of it, which was distinguished from the
other villas in town by its size and style. The thought had occurred to him
that his secret lover might live in this beautiful, stately house. But no matter how often he passed it, no human being had ever appeared there. Now
his heart was pounding. He imagined the woman he longed for suddenly
coming out of the door to meet him.

Reluctantly, he pressed the bell button next to the closed door of the
front garden. It burst open, and as he climbed the stone stairs of the villa,
the front door opened as well. A servant welcomed him, took his hat and
coat and asked him to sit down in a leather armchair in the comfortably
warm hallway. As the servant, to whom he had given his card, moved
away, he settled into a deep chair. Through an open double door, he could
see into an adjoining room.

Suddenly startled, he held on to both armrests of the chair. Just in
front of him on the opposite wall of the open room hung a life-size painting. From the heavy gold frame, a girl's figure seemed to want to step into
the room. It was her!

It was as if he were seeing an apparition. She was walking down a
gently sloping, sun-soaked forest path, in a light, florid, footless summer
dress, her hat on her arm, a few flowers from the meadow gathered in her
hand.

Then he jumped up and hurried toward her. She smiled at him kindly,
as if she were happy to see him again.

The servant came back with the message that the Councilor had given
him.

"Who is the lady?" he wanted to ask. But partly out of fear of betraying his secret love, partly out of an inexplicable oppressive angst, he could not bring himself to utter a word.

With trembling knees, he followed the servant up the stairs. On the turn he stopped and looked back at the picture. Only the dainty feet and the enchantingly beautifully formed ankles were still visible. The rest of the figure was hidden by the door frame. The servant smiled. Hermann noticed it and now walked resolutely up the rest of the stairs.

The Councilor sat at his desk, looking over letters, and received him very kindly. Without getting up, he asked Hermann to take a seat in the club chair directly opposite the desk. After inquiring about Hermann's condition without being particularly concerned, he said abruptly:

"So you want to give up being a professor?"

"I would love to go into practice, that is, if I can find a position."

"Understood. With a professorship, nothing looks right after all. And why shouldn't you find a position? You've learned something, you're a doctor, a professor..."

"Pardon me," Hermann interrupted him, "I am only a private lecturer. I don't even have the title 'professor' yet."

"What's a private lecturer! What's a professor! You are something and you can do something, that's the main thing! That's what gets you into a practice! I guarantee it!"

Hermann was beginning to get carried away. The Councilor was suddenly waving his hands in the air and mumbling like a Galician Jew. The thought that had oppressed him earlier, that he could or must be the father of the girl he adored, now only amused him. With a certain comical joy he thereupon followed the gesticulations of his counterpart.

"You're speaking as if you already have a job for me!" he laughed.

"I do! I do have one! That is, depending on the circumstances!

"What do you mean?" asked Hermann curiously.

"Do you know anything about colors?"

"I was very interested in the chemistry of dyes as a student. But in chemistry you must quickly limit yourself to a special field. As I told you the other day, I am a protein chemist."

"That's good too, protein chemist! Very good! Has a great future! I can tell you! If we make flour and sugar from wood shavings! You can become a millionaire, if you invent that. But do you know anything about dye chemistry?"

"As I just told you, I..."

The Councilor did not let him finish the sentence. He jumped up from the desk buoyantly and stepped close to Hermann.

"Look here, doctor! I produce, to be specific, tiles, as strong as iron! Look here!" He took a thin, light gray, rhombic-shaped disk from a side table. "Here! Look!" With his hands, covered in black hair, he made strenuous movements, as if he were trying with great effort to break the object.

"Break it!"

He handed the tile to Hermann, who now also tried in vain to break it.

"Well? Can you?" grinned the Councilor triumphantly. "You can't!"

He took the object from Hermann's hand again and threw it to the ground with force. It did not break.

"Well? See?" he exulted.

"That's certainly amazing," said Hermann with honest admiration. At this, he bent down, picked it up again and threw it back on the floor with somewhat lesser force than the Councilor had done, as if he feared it might break after all. But again it remained whole.

"And that's nothing!"

With these words, the Councilor attacked the slab in a downright angry manner and stomped it violently with the heel of his shoe. "Do you see? Do you see? Now try and see if you can do it!" He asked Hermann, with animated movements of his arms and hands, to step up now and try the work of destruction for himself.

Hermann hesitantly raised his hobnailed mountaineering boot to strike.

"Only Kurash! Only Kurash!" the Councilor urged him.

Hermann stamped on the plate strongly. Again it did not break. He now wantonly gave it several strong kicks in quick succession. It remained whole as before.

"So? So? What do you say now?" the Councilor asked the very astonished Hermann, almost with a sneer. Instead of an answer, he picked up the plate and, turning it in all directions, examined its structure with scientific zeal.

"What is the tile made of?" he asked, tapping it with his index finger. It gave a bright sound.

"Yes, what's it made of!" grinned the Councilor. "That is my secret patent!"

"It can't possibly be a secret," Hermann said nonchalantly. "Even if the tile is patented. Its composition can be easily determined by chemical analysis. Here, by the way, you can see with the naked eye that it contains asbestos."

With these words, Hermann pulled out his pocket knife and exposed an asbestos fiber on one edge of the slab.

The Councilor made a respectful face.

"And I'll bet there's lime in there, too. Carbonate of lime, of course." With that, he took the vial from the geology testing kit out of the pocket of his sports coat and placed a drop of it on the plate. Immediately, numerous gas bubbles developed on the moistened area, proving that he was right in his assumption.

"There! Look!" he said to the Councilor, "hydrochloric acid!" Looking closely at the tile, then he added: "The binding mass probably consists of cement, otherwise it would react much more vigorously from the acid!"

The Councilor listened to these explanations in amazement.

"Well, am I right?" asked Hermann with a smile.

With a mixture of respect and distrust, the Councilor blinked at him for a while out of his pinched eyes. Then he suddenly said, jovially patting Hermann on the shoulder:

"You are my man!"

"What are you trying to say?"

"That's all I'm saying! I'm just saying, you're my man! But now tell me! Is that a tile or is that not a tile? Hey? What?"

"You spoke earlier about artificial slate. I assume that the tiles are to be used for roofing. That is certainly quite an excellent roof covering and, on top of that, completely weatherproof and fireproof!"

"You guess everything, Doctor! Of course, this is a roof covering! But what you don't guess: It's my invention! My invention!" With that, he triumphantly stuck both his thumbs into the armholes of his vest and bobbed up and down on the tips of his feet.

"You are to be congratulated!" said Hermann honestly. "How do you fabricate the tiles, then? Are they pressed, drawn, cut?"

"Yes, how do I fabricate them! But you also want to know everything!"

"I don't want to penetrate further into your secret! But if I wanted to, all I would have to do is read the patent specification!"

"There is nothing can you read in the patent specification! Nothing at all! Yes, you can read the writing! But copy it? Others have already tried to copy it! The tiles fell apart like dirt!" the Councilor of Commerce shouted at the inquisitive questioner.

Hermann remained silent, shocked. The Councilor bored his eyes into Hermann's, as if he had an enemy before him. But then he slowly twisted his face into a good-natured grin and said, patting him on the shoulder again:

"Visit me once you are in Berlin! Maybe I'll show you then how the tiles are made!"

"So, you live in Berlin?" asked Hermann with lively interest, and a crimson flush covered his face. Forebodingly, he connected the word "Berlin" with his secret love. For it was obvious that the girl, whose picture hung in the room below, must also live where the Councilor of Commerce lived, even if he could not and would not consider it possible that he was her father.

Hermann's query did not escape the attention of the Councilor. He looked at him again suspiciously, even hostilely. "Why are you surprised?" he asked coldly.

Hermann hesitated for a moment. Then he lied: "I want to go to Berlin soon anyway, to look for a position. That would be wonderful if I could visit you there on this occasion. I suppose you have your factory in Berlin, too?"

Now the Councilor laughed. "My factory? Which factory do you mean?"

"Your factory where you fabricate this excellent tile!"

The Councilor looked at Hermann almost pityingly.

"So far, you are quite bright, my dear good Doctor! But not yet entirely bright! What's a factory? I don't have a factory, and yet I have seventeen!"

"I don't understand."

"You'll just have to get brighter, Doctor! Why do I have my patent? Where am I going to burden myself with the noise of a factory, with machines and people and houses and risk? I give licenses! Licenses for Germany, for Austria-Hungary, for France, for Italy, for Spain, for Portugal, for England, for America, for Australia, licenses for the whole world! Of course I have shares in the factories! Even a lot of shares! Almost all of the one in Berlin! That's why I don't have a factory, and yet I have seventeen of them! Have you ever heard of Evonite?"

"Of what?" asked Hermann in surprise.

"Well yes! Of Evonite!" With that, the Councilor of Commerce pointed to the tile.

"Oh, I see! Now I understand!, You call the material from which you make the plates, or have them made, 'Aevonite'! An apt name indeed! From 'aevum,' in German: *Ewigkeit*! Meaning eternal! Truly, a quite brilliant designation! Did you invent it too?"

"Well, what do you mean invented? Where did he get his lawyer? He took enough money from me for that! The rascal demanded five thousand marks for a few letters! And he didn't even make the word himself! He took it from Italian!"

"You mean to say from Latin!" interjected Hermann.

"Well, from Latin or Italian. I don't really know anymore. It's been over ten years. But I only gave him four thousand five hundred. And he only got it for the first letter, for the "E", which he made from the "Ä", because otherwise the patent office wouldn't have patented the name. The name of my invention is "Evonite", not "Aevonite", with "an E" and not with "an A". He wrote the letters E and A with his finger on the tile.

"I understand!" Hermann smiled. "But now tell me," he continued at once, "since it was not you, but someone else who came up with the name, are you in the end not the actual inventor of the substance that bears this name?"

The Councilor of Commerce glared hostilely at the questioner.

"I mean," Hermann explained, "that you bought the invention yourself from someone else, so it's not really your invention at all?"

"How is it not my invention?" drawled the Councilor. "If I can pay the inventor with my money and buy the invention from him for cash, isn't that my invention? What could the inventor have done with it without my money? And doesn't he still have his percentage of the invention? Ten percent of everything that the licenses carry? And didn't he get from me, besides the percentage, a hundred thousand marks that I paid him beforehand, cash on the table? And this, then, is not my invention?"

Completely oblivious to his position as Councilor of Commerce, Burghamer gave the purest Jewish performance. Hermann could not refrain from laughing out loud.

"So? What are you laughing at?"

"Forgive me, Mr. Councilor! You misunderstand me! I have no doubt whatsoever that you are the rightful owner of the invention! But now I think I ought to say goodbye, it's already getting dark."

Ignoring Hermann's intention to leave, the Councilor turned on the electric light and rang a bell.

"But you see, doctor," he then continued, composing himself, for he had obviously become aware that in the heat of the moment, as often happened, his Galician ancestors had run away with him once again. "Sit down, the Evonite still has one big flaw, it's too light. People want black or red roofs, especially in Germany. It's actually ridiculous, but what are you going to do! Germans are like that. That's why the Evonite has to be colored. But the color doesn't last, the rain washes it off again and again. I have already tried everything possible, but..."

He suddenly stopped, because he perceived that Hermann was not listening at all.

When the room was suddenly illuminated, Hermann's gaze had fallen on the life-size bust portrait, painted in oil, of a woman who bore a striking resemblance to the girl of his desire. She was equally beautiful and blond, only more mature and fuller, and might have been about forty years old. Undoubtedly she was the mother of the girl.

"You're not listening at all, Doctor!"

"Excuse me. I have heard everything. So the Evonite is to be dyed," said Hermann, now turning back to the Councilor.

"That's right. But the paint doesn't hold."

"You must not coat it with the dye, of course, but dye the fibers directly, preferably chemically producing the dye directly in the fibers!"

"You can do that?" asked the Councilor in amazement?

"For a chemist, this is - well, in this case, where we are dealing with the dyeing of a mineral substance - perhaps not a trivial matter, but in any case a thoroughly solvable task. Haven't you ever consulted a chemist?"

"That's just the catch! Who can trust anyone these days! The rascals all look like regular people! Who can guarantee that a guy like that, won't just back out and snatch the invention right out from under my nose, before the process is patented?"

Hermann could not help smiling pityingly. How this person was the slave of his greed and mistrust!

"All men are not crooks, after all!" he said. "Besides, I am convinced that this tile here can be chemically dyed so jet black that no rain will be able to wash away the color."

"You're kidding me!"

"Not at all!" I can prove that to you right away, provided that I can procure the necessary reagents for the experiment. I will see if they are available in the local pharmacy. If that is the case, I will come back tomorrow, if you wish, and dye the tile here before your eyes!"

The Councilor listened with wide, even greedy eyes.

"If you get this done, you're a made man! I guarantee it!" he said incredulously. But immediately he added, "You will come back, won't you, Doctor?"

"If I make you a promise, that should be enough! But if you distrust me, then…"

"Who's talking about mistrust? Who? Who? So it's agreed, you will come back tomorrow at the same time and bring the chemical things with you? We're in agreement? Shake on it!"

With these words he held out his hand to Hermann. With a feeling of uneasiness, he put his hand in it. He stood there as if on coals. He felt as if one of the two women was going to enter the room at any moment. He heard light footsteps in the hallway. The door opened, but only a maid entered, holding a silver tray with two steaming tea glasses and a plate of pastries. She was a petite, slender young thing. The white bonnet on her luxuriant blond hair was very lovely.

Strange! All the people in this house were blond, except for the master of the house! Even the servant was blond, as Hermann subsequently noticed.

The girl put the tea tray on the table and left the room as quickly as she had come. Hermann clearly noticed that the eyes of the master of the house followed her with pleasure.

Without asking for Hermann's consent, the Councilor pushed a tea glass toward him. At the same time, he threw two, three, four, five pieces of sugar into the glass, so that Hermann anxiously held his hand over it. Then he helped himself and sipped the hot drink with a loud noise, his unkempt mustache hanging down into the liquid. Every now and then he dipped a piece of a cookie into the tea and, after taking a bite, dropped it in, only to fish it out again with his fingers and devour it with smacking sounds.

"You'll be a made man when you get that done with the tiles," he said in between, winking merrily at Hermann with his small, pitch-black eyes.

A turbulence that could no longer be contained ran through Hermann's limbs. He gratefully declined the imported delicacies offered to him by the Councilor after tea and pressed him to leave in the vague hope of meeting the ladies. He did not dare to ask about them. The Councilor accompanied him down to the front door. But Hermann's hopes remained unfulfilled, neither of the ladies showed themselves.

"You will definitely come back tomorrow, won't you?" asked the Councilor of Commerce again suspiciously. At the same time, he held fast the hand of his interlocutor.

Hermann had trouble overcoming a feeling bordering on disgust that trickled over him from the cold, damp hand of the Councilor. He felt as if he were holding a frog in his hand. Slowly, so as not to appear rude, he freed his fingers from the amphibious grasp.

"I promised you, after all!" he said, and quickly moved away.

About fifty paces from the villa, Hermann stopped and looked back.

"What if she was looking out at him?"

The house was silent and dark. Only the windows of the lower ground floor, which might have contained the utility rooms, were illuminated. The Councilor's study was in the back, facing the garden, probably also the private rooms of the ladies. Sirius sparkled like a giant diamond immediately above the roof. Clouds of smoke curled from the chimneys. But nothing moved in the windows.

Ashamed of his childish thought, Hermann quickly continued on his way. Nevertheless, he had to force himself not to look back again.

Once at the hotel, he locked himself in his room, as he always did when he wanted to make up his mind about something.

That his secret love should be the daughter of this repulsive man was unbearable and at the same time incomprehensible to him. And yet there was hardly any doubt possible. The two portraits of the ladies confirmed it. The older one was the wife of the Councilor of Commerce and the girl was the daughter of them both. Both?

A new hope rose in Hermann. It didn't have to be his daughter at all! She could have come from a previous marriage of the mother! Yes, the mother did not even have to be the wife of the Councilor! Who knows how the old man came to possess these two pictures! He seemed to take particular pleasure in blond women, and indeed in blond people in general. Perhaps that was why he had taken a liking to himself. Perhaps he had bought the two portraits of the women in some art exhibition. What silly foolish fears he had talked himself into! Was the Councilor married at all? Hermann could not remember noticing a wedding ring on his hand. He probably did not even know the two ladies personally, and perhaps did not even know who they were!

This thought now troubled him greatly, and he reproached himself for not having found the courage to ask whom the portraits represented. He could hardly wait for the next day. That same evening, he went to the pharmacy and was happy to obtain the reagents he needed for the experiment.

At the stroke of three the following day, he returned to the villa. The servant had orders to take him immediately to the Councilor's room. Impatiently, curiously, and suspiciously, he was already waiting for him. He was only able to catch a glimpse of the picture of his secret love as he passed. She smiled at him pleasantly like the day before.

Hermann suggested to the Councilor that the experiment should be carried out in the bathroom, since plenty of water, a rinsing device and the like were needed for this purpose and, in the event of any splashing of the chemical liquids, the least harm could be done there. Secretly, he hoped that in this way he would somehow come into contact with the ladies of the house, for the thought that they must surely belong to the house had again become powerful in him on the way there.

The Councilor accepted his proposal without further ado, but Hermann did not catch sight of the ladies.

He now went to work without further delay. He asked for two wash-basins. He poured a greenish liquid into one and a yellowish liquid into the other. Then he added just so much water into each bowl that the tile placed in them were covered. After it had been treated with one liquid, he lifted it out, let it drip off, and then put it into the other liquid. Instantly, it turned jet black.

The Councilor of Commerce was speechless.

Hermann now took out the colored tile and rinsed it vigorously under the water pipe. It retained its deep black color in the process.

Astonished beyond all measure, the Councilor took the tile in his hands and wiped it with his finger. It did not stain at all.

"Marvelous!" he exclaimed.

Hermann now explained to him the secret of this intimate connection between color and mineral, as far as it was possible to make it comprehensible to the layman. Then he continued:

"We will now take the plate outdoors and leave it outside for a while to see if it changes in the air. If this is the case, the experiment would have to be repeated with other solutions. There would be a whole series of possibilities to reach the goal, but one would have to be strictly methodical and not spare any effort or patience.

The Councilor of Commerce shook his head in astonishment repeatedly. He looked at the plate, rinsed it with water, wiped his finger over it, again and again always with the same satisfactory result. Finally he said:

"Come up to my room!"

Upstairs, the Councilor sat down at his desk and asked Hermann to take a seat opposite him.

"Is the material you're using to dye expensive?" he asked.

"I don't think there is a cheaper one," replied Hermann. "One liquid was an iron solution, the other an extract of gall apples."

"What do you want for the invention?" asked the Councilor hastily, and fixed a furtive, almost spiteful glance on Hermann.

"It's not an invention at all," he replied calmly. "The process has been known for a long time. The two substances are the material from which ink used to be made. Every student knows that nowadays."

The counsellor's face twisted into a grin.

"So anyone can copy it and you don't even have to patent it?" "Creating the black color in the primitive way I just showed you is not patentable, of course," Hermann replied with even calm. "But it is not as simple as you seem to imagine! It will take months, maybe years of trial and error to find the right method that can be used in practice. What I have just shown you was an initial superficial laboratory experiment, which was only intended to prove to you that the problem can fundamentally be solved by chemical means. Presumably, a whole series of patents will have to be taken out on the process if anything useful is to come of it."

This made sense to the Councilor.

"Do you want to do it?" he hurried out after a while.

"Why not?" Hermann replied with restrained excitement. A whole series of future images suddenly appeared before his soul. He thought of his beloved and the possibility of winning her. He had to earn money, whoever she was, in order to be able to offer her an existence worthy of her, and here was the opportunity!

"And what are your conditions?"

"We haven't got that far yet. That will come naturally in the course of the work. For the time being, pay me a salary in the amount of my current income, and we'll come to an agreement about the share of the profits that I'll receive from the invention.

"How much do you currently earn?" blurted out the Councilor.

"With my college funds, I stand to make about two thousand five hundred marks a year with free housing, lights, and heat."

The Councilor burst into loud laughter.

"And for that you play professor?"

"So far, the income has been quite sufficient for my needs," Hermann replied.

"Well, you won't get around Berlin with it, my dear fellow. You'll have to move to Berlin, of course. I will set up a laboratory for you in the factory there, so that you can do the tests on the spot. Let me tell you something: I'll pay you an annual salary of five thousand marks and ten percent of whatever the invention earns. Do you agree to that?"

Hermann hesitated. The salary seemed princely to him, though the profit share was low enough. But after all, if the thing succeeded, he could earn a lot with it even then.

"Well? I want say even fifteen percent (he always said 'per-zent' instead of 'percent' in memory of Galicia), but on my honor, if I say more, it's my bankruptcy!"

Hermann's gaze fell on the portrait of the woman and he quickly reached out his hand to the Councilor.

"So it's done!" said the latter, slapping the proffered hand, reaching for paper and pen and drawing up the contract.

Hermann was like in a dream. When he saw the Councilor sitting there and scribbling on the paper, it was as if he had lived through the same situation before. Just like that, on that fateful Easter Sunday, the Jew sat at the table and drew up the contract that destroyed the happiness of his parents' home and killed his father, mother, and sister. A suffocating feeling of fear, the premonition of something terrible suddenly came over him and he was on the verge of falling into the pen of the Councilor and tearing up the document. Then his eyes met the portrait of the woman again. He saw in his mind's eye how his beloved passed by him on Christmas Eve, looked at him, hardly noticeably stopped, continued walking, turned around and threw the paper shackle at him as if she wanted to chain him to herself, how the paper tore and how she then walked away with an indescribable look without turning back to him. A soul-consuming longing rose up in him and a foreboding of immeasurable happiness mixed with fear, hope and trepidation.

Now the Councilor stood up and handed him the pen to sign. It was the same movement, the same look with which the father was asked to sign his misfortune. And the words were the same: "We will make the notarized contract tomorrow!"

Hermann stood as if paralyzed. The Councilor's gaze clung to him like that of a snake transfixing its victim.

"Well?!" he said in amazement when Hermann hesitated. "If you don't want to, then don't! Then I'll look for someone else!"

An abrupt jealousy struck its claws into Hermann's chest. And another one! With a sudden, even wild decision, he took the piece of writing in his hand, flew through it and inscribed his name to it.

Breathing a sigh of relief, he stepped away from the desk and stopped in front of the portrait of the woman. As if it were a matter of course, he said:

"I suppose this is your dear wife?"

The Councilor, drying the signed document with a blotter, looked up and confirmed, "My wife." And with more boasting than with understandable pride, he added "A very beautiful wife! Yes?"

Hermann nodded. Then he continued to ask in as indifferent a tone as possible, without looking away from the picture:

"And the young lady whose picture hangs in the room below is your daughter, then?"

"Have you already discovered her?" laughed the Councilor. "It is my daughter," he continued boasting. "And she is as clever as her mother! Plays and sings and is solid in every sport and speaks four languages perfectly!"

The words of Councilor ran down Hermann's spine like blue lightning. The question hovered on his lips whether the daughter was engaged or married, but he did not dare to say it. Only with extreme difficulty did he control his excitement, and only to conceal it did he continue to ask:

"And you don't have any other children?"

The Councilor's face darkened.

"None," he replied.

Now Hermann dared to ask whether he could pay his respects to the ladies of the house. Then he learned what he already feared, that they had already left. Right on the first holiday, for the Riviera.

The servant entered and brought the mail.

The Councilor went through the addresses. Suddenly, his face took on a surprised expression. With the words "from my daughter" he took out a letter, tore it open and took out a card. At one point he faltered, as if he could not decipher it. Finally, pointing to a particular word, he asked Hermann if he could read it.

With a beating heart, Hermann picked up the letter. It was clear, steep, big writing. Only the one word had been edited several times and was illegible. Perhaps the word would be obvious from the context, Hermann thought, and asked if he could read the contents. The Councilor answered in the affirmative, and Hermann read:

> Bordighera, Villa Monfalcone, January 7.
> Dear Papa!
>   I left a novel in my room, a paperback, with a yellow cover, it is half uncut. Please send it to me immediately, I'm in the mood to read it right now. I can't quite remember the title and the author, I think it's by … (and here followed the illegible word). Please don't mix it up with the other novels

that are still lying on my writing table. I'm sorry to bother
you with this, but I'm afraid the girl will send me the wrong
book. I thank you in advance for your trouble. I have received the information, thank you very much for that as well.
Mom sends her regards and so do I.

Elisabeth.

The illegible word could be Dostoyevsky. Hermann's suspicion was confirmed when the chambermaid brought all the books in question, about a
dozen, on the order of the Councilor of Commerce.

"Elisabeth!" So that was her name! Like a precious stone that had
fallen into a deep well, this name now rested in Hermann's heart. However, he wondered at the meager, almost businesslike manner in which the
girl wrote to her father. This realization, however, only served to make him
happy. The letter proved that she was not close to the Councilor, to whom
she was outwardly as dissimilar as possible, even inwardly. When Hermann asked the Councilor if he was not worried about the ladies when they
traveled alone, he responded that business prevented him from accompanying them. From the answer, however, it was clear that this was only an
excuse. By the way, the Councilor added, the ladies were in good hands,
Government Assessor Baron von Werheim, a good acquaintance, was accompanying them.

This statement hit Hermann like a thunderclap. Who was this Government Assessor? Undoubtedly, the monocled man who seemed in
particular to be courting her among her companions on Christmas Eve. A
wild jealousy suddenly reared its head in Hermann. Unable to converse
any longer, he quickly departed. The Councilor urged him to be there tomorrow in time for the notarial execution of the contract.

On the terrace of Villa Monfalcone, Elisabeth Burghamer was comfortably stretched out in a deck chair. She was reading a book. But she did not seem to be particularly captivated by the reading. She often let the book sink into her lap and looked out to sea, pondering and dreaming. Spring had arrived on the Riviera earlier than usual this year. It was only the beginning of February, and the gardener was already dragging the palm trees out of the greenhouse and into the open air. In the fresh green grass of the meadow, the magnolias were resplendent with their giant blossoms and the trees of the park were covered with soft yellow buds. The cheerful chirping of birds drifted over to the terrace. A fine haze lay over the landscape, and from time to time, when a gentle breeze blew in from the deep blue sea, in whose smooth surface the mild spring sun bathed pleasantly, it brought an indescribably delicious fragrance that the young girl inhaled greedily. Then male footsteps approached her from behind in the villa. Immediately she picked up the book again and immersed herself in reading.

"Good afternoon, my gracious lady!" now sounded behind her.

Without returning the greeting or even looking up from the book, she casually stretched out one hand in the direction from which the voice came.

Baron Dr. Edgar von Werheim, a young man about 28 years old, hurriedly jumped over. He dropped his monocle and greeted her with a somewhat more than social kiss on the hand.

"May I inquire how yesterday's ball fared for the gracious lady?"

"Thanks. I had quite a good time."

Meanwhile, she continued to look into the book as if reading.

The Baron put the spectacle back in place. Then he said in an embarrassed manner:

"I must be interrupting!"

"Not at all!" was the answer. At this, Elisabeth closed the book and, looking at him, asked:

"And you? Having a good time too?"

"Frankly, no. I was plenty bored."

"You have only yourself to blame, my dear! You have to come to a masked ball in disguise, otherwise the so-called fun is over! By the way, the cabaret we presented after the unmasking was quite respectable! The

Chat Noir in Berlin or even the Parisian Moulin Rouge are hardly more authentic and tantalizing! How could you stay there for so long?"

"I admit," smiled the Baron, "that was a pretty good thing. However…"

"Oh, you mean that the performers were all only ladies of the best society? That should actually heighten the experience for you Lords of creation, who enjoy the haut-goût to excess! Just because of the novelty!"

"I didn't mean it like that at all! On the contrary, I wanted to say that if one applied the standard of strict correctness…"

"Don't pretend, little Baron! You're trumpeting morals like a professor of ethics! Today we are red, tomorrow we are dead! Actually, the mere thought of it is horrible. But that's why! I can tell you, if I were a man, I wouldn't do it any differently than you all!"

"You still don't understand me, madam! Of course, I do not have the slightest inner objection to such choices. I mean, of course, a purely external standard. You see, I am a government official and I want to have a career. Therefore, I strive to be a thoroughly correct person, at least to make the impression of such. That is, so to speak, it is a need for me, but it also has it's advantages. Both outwardly as well as upwardly. For example, at the moment I should be fortunate enough to call you my fiancée, I would be extremely embarrassed if you…"

"If I performed as a Tingel-Tangle singer, as I did last night, you want to say."

"Not at all, my dear lady! I do not think in such philistine terms. Especially not when it concerns ladies of the very best society, where any haut-goût, as you so aptly called it earlier, is quite out of the question."

"Well, well!" the young lady interrupted him. "Do you always know that without a doubt?"

"That's not what matters at all! The main thing is that outwardly the form is correctly maintained! I mean…"

"Now I'm really curious to know what you're actually getting at!" the girl interrupted him again.

"I mean, it might have been noted badly by correct-thinking people, the high and highest officials, for example, that you treated me all evening yesterday as if I were not present, so to speak, yet everybody knows…"

"Now allow me, my dear highly correct Mr. Government Assessor and Baron Dr. Edgar von Werheim! First of all, we are not that far along yet, and secondly, you should not expect me to monopolize myself for you at a Venetian carnival, whether you are my admirer or bridegroom, or even my dear lord husband!"

"Of course not. But nevertheless, correctness demanded it, especially since everyone here knows that I am courting you, that you should have taken a little notice of me, especially since I was not masked. Forgive me, Madam, if I present this to you in all due form, without wanting to reproach you with it!"

"Well, you are good!" the beautiful girl laughed at him. "Besides, this goes completely against our agreement!"

"Indeed! But…"

"What do you mean by 'but'?" said the young lady quite angrily. "When you proposed to me at Christmas, I asked for three months to think it over. During this time, each of us should be allowed to follow and do whatever we want! Is that true or not?"

"Indeed! But…"

"'But' nothing! 'But' nothing at all! Are the three months over?"

The Baron wanted to object again. But she didn't let him get to that, and continued:

"You promised not to press me again before this time was up! It was only under this condition that I allowed you to accompany us here at all. You admit that, don't you?"

Now the Baron stepped close to her, grasped her hand, and said with a passion whose genuineness was difficult to ascertain:

"Elisabeth! Don't torture me any longer! Put an end to it! Make up your mind one way or the other!"

Gently wrestling her hand from his, she said with smiling calmness:

"Now, first of all, pull up a chair there and sit down here nice and quiet, and then we'll continue to talk to each other openly and honestly."

The Baron complied with the request. The beautiful girl, whose cheeks had taken on a vivid color, rose from the lounge chair, sat down across it as if on a bench, and began:

"When you proposed to me at Christmas, you knew little more about me than my father's bank account."

The Baron made an imploringly negative gesture.

"Please. You don't need to deny it or even apologize for it. I don't hold it against you at all and find it quite 'correct' and quite in order. What else could you and did you need to know about me if you wanted to marry me? We had already known each other for three weeks, had tobogganed and danced together a few times, and were otherwise very bored with each other. Wasn't that enough?"

The Baron wanted to object, but she again did not let him get a word in edgewise.

"Please. After all, there's no point in denying it, and it doesn't do any harm! On the contrary! Pretty good auspices for a modern marriage, as I need it and you do too probably. Please, don't interrupt me! There is no point in us pretending to each other! A government official who wants to make a career nowadays must first of all marry well, and this marriage with me offers you the very best prospects of that. And as for me, well, the matter is similar. I have to continue playing the role that was assigned to me willy-nilly from the theater of the top ten thousand, because one has to play some role in life, since one is no longer able to live life for oneself. You look surprised. You probably don't understand me at all and think I'm crazy. There is no harm in that. Just keep on listening to me. For my part, I am thoroughly fed up with all the nonsense of our so-called life. I can only tell you that I am choked with disgust just hearing talk of clubs and dancing, charity parties and premieres, Venetian nights and horse races, bobsleds and automobiles! The question, repeated several times a day, what should I wear, can make me furious! And all the insipid chatter about Reinhard and Richard Strauss, Liebermann and the Secession, about monism and futurism, Wedekind and Strindberg, and in one breath the raving about Bach and Beethoven, Lissauer and Sternheim, Puppchen and Goethe, it can make one sick! I don't have a girlfriend, at least not the kind I need, an honest, like-minded soul. Where should honesty come from nowadays! No one wants to be what he is, but at any price wants to seem something he is not and can't be! That's why there is all this nonsense and high-trotting chatter!

"In truth, all the interests of our girls revolve only around the question of how I will outdo my dear friend, how I will steal her flirtation and how I will finally make a good match. They don't want to have children, the only thing that could finally give our lives substance. And if, against their will, they do give birth to one or two, then these poor worms are delivered to the nurses and governesses and go as soon as possible to a boarding school. The only glorious happiness that is granted to a woman by nature, to bear, nourish and educate children, is considered shocking and is also so exceedingly tiresome and inconvenient! In short, my dear Baron, I am pretty much on my own and feel as if I am swimming forlornly in a swirling ocean. Of course, I have already tried to come ashore and build my own life. I have tried to study in order to do and become something useful and to be of some benefit to people.

"But there is something in my blood that does not let me persevere or come to logical decisions. This may be due to my upbringing, my being spoiled or my lack of talent, in short, I don't know. The only thing that could save me would be the honest love of an honest man. But I cannot buy this with all my money. I can tell you that last year I was about to marry a healthy, handsome peasant boy who had honestly fallen head over heels in love with me. It would have been a joy to me to let him make me a wife and a mother, to give birth to half a dozen strapping boys, and in between to grow cabbages and milk the cows. Such a life would still have had a meaning and a purpose and I would have been rid of all this stupid social insanity.

"But as I told you, there is nothing whole in me. A kind of half-heartedness or cowardice, or call it what you will, always keeps me from doing what I am actually driven to do. Don't think that so-called good manners would have kept me from it! Good manners! Such a lie again! We don't have any good manners at all! Pathetic hypocrisy and mendacity is what we call good manners in our circles! Appearance, lies, deceit is everything and even more so our morality! I bet—I don't even have to bet, because I know it—not half of the girls of our so-called good society, which has this so-called good custom of perpetual lease, still enter into marriage as virgins, and from the hundreds of married people, hardly one remains faithful to her husband. They smile! They know it! Is it disgusting or not? No! It is not the so-called good custom that forces us into the social spell! It is the lie! It is the tyrant that none of us dares to slap in the face! It is the one that holds us and does not let us go! We are slaves to it with skin and hair, with body and soul, until we are forced to resign behind the black backdrop, where nobody really knows what it looks like behind it, despite Häckel and Ostwald!

"So, dear Baron, there is nothing left for us but to resign ourselves to these things and to make them as tolerable as possible, and for this you need a lady representative for your house and I need a legitimate chaperon, *violà tout*! The only question is whether or not we can agree on the mutual conditions for entering into such a community of interests."

"But my dear lady," the Baron interrupted her almost indignantly, "do you doubt the honesty and sincerity of my love?"

She smiled.

"Don't rush into the unforeseen expenses, my dear Baron! As far as you are capable of a warmer sentiment at all, I gladly believe that you are giving it to me. But to describe the feelings which you find it advantageous to devote to me, with the weighty word 'love' would be as silly as it is tasteless. What would have become of your irresistible "love" for me if the information you obtained about me had not confirmed the data of your marriage bureau that my dowry consists of a seven-digit number?"

Without being embarrassed in any way, the Baron replied with a smile:

"You are too clever a young lady to expect an answer to this from me. You have undoubtedly learned by now through your own information office that my fortune is not inferior to yours, even if my correctness forbids me to emphasize that. And I doubt very much whether you or your parents would have allowed me to accompany you here if the information about me had not been satisfactory in every respect."

"Maybe!" replied the young girl with a flippant shrug of her shoulders.

"So if you find it so difficult to decide on my proposal, surely the cause cannot lie in my circumstances!"

"You're quite right there!"

"There you go! Do you have something to say about me personally?"

"You seem so convinced of your own perfection that you don't even think such a thing is possible!"

"What do you mean, my dear lady? What do you find wrong with me?" asked the Baron, visibly astonished as he put in his monocle.

"I already told you when you proposed to me that I like you quite well. You are no more unsympathetic to me than all the irreproachable cavaliers who honestly or dishonestly confuse their love for my purse with their love for my person. Also, the information that I have obtained, especially about your past morality, has turned out to my satisfaction. You seem surprised about this yourself? My God, the fact that you put up with the little actress for years and had another relationship besides, even two of them at times, one with, one without a child, doesn't bother me at all. This does not play the slightest role in the community of interests that we want to enter into together. You have not yet been in conflict with the penal code and you have not yet had to be vaccinated with Salvarsan, that is the main thing for me. Everything else of your past does not interest me. Or maybe something does, but you can't help that."

"What do you mean?" asked the Baron, smiling.

"May I be blunt?"

"I insist on it!"

"Well, it's your name I don't like."

"My name?" asked the Baron with astonishment.

"Does it bother you that I'm noble?"

"Not so much. But you can clearly see in the name what a hefty sum your blessed father spent to shorten the first syllable of the name by one letter. I admit that Baron von Werheim sounds better than Baron von

Wertheim. But the pruning of the thing is too noticeable, and that displeases me."

"Excuse me, my very honored madam," the Baron replied, affirmatively pressing his right hand flat to his chest, "I was born a Christian just like you!"

"Yes, of course! So it shouldn't be necessary for your name to suggest the opposite. You yourself look quite Christian, except for the suspicious black frizzy hair and the obligatory black mustache, especially when you stick that cursed shard of glass in your face. But as I said, I am not yet beyond a certain disgust for the matter. It's possible that it will subside with time, but I'd be lying if I said it was already the case today."

"May I now, in all modesty, also take the liberty of making a remark about you, my dear lady?" said the Baron, with a smug expression and tone, who was by no means offended.

"But of course!" she sounded back challengingly.

"Well, I mean, people who live in glass houses should not throw stones!"

"May I ask you to express yourself a little more clearly, Baron?" said the beautiful girl with piercing coldness. With this, the light blue of her eyes turned to ashen steel.

The Baron hesitated.

"Now please!" she sneered razor-sharp in his face.

The Baron ran his index finger back and forth between his throat and his turned-up collar. As he did so, he grimaced with a wrinkled nose, so much so that he dropped his spectacle. Curling his thick-lipped mouth into a jaunty oval, he put the glass back in with well-played indifference and smiled mischievously at his beautiful counterpart.

"Courage does not seem to be your forte, Baron von Werheim!" said Elisabeth contemptuously, with special emphasis on the first syllable of his name.

That worked.

"If you absolutely want to hear it, my dear lady…but far be it for me to offend you!"

"You can't offend me at all, Baron! And if you do not speak now on the spot, I will leave you!"

At this, the beautiful speaker, flushed with anger, stood up and made an effort to carry out her threat.

"Well, it concerns your name, too, my dear lady!" said the Baron with superior calm.

"My name?" asked the young girl in utter amazement. "What do you find wrong with my name?"

"Find wrong? There is no question of that at all! But since you so kindly instructed me earlier about the etymology of my name, I am gladly prepared to render you the same service concerning yours, if you wish, that is."

"Yes, I wish that!" the girl, quivering with excitement, snapped at the Baron.

"Good," said the latter and, grimacing, inserted the spectacle anew.

"Now I am really curious!" Elisabeth laughed convulsively. "Burghamer! Isn't that a very beautiful name? Doesn't it sound almost old Germanic? And doesn't it sound much more aristocratic than yours, even though it still lacks the "von" for the time being?"

The Baron smiled.

"What are you laughing at?"

"I really don't know, my dear lady, are you serious or are you joking? Surely you do not believe that your ancestors - on your father's side, of course, I mean - come from an ancient Germanic family of knights?"

"Why shouldn't they? However, I haven't thought about it any further," she added, blushing vividly, somewhat meekly.

"You are delightful, my gracious lady!" Charmed, he kissed her hand.

"Now please! What do you have to tell me about my name?"

"Let's not do that. I don't want to destroy your illusions," the Baron said warmly.

"Now I just want to know!" cried the unsuspecting girl, stamping her foot.

"Well then! - Do you remember your grandfather? I mean your paternal grandfather, of course!"

"No. He died the same year I was born."

"Aha! His name was not Burghamer!"

"It wasn't? Well, what was his name?" asked Elisabeth, amazed beyond measure.

"Well, his name was similar. For when he had earned so much from his rag and second-hand clothes business, which he inherited from his father, that he could start a business befitting his station, he performed a similar operation with his name as my blessed father did with his."

"What?! Did he also let himself be ennobled? Then why don't we have the title of nobility?"

The Baron could not help but laugh out loud.

"Mammon was not enough for nobility at that time!" he said, only forcing himself back to seriousness with difficulty. "But a small operation on the name doesn't cost the earth."

"So he only dropped one letter?" asked Elisabeth, now disappointed. "But that's unthinkable! What kind of letter would that be?"

The Baron burst into new laughter.

"I think you're just making fun of me!" Elizabeth said now in flaming anger.

"Not at all, my dear lady! One need not exactly drop a letter to give one's name a...well, let's say a more pleasing sound! One can also make a small change of syllables!"

"A change of syllables? So his name was Hamerburg?"

"You are delightfully naive, my dear lady!"

"I think I am anything but naive, my dear Baron! And now I urge you to stop teasing me, otherwise we are estranged!"

"So, in a nutshell! Your blessed grandfather's name was Isidor Hamburger."

Horrified, the blonde girl backed up. Her eyes moistened.

"You are disgusting!" she said then.

"I only did it on your orders!" replied the Baron, embarrassed.

But when he saw that she was seriously fighting back her tears, he moved towards her and took her hand.

"What else is there to it, Elisabeth! Society has no idea about the history of your name and mine! And that is all that matters! And by the way, it is good that you know now. That will make you more forgiving towards my name. We both have nothing more to reproach each other with! Isn't that so, Elisabeth?"

"Oh, allow me!" she exclaimed, pushing him indignantly away from her.

"That's something completely different! I don't want anything from you, but you want something from me! Since you proposed to me, and not I to you, I must assume that all my circumstances, including my name, suit you! If not, then please withdraw your proposal, and God knows, I am not angry with you about it! But if I am to become your wife, then I will probably still take an interest in the name I'll have to bear one day! Then I'll take mine off!"

The Baron made a silent bow.

"Or is it somehow obvious that my father was baptized? How?" the girl flashed her eyes at him. "And my mother comes from a purely Christian family."

Instead of answering, the Baron kissed her hand ardently.

At that moment, a servant appeared with the message that the Madame Councilor was asking for tea.

With a bow, the Baron offered Elizabeth his arm, which she took without hesitation, and they both walked toward the entrance of the villa.

Madame Councilor was waiting for the two young people at the tea table. She was indeed the beautiful blonde woman in the picture of the Councilor of Commerce's study. Looking at her next to her daughter, she could have been mistaken for her older sister, so youthful was her appearance and so surprising was the resemblance. Her beauty only seemed richer and more mature than her daughter's through her womanhood and internalized by a touch of quiet sorrow. It was obvious, all the wealth that surrounded her didn't make her happy. A careful observer could also see the following difference between mother and daughter. While the beautiful mouth of the mother was formed in the most perfect symmetry, the lower lip of the daughter appeared slightly thickened and somewhat drooping. She seemed to be aware of this small blemish, which was hardly perceptible to the average eye, because she was visibly anxious to pull in her lower lip a little and press it against her upper lip when she kept her mouth closed. This seemed to be the only physical trait she had inherited from her father.

"Well, you've been bickering again!" said the Madame, noticing her daughter's terse diction.

"Not at all, mamma! The Baron only complained that I didn't attend to him very much last night, and I made it clear to him that he doesn't yet have the slightest right to be favored by me in any way. Isn't that right, my little Baron?"

At this, Elisabeth waved her index finger over the Baron's nose and, even before serving her mother, poured him tea.

"Indeed, Madame! Miss Elisabeth treated me miserably last night. You must admit that! She even seems to realize it herself now, since she is visibly trying to make amends."

"That did not even occur to me!" said Elisabeth laughing, took the cup she had just filled for the Baron, handed it to her mother and put the empty cup in front him. Then she poured herself a cup and looked triumphantly at Werheim. But before he understood the changed situation, she took the empty cup away from him again and gave him her own cup, which she had just filled. Smiling, the Baron kissed her hand.

"Well, are you satisfied now?" said the Madame with a smile. Instead of answering her, the Baron kissed her hand as well.

"Now that this incident has been correctly settled," at this word Elizabeth, bowing her head, paused for a moment and looked at the Baron from below with ironic devotion, "to everyone's satisfaction, I think we can proceed with the order of the day. Baron Dr. Edgar von Werheim, future Minister of Culture, has the floor."

"I am so touched by your extraordinary kindness, my dear lady, that I am indeed at a loss for words to say anything," the prospective Minister of Culture replied with a smile. "Besides, I have already said everything I have to say to you in the garden!" he added with a meaningful look.

"No rollicking, Baron! For God's sake, no rollicking! That is excessive and highly incorrect!" interjected Elisabeth briskly. "The matter is settled! Here, light your peace pipe!" She handed him a silver tin of cigarettes from the nearby smoking table and lit one for herself. She held the burning match still in her hand, so that the Baron hurried to comply with her request. When he tried to take the match from Elisabeth, she refused and held the flame to the cigarette herself.

The Baron acknowledged this new attention with a silent bow and obvious pleasure, while the Madame followed the play of the two young people with a satisfied smile. In order to leave them completely undisturbed, she soon took her leave under a suitable pretext.

How she envied her daughter! How free and independent she was in the choice of her husband! On the other hand, what a bitter constraint she had been under when, 23 years ago, she followed her detested husband into marriage as an inexperienced seventeen-year-old girl!

Her father was a schoolmaster in a small town in Schleswig-Holstein. She was the youngest of seven surviving children. With limited means, her good father had provided for the education and advancement of the children as far as he could. Like her four older sisters, she was to take up a profession in order to stand on her own feet and to be able to save herself a dowry, however modest, in the event of her marriage. She had attended commercial school since the age of five, and at the age of 17 she took up her first position in the office of the grain agency Burghamer and Company in Hamburg. The son of the head of the company, her husband, had his eye on her at that time. Without feeling the slightest affection for him, she let him court her. This gave her a childlike happiness she had never known before. After all the misery and inadequacy of her childhood, she drank in thirsty draughts of the big city life she got to experience through him.

One day after a visit to the opera, to which he had invited her, as he had so often before, she had followed him to dinner in one of the glittering restaurants at the Alsterbecken, despite her initial stubborn resistance, whereas he had usually taken her back to her modest pension immediately after the theater, without being intrusive. How it happened, she did not know, but that night for the first time she had not come home and had woken up the next morning in an apartment that was complete strange to her. Who can describe her horror when she came to her senses and realized what her seducer had done! In her fright she dressed and ran away.

She returned to her parents on the next train, threw herself at their feet in tears and confessed what she hardly knew herself. Her father wanted to chase her out of the house, but her mother would not permit it. When her and her parents' fears were confirmed, the father took a vacation and went to Hamburg. He was received with piteous smiles by father and son Burghamer. Marriage was out of the question because of the girl's lack of assets, but they were prepared to pay "compensation." The father returned from Hamburg, aged twenty years. Her brother Kurt, the lieutenant, was just visiting. Without saying a word, he took his riding crop and revolver, and soon returned from Hamburg with a written promise of marriage. Shortly thereafter was the wedding. Elisabeth was the child that the young woman, not yet eighteen years old, gave birth to a few months later in Switzerland. In the meantime, her husband had moved to Berlin, where he opened a brokerage business and over the years earned millions.

It seemed lucky to the young mother in all the misfortune that her child did not show the slightest resemblance to its father, but was entirely in her image. Only when she grew older did the small similarity of the lower lip emerge. It was another joy for her that the girl, who was maturing into a young woman, shared her aversion to the father without having the slightest inkling of the circumstances to which she owed her existence. She anxiously guarded the secret and was careful that it should remain closed to Elisabeth forever. Mother and daughter kept as far away from her father as possible. They had tacitly agreed never to speak of this reserve. In their interaction with him, however, especially in front of others, they maintained their form. Since they usually traveled and almost always met with the Councilor only in the presence of strangers, this was not too difficult for them, and the few close friends they had, suspected quite different reasons for this cool relationship and were considerate enough never to touch it.

However, neither mother nor daughter were clear about the real reason for their deep dislike of their husband and father. Educated in the conventional biblical views of the schools, which ignorantly and uncritically pass by the problems of the Old Testament and are blind to the unbridgeable, racially conditioned spiritual abyss that gapes between the Old and New Testaments, arbitrary dogmas were to them synonymous with religion, and religion again synonymous with some pedantic creed. So, the good and honest father of the seduced girl and her unsuspecting, dashing brother had not the slightest scruple about chaining this unhappy creature to the desecrator of her body and soul for life by marriage, since he was, according to external confession, a Christian like themselves. Against this brutal act, the inner feelings of the girl's mother as well as all mental and physical organs of the girl herself resisted. But that the seducer had only been baptized and had his name changed in order to be able to carry out his craft of exploitation on Christian fellow believers all the more inconspicuously, the thought had never crossed their minds, and if anyone had spoken of it, they would have ignored it harmlessly in disbelief. Or if someone had told them that all the water and fire of heaven and earth are not able to wash away the facts of blood and soul and of a past of many thousands of years, they would have looked on uncomprehendingly, and smiled at him, pitying him for his unchristian faith, and prayed for his salvation.

So neither mother nor daughter suspected that it was in truth their Germanic blood, which resisted being sullied by impure foreign blood, that had sprung from the darkest chaos of nations. The mother explained her dislike, even her hatred of her husband by the crime he had committed against her, the daughter her dislike of her father by the love she had for her mother, as well as her misgivings about marrying the Baron, by the social prejudices people had against Jews, even the baptized ones, and against which it was embarrassing or uncomfortable to oppose. Mother and daughter had neither the impulse nor the occasion to think more deeply about these things, for their originally healthy instincts had become so dull and perverted through an uncritical upbringing, through effeminacy and comfort, through the most insipid and at the same time enervating pleasures, that they felt the unnatural to be natural. A last remnant of healthy and original feeling, which sometimes still reared up powerfully in Elisabeth, was held down by the social pressure to which she was subject and which she lacked the strength and resolution to break. So she staggered along between pleasure and disgust of pleasure and at the same time lust for pleasure. Depending on the weather and the mood and the most random circumstances, she expressed these feelings, and thus domineered over herself, her surroundings, and the whole world.

When she met Hermann Kämpfer that Christmas Eve, the untainted remnants of her blood stirred for a moment. The serious blond young man with the fresh cut across his cheek, in the weather-beaten sports suit, who didn't seem to care about all the insipid society stuff, had done it to her for a moment. But since the silly young man did not respond to her game, she had carelessly moved on. Since then she had hardly thought of him. Now and then, when she was walking idly, she saw in her mind's eye his serious, sad, yet fiery eyes, just like when she was dreaming on the deck chair by the sea. But she paid no further attention to the dream image. What should a young green student do to her? The Baron was a completely different man. She was impressed by his self-confidence, whose well-played pose she did not see through, and liked his "correctness," though only the mask for his own inner helplessness, which she derided.

She did not doubt the Baron's love. His jealousy was boundless! And genuine! She understood it. After all, her whole life since joining society had been nothing but flirting, raising hopes, making people jealous, and handing out rejections. She also enjoyed making the Baron squirm and fidget, even though she had long since decided to accept his proposal. Did she love him? Maybe! She was not sure about that. A dark hunch seemed to tell her that true love must be quite different. But she had not met it until now, and she was already entering her twenty-third year! What a terrible age! It was high time that she got married and did not give her friends, who had long since been engaged or married, any more opportunity to tease her.

Moreover, the game was such that a similar opportunity would not present itself again anytime soon. How often had she experienced real Barons from old noble families courting her in all seriousness, but withdrawing again as soon as they met her father. That had already made her angry. But she was smart enough not to dwell on things that couldn't be changed. It was for this reason alone that she was chagrinned by the fact that the Baron von Werheim clearly showed both his own descent and that of his nobility. But she did not think of turning him down because of that. He would undoubtedly make his way. He was ambitious, after all, and she wanted to see to it that his striving for the heights would not diminish, once she was his wife! He should advance at least to Minister! When she often laughingly called him "Minister of Culture," it was more than just a joke. To the haughty countesses and baronesses, whom she and her mother did not take seriously socially, she still wanted to show it off! She could hardly wait for the day.

However, she had asked for a three-month cooling-off period to think it over. But that was only an impulse that her feminine instinct gave her, not to throw herself at the irresistible suitor, whom she had known for barely three weeks. However, since she observed that the Baron seemed to take more than a passing interest in the little Countess von Witzleben, whom he had met in the last few days and whom she herself had found delightful against her will, she regretted that she had set herself the long deadline. Her pride and instinct forbade her to shorten it voluntarily. The Countess was penniless, as her unfashionable costumes and her whole standard of living revealed. But she was of the senior nobility and her father was a member of the Prussian House of Lords and of influence at court.

All these circumstances must have induced the Baron to consider a marriage with the Countess, despite her lack of wealth. And it was quite obvious that the very rich Baron was not unlucky with the countess and her Lord . Now it was time to be smart and to act and, above all, not to let anything be noticed. The only way to keep the Baron in line under such circumstances was to increase his jealousy to the extreme, and to her great satisfaction she was by no means mistaken in this calculation. The success of the previous evening proved this to her. She had certainly counted on him to urge her again to shorten the reflection period. But it did not seem advisable to her to respond so quickly. If, however, after she had rebuffed him earlier, he should again urge her to make a decision, she could now dare to give in to him "out of pity" or as "proof of her love" without giving up anything in the process. It was therefore highly desirable to her that her mother now leave her alone with her admirer, who was more impatient than impetuous, after she had encouraged him to make a new advance.

"May I ask you a question, Elisabeth?" said the Baron quite abruptly, when they had been talking about the most trivial thing for over half an hour.

"Please!" she replied with carefully concealed curiosity.

"Will you also promise me to answer the question as frankly and freely as you made your confessions about yourself to me in the garden earlier?"

The solemn manner in which the Baron asked this question disturbed her somewhat. What was he up to?

"But of course!" she replied nervously.

"I already indicated to you earlier in the garden that the cause for your indecisiveness about my proposal must not lie in me and my circumstances, but solely in you. The explanations you were kind enough to give me in response have in no way invalidated this assumption of mine."

"So? Now I'm truly curious!"

"Be completely honest, Elisabeth! Does your heart belong to someone else?"

The girl had struggled to hide her triumph.

"What makes you suppose such a thing?" she said in a tone that could not but strengthen the jealous man in his assumption.

"I remind you of Christmas Eve. I think I must assume that you are not entirely indifferent to the blond student in the menacing, disheveled clothes!"

"And what makes you assume that?" she said indignantly.

"Well, you did distinguish him in quite an outrageous way! And what's more, in my presence, a few hours after I asked you to marry me!"

"Did that violate our agreement?"

"Admittedly, that is not the case. But it was quite striking, especially since you usually exercise a very correct reserve towards strangers. I am forced to assume that you know the student personally, and that you care for him!"

Elisabeth's self-control was severely tested. She would have loved to laugh out loud. Her heart cheered. She had not expected the Baron to make it so easy for her to win the game and to play such trumps into her hand. She threw herself back in the armchair, tapped the tips of her toes up and down, and blew smoke from her cigarette out in slow puffs. She pondered how best to tactically exploit this unexpectedly favorable strategic position. Should she play the offended, the indignant, or just the mortified part, or should she keep a meaningful silence and let the poor man flounder even longer? Or should she even throw him some nugget, on which his jealousy had to gorge and swallow anew? A bitter lump or a sweet one, half or completely poisoned? Doing the latter made her blood tingle. Or was she ultimately mistaken about the favorable situation? Did she perhaps under-estimate the strength of her opponent? What if this was just the prelude to the decision he was determined to make at that moment, one way or anoth-er? Or was that perhaps already the signal to retreat and that the decision was no longer important to him? That would be an unbearable disgrace! The faces and the sympathetic words of her friends! She thought of Witz-leben. The mere thought infuriated her. And that solemn, measured tone in which the Baron spoke, she had never noticed in him before! No doubt, she had already stretched the bow too tightly. Now was the time to give in if he wasn't to break.

With quick, short puffs, she finished the cigarette, tapped out the burning residue in the ashtray, crossed her hands behind her neck, and bouncing both feet again up and down again, she began slowly whistling the tune "You're crazy my child!"

"What is that supposed to mean!" said the Baron, highly indignant.

Then the Madame Councilor entered the room again. While the Bar-on rose with a bow, Elisabeth suddenly jumped up, took the Baron by the hand and leading him to his mother, she said:

"May I introduce you to my fiancé here?"

The Baron looked at her speechlessly. The Madame looked from her daughter to the Baron in amazement, as he stood there in comical astonishment.

"Now look, mama, now he doesn't believe it! There's no way to please this person!"

"Elisabeth!" came joyfully from the lips of the dumbfounded bridegroom. He hurried toward the beautiful girl to embrace her, but he remembered his correctness in time and only kissed her hand, but more intimately than usual. He also kissed the hand of the Madame Councilor.

Immediately after the execution of the notarized contract, Hermann Kämpfer had gone home again. For a while he had still been wavering whether he should travel on to Bordighera, in order to somehow bring about a meeting with Elisabeth, or even just to see her again. But the holidays were over in three days, and to ask for a leave of absence beyond that and to cancel his lecture was contrary to his sense of duty. When he stood in his laboratory again and realized that he was now to leave these rooms, in which he had worked day and night for ten years, forever, he felt quite strange. He did not dare to open the cupboard and look for the crystal bowl in which his beloved science was now buried, for fear of becoming indecisive again. At first, he wanted to tell his boss that he would be resigning from his post at Easter and withdraw from the union of the university, in order to seal his decision, and as it were, to make it irrevocable and to burn all bridges behind him. But this turned out to be more difficult for him than he had imagined.

After it had happened and he had steadfastly rejected the well-meant advice of his bosses and colleagues not to rush things and to think things over carefully again, he did his job and continued to lecture as if everything were the same as before. Only he no longer took up his private scientific work. The crystal bowl remained locked in the work bench. He wanted to hand over all his material, including his scientific ideas, to a colleague who, like him, was working in the field of protein chemistry, but not until the end of the semester, shortly before his departure. Instead, he now eagerly set about his new technical task.

Since the conclusion of the notarized contract, the Councilor of Commerce seemed to trust him unreservedly. He had willingly sent him the patent specifications and given him all the information he wanted. Soon Hermann was very familiar with the composition and the manufacturing process of the Evonite and the production of the tiles. With the scientific method and his characteristic thoroughness, which penetrates to the core of every matter, he now devoted himself to his new work.

Incessantly, his thoughts were with his beloved. Whatever he undertook, he did it only with the thought of her and for her. He related even the most insignificant action to her. "Elisabeth!" he often whispered to himself. All organs of jealousy broke loose in him when he thought of the Baron who was allowed to accompany her. That she could have a thing for "such a peacock" seemed to him, on calm reflection, so unrhymed that he laughed at himself.

When the laboratory work was done, he used to study the literature of his field. Now he read Plato. At school, he had only glimpsed the divine. But that had been enough for him to kindle a deep love. As a student, he had heard a lecture on Plato and also on Kant. As much as he was fascinated by these philosophical studies, his devotion to his specialized science had never given him time to pursue them consistently, and yet it was in his nature, indeed it was his nature in general, to do everything, once he started, completely, rigorously and methodically. Given the diversity of his lively interests, this brought him into the hardest of situations and most painful conflicts.

But it was of no use. If he wanted to make it in his science, he had to humble himself to his concentration. This merciless discipline was a juggernaut, which devoured him and all his other gifts and desires. Other gods next to it were not tolerated. As a student, he had once calculated with horror that the day would have to have 32 hours if he were to be able to study only the chemical literature that appeared daily! At that time, he was close to despair, because it was quite impossible to completely master even one special field of natural science, such as chemistry. And he wanted to devour not only chemistry, but all the natural sciences and also its neighboring fields, including philosophy! He had to be content with the most miserable piecemeal work and had to cut out a narrowly circumscribed special field from a special subject in order to achieve some mastery and tangible results.

But now he was free! He had been a fool not to break this scientific slave bondage long ago, in order to finally be able to be a human being! With what delight he imagined how he would read Plato's Symposium to his beloved! Truly, life was glorious and worth living! Only it wanted to be experienced and not speculated! He was happy to see that he still knew enough Greek from school to understand the works in the original. It was an unparalleled pleasure for him to read aloud the most beautiful passages in the original text, and even to learn them by heart, after he had precisely grasped their meaning by means of excellent translations. Elisabeth had to learn Greek, that was certain. How he looked forward to teaching her himself!

Individual thoughts of Plato reminded him vividly of the New Testament. He took it up again, and for the first time in his life the content and meaning of the Christian doctrine of salvation dawned on him. How tedious schoolmasters and dull-witted priests had stifled his living sense for

the Word of God as a child! Relations with God were degraded to the sad-
dest business! Reward for good, punishment for evil! An eye for an eye, a
tooth for a tooth was said there, exactly as in the Old Testament, only in
another, the same sense roughly veiling form! The relations to God became
a very foolish calculation, which one had to solve, if one did not want to
get the greatest inconveniences. Anxiety and fear were its prerequisites,
cunning, at best cleverness its method, and plus or minus, depending on the
skill of the calculator, the result. Such was the "good news" drilled into the
childish brains and hearts! God, who according to the Gospel is our Father
and Love himself, appeared as a terrible judge and avenger! "I came forth
from the Father and return to the Father, so you also shall find your way
back to the Father, whom you have lost," this simple, world-glorifying and
world-conquering meaning of the doctrine of salvation, how it was de-
formed and contorted and twisted and misinterpreted! And four hundred
years before Christ, Plato had already taught it in his way, when he said
that our longing for beauty and truth is only the memory of the view of
God, which we had before entering this life, but which we lost through
arrogance!

To find the way back to the Father, that was the only possible meaning and purpose of this earthly life, which no science and no worldly wisdom could uncover and find, that was the revelation of the Good News,
which Hermann Kämpfer had gotten in his thirtieth year. But he did not yet
understand the whole depth of its meaning, otherwise he would now have
quietly and humbly submitted to the simple demands of the day, which his
profession and life made on him. He still wanted to go beyond himself and
his earthly task. The passions and transitoriness of this temporal world still
clouded his view of the eternal and imperishable, and therefore he still had
to experience immeasurable suffering before he was ready for the deepest
insight.

One day, when he was again indulging in vain thoughts of the future,
imagining how having become rich in fame and money he would appear
before his beloved and ask for her hand, Röschen Brunner came into the
room and brought him the mail.

The only correspondence he had was with the Councilor of Commerce. He had long since agreed with him to carry out the practical evalua-
tion of his experiments himself by setting up a factory in Germany and
only granting licenses for foreign countries. He now reported to him regularly on the progress of his work and received new technical and commercial information and explanations of all kinds from him. The letter he had
just received also bore the Councilor's handwriting, but the format was

larger than usual and the company name was missing from the envelope. When he tried to open the letter, he discovered that it was not closed at all. It was just a printed matter. Curious, he took it out of the envelope. Then he thought the sky was falling in on him. He read:

> Councilor of Commerce Karl Burghamer and Mrs. Elisabeth née Wicking are honored to announce the engagement of their only child Elisabeth to Baron Dr. Edgar v. Werheim, Royal Prussian Government Assessor.

Hermann felt as if he had been struck by lightning. It took several days before he even came to his senses. A horrible pressure lurked just below the top of his skull and crept up between his forehead and his eye. Unable to perform his duties, he called in sick. A nervous crisis came over him and he had to seek clinical treatment.

But the doctor could not get anything out of him. He stubbornly resisted all questions about what he had experienced and all requests to confide in the doctor in order to relieve himself and to give him the opportunity to have a psychological and appropriate clinical effect on him. After three weeks he asked to be released from the clinic. He would now be able to cope with himself.

For a long time, he had brooded over whether, under the new circumstances, there was any point at all in continuing the contract with to the Councilor of Commerce. After all, he had only done it in order to find the opportunity and possibility to lead to his beloved. This possibility no longer existed. What did he care about the artificial slate and the problem of its coloring or about the money that could be earned with it! Despite it's notarial execution, the contract itself would not prevent him from reversing his decision. He had already worked diligently on the matter and had obtained valuable experimental results. If he left them to the Councilor for further exploitation without compensation, the latter would certainly agree to an amicable resolution to the contract. He would not have to give up his academic career if he now set himself more modest scientific goals. To be a teacher of the young, to introduce them to the wonders of science, was also a wonderful task in life.

And if working in a narrowly defined subject area was too one-sided for him, he could become a senior teacher. He had studied the individual subjects of natural science thoroughly and had passed all the necessary examinations. So why should he forcibly break with the profession he had once chosen, if the goal that could be achieved by doing so no longer existed? The allure of the big world had lost its attraction for him just as quickly as it had suddenly seemed desirable to him. Only for the sake of his beloved, who belonged to this great world, did he yet strive to conquer it. Now this prospect had disappeared, what was the use of the vain endeavor? His world lived deep inside his chest, what did he have to do with this fickle, ever-changing, restless and troubled outside world? And yet, in spite of all this, he was drawn to this drowned world as if by magnetic forces. He often felt as if he would not be released from his longing for it until he was thoroughly immersed in it.

It was primarily this ebb and flow of indecision that caused the prolonged state of illness into which the announcement of this engagement had plunged him. Hermann Kämpfer's way was to face dangers and unalterable things firmly and fearlessly and not to dwell on fruitless musings. But no matter how quickly and confidently he was able to act, in moments of danger or in situations in general that made prolonged deliberation impossible—he had proved this more than once during balloon rides, which he often undertook with a meteorologist friend of his—it was just as difficult for him to come to a decision when he had been given sufficient time to consider the pros and cons. His scientifically trained, methodically thinking mind was then at war with his impulsive temperament and instinctive feelings, which, in spite of all calculations, usually made the right decision and often just when all rational reasons seemed to demand the opposite. This inexplicable but irrefutable fact was always proof to him that beyond all reason there are powers at work in us that we are just not aware of. So, this time, too, he had come to the decision, obeying a flash of inspiration, to follow the new path of life that had been pointed out to him by the contract with the Councilor and not to let himself be diverted from it by external influences.

From that moment on, he was inwardly reassured and, in a few days, he was as healthy as before. He even managed to calmly wish the Councilor good luck on the occasion of his daughter's engagement, apologizing for the delay in his congratulations with the illness he had overcome in the meantime. As if nothing had happened, he resumed his duties, his lectures and his technical work, even though the semester would end in a few weeks. Fulfilling his duty until the last moment was a natural requirement for him.

A few days before the end of the semester, without a trace of remorse or wavering uncertainty ever coming over him again, he handed all his experimental and handwritten material for further scientific use to the only colleague besides himself at the university working in the field of protein chemistry, the private lecturer Dr. Siegfried Salomon. He had finished with science, and from now on all his energies were to be devoted to the practical life. He then made preparations to move to Berlin.

Röschen Brunner provided him with loyal help. Snowdrops and first violets were on his desk every day. She took special care in packing his library, as she had observed with what love he treated each book over the years. She carefully wrapped each book in its own newspaper, and even the books that had cardboard covers were wrapped with special care. The packing of the books into the boxes, however, was done by Hermann himself and Röschen handed him each book. Sometimes her hand touched his and it ran boiling hot through her young body. One box, however, she had dared to pack all by herself, when Hermann had been called to the boss for some time, who still had something to discuss with him. Proud but also fearful that she might not have done well enough for him, she awaited his return. When he praised her, however, flaming crimson flooded over her pretty face. She hurriedly bent over one of the still empty boxes so that he would not notice.

Spring had come with a vengeance overnight. Nightingales were already singing in the university park. When Hermann unexpectedly returned from the city on the eve of his departure, where he had run some last errands, he found Röschen in his room at dusk. Leaning her head on her arm against the cross of the window, she stared into the spring evening with big, tearful eyes. He had entered unnoticed. When she saw him, she tried to hurry past him out the door. He caught her in his arms. Suddenly, she let herself be covered by his hot kisses, and that last night brought the two young eager people the fulfillment they had both so firmly resisted for many years.

Hermann had now been living in, or rather near, Berlin for half a year. The Evonite factory, in whose adjoining rooms the Councilor of Commerce had a laboratory set up according to Hermann's plans, was located in Groß-Lichterfelde. Nearby, he had found a furnished two-room apartment that suited him. The difficulties he encountered in solving the dyeing problem were greater than he had foreseen. The path he had taken on the basis of the first experiment proved to be impracticable. He had to devise new methods with new materials. He did succeed in producing a weather-resistant coloring for the tiles.

But after a long time, white spots of exuding quicklime formed on the black surface, which hardened in the air to white crusts of carbonic acid lime. Attempts to reduce the lime content of the base compound in such a way that these exudations would be eliminated failed, since an excess of quicklime was required for the cement to set, and new quantities of quicklime were always formed by the setting process. A way had to be found to convert the excess quicklime into insoluble carbonic acid lime after the setting process in the cement had been completed and before the tiles were colored. Since, for economic reasons, the carbon dioxide in the air had to be used for this purpose, the process was rather cumbersome. The tiles had to be stored for a long time in suitably shaped rooms through which air was constantly drawn until they were saturated with carbonic acid. But finally Hermann had mastered all the difficulties and the patent could be registered. He immediately set about establishing the factory in order to exploit the patent for Germany itself. The Councilor of Commerce, who could not admire Hermann's scientific and practical activities enough, went along with all his plans and suggestions. Hermann was to be employed as the technical director of the factory with a special salary and a full third of the net profit.

Now a busy and enjoyable time began for Hermann. He himself took care of the selection of the building site, the negotiations with the contractors and architects, with the machine factories and other suppliers. He felt powers stirring and growing, of which he had previously had no idea. This was a different kind of life and work, of planning and creating, than the sedentary scholarly life.

Autumn had come without him seeing Elisabeth. It is true that he soon paid a visit to the luxurious Grunewald Villa of the Councilor, but the gentlemen traveled throughout the spring and summer. Of course, Elisabeth's image had not yet disappeared from his heart. But he thought of her less and less often, and then only with the resignation of a man who has finally ended with a love affair. Instead, his thoughts often turned to Röschen Brunner. In his dreams he often held the young creature trembling with love in his arms, and he reproached himself most bitterly for having robbed the girl of the peace of her heart and for not having remained master of his senses in the last hour. Three more times she had written to him, whole pages full of sweet, awkward words of love. He had not answered her. This seemed to him the most painless way for the girl, to break off relations with her that could not lead to any result. Of course, he would not have wanted his mother to judge him. A few months later, Röschen had sent him two more letters, but he had left them unopened in his desk. To burn them seemed to him unloving, to read them pointless. He was also too ashamed of himself. Since then, she was silent.

Business often took him to Berlin. In the hustle and bustle of the big city he always felt suffocated, and he was always glad when he could return to the quiet rural suburb. There was air and light and sky and sun and some trees! Yes, even waving fields of ears of corn lay in the immediate vicinity! When he often roamed through them in summer, he always ran his hand lovingly over the golden stalks. But each time the memory of his childhood was then so painfully awakened in him that he refrained from these walks, However, he liked to spend time in the Tiergarten in Berlin, and spent whole afternoons in the zoological garden. He never tired of looking into the eyes of the animals and reading from them the silent wisdom of their millions of years old past. A main attraction for him was the geological and paleontological museum. The whole history of creation, whole eons he wandered there in the spirit.

One day, looking at the riders in the zoo, he felt like riding again. He calculated how long it had been since he had had a horse under him. Twelve years had passed! It had been for the last time during those fateful Easter vacations, when the Jew had brought misfortune upon his father's house. With a quick decision, he went to the riding school at the Tiergarten, borrowed a pair of riding boots and spurs, and mounted the horse as he walked and stood. But this was only a moderate pleasure on the sullen rented nag. As often as the Hippodrome's riding arena crossed the path leading back to the stables, the stubborn drudge tried to break out. Hermann had never had riding lessons. As was customary in the country, he had mounted and ridden away as a boy. So he was more of a bold, even daring, rider than a good one. Nevertheless, he remained master of the nag, and at the end of the hour for which he had hired it, he happily brought it back to the stable. He quickly decided to keep his own riding horse. He could afford it now.

After a few days he had found what he was looking for. He bought a magnificent five-year-old half-breed gelding, a Kohlfuchs, called Romeo. Now he hired a riding instructor to methodically learn this art according to all the rules. Soon he had achieved respectable results and even won a second prize at a riding school competition. He was passionate about jumping. No ditch was too wide and no obstacle too high for him. He could hardly wait to take part in the first scavenger hunt, of which the riding school organized several every autumn. He had made for him an elegant red coat and white breeches. To his surprise and dismay, he also read the name of Elisabeth and her fiancé in the registration list for the hunt.

Now he lapsed again into agonizing indecision. Should he avoid the encounter? Should he cancel the hunt? If he met Elisabeth, would he not expose himself to new useless torments and struggles? The wound in his heart was certainly closed, but not yet healed. Why tear it open anew? But an encounter with the lost love could not be avoided in the long run. After all, he had paid a visit to the family of the Councilor. So why avoid a matter that sooner or later would happen? Besides, Elisabeth would most likely not recognize him at all! Despite all these reasons, he could not come to a clear decision. But when the day of the hunt dawned, he put on the red coat.

On a sunny September morning, the field of about thirty to forty gentlemen and ladies gathered in the courtyard of the riding school. But neither Elisabeth nor the Baron were there. A few high carriages stood ready for the spectators to accompany the riders to the Grunewald and then await the exit on the Halali Square. Led by the director of the hunt, the "Master," the company moved along Kurfürstendamm via Halensee to Grunewald. Hermann rode at the head close behind the leader. At the end of Kaiserstrasse, where the path turns off to the lake, a group of five horsemen awaited the company. They were some participants from the Grunewald district, who wanted to join the field from here to save the detour via the riding school. Hermann felt a stab in his heart when he discovered Elisabeth at her bridegroom's side.

They greeted each other. Neither Elisabeth nor the Baron recognized Hermann. A pause of about fifteen minutes was held, then the hunt started to move. A few hundred yards ahead rode the fox, scattering the schnitzels. The bridal couple, who had in the meantime greeted some acquaintances, now rode with them in the front half of the field. Hermann arranged it so that he rode directly behind Elisabeth. First at a walk, then at a light trot, they rode along the shore of the lake, past the Hubertus Castle and the Seeschenke. From there the trail led across the forest in the direction of Uncle Tom's Cabin.

Elisabeth sat brilliantly on horseback. She rode a golden chestnut mare of the noblest blood. Her groom, whose aspiring stoutness cut a less attractive figure, rode a black horse of no less noble blood. Elisabeth sat in a side saddle, in spite of the fact that the loathsome convention of riding in the manner of gentleman had just become fashionable among the ladies. Her figure was magnificent in the tight-fitting black riding costume. In dense waves held together by a fine net, her blond hair flowed abundantly out from under the stiff gentleman's hat. She masterfully ruled her fiery horse, while the Baron clenched at his reins with a visibly hard hand. He had a crooked seat leaning to the left and, despite spasmodic efforts, no proper thigh closure. His squirming restlessness was transmitted to the horse, so that it lurched back and forth.

Now the leader progressed into a light trot and then, after momentarily slackening to a walk, reached the first gallop. Immediately from the top some gentlemen were left behind. Elisabeth kept herself directly behind the leader, the Baron with effort beside her. Hermann rode at all times close behind his lost love, as if he still wanted to catch up with her in life. Soon the first artificial obstacles appeared, simple hurdles and low poles. Elisabeth flew over them like a swallow, as did Hermann. Behind them both, the Baron was like a clumsy chicken. Each time, at the approach of an obstacle, he vacillated and awkwardly scrambled over it. Now Hermann bridled his horse lightly, to order to let the Baron go ahead again. At most eight to ten riders, including three ladies, were still ahead. Then the leader raised his hand and came to a dead stop, gradually the widely separated field gathered together again.

Panting, the Baron wiped his brow. A large stain appeared on the broad back of his hunting coat.

"Well, little dumpling? Survived well?" his bride laughed at him.

"My flayer is all out of shape," he sighed, reinserting the long-displaced monocle.

"Of course, the flayer!" laughed Elisabeth brightly. "But if it's too much for you, dumpling, stay back. I won't hold it against you. But I'm staying here in front! I won't come home today without the fox's tail!"

"It's a matter of honor that I stay with you, Ellichen!" he mumbled to himself.

Hermann felt like he was going to swallow a frog. He called her "Ellichen"! And she bore the most glorious of all women's names, Elizabeth!

Now the Baron rode close to the leader.

"Tell me, rider," he murmured to him, "how long is this hopscotch going to last? Confidentially! Do you also have another or even more trenches on the program?"

"Officially, my secret, Baron!" the latter smiled authoritatively.
"Trust for trust! If you don't tell anyone, three trenches are provided, two with water, one without."

"God save us!" sighed the monocle man and went back to his bride's side.

Hermann, who had followed the process with a grin, now held back and let some riders ahead so as not to attract attention. His Elisabeth now belonged to this fat swollen peacock! With a mixture of rage and woe in his heart he rode along.

In a sharp hunting trot, they went now in a wide arc around Uncle Tom's Cabin. After fifteen to twenty minutes, they walked again for a similar length of time, then continued again into a really vigorous hunting gallop, in which some tree trunks lay across the track, respectable hurdles and poles and the first wet ditch were taken. Only five or six riders managed to keep up with the leader, including Hermann at the foremost lead, with Elisabeth to one side behind him. The Baron was far behind. When they rendezvoused, he wheezed like a freight train locomotive. He claimed to have lost his hunting cap. The string had broken, he said, and he had had to ride back and look for it. The lie stood rank on his sweat-soaked forehead.

"Poor dumpling!" said Elizabeth with a distinct sneer. "Now stay back, so you don't lose your cap again!"

But again they went into gallop. The narrow, dry ditch followed, which the Baron took tolerably well with a desperate courage, so that Elisabeth shouted a loud "Bravo! Then came a picket fence, which the Baron's black horse took in a stride. Just before he jumped, however, his master, who was crouching on him like a monkey, fearfully groped at his reins in his mouth, and with a hindquarter the animal broke free around the obstacle.

"Bravo!" exclaimed Elisabeth tauntingly to him, flying like a Valkyrie past him over the obstacle, at the same height beside her was Hermann.

The leader maliciously slowed the ride a little bit to give the Baron the opportunity to move into the front field again, because now a wide moat had been created very mischievously and surprisingly for the riders, of whose location none of the hunt participants except the leader had an idea. The Baron should be there! Marking the breakout of the horse was not possible there! There it was a matter of showing one's colors!

"What a bitch!" gasped the Baron as he approached. "Erupts at the last moment!"

"Bad luck!" cried Elisabeth to him derisively.

Now, however, the leader set off what the flanks held! Suddenly, there was the trench, until then covered by a light wave of earth, enclosing the riders in a horseshoe shape. Now it was time to give prongs! Hermann smoothly leaped over at the same level as the master, as did Elisabeth's horse a length behind them. Then the unfortunate Baron followed, unable to hold his horse glued to the horses in front. In fear of death, he yanked at the poor animal in the mouth once again, and, with a start, he overturned with it in the middle of the ditch.

But for the luckier riders there was no stopping now. Barely 300 meters were left to the parade ground, where the run was and in the middle of which the fox had already stopped. Now it was a matter of victory!

A gentle hill went up to the edge of the parade ground. Two other riders had taken the ditch smoothly and now sat close on Hermann and Elisabeth's heels. Nevertheless, Hermann could not refrain from looking around. With hearty glee he noticed how the Baron was crawling on all fours like a wet poodle out of the ditch onto the shore.

"Nothing else happened to the Baron!" he called to her, lying close beside Elisabeth at a stretched gallop. She thanked him with a quick nod of her head. Then Hermann put in his spurs, and one or two horse-lengths ahead of the other riders, he headed toward the fox. The leader had meanwhile stepped out of the field.

But at the last second, Hermann came to his senses. She should win! Shortly before the fox he stopped and he turned a little to the side, and he as if he couldn't control the horse. Then Elisabeth rushed between him and the fox, and with a little cry she snatched the fox's tail as she flew past, which was attached to the back of the rider representing the fox. Triumphantly, she held it high in the air, gradually parrying her courser while the hunting horns blared the tallyho through the clear autumn air.

Now something unexpected happened. Elisabeth rode up to Hermann, near whom she had brought her horse to a halt, and silently handed him the trophy. She was out of breath and could not speak a word. Astonished, Hermann refused the offer. She, however, still wordless and struggling for breath, shook her head and tried to hand him the booty. "You've won!" she finally said haltingly. "I saw, of course, that you swerved to let me go first. I can't accept that!"

Blushing deeply, Hermann pulled off his hunting cap and affirmed that the madam must be mistaken.

Suddenly a strange movement ran over Elisabeth's face. She looked thoughtfully at Hermann and said:

"Don't we already know each other? I wouldn't know at the moment, however..."

Then Hermann gave his name and added in short words the time and circumstances of their first meeting.

"That's right!" she replied. "I remember it perfectly. But now, more than ever, I ask you to receive the sign of victory that is coming to you!"

Then Hermann found the courage to ask her to keep it as a souvenir of that Christmas Eve encounter.

Without thinking, she accepted and extended her hand to him.

"By the way," she added, "like you, the name of a young doctor who is my father's associate. Are you perhaps related to him?"

All the while she steered her horse back to the company at a walk, asking him to accompany her. Hermann had introduced himself only with his name, without adding his title.

"That's me!" he replied.

"That's wonderful!" she exclaimed, looking at him more closely now. "But why don't we ever see you here?"

"I don't think it's up to me, my dear lady! I have already paid you, that is, your parents, my visit long ago, but you were probably still traveling at the time."

Before Elizabeth could say anything in reply, several members of society had ridden up and congratulated her on her victory.

"Here stands the victor!" she said pointing to Hermann, introducing him to the acquaintances. "It is only due to his chivalry that I owe my so-called victory!" At this she looked at Herman with the same look that had struck his heart on Christmas Eve! This second look hit him no less deeply. In the meantime, servants had rushed over to receive the horses of the now dismounted gentlemen and ladies. They went on foot to a table set up outside, where tea, punch, schnapps, and a light snack were ready for the gentlemen. A band played light tunes and brought a flourish to the victor as she approached.

At the table, soaking wet and wrapped in an Ulster, sat the Baron. He was eagerly tossing back the hot tea and cognac. The ridicule he received from all sides seemed to fill him with great satisfaction. He felt immensely important and was pleased to see the general attention focused on him. He called out "Congratulations!" to his bride from afar, and when she approached the table and mockingly asked him how the bath had been for him, he rose and, chewing a caviar dumpling, kissed her hand.

"*Fi donc!*" raged Elisabeth, giving him a light smack on his cheek, which he acknowledged with a smug grin.

Hermann noticed that Elisabeth did not introduce him to the Baron, although he was standing in her immediate vicinity. Hermann towered over Elisabeth by half a head's length, while the Baron was almost a hand's breadth shorter than her.

"By the way, Ellichen," said the Baron, on his sixth caviar dumpling, after he had already downed the same amount of cognac, "I've had my car brought around and I'm going home as soon as possible to get something dry on my body again. I hope you will accompany me!"

"Don't mind me!" was the somewhat irritated reply. "I'm riding!"

"Bong!" coughed the Baron, choking.

"But who will take you home?"

"I'll find a way. In case of emergency, Wilhelm is there." She was referring to her riding valet.

"Fine! You're not mad at me, are you, child?"

"*Ich wo wer ik denn!*" snapped the "child" back in the Berliner fashion, obviously pleased to be rid of him.

"Well, then I will excuse myself. And please, give your mother and father my greetings." With these words, the Baron took leave of his bride and, saluting to all sides, boarded his twenty-horse chariot, which was already rattling in the immediate vicinity.

Half an hour later, however, Hermann Kämpfer, dizzy with happiness, rode back through the autumn forest at Elisabeth's side.

— 15 —

The very next day, Hermann received an invitation to tea from the young Madam Councilor. The Burghamer motor car picked him up from his office. Elisabeth received him. He was the only guest. A short time later the Madame Councilor appeared, half an hour later the Baron. He was quite astonished to see the "student" again so unexpectedly, and at the family table of his parents-in-law! During the scavenger hunt, he had not recognized him in the red jacket, least of all had he suspected in him the sporting rider. He clearly expressed his astonishment and discomfort at the unexpected encounter. Where had he left his "Schmiss", he asked maliciously. Hermann calmly explained that he had only suffered a very superficial scratch in a skiing accident, which had long since healed without a trace. But when Elisabeth introduced Hermann as the inventor of the new dyeing process and as her father's successful business partner, he had to put a good face on the matter. Elisabeth, however, was of such unselfconscious, easy-going cheerfulness and so warmly attentive him that he soon recovered his spirits. Hermann suffered hellish agonies in the process. He did not see through the well-calculated game the beautiful girl played to make him jealous of her.

That Hermann loved her, of course, had not escaped her notice. She savored this triumph and, with true feminine cruelty, strove to push it to the extreme.

Unable to speak a word, Hermann sat there as a starry-eyed guest. Suddenly he was struck again by the same look that had opened all the floodgates of bliss for him on Christmas Eve and had set his heart on fire anew at the end of the scavenger hunt. She asked the Baron for a favor. When he moved away for a few seconds into the next room, she apparently harmlessly in the presence of her mother, put her hand on Hermann's head, looked deeply into his eyes and said in a tone of heartfelt sympathy, "Doctor, what's the matter with you?"

Hermann lost his hearing and sight. It was only with extreme effort that he was able to control his excitement. He would have liked to jump up and hurry away, although he knew how ridiculous he would have to make himself.

When the Baron re-entered, Elisabeth took her hand away and placed some morsels on Hermann's plate. "I suppose you don't like sweets, Doctor?" she said unabashedly. And now she turned the game. From then on she was only attentive to Hermann, handed him dried bread and caviar, spread him a sandwich of butter, sweetened his tea, and bubbled over him with teasing and merriment.

When the Baron asked in an ironic tone if he might also ask for a cup of tea, she said:

"Help yourself, dumpling! I have to take care of the company. Father recommended that to me, in particular."

Hermann could no longer remain silent now. He gradually thawed under the sunny gaze of the cheerful girl, and after a short while, he became a lively participant in the conversation.

Elisabeth, who was adept in all areas of social chatter, brought up the subject of natural science. She attached such great importance to it that she wanted to see this field of knowledge made the basis of all education.

Hermann contradicted this strongly.

"So you want to make the random, the incidental, the ever-changing the basis of human learning? Would you build a house on rolling sand or on blowing snow?"

"You obviously don't understand me, Doctor! I have the laws of nature in mind, which are eternal and unchangeable after all!"

"I suppose so. But these eternal and immutable laws do not arise from the substance which they govern, but from the spirit which creates them and the substance in the first place!"

"You say that as a natural scientist? Isn't matter eternal, indeed the only thing that is eternal?"

"Matter is the only thing that is certainly not eternal. There is not the slightest doubt about that for me, my dear lady," said Hermann with calm seriousness. "Only the spirit is eternal! Spirit is the original, the first, the un-generated, the generating. Substance is that which has come into being only through the movement of the spirit, the second, the generated."

While Elisabeth listened to Hermann's words with wide-open eyes, the Baron laughed out loud.

"Please, explain this to me in more detail, Doctor!" said Elisabeth then, visibly disturbed.

"There is nothing more to explain, my dear lady. It is a conviction that one comes to through study and reflection in the course of time, without being able to say how."

"But there must be some way to prove this view!" interjected Elisabeth.

"Prove? Can a worldview be proven at all? Can the materialists prove their worldview?"

"Of course, the materialistic world view has been proven!" interjected the Baron with a pitying grin. "It has long since been proven!"

"Then I would be quite grateful if you could give me this proof, Baron," Hermann replied calmly.

"Well, haven't you ever heard of Darwin, Häckel, and Ostwald?"

"I know every line of Darwin, Häckel, and Ostwald."

"There you go! Then you know the evidence!"

"Excuse me, Baron. Darwin communicates in his steps merely a tremendous amount of observational material. To the observable facts collected by him, he now gives his well-known explanation, with which he is undoubtedly right, as far as the development of the living beings from lower to higher forms is concerned. Before the emergence of the first living beings, however, he also stops reverently, and says: "About this we know nothing!"

This Darwinian theory of development does not contradict at all the idealistic view that the spirit is the generating and the substance the generated! On the contrary, it is one of its strongest supports! It is the spirit that first creates the organic form out of the substance and leads it from step to step to ever higher development, until it has finally built for itself in the human body the dwelling in which it is able to live in order to fulfill its earthly task. The plan, by which the spirit works, can be grasped with your hands! If you pick up any work on the newest results of the biological sciences, you will come across the view, even among materialistic researchers, that that which gives the cell the impulse to change and develop, must be a mysterious something, which cannot be explained and understood materially! But Häckel and Ostwald, his sworn assistant in physico-chemistry, make such arbitrary, one-sided, completely unprovable assertions about this that they cannot be taken seriously by a level-headed and dispassionately thinking mind.

No, my dear Baron, it remains with what Kant taught us and proved, namely, that a certain world-view cannot be proved at all! One has a certain world view or one does not have it! Prove of the materialistic as well as of the idealistic world-view cannot be found! But the idealistic one, to which I adhere, has the advantage that it does not lead to contradictions, but makes possible a uniform conception of the world as a whole and of its meaning and purpose, while the materialistic one has such contradictions of meaning as its presupposition and consequence that only uncritical fools can adhere to it!

"Well, allow me, Doctor! I am also a follower of materialism!" replied the Baron, speechless, so to speak.

"This is your responsibility, not mine," Hermann explained with a calm smile.

The Baron wanted to retort irritably, but Elisabeth did not let him.

"You must first explain to me how you of all people, as a natural scientist, have come to such peculiar views!" she interjected.

"This may be because a professional who pursues natural science with open unprejudiced eyes is more likely to recognize the limits drawn by this seemingly all-powerful science than the layman who is easily baffled."

"What are these limits? Please explain it to me!" said Elisabeth in honest curiosity and passionate impatience.

"It's very simple, my dear lady! Natural science cannot get out of matter, that is, out of the secondary, the second, the produced. It can only investigate the relations that exist between the material, only the laws that are valid within the material and for the material. But it can never penetrate to the actual being, to the original, to the first, to the non-produced, to the eternal, in a word, to the spiritual. But also its actual area, the material, is accessible to it only in the most limited measure. Namely, only insofar as it is accessible to our senses. However, our senses are able to perceive only a very tiny fraction of the world of appearance. Surely you know that!"

"No, no! I am not aware of that at all! Please explain it to me further!"

"I trust you have studied natural science in depth, my dear lady?"

"What one picks up at school or in the lecture hall, as it were, in passing. I never managed to study it properly," Elisabeth confessed with unreserved frankness.

Hermann was only too happy to comply with her request and continued, "In any case, you know that sounds are vibrations of the air?"

"Certainly. But it's not really clear to me either!"

"You'll quickly realize that, pay attention!"

And now Hermann explained the basic acoustic laws to her on a violin and came to the conclusion:

"So, every sound is produced by the movements of air caused by a vibrating body hitting your ear. And indeed, to each tone corresponds a quite certain number of oscillations per unit of time. We call this number 'frequency.' The larger the number of vibrations, the higher the tone, the smaller the number of vibrations, the lower the tone. However, our ear is only able to hear air vibrations as tones whose number of vibrations is approximately between the range of thirty and thirty-six thousand per second.

All air vibrations, i.e. tones, which lie above or below this limit, cannot be felt by the ear, so they practically do not exist for us.

"And exactly the same applies now to the oscillations of the ether, which cause light and color sensations in us. Our eye is only capable of impressions for the colors which lie within the borders of the rainbow. All light vibrations, i.e. colors beyond these limits, we do not perceive at all. But that outside these limits there is still an infinite flood of colors, we recognize by the fact that they attack light-sensitive plates, and can therefore be photographed.

"And it is the same with our other senses. Beyond the realm of our senses there is a whole infinity of phenomena that we simply cannot perceive because we lack the senses for them. We can assume with certainty that the actual world of phenomena lies beyond our senses and that our senses convey only a very small fraction of the world of phenomena. For example, we are not able to directly perceive electricity, magnetism, X-rays, etc. We get knowledge of these phenomena only by chance, because they are able to cause other phenomena, which are sensually perceptible for us, for example, the deflection of the magnetic needle by the galvanic current, the attraction of iron filament by the magnet etc. If you represent the whole area of natural phenomena by a circular surface, the diameter of which you can imagine as large as you like, then the part of this circular surface accessible to our immediate and direct perception corresponds to only a tiny dot, which you place somewhere on it. So tiny and so indeterminate is the part of the world of appearances that is accessible to us by natural science.

"Thereby it is still very questionable whether you are justified to let the point coincide with the center point of the circular surface. Because, of course, one cannot rely at all on our senses, since they do not reflect us the things and facts themselves, but only the impression which we receive from the things and facts. There are people who see green instead of red and vice versa. And there is no doubt that we would perceive a completely different world-view, if the perceptual threshold of our senses would be modified even slightly. Only a slight shift of our senses would be needed, in order to cause us to hear colors and to see, feel or smell sounds."

"This is all just wonderful!" exclaimed Elisabeth, visibly moved.

But the Baron said, with a superior smile:

"Surely you will not want to deny that we have seen enormous advances in the last few decades, we owe solely and above all to natural science the vastness of our modern culture!"

"Culture? We don't have any culture! We have only civilization! Railroads, dynamos, automobiles, giant steamers, airships, radio telegraphs and all the other things you want to mention are not achievements of culture, but only of civilization! Essentially, these achievements are no different from what the ant and the bee also accomplish! And from a cultural point of view these inventions have undoubtedly not brought us forward, but rather a quite considerable way back, since they have led us deeper and deeper into materialism, instead of helping us overcome it! Because all these inventions prove that it is the spirit and not the material that has command!

"Permit me to say, Doctor! You have downright barbaric views!"

"I don't see it like that," replied Hermann Kämpfer with a quiet smile.

"Well, what do you actually mean by culture?"

"By culture I understand the activity and purposeful cultivation of everything human from the point of view that man is a spiritual being, which comes out of eternity and is created by God, and returns to eternity. National and state unity, social welfare, science, technology, politics, war, and all that is connected with it, arise only from the purely vegetative instincts, which man also has in common with animals. They only become culturally valuable when they serve the conscious cultivation of the divine-spiritual in man. With religion and art, which both originate from the same metaphysical source of our being, man only begins. The idealist is the true realist, because he grasps the core and essence of the world of appearance, but the materialist is eternally deceived, because he considers the unessential to be the essential."

"So you really believe that man has a so-called immortal soul?" replied the Baron with a pitying smile.

"This is not only my opinion or even my conviction, but it is my deep inner certainty. Apart from that, there is the only thing that is able to give meaning and purpose and a goal to life. But even completely detached from such a purpose of life, I am deeply imbued with this certainty."

"Truly?" interjected Elisabeth with joyful astonishment.

"How can you doubt it, my dear lady! Just look up at the starry sky! Descend just once into the depths of your heart! Just take a single thoughtful look into the world of crystals, plants, and animals, into the inconceivable, incomprehensible, planned harmony, which permeates all these earthly and stellar worlds and forms them into one great, meaningful and sublime thought! Can you then doubt that a rational will has created all this, and could this will be rational if it were not immortal? Otherwise, would our existence have any meaning and would these innumerable starry worlds have a sense? Or are you so short-sighted to believe that the planet we dwell on is only the planet populated by reasonable beings, and that the countless suns of the starry sky with their planets and satellites, the whole army of billions in the Milky Way is only a pastime for scholars and fools?"

"Yes, yes, you are right!" exclaimed Elisabeth. "When I sometimes suddenly think that to myself, then it's an inner certainty for me too, then I can't doubt it either!"

"Well, there you are!"

"You're not going to believe in such fantasies, Ellichen!" the Baron shouted angrily. "That is nothing but a fantastic dream, in which the wish is the father of the thought! Wouldn't it be nice if it turned out that way! But one blow to the skull, and that's it with us and the dream!"

"Who's to say we'll be finished then?"

"My mind!"

"Then I feel sorry for your mind, Baron!"

"And I yours!" replied a very irritated Baron von Werheim.

"Edgar!" cried Elizabeth, rebuking him.

"I'm sorry!" said the latter, excitedly pacing up and down. "But I ask you!"

Hermann sought to pacify him: "Forgive my brusqueness, Baron, and allow me one more calm word!"

"Please!" he sounded back unkindly.

"We want to distinguish between understanding and reason. I don't know whether you have studied Kant," Hermann now continued very calmly.

"Kant, Kant! Who is Kant!" exclaimed the Baron very angrily, waving his hands through the air. "Kant is an old long-suffering moral trumpeter with whom I want nothing to do!"

"Then it will be difficult for us to come to an understanding," said Hermann with an even calm. "But perhaps you have read Plato, who calls understanding an earthly product, but reason a divine one?"

"For God's sake, stay away from me with these tedious paper philistines! I have studied law and *cameralia* and that is it! I am a practical man who looks at life in a practical way and not a fantasist! I have neither the desire nor the time for such unprofitable arts!"

"But I would like to learn more about these things," said Elisabeth. "Please, Doctor, tell me something about Kant and Plato!"

"Tell?" Hermann replied with a smile, "we won't get by with simple telling. In order to understand Plato, let alone Kant, a very logical study is required. But I suggest that we read together some chapters from the writings of these great minds, then we will make progress!"

"Wonderful, simply wonderful!" exclaimed Elisabeth, beaming with joy.

"When do we start?"

"As soon as it is convenient for you, my dear lady!"

"This is indescribably beautiful! Then let's start right away tomorrow! Please come again tomorrow for tea and in general every day! Then we will read together for an hour every day and you will explain it to us!" exclaimed Elisabeth enthusiastically. Then she turned abruptly to the Baron: "You will join us, won't you, dumpling?"

"Don't even think about it!" was the annoyed reply.

"Fine! Then we'll just read with the Doctor alone! Right, Mamma?" The Madame Councilor, who, busy with a manual task, had followed the conversation with silent but lively interest, looked questioningly at the Baron.

"Eh, allow me, Elli! That won't work!" he said very formally.

"Why shouldn't I be able to do it? Are you trying to tell me what to do, or even forbid me from continuing my education?"

"That's far for me! But…"

"There you go, but what?"

"What do you think, Madame?" the Baron now turned to the Councilor's wife.

"I mean, this could get pretty interesting and you'd do us the favor of being there."

"So!" sighed the Baron. "Fine! The enthusiasm for this new thing won't last for too long anyway!"

"I even hope that you yourself will acquire a taste for these studies," said Hermann with sincere cordiality. "As a future Minister, you should know at least Plato's treatises on the state and the laws," he added with slight irony.

"He wrote something about that, too?"

"Indeed! I would suggest that we first read the most beautiful chapters from *Phaedo*, *Phaedrus*, and the *Symposium*, about immortality, beauty, and love, then the basic chapters from the *Republic* and the *Laws*. This will give you the quickest idea of Plato's world of ideas."

"Alright, I'm really eager!"

"In the meantime, I would like to appeal to your reason once again, as far as our existence before our birth and after our death is concerned. Will you please pay attention to me for a few more seconds?"

"Yes, please! What do you want to say?" Elisabeth eagerly replied in place of the Baron. The latter had meanwhile sat down again and now looked on with mocking superiority.

"You know what a shooting star is!" Hermann now turned to Elisabeth.

"Now I actually know that! They are debris from celestial bodies flying through the atmosphere of our Earth, becoming incandescent as a result of friction with the air."

"Quite right. Imagine a very simple, uneducated person now, who has no idea of physics and astronomy, perhaps a primitive man, who sees a shooting star for the first time. If he observes quite superficially, he will believe at first, that a star has fallen from the sky. But if he observes correctly, he will recognize that it is not just any star that suddenly starts to move, but that in the night sky a shining point arises anew, covers a certain distance in the sky and then goes out again. Such a naive and crude person will, of course, not be able to form any idea of the essence of the phenomenon, he will believe that it is exhausted with the sensual perception of the luminous distance. It will never occur to him that the short distance traveled by that luminous point in the sky has a continuation into infinity beyond the beginning and end point of its course. Hundred thousand years of mental work were still necessary to fathom the nature of this celestial phenomenon."

"Oh, I understand this picture very well!" exclaimed Elizabeth with delight. "The path that the shooting star follows before it enters the earth's atmosphere is our life before birth. The trajectory after its extinction is our life after death, and the luminous stretch itself this our earthly life! Yes, you are right! Man is such a shooting star!"

"You have understood that correctly, my dear lady! If we assume that man comes into being only at birth and passes away again at death, we would be making the same mistake as an astronomer who wanted to limit the existence of a shooting star to its luminous orbit and considered it only an atmospheric-terrestrial phenomenon, rather than a cosmic one. If we consider the existence of man only as far as it appears in the light of sensible consciousness, we commit the grave error of addressing him only as an earthly issue, when he is a cosmic one."

"That is all quite beautiful! The only thing missing is the proof!" mocked the Baron. "With the shooting star I know that it behaves in such a way, because one can calculate its course from the terrestrial fragment! In the case of the humans, however, everything is mere conjecture!

"Allow me to draw your attention to a mistake in your reasoning, Baron! In order to calculate the cosmic orbit from the earthly fragment of the path of the shooting star, you must first make the assumption that the orbit goes on into the cosmos, otherwise your calculation would have no sense at all and could not take place at all! So you come to know the path of the shooting stars through a pure act of thought! And in spite of the most exact calculation you can never see the path of the shooting star! But you only deduce the existence of the path of the shooting star from your observations and calculation! Calculate means after all, to infer from one quite certain position to another!

However, you do exactly the same thing only if you conclude the cosmic position of man from the earthly situation! And you must make this conclusion with the same necessity as that astronomical one if you want to come to a solution that is just as satisfying as in the case of the shooting star! Quite apart from that, however, in the case of man we have proofs, while in the case of the shooting star we always have to rely on the correctness of our premises and calculations!"

"Well, I'm curious about that evidence!" scoffed the Baron.

"You are a Christian, aren't you, Baron?"

"What are you trying to say?" replied von Werheim nervously.

"Nothing other than what the question means, do you profess the doctrine of Christ?"

"What does confess mean? Of course, I avow it! That is, I'm not making any active use of it right now, but it goes without saying that I'm a Christian!"

"Well, then you know the evidence!"

"Meaning what?"

"I mean the evidence given to us by Jesus Christ through his whole personality, his life, his teaching, his suffering and his death!"

"How?" asked the Baron with astonishment bordering on horror. "Surely, as a modern man, you do not believe in the fables that Christ really lived?"

"Believe? Why do I have the choice to believe in the existence of Christ or not? You might as well ask me if I believe in the reality of the sun. A whole world collapsed under the appearance of Christ, a whole new world was born of him, and you doubt that he really lived? Not to speak about the testimony of the Gospels and the eyewitness of John, which even skeptical science recognizes today! But good! Let us take another example. For example, the Christian martyrs or Giordano Bruno or if you want to disregard Christianity completely, think of Socrates. Or do you also doubt that Socrates lived and died for his conviction?"

"Socrates is undoubtedly a historical figure, and that he died for his beliefs is also certain. But what does that prove?"

"This proves that the invisible world has just the same practical reality as the visible one! Yes, a far higher and stronger reality, because otherwise it would not be able to triumph over the visible world!

"Surely this proves, at most, that these people perished on foolish fictions!"

"You are sticking to mere words instead of facts!" continued Hermann Kämpfer with unflinching equanimity. "Whether you call what enabled people to lay down their lives for their convictions fiction or foolishness, conviction or duty or anything else, the fact remains that there was alive in them a force to which the outside world was subject. And in the simplest volunteer, who spills his blood for the fatherland, something outrageously real must be alive, against which the sensual world simply shatters, no matter whether he is aware of it or not! What words you use to describe this, it doesn't really matter at all! Force can be overcome only by force! The real only through the real! Being only through being!"

"You must realize that!" exclaimed Elisabeth with flaming cheeks to her fiancé.

"I have nothing at all to realize! Absolutely nothing! This is all crazy stuff! I ask to be allowed to take my leave!"

With these words, the Baron stood up, highly agitated and annoyed, kissed the hands of the Madame Councilor and his bride, and very coolly said goodbye to Hermann. He met the Madame's request to stay after all with the assurance that he had no time, that he had to go to a conference at the ministry.

Elisabeth made no attempt to hold him back, and even seemed pleased at his departure. But when Hermann also wanted to excuse himself, she asked him vigorously to continue their conversation.

Hermann was only too happy to accept this heartfelt request.

Elizabeth asked him to tell her something more about his view of the personality of Christ. What she had heard in the religious instruction she had received on this subject had been so boring and inadequate that she had not been able to gain any inner sympathy for the matter.

Hermann gladly complied with her request. But when he asked for a copy of the New Testament, in order to explain his view on the basis of the living words of Christ, it turned out that the book of God was not available at all in the Councilor's house. Elisabeth blushed a fiery red, when she returned with this admission after a long search.

Therefore, Hermann contented himself at first with explaining to the two ladies the difference between the synoptic Gospels and that of John, and made the suggestion that instead of Plato, they should first read the Gospels together, since these were the main basis for the doctrine of immortality, to which Plato appeared only as an inconsequential rhapsody.

The proposal was enthusiastically received, and Hermann departed with a sense of unspeakable happiness for the future.

— 16 —

When Hermann appeared punctually for tea the next day, the Baron was not yet there. They didn't wait for him either, since his lack of punctuality was part of the daily routine, and when he still didn't show up after taking tea, Elisabeth said impatiently, "Let's get started!"

Hermann had brought his own personal copy of the New Testament. It was a Greek-German edition. The original Greek text was on one side, the German translation on the other. He loved to read certain passages, whose tone and color could not be reproduced even by the best translation, in the original Greek text.

Now he read to the two ladies the good news that God is our Father and we are His children. That our immortal soul, created from the love of God, but having rebelled against God's love, is bound in the bondage of this earthly body to find its way back to God through suffering, experience, and insight. That we children of God should love each other with the same love with which God loves us, and that love is the first and last and only one of all commandments, which includes all the others. That simple insight and contemplation into our deep inner connection with God and therefore selflessness and readiness to help our brothers and sisters, love, love and only love can bring us salvation and allow us to find our way back to the divine home from which we originated and which we have lost through our own fault by the arrogance and blindness of our will which was created free by God. Again and again, we have to be born in the flesh until we are cleansed and purified and become perfect again, as God's love had created us perfect.

Hermann read with a melodious, even, powerful voice, which swelled like an organ in tone and increased to a stormy roar in those powerful passages that shake the reader like primeval thunder:

"Father, wherever I am, I want those you have given me to be with me, that they may behold my glory which thou hast given me: for thou loveth me before the foundation of the world. Righteous Father, the world does not know you, but I know you, and they know that you have sent me. And I have made known unto them thy name, and I will make it known; that the love wherewith thou loveth me may be in them, and I in them."

And:

"These things have I spoken unto you, that you might have peace in me. In the world you have trouble and fear; but be of good cheer, for I have conquered the world."

"I went out from the Father and came into the world; and again I am now leaving the world and returning to the Father."

"And now you, Father, you transfigure me yourself with the clarity that I had with you before the world was."

The two women could not escape the tremendous impression of these cosmic primal words, their incredible self-confidence. Hermann intensified the effect even more by repeating them in the sounds of the original language. They may have sounded even more elementary and powerful in the Aramaic in which Jesus spoke them.

Silently and deeply stirred, the women listened. After a while, Elizabeth asked how it could be that we didn't bring any memory into the world of our spiritual life that we had led before birth.

That is the meaning and purpose of this life, Hermann replied, that we have to start all over again, in order to reach a new insight into our actual destiny in the hereafter through work and experience, through pain and suffering, and thus to come to contemplation and conversion. But we are by no means without any memory of our spiritual past! It lies only in our subconsciousness, and often it flashes and twitches through our mind like a premonition! The more internalized and spiritualized a person is, the more conscious they are also of their relations to the world beyond, from which we originate.

Plato pointed out these relations long before Christ. He even goes so far as to say that all our sensations and thoughts, ideas and concepts are only more or less clear images of memories from the spiritual world in which we lived before our birth. One must imagine that through our incarnation a veil, as it were, is spread over our memory of the world beyond, which is more or less dense depending on the stage of development of the incarnating spirit. The more spiritual and ingenious a person is, the thinner and more transparent is this veil.

One can assume, said Hermann, that with Jesus, who had never abused the freedom of his will to turn away from God—in contrast to the rest of us "Sons of God", as Jesus himself calls us—this veil had remained as fine as cobwebs, that even as a man he had an almost unclouded memory of his life before his incarnation, indeed, that in certain heightened moments it rose to a clear vision. For the purpose of his incarnation was not to cleanse and purify himself in order to find his way back to God, but to bring the message of the Father to us, to make us aware of the meaning and goal of this existence on earth and to be a powerful example for us. The view, which is still held by many Christians today, that Jesus, by his suffering and death, offered God a sacrifice of atonement for our sins and thereby obtained, as it were, a kind of general pardon for all sinful humanity, is of course only an uncritical transfer of barbaric Old Testament ideas to the teachings of Christ.

The first Christians, caught up in Jewish ideas, were not yet able to comprehend the unprecedented selflessness of Jesus' life and suffering as an example. They could not free themselves from the Jewish concept of "business" associated with sacrifice. Jesus himself never taught such things, but he repeatedly pointed out that he had come to give us an example. Yahweh, the vengeful and acquisitive god of the Jews, could probably be reconciled by sacrificial offerings and be made inclined to conclude new business deals. But what sense should such sacrifices and even the sacrifice of death have to our God, who is our father and love?

"How wonderfully you put all this into a natural and easily comprehensible context!" exclaimed Elisabeth enthusiastically. "Now I see everything that we were told and taught in school in such an incomprehensible and contradictory way, all at once in a completely new and clear light!"

The Madame Councilor expressed herself somewhat more skeptically. She asked whether Hermann also believed in Jesus' healing and miracles.

"Most certainly!" replied Hermann. "What do we mean by a 'miracle'? That's what we call any event that contradicts the laws of nature as we know them. But do we know all laws of nature and all forces of nature? New ones are discovered all the time! Yesterday I explained to you, how our knowledge of nature is and will always be quite infinitesimal! An event appearing to us as a miracle would lose all miraculousness, if the forces and laws according to which it takes place were known to us. If a magnet lifts a piece of iron into the heights, contrary to the laws of gravity, a person who has never heard anything about a magnet would at first address this phenomenon as a 'miracle.' It is not difficult to understand that Jesus, who stood in such intimate connection with the Father and the spiritual world and all the powers and forces of existence, had completely undreamed-of knowledge of the forces and laws of nature!

"Such healing and miraculous deeds are reported not only by him, but also by others of his contemporaries,[1] indeed, we know such reports from the history and literature of all peoples and times. Much of it may be fic-

---

[1] Ed.: There are in fact no contemporaneous reports about Jesus, meaning, from during his lifetime (0 to 30 AD) or for decades afterward.

tion, and even in the evangelical reports about the healing and miraculous deeds of Jesus truth and fiction may be interwoven. But we can still see today in individual people forces and powers that are active, which seem to contradict the laws of nature known to us. The facts of suggestion and hypnosis, of somnambulism and spiritualism, of psychokinesis and magnetic healing therapy, can no longer be doubted. Our exact sciences are already beginning to treat them seriously and by no means only in the negative sense!

"It is not surprising that our one-sided materialistic science and its daily press attach their doubting and scornful remarks and considerations to such phenomena, because the entire worldview and domination by those circles of meaning would collapse, if it were proven that there is an afterlife and a continuation of our existence after our death. It is understandable that these facts and phenomena caused by super-sensible forces give uneducated and profit-hungry people the opportunity to lie and deceive.

"But today no prudent and unprejudiced man of science can pass by the truth at its core. It is amusing enough to see with what stubbornness the materialists insist upon their inadequate way of explanation! By accepting arbitrary assumptions and absurdities, by setting up new scholarly word monsters and conceptual frameworks, they imagine that they are "explaining" facts, instead of correcting their rigid and outdated ideas! Our old master Goethe has already made enough fun of this kind of scholars and researchers:

> *For precisely where terms are missing,*
> *That's where a word comes at the right time!*

But even Jesus fought in vain against these eternally incorrigible scribblers and rigid dogmatists and actually fell victim to them."

"Jesus? Why? Who are you talking about?" asked Elizabeth eagerly.

"I mean the Jews, of course."

A flaming blush poured over the young girl's beautiful face, and the Madame also seemed embarrassed. But Hermann paid no attention.

"But Jesus himself was a Jew!" said Elizabeth.

"Jesus, a Jew?!" retorted Hermann briskly. "Rather, an eagle might hatch from a clutch of crow's eggs, or a hyena give birth to a lion!"

"But in the Gospels, the entire Jewish genealogy of the Savior is mentioned," interjected the Madame Councilor in great astonishment.

"This is of course a pious rewriting of the Evangelist, who is still completely under the spell of the Jewish Old Testament. You can see that already from the fact that in the Gospel of Luke a completely different family tree is found than in the Gospel of Matthew. But even if the Jewish descent of Jesus could be notarially attested to by all 42 families mentioned there, then I would rather consider these 42 notaries as crooks or themselves victims of a swindle than that I could believe in the Jewish descent of Jesus".[2]

The two ladies looked at Hermann in amazement. But he continued undeterred:

"Just imagine the irreconcilable spiritual contrast between Jesus and the Jews from the beginning of his appearance until his death! Just hear how he thunders against the Pharisees and scribes, these archetypes of racial Judaism!"

And Hermann reached for the Gospel of Matthew and read from Jesus' denunciation in Chapter 23 that hammers down like a rain of fire on the "brood of snakes and vipers."

"Can you imagine a deeper gulf than that which yawns between his thinking and feeling and that of the Jews? Jesus is total inwardness, selflessness and truthfulness, the Jews embody outwardness, selfishness and mendacity! Clinging to the rigid letter of a law directed at sheer transience. He carries his law, aiming at the eternal and imperishable, unwritten in his breast! Jesus directed all his reflecting and longing, his thoughts and actions to the inner world, the Jews cling to money and gold, and even degrade the temple of God to a place of money changing and usury, indulging only in the miserable moment, simply unable to follow his high flight of feelings and thoughts. Jesus taught of a God who is our kind father, the fountainhead of all love and mercy, the Jews formulated a God who mercilessly insists on the letter-perfect fulfillment of a purely business contract, for which he promises them good profit under the condition that he himself will have a ten percent share in it.

"What did this horrible, vengeful, profit-hungry Jewish God not promise his "chosen" people! "All the nations of the earth shall you devour, and you shall not spare them!" (Deut. 7:16.) "Strangers shall build thy walls, and their kings shall serve thee!" (Isa. 60:10-12.) "Thou shalt gather up the milk of all nations, and the breasts of kings shall suckle thee!" (Isa. 60:16.) "Strangers shall stand and feed your flocks, and foreigners shall be your husbandmen and your vinedressers! The goods of the nations you will consume and make their glory your glory!" (Isa. 61:5-6.) "You may take advantage of the stranger, but not your brother, so that

---

[2] Ed.: By all accounts, Jesus was indeed a Jew; see the Introduction.

Yahweh may bless you in all that you undertake, wherever you come to take it!" (Deut. 23:20.) Etc. Open the Old Testament any place you like, everywhere the religious thinking of the Jews is revealed, which is directed to deceit and fraud, business and profit.[3]

"And Jesus opposes this insatiable greed for money and power with the simple confession: 'My kingdom is not of this world'."

"Jesus himself soon realized that the Jews were incapable of understanding his teachings. There are numerous passages in the Gospels that show how painful it was for him to find a greater understanding among the Gentiles than among the Jews. The Canaanite woman, the centurion of Capernaum are examples of this. So, he soon sent his disciples into the lands of the Gentiles, while he had originally commanded them to enter "no Gentile road and no Samaritan city," but to convert the "lost sheep of the house of Israel." Finally, he realized that the kingdom had to be taken away from the "chosen" people and given to the heroes! "The sons of the kingdom will be thrown out into the darkness outside" (Matthew 8:12.). In the Gospel of John, the Jews are constantly spoken of as strangers.

"This irreconcilable spiritual contrast between Jesus and the Jews can only be explained and understood by reference to their race, because the way we feel and think is intimately related to the nature of our blood and nervous system. Just as a blackthorn always bears sloes and never apples or pears, so the precious fruit of Jesus' teaching can never grow on Jewish stalks. And in fact, there is a whole series of clues, even proofs, that Jesus was not a Jew, but an Aryan, or what is the same, an Indo-German. He was a Jew only by his upbringing and his religious confession, but never by his race![4]

"References to this can already be found in the Gospels. Jesus came from the northern province of Galilee, which has always stood in ethnic contrast to Judea. The prophet Isaiah already calls this landscape the "Galilee of the Gentiles", and the word "Galilee" itself means "pagan region". The Galileans were recognizable in Judea by their peculiar pronunciation. "You are a Galilean, for your accent gives you away!" says the serving girl to Peter. Because of their peculiar sounding pronunciation, which aroused laughter among the Jews, the Galileans were not permitted to read aloud in the synagogue.[5]

---

[3] See Appendix.

[4] Ed.: Again, this seems clearly false, if only from the NT passages alone—not to mention the general presumption of exclusively Jewish characters.

[5] Ed.: Galilee is now widely seen by scholars as a predominantly Jewish region during the time of Jesus. See M. Chancey, *The Myth of a Gentile Galilee* (2004).

"They were unable, for example, to speak the Jewish guttural sounds, just as the Jews, conversely, are unable to cope with our Aryan tongues to this day. The Galileans are said to have been completely unable to learn Hebrew. This linguistic inability, however, is based on racially conditioned differences in the structure of the larynx. The words with which Nathanael greets Philip's message in John's Gospel, "What good can come from Nazareth?", which apparently forms a standing expression, also point to a sharp contrast between Judea and Galilee.

"Historically, there is no doubt that the base population of Galilee was not of the Jewish race.[6] The Jews had advanced in Palestine from south to north. However, not even the countryside of Samaria, lying inside Galilee, was completely Judaized in Jesus' time, and the Samaritans were regarded by the Jews as strangers and misbelievers. For the Jews, accepting a piece of bread from a Samaritan was considered the equivalent to eating pork. Jesus' well-known parable also points to the contrast between Jews and Samaritans.

"The northern border province of Galilee, the "pagan region", was already regarded by the Jews as a foreign country. This region was so sparsely inhabited by Jews already in King Solomon's time that he ceded twenty Galilean cities to King Hiram of Tyre as payment for materials Hiram delivered to build the temple in Jerusalem. In view of Jewish ethnic solidarity, this act would have been quite inconceivable if these cities had been inhabited by the children of the chosen people. In the following centuries, Aryan blood was repeatedly transplanted to northern Galilee: In the eighth century B.C., the Assyrian rulers Sargon and Tiglath-Pilaser sent Prince Dejokes of Medes as a hostage to the Sea of Galilee. Shortly thereafter, all of Galilee, including Samaria, was settled by Assyrian colonists.

"This ruler and master race, however, was closely related to the Indo-Aryans and must be regarded as a semiticized opening wave of the flood of Indo-Germanic peoples. Its literary and artistic monuments, which can be traced back to the intellectual patrimony of the ancient Aryans, leave no doubt about this. It had originated with the purely Aryan Sumero-Akkadians, who were flooded by Semites and merged with them. They were also the ones who supplied the Jews with the foundation stones for the building of the Old Testament, who in their unimaginatively sober manner, devoid of any introspection, chopped it down to fit their special purposes by stripping the Aryan myths of their deep symbolism and degrading them to trivial chronicles. They were simply incapable of grasping

---

[6] Ed.: Again, now seen as a mistaken presumption.

their symbolic sense of eternity. The history of creation, the legend of the Flood, even the psalms and the hymns of the Old Testament have their origin and archetypes in the Babylonian-Assyrian literature, in which they were already contained thousands of years before the origin of the Jewish Bible![7] The fall of man, man and woman and serpent under the tree of knowledge, and winged angels were all already depicted on Babylonian-Assyrian clay tablets thousands of years before the origin of the Bible, as were floating deities and winged sun wheels, demons, and devils![8]"

"That's amazing!" exclaimed Elizabeth. "And we are brought up to believe that the Jews are the creators of these foundations of the Christian religion! Why aren't we told about this?"

"Yes why!" interjected Hermann. "That's probably omitted for the same reason that one does not want to admit that Jesus himself was not a Jew. One fears for the international authority of the church without considering that nothing undermines authority more than the fearful concealment of the truth. This is not wise, for truth cannot be stopped and the Church has itself to blame if the best spirits defect from it. For us Germans, it is really not irrelevant that Jesus was of Indo-Germanic stock! Because the fact that an Indo-European peoples lived in Palestine alongside and among the Syrian-Hittite peoples is evident from the Bible without a doubt!"

"What people do you mean?" asked Elisabeth in amazement.

"The Amorites," Hermann replied. "Amurru, the people of the north country," as they are called in the Egyptian documents.[9] East of the Jordan they had founded a powerful empire with which Israel was in constant struggle. They were a tall, blond, blue-eyed people of fair complexion. The preserved images remind us of the portraits of Germanic princes. "Like locusts" the scouts felt toward them (Genesis, 13). These "sons of Enak" are referred to as "giants" by the spies of Moses, and as "people of great length." I am inclined to think them a southern branch of the noble Sarmatians native to the Black Sea, a tribe which in later centuries produced the Goths. These Amorites also formed an essential component of the Philistines, who had also already received Aryan blood from the Hellenes.

---

[7] Ed.: Indeed, Akkadian literature dates back to 2200 BC.

[8] On this topic, compare *Babel und Bibel* by Friedrich Delitzsch, (Stuttgart, Deutsche Verlagsanstalt, 1903) and the works of Kaulen, Lauth, Lepsius, Sayce, Schrader, Wahrmund and others that appeared decades before this work. Examples from the pre-Jewish writings, which are unmistakable models for the most beautiful parts of the Old Testament, can also be found in Theodor Fritsch's book, *Der falsche Gott.*

[9] Ed.: Amorites came from the region of present-day Syria and Iraq.

One of their people was the brave Goliath, who challenged the Israelites to a chivalrous duel, but was struck down by a treacherously hurled stone. Also the "sons of Raphas", mentioned in the second book Samuel, who carried gigantic spears and heavy iron armor, were of the same tribe. Just as Germanic tribes could only be defeated by Germanic tribes, so the Amorites and Philistines could only be defeated by their own kind. Israel did not become their master until it had succeeded in winning voluntary allegiance of the Amorite tribe the Gittites. The city of Jerusalem was founded by an Amorite. The king of Jerusalem who goes against Joshua is an Amorite, and the prophet Ezekiel calls out to the city of Jerusalem: "By origin you are a Canaanite; your father was an Amorite, your mother a Hittite!" Only with the help of the Philistines did David manage to take the throne. After their defeat, they formed the core of his army and provided him with commanders and generals, as the Germanic tribes did later for the Romans. The Aryan element of the Amorites and Philistines is still effective in the Jews to this day. The blondness of some old Jewish families goes back to this blood mixture.

In addition, in the last centuries before Christ, there was active Greek immigration throughout Palestine, which was especially beneficial for the more accessible and fertile Galilee. Alexander the Great had also populated nearby Samaria with Macedonians. Through these immigrations, numerous Aryan proselytes were introduced to Judaism. In the Maccabean period there were even high priests who bore Greek names! Yes, scholars have raised the question whether or not Jesus spoke Greek! Also, the Gauls that crossed the Hellespont in the third century B.C., wandered through Asia Minor, and finally founded the colony of the Galatians at the Halys, may very well have brought new Aryan blood to Galilee as well. These Gauls also easily found their way there as mercenaries.

To turn the pagan population of Palestine into Jewish believers became the burning desire of the Jewish priests and prophets. How cleverly they went about it is known from the 2nd book of Kings. After the Babylonian captivity,[10] which resulted in the breeding of the pure Jewish race, the ethnic antagonism between Jews and Galileans had become so great that marriage between them was considered unthinkable. This feeling was still so strong that even in the Maccabean period, a century and a half before Christ, the few in-country Jews who could not marry Jews who had migrated to Galilee, were gathered by Simon the Maccabee and brought back to Judea in their entirety. According to this, Galilee was therefore completely

---

[10] Ed.: The captivity ran from 597 to 538 BC.

free of Jews 150 years before the birth of Christ. But even during Christ's lifetime the ethnic contrast between Galilee and Judea was so sharp that Herod Antipas did not succeed in winning Jewish settlers for the city of Tiberias at the Sea of Galilee, which he had founded, either by promises or by force. These facts alone make it seem impossible that Jesus was a Jew by race.

That he was of pure Aryan stock, however, becomes an unequivocal certainty on the basis of a mental analysis. This is, like the *aqua regia* in chemistry, the sharpest means of testing the race.

To consider Jesus a Jew, and the Jews as the founders of our Christian religion, is one of the greatest and most fatal failures of world history![11] Jesus was no more a Jew than was the Galilean Ezekiah, who during Caesar's lifetime revolted against the slavery of the Jewish doctrine in Galilee, or like the famous Judas the Galilean, who some decades before Christ proclaimed: "God alone is Lord, death is irrelevant, freedom one and all!" or like his sons, who were crucified as dangerous agitators against the state! Or like that Galilean Menahem, who destroyed the Roman garrison of Jerusalem in Nero's time and was executed for it by the Jews under the pretext that he had pretended to be the Messiah! Or like the Galilean John of Gischala, a city at the extreme northern border of Galilee, who led the desperate defense of Jerusalem against Titus, or like the Galilean hero Eleazer, who for years after the destruction of Jerusalem entrenched himself with a small troop in the mountains, and ultimately, with his followers, first killed the women and children and then himself. Is such behavior Jewish?

The Jews, wherever they were in Alexandria and Rome, knew then, just as they do today, how to get along with their Gentile governments, to find their advantage as peddlers and junk dealers, merchants and money lenders, scholars and lawyers, swindlers, and actors. But to offer the hopeless resistance of death in order to save honor and conscience, that is really not the Jewish way!

There is an important document which also throws a flash of light on the origin of Jesus' hometown of Nazareth. Pliny tells about the "Nazarini" in the area of the Caucasus. Their descendants are the Nossair, who still live today in Lebanon, that is, in the mountains bordering on Galilee to the north. The Nossair, however, belong to that Aryan sect of the Sufis, who believed themselves to be one with God, sinless and lords over all things. Everything indicates that it was these "Nazerini" who founded Nazareth as a city or a religious sanctuary. The name Nazareth shows no other word

---

[11] See Appendix.

relationship, while all the other place names and river names in Palestine are related to, or even synonymous with, others in the Mediterranean area. Thus, the word Dan in Jordan is also found in many river names in the territory of the Kassites, in Don, Düna, Donau, Donez, Rhodanus, Eridanus. Also Tabor, the mountain of transfiguration, is not Jewish at all! In Greek it is called Artabürios and it occurs in exactly such a way on Rhodes as well!

Whoever looks critically at all these historical, ethnic, and linguistic connections in combination with a mental analysis, is forced to realize that Jesus could not possibly have been a Jew. There is no doubt in my mind that the Savior had chosen the tribe of the Sarmatian Amorites for his embodiment, that from their noble Gothic blood his spirit formed the body in which he walked on earth to bring the good news of the Father to the people. Only a body of the purest and most highly developed race was able to provide his soul with the instrument from which it could sound its heavenly notes. In a body of a less noble race, they would have been smothered or only expressed imperfectly.

The disciples of Jesus were also Galileans, with one exception![12] Leaving home and family, fortune and business, to follow an inner confession, a useless ideal, is something no Jew can manage to this day. Judas Iscariot was the only Jew among the disciples of Jesus, and he betrayed him for money!

Just as Jesus and his faithful disciples were not Jews, neither were most of the prophets of the Old Testament![13] The fact that Judah made the peoples "interest-bearing" to itself, is mentioned everywhere in the Bible. From the prophets, the voice of despair speaks from the exploited, original race against the foreign Jewish oppressors.[14]

The story of Jacob and Esau, which is told in the first book of Moses, is clear proof that two different races lived in Canaan. The land of Canaan itself is symbolized by their mother Rebecca. "Two peoples are in your body and two kinds of people will separate from you. One people will be superior to the other, and the older will serve the younger." Esau, the older, a huntsman and tiller, according to the story of the Bible "has reddish hair, like fur, and is quite rough." Jacob, the younger, is "smooth" and "dwelled in the tents." So he did not go hunting and did not work the field, but went about his business "in the tents".

---

[12] Ed.: Again, incorrect. All the disciples were surely Jews.
[13] Ed.: Again, incorrect.
[14] See Appendix.

Esau, synonymous with Edom, symbolizes the established tribe of the earlier Aryan population, which is designated here with the collective name of the Edomites. Jacob represents the tribe of the immigrated Jews. Jacob means in Aramaic the rogue, the deceiver! He uses Esau's hunger to cheat him of his birthright for a bowl of lentils, and the Jewish god Yahweh helps him! The allegory says that he took Esau's right of inheritance, his claims to his father's house and farm for a dish of lentils, we would say for a sandwich. Of course, fraudulently taking advantage of Esau's plight, because no one would voluntarily sell his paternal inheritance rights for lentil soup. This is the well-known method that Jacob's descendants still practice on our peasants to this day. They use the Gentile's misery to persuade him to mortgage his movable and immovable property.

Jacob, however, is not satisfied with cheating Esau only once. He also steals the fatherly blessing from him with the help of his resourceful mother Rebecca. When Esau comes home and asks for the blessing from his blind father, the duped patriarch can only comfort him with the promise that he will have part "of the dew from heaven above". From now on he must live by his sword and be of service to his younger brother! What profound words! The promise, however, that Esau received from his father, ends profoundly! "It will come to pass, if you make an effort, you will shake off his yoke from your neck!" And Esau did exert himself. Since he was cheated of all legal titles by Jacob, there was nothing left for his deliverance but brute force: he wanted to strangle his so-called brother Jacob! Not slay him with his righteous sword, but strangle him with his hands! The *furor teutonicus* had finally awakened in him for the slick con artist.

But his mother Rebecca immediately raised a loud cry for her favorite son Jacob, like always when someone harmed by the Jews tries to defend his own skin. Nowadays the *Berliner Tageblatt* and the *Frankfurter Zeitung* would immediately accuse Esau of "anti-Semitism" and "religious intolerance." But since Esau did not forgive the trickery, she helped her darling flee as fast as possible to her brother Laban. Esau, freed from Jacob, was finally allowed to live in happiness and peace.

Jacob, however, continued to lie and deceive even in a foreign country, and his God Yahweh faithfully helped him as always, of course, in return for his agreed upon ten percent stake. He even cheated his father-in-law Laban quite properly. With Yahweh's help, he performed the well-known hocus-pocus on Laban's flocks with the piebald and un-piebald lambs, and thus brought the good half of Laban's property to himself. But Laban was well worthy of his wily son-in-law Jacob. With his two daughters Rachel and Leah, he outmaneuvered and entrapped him. Which is known delightfully from the further narrative of the 1st book of Moses. The idyllic family life described there sheds a pleasantly clear light on circumstances during the patriarchal era.

Jacob, however, became "rich beyond measure", and soon had every reason to run away again. Trusting in the generosity of his brother Esau, he decided to return home, not without taking with him the golden household gods of his father-in-law Laban. When Esau learned of his approach, he went to meet him with four hundred men. It is not clear from the biblical narrative whether his intentions are good or bad. Jacob, pushing women and children before him as a shield, came to meet him, serving and bowing down, offering gifts and beautiful speeches.

And there Esau, in his blond innocence, committed the same mistake, we can calmly say the same stupidity, which we Aryans have committed regarding the Jews repeatedly for thousands of years: we do not become wise through harm and fall from endless Jewish tricks and whistles. Esau said to him, "I have enough, my brother, keep what you have," and magnanimously took him back. Jacob then had free play again and his old practices flourished and thrived with his children and his grandchildren to this day, under the constant and copious help of Yahweh, the God of the Jews.

The Old Testament is an unambiguous diary of these Jewish lies and deceptions, and we are taught in school that it is the foundation of the New Testament and Jesus Christ is its fulfillment! On the contrary, Jesus nullifies the Old Testament and the business operations glorified there, he destroys and annihilates all Jewish materialism, and the historical foundations of Judaism, which are composed of the basest greed for possessions and selfishness, lust for power and domination![15] Without the appearance of the Aryan Jesus of Nazareth, these would have remained the foundations for the further development of the whole mankind! The Old Testament principle of "an eye for an eye, a tooth for a tooth" had to be eradicated, if mankind should enter the higher realms of spirituality. Jesus carried out this eradication, and selfless love has taken the place of selfishness. If this is not yet the general basis of morality and society and of mankind today, it is largely due to the fact that the teachings of Jesus were artificially grafted onto Judaism and saturated with Judaism by his disciples, who were still completely caught up in it.

---

[15] Ed.: Jesus "nullifies" the OT because he (as Paul's creation) must appeal to the Gentile masses. Therefore, he cannot simply parrot the OT; he must appear to be its opposite, even as he works for the benefit of "Israel."

Thus, the Jewish dragon, which Christ had slain, awoke to new life and to this day we are not rid of the Jew in us and around us. Is the division of Christianity into different confessions and sects based on something other than the remnants of Judaism, which were taken over from the Old Testament by the church? The division of German Christianity, to which we owe all the misery of our inner turmoil, begins with the most trivial of the trivial! And Jews and Jewish comrades triumph in this!

The Jews feel only too clearly in their sure racial instinct that Jesus of Nazareth is the destroyer of the historical foundations of Judaism, and that is why they put him on the cross, and that is why they persecute him and his confessors up to the present day with indelible hatred.[16]

The Talmud, the law book of the Jewish religion, which is still binding for the Jews today, assigns Jesus Christ such foul names that a Christian tongue resists pronouncing them. He calls the Christians "cattle", that stand outside the law![17] Also in the *Shulchan Aruch*, the more recent law book of the Jewish religion, they are repeatedly compared with animals, the consumption of which is forbidden to the Jews.[18]

Adultery with a Christian woman is permitted, because she is not a human being, but rather an animal![19] The Talmud and the *Schulchan*

---

[16] See Appendix.

[17] Talmud Jebamoth 98a: "The Torah has set the children free from them (from the Akum) because it says: "their flesh is donkey flesh and their seed is horse seed."

(According to the testimony of court-sworn experts, "Akum" and "Goi," plural "Goyim", mean the gentile, "specifically" the Christians).

Tosephot (the medieval supplement to the Talmud) to Talmud Kethuboth 3b: "His (the Akum's) seed is regarded as the seed of cattle." etc.

[18] *Shulchan-Aruch*, Orach hajjim 576:3, Eben ha' ezer 26.1 Haga etc.

[19] Moses said: "You shall not covet your neighbor's wife" and "whoever commits adultery with his neighbor's wife is guilty of death. The Talmud, Sanhedrin 52,2 teaches, Moses only forbids for the Jews adultery with his neighbor's wife, meaning the wife of a Jew, but the wife of the Akum is excluded from this prohibition! In Tosephot, Raschi remarks (Leviticus 20:10) that one learns from this that the Akum has no marriage! (According to Rohling, "Der Talmudjude" [The Talmud-Jew], new edition by Carl Paasch, 13th edition).

Tosephot to Talmud, Sanhedrin 74b: "*Concubitus Akum* (sexual relations with the gentile) is like *concubitus bestiae* (sexual relations with an animal)"!

It is not possible to reproduce here all the shamelessness of the Talmud which justifies adultery with Christian women. The reader will find more detailed information in Chapter 7 of the work, "*Der Talmudjude*" by Professor Dr. August Rohling (new edition by Carl Paasch, Leipzig, Hammerverlag). However, after these examples, one understands that the Jewish young men and husbands, who seduce thousands of German girls and women every year, are acting entirely in accordance with their religious norms!

Aruch contain countless instructions to harm and exploit Christians. Lying and deceit, theft, and embezzlement, even assassination of a Christian is not only allowed, but even prescribed in certain cases![20]

Perjury is permitted, if a Jew can thereby evade being punished by a court! Every year at the Feast of Atonement, the Jewish community firmly prays together the Kol Nidre prayer, by which all oaths and vows to be taken in the coming year are declared invalid in advance![21]

And such a religion was elevated in our German fatherland to a state religion on an equal footing with Christianity! You scratch your head and wonder how such a thing is possible! It can only be explained by the fact that Christians do not read the Old Testament with open eyes, and that the true essence of the Jewish religion has remained completely unknown to them. Jewish religious laws, written in Hebrew, are kept strictly secret by the Jews, and all attempts to arrange for a German translation by the state have so far been successfully thwarted by them.[22]

Every race has own religion, peculiar to its nature! Christianity, which originated in the midst of the Jewish people, has been rejected by the Jews to this day. Individual proselytes prove nothing at all, quite apart from the fact that such conversions from Judaism to Christianity are usually made only for practical advantages and not out of inner conviction.[23]

---

[20] See Appendix.

[21] See Appendix.

[22] In the essay "On the Jewish Question" in the "Franco-German Yearbooks" of 1844, Karl Marx wrote, among other things, the following: "If the Jew is to be emancipated from the Christian state, he demands that the Christian state give up its religious prejudice. Does he, the Jew, give up his religious prejudice? Has he, then, a right to demand of another this abdication of religion?... The Jews have emancipated themselves to the extent that Christians have become Jews. What, in and of itself, was the basis of the Jewish religion? The practical need, the egoism. Money is the zealous God of Israel, before whom no other God may stand."

Prof. Mandelstam was fully justified in declaring at the Jewish Congress in Basle, August 28, 1898: "We Jews reject with all our energy, absorption into the other nationalities and hold fast to our historical hopes." (According to the report in the pro-Jewish Paris newspaper "Le Temps", Sept. 2, 1898.) This historical hope of which Prof. Mandelstam speaks is that of world domination. "The Jews are right to aspire to it; but all of us who have never thought of world domination and who are content to be and remain masters in our own house, we have the right and the duty, without being unkind, to take vigorous protective measures against such a dangerous guest." (Houston Stewart Chamberlain, "Race and Nation" in *Deutschlands Erneuerung*, issue 7, July 1918, Verlag J. F. Lehmann, Munich.)

[23] See Appendix.

Where whole Semitic communities have converted to Christianity, as in Syria, Mesopotamia, in North and South Arabia, Christianity has not persisted and most of these Christian communities have disappeared again in those regions. Only a few hundred thousand Nestorians and some Christian Arabs in Syria remain. Conversely, only Jews profess the Jewish religion. The conclusion cannot be avoided that the personality and teachings of Christ were and are felt by Semites to be alien to their nature. "You resemble the spirit you understand!"

The bearers of the Christianity are quite essentially the Aryans, namely the occidental Indo-Europeans! All other races, which have professed Christianity, do not yet make up one twelfth of the total number of all Christians! In the cases of non-Aryan exceptions, it should also be considered that the Hungarians and Finns have absorbed a lot of Slavic and German, i.e., Aryan blood, and that the Negroes and Indians succumbed by necessity to the culture of their conquerors and thus to Christianity, but that Christianity has hardly penetrated skin-deep into these peoples and that any deeper and active participation on their part is missing.

"Brahmanism has never conquered any peoples other than Hindus. The word of Zarathustra has spread only among the Persians. The teachings of Confucius have always been limited to East Asia. The Buddha claimed to redeem all the peoples of the earth. But after a victorious run of more than two thousand years, it has gained validity only among the people of Mongolian blood.

"The connection between religion and race is unmistakable everywhere. The only apparent exception is Islam. But it is not original itself and neither are its adherents. It originated in a country whose population was mixed with Semites, Hamites, Negroes, Persians, and other racial elements. Aryan Spain, which had completely succumbed to Islam under Arab rule, has thrown it off again and has returned to Christianity.

"No matter where you look, the essence of every race is always reflected in its religion! The sobriety of Confucius is the soberness of the Chinese! The exuberance of Shinto reflects the fantastic of the Japanese spirit! Buddha is the Indian-Tibetan dreamer! Yahweh the embodied principle of trivial Jewish materialism! Christ the shaper of the idealism of the Aryan, springing from the depths of the soul, tearing apart the deceptive appearance of this world, overcoming the world and death! Luther, the watchful conscience and the ruthless defiance of the Northerner, who came to restore the teachings of Christ to their original purity, which had been falsified by Judaism! Unfortunately, however, he stopped at the Old Testament! When will we German Christians finally see the new Luther, who will bring the deeds of the first Luther to completion, free our Christian religion from Judaism and ourselves from the Jew in us and around us, who will cut off the head of this Jewish Gorgon once and for all?"

Now Hermann was silent, and the ladies were silent, too. After a while, Elisabeth silently squeezed his hand and left the room in deep excitement. The Madame Councilor also seemed seriously moved.

Then the doorbell rang and shortly afterwards the Baron entered.

"Well, where's Elli?" he asked in surprise after greeting Madame Councilor and bowing carelessly to Hermann.

The Madame remained silent.

"What's that supposed to mean?" he asked irritably.

"We have read and the young lady has just gone out," said Hermann very calmly.

Then Elisabeth entered again. The Baron kissed her hand. She let it happen carelessly.

"Why are you so late?" she asked calmly, not wanting to say anything at all.

"I was on duty, my child. The Ministerial Councilor wouldn't let me go. You must excuse me!"

Elizabeth rang the servant and ordered fresh tea for her bridegroom.

"Don't be angry, Ellichen!" said the Baron. "I actually didn't have time. Next time, I will be more punctual. I promise you." He kissed her hand again. This time, however, she withdrew hers from him.

Shrugging, the Baron sat down and lit a cigarette.

Dusk was already falling.

Quickly Hermann said goodbye, without setting a time for the next reading session.

Elisabeth was agitated in every depth of her heart and soul. At first, she was unable to account for what was going on inside her. She felt as if she was staggering blindly along an abyss into which unseen forces threatened to pull her down. It seemed incomprehensible to her that she had not long since fallen into this abyss, and it was as if she could, indeed must, fall to her death at any moment. But she clearly felt that only one person could help and save her, Hermann Kämpfer. And she also felt that she had fallen for this strong blond man, body and soul. This was the hero she saw in her dreams, the man from whom she longed for children, the husband for whom her blood cried out in her sleepless nights. For the first time she was sure that she did not love the Baron, that she had not known the feeling of love at all. But now she knew what love was!

But she also had no doubt that she would not be able to buy the love of this man drunk with fire for all the treasures of the world, unless he gave it to her voluntarily. She had noticed as well, that he had not remained indifferent to her. It was precisely that, that had tempted her to play her coquettish game with him. But what, if he had now seen through this game! The blush of shame rose hotly on her face at the thought. She was certain then of his contempt, she had lost him irretrievably, even before she had possessed him! If she had known that her fear was groundless, that he loved her and suffered for this love, she would have rushed to him on the spot and thrown herself into his arms, surrendering herself to him as his pliant property without regard for society and manners, indeed precisely in opposition to them and out of defiance against them. She would have been capable of such an elementary deed, and she would have committed it rejoicing.

The will to live of her mother's pure Germanic blood was not diminished by the dark chaotic flow from her father's veins, even if it was inhibited in all its nobler instincts. Passion and sensuality, lust for pleasure and licentiousness, the remains of our animal development, were heightened by this accursed mixture of blood, everything great and good, pure and true, noble and profound, striving out from animality into spirituality, was degraded, paralyzed or even suffocated. This was the curse of sin against the blood to which she owed her existence.

Because of the imbalance and volatility of her nature, Elisabeth had often felt bitterly that something that was originally whole in her had broken and gone bad. But it had never occurred to her to ask for a reason for this. Now, however, Hermann described to her with such vivid colors the contrast, even the hostility of the elements from which her blood was mixed, that she began to suspect the cause of the incompleteness in which she stumbled through life. She began to feel vaguely that she was a flawed creature, and helplessly she resisted this increasingly clear realization. Now she understood why she had lost any deeper feeling for her father, indeed why she hated him! He was to blame for the curse under which her existence stood! But was her mother not also guilty? Something un-childlike and hostile to her mother also began to stir in her and threatened to increase into hatred, no less so than against her father.

This change in her daughter's mind was not lost on the mother. She suspected its cause, only too clearly, and when the two women sat next to each other in silence for a long time one late afternoon in the twilight hour, and Elisabeth suddenly threw herself around her mother's neck, sobbing loudly, she told her the sad circumstances from which her life had sprung. From that moment on, Elisabeth only felt a more intimate bond with her mother. But the dull desperation did not leave her. The stain remained and clung to her life, and all her mother's blamelessness and all her love could not erase it.

There was only one person in the whole world who could redeem her from the curse, and that was Hermann Kämpfer, if he loved her! His love would wash her clean and tame the demons of half-measures and restlessness in her, in his love she would find the power to move mountains and break even the barriers of her father's blood! Her whole being would be decontaminated, purified, and refined and reborn by his love! The bliss of becoming good and pure oneself in the love of this good, pure man must have been unthinkable! The drive for ennoblement, deepening and internalization had always been alive in her! That is why she hated and despised this superficial, flighty, even vicious life of sensuality and pleasure, which she was socially conditioned to lead, and which she nevertheless could not find the strength to renounce. Hermann's love, however, would snatch her away from this maelstrom and quench the longing of her soul! But if she became the wife of this Jewish Baron, her fate would be to degenerate and perish spiritually!

How she hated him all of a sudden, and how disgusting his striving seemed to her now, in which she had always encouraged him, since she was driven by a desire bordering on frenzy to pile higher and higher the

balconies of her vain desire for fame and splendor! She would now exchange this mendacious life of appearances for a true and genuine life at
Hermann's side, whose purer and nobler joys filled her with a promise of
bliss.

A deep inner exultation suddenly came over her. She felt free like an
eagle floating calmly and steadily on strong, secure wings over mountains
and valleys, ravines and chasms, carried by a certain momentum and
strength, not blinded by the flood of sunlight that is its element and its
home. But all of a sudden it was again as if her resilience was breaking and
she were falling into the whirling depths from the bright heights to which
she had soared on the wings of her love. Would Hermann, who was so
completely made from one untainted cast, resign himself to her half-
heartedness, would he not feel repelled by her, once he saw through her
true nature? Would he, who was so completely filled with high and pure
feelings and thoughts, find satisfaction in a creature who was only at home
in the lowlands of the life of feeling and thought and perhaps was no longer capable of finding his purity and clarity to get through? With a grinning
grimace, reality suddenly stood before her again: she was, after all, her
father's daughter and the bride of this Baron! In a few weeks she would be
his wife and in a year the mother of his child!

In this way, the sensations surged up and down in Elisabeth. Especially in the morning, when she woke up, they stormed at her powerfully.
Then, quite contrary to her usual habit, she stayed in bed until late in the
day, tired and worn out, and had breakfast brought to her bedside, while
she was usually on horseback by 9 o'clock.

A few days after that last meeting with Hermann, she had again not
gotten up until around noon. She had not been able to get any sleep almost
all night long. Half dressed, however, she had once again succumbed to
despair and had thrown herself back on the bed, weeping bitterly, her face
and hands clutching the pillows. In this state, the Baron surprised her.

In vain he had tried to reach her in the last days by telephone. He had
always received the message that the madam was not yet available or had
already gone out. Finally, he showed up himself. Since he learned from the
servants that Elisabeth had not yet left her rooms and that the Madame
Councilor, from whom he could have obtained information, had gone out,
he went up to Elisabeth's private quarters, angry and worried at the same
time. As her soon-to-be husband, he believed he had the right to do so.
Since he found her neither in her anteroom nor in her living room, he
knocked softly at first, then a little louder at her bed chamber, and when
even then nothing stirred, he carefully opened the door.

Startled, he called Elisabeth. Only then did she become aware of him. Outraged by his audacity, she asked him to leave. He, however, played the tenderly concerned one and approached her impudently. She threatened to scream. He paid no attention. But when he put his arm around her body and began to cover her free neck with kisses, she wheeled around and up as if stung by an adder and ordered him to leave the room at once. Highly erect, like Pallas Athena, she stood imperiously before him and pointed with her hand to the door.

Like a poodle fearing his master's blow with a stick, the Baron slipped out the door. When he was gone, Elisabeth locked her rooms, quickly sat down at her desk and wrote and sealed a short letter. Then she rang her maid's bell and ordered her to have the letter delivered immediately to the address by her driver.

Furious, the Baron left the house. Shortly thereafter, Elisabeth's new Mercedes automobile rattled out of the garden gate to Gross-Lichterfelde to deliver the letter to Hermann Kämpfer.

Hermann, too, could not find peace since that afternoon. But his restlessness was different from Elisabeth's. He reproached himself vehemently for having once again unthinkingly let his feelings and thoughts run wild. How his remarks must have hurt and outraged the two women! Must they not assume that he presumed to hold up a mirror to them and criticize them, their lives and the unfortunate but unchangeable foundations on which they were built? What did this life matter to him? Was he called to play the apostle and, by his daring honesty, to lose again and again the favor of the people who meant well with him?

And it was not even his intention to influence the conscience of the women in any way! What would have been the point of that! He was not able to change the tragic facts! And that the ladies resented his boundless carelessness and felt it as tactlessness, there hardly seemed any doubt, because otherwise they would have asked him to come back! But they had omitted this, although originally it had been agreed that he should appear daily for tea and to read with them! Elisabeth herself had wished it, but when he left, not a syllable was spoken to remind him of this agreement! She had indeed shaken his hand warmly as a farewell, and it had seemed to him as if she had held his hand more intimately and for a moment longer than usual. But, of course, he was only imagining this, just as all the attentions that the lovely girl showed him, existed only in his imagination from their first meeting on Christmas Eve until that last handshake. This would probably be the last touch of her hand. For if she had not deliberately failed to remind him of the agreement, or if she had only neglected to do so out of carelessness, she would have had the invitation in writing again by now, especially since he had not come back. But almost a week now had passed without his being remembered.

Or had she refrained from repeating the invitation out of considera- tion or even love for the Baron? A wave of blood rushed into his head at the thought, and involuntarily he clasped both hands around the oak arm- rests of his desk chair, as if to prevent them from committing an act of vio- lence. At the same time the whole hopelessness, even sacrilege and ridicu- lousness of his love for Elisabeth appeared before his eyes. He loved the bride of another! Now he began to rage against himself anew.

What did he actually want? Maybe alienate the Baron's mistress away from him, to try to outdo him? Who was he compared to the Baron! A poor devil, who earned very nice money at the moment, but still only an adventurer, who lived from hand to mouth! Admittedly, he trusted himself to take on this windy monocle-wearer ten times over as a human being and a man! If he had set himself similar life goals as this hallow striver, he would have crossed the finish line ten lengths ahead of him! He was cer- tainly not lacking in practical life skills! If he had wanted to live only for the outer world and not just for his inner world, he would have been able to climb to the highest rungs on the ladder of a firm and securely established state career, if it had been worthwhile!

But what did he care for rank and title and medals and decorations! He wanted to be free! He only wanted to serve his inner truth and veracity in order to become completely and utterly what he must become out of his innermost necessity! All the temptations of the world would not have been able to throw him off the course which his inner laws prescribed for him! He would have climbed over dead bodies, if his inner goal demanded it of him! Out of the self-assured exhilaration of his whole undivided, indivisi- ble and indestructible personality, he felt it as a pitiful disgrace that he had even compared himself with this distorted caricature of a human being and a man. And to be compared by others! By others? By whom? He had to confess it to himself, by the woman he loved!

And continuing this chain of feelings, he was again overcome by doubts about the inner worth of his beloved. It seemed downright incom- prehensible to him that she had chosen this nullity to be her husband and the father of her children! What could be so great about her? Certainly she was beautiful, beautiful like a goddess! But what was this outer beauty worth, if the inner beauty was missing? Did he not commit anew the mis- take he always made in judging people, that he unconsciously attributed to others everything that lived so great and glowing in his own soul? And especially in people he loved? How often had he not wasted his heart, even thrown it away! What painful disappointments had he not already experienced! He always received nothing in return for all that he gave but threshed straw! But he did not become wise by injury! With a certain malice he wholeheartedly indulged himself in this new experience. Why had he not followed the inner voice, which had never betrayed him, and stay away from this fateful scavenger hunt? Now, as he had foreseen, the barely healed wound had broken open again and was bleeding more than ever. If he didn't bleed to death completely, it was now a matter of putting an end to it quickly and irrevocably.

With a sudden jerk he rose and paced up and down in great excitement. A closed motor car drove up. It was Elisabeth's car! Surprised, he stopped at the window. Was he supposed to go and see her himself? Unthinkable! His gaze was fixed tensely on the car door when the driver climbed out. He did not close it, but turned off the engine. Then he took a letter from the leather bag at the side of the driver's seat and went to the house.

The letter could only be from her, because the Councilor of Commerce was not at the house, indeed not in Berlin at all. And right! He heard the servant's footsteps, while the driver of the carriage was already leaving the house. But he did not board the carriage, but waited. For an answer? Or even for himself?

The report of the servant entering confirmed Hermann's suspicion. Hastily he tore open the letter and read:

> Dear Doctor!
>
> I need your friendly advice on a personal matter. I would like to ask you to visit me as soon as possible and to let me know when I can expect you. I would prefer you to come at once. I will have the car waiting for you. Please announce yourself to my mother, whom I will inform of my request.
>
> With warm greetings,
> Elisabeth Burghamer.

Hermann read the letter three, four, five times, undecided what he should answer. He felt that once again a momentous decision had been placed in his hands. If he refused now, with any excuse, to comply with the request, then he had taken the irrevocable step that could only lead him back his inner freedom and peace. His inner voice clearly told him that this was the right thing to do. He already sat down at his desk and took up his pen. He had more than enough reasons for excuses, because the full responsibility for the new factory enterprise was on him. A trip to the province lasting several days could not be postponed any longer anyway. He could start this journey immediately. He read the letter again.

"I need your friendly advice on a personal matter."

It was a request, a heartfelt and urgent request, because it was expected to be fulfilled as soon as possible. Could he, as a human being and a man, refuse this request, which a friendly, even beloved lady, had addressed to him? His advice was requested! And moreover in a personal matter! No! There was no thinking about it! The simplest knightly duty demanded he fulfill the request.

He rang the bell for the servant. The driver should restart the automobile, he himself would come immediately.

While he was still signing some papers, he racked his brains as to what kind of personal matter this could be. He stumbled when he realized that Elisabeth was seeking his support and not that of her bridegroom. A surge of liquid fire raced down his spine at the thought that the beloved girl was evidently honoring him with a trust that she did not place in her bridegroom.

Quickly he put on his overcoat and left.

Elisabeth waited impatiently for the return of the car. It took a good five-quarters of an hour to get from the Grunewald district to Gross-Lichterfelde and back. She did not doubt for a moment that Hermann Kämpfer would immediately come himself, provided he was present at all and not on a business trip. But the nearer the time came for him to appear, the more anxious she felt.

She had written the letter to Hermann without really being clear about what she actually wanted from him. She had acted only out of the irresistible urge to see him again, accustomed to fulfill every wish in an instant. In doing so, she not only followed the course of her heart, but also the need to bring order back into her thoughts and feelings. But this could only happen through the one who had so powerfully stirred her inner being. She felt as if his blond presence would calm her down and bring her clarity. She had hoped in vain during the last few days that Hermann would come by himself, since in the excitement of that hour she had failed to ask him to come back. She was afraid to do so afterwards. For from the moment that this sudden love for Hermann had swelled up in her, her feminine instinct kept her from doing anything that might betray her love. But she had finally succumbed to the peculiarity of the female sex to be logical in feeling and insight, but not in action, and had written the letter. The closer the moment

came to when Hermann would arrive, the more passionately she reproached herself for having acted so rashly, thus betraying the secret of her
heart. She flushed red with anger and shame. God knows what she would
have given if it had been possible to retrieve the letter.

Involuntarily, she stepped in front of the mirror. How she looked! She
had fixed her beautiful hair right after the letter was sent. In spite of all her
cunning feminine arts of beauty, she had not succeeded in completely eras-
ing the traces of tears and excitement on her cheeks. It was impossible for
her to receive Hermann like this! And what should she to say to him! With
what "personal matter" should she bother him! A sudden fear came over
her. What should she do! Let herself be denied? Feign a sudden indisposi-
tion? If only her mother had still been there! She had not even thought of
having Hermann received by her mother! Only for the sake of social form
and in consideration of the servants, had she requested him with this kind
of declaration. The whole pointlessness of the plan suddenly became clear
to her. And on top of that, she had sent her own car to fetch the longed-for
man! How foolish that was! How silly! Ridiculous, she had made herself
completely impossible in front of Hermann! Of course, she had no idea
that Hermann, who lacked any deeper experience with women, was thinking quite different thoughts.

While she was handling paste and powder at her vanity in despair,
and always finding still something to dab and wipe, she heard the car drive
into the garden below. In abject terror, she rushed to the window. Before
the carriage had even stopped, Hermann jumped out with a spring and
walked briskly toward the front steps of the villa.

Her heart was beating up to her throat. But now was not the time for
hesitation! Now it was time to act decisively!

When the girl told her that Dr. Kämpfer wanted to pay his respects to
the Madame Councilor, and asked what she should tell him, since she had
gone out, a saving thought flashed into her mind. With perfect composure,
she said: "I will receive the doctor in Mamma's place.

Having grown up in the world of social guile, she took refuge in lies,
and when Hermann, entirely unprejudiced, modestly asked her what he
could do for her, she first thanked him warmly for coming immediately.
Then she said, with a manner and certainty, as if she were dead serious:

"I would like to educate myself with scientific thoroughness on the
issues you recently touched upon, and I intend to study theology for that
purpose. I would like to ask you to help me draw up my study plan."

Hermann could hardly believe his ears. How thoroughly wrong he
had been in the effect of that reading lesson, and even more so in his as-

sessment of Elisabeth! What a grave injustice he had done to her! He answered warmly:

"There, I think it's splendid of you, my dear lady! But you don't need to study theology for that! It will be enough if you listen to one or another lecture. You don't want to become a priest, do you?" he added jokingly.

"Certainly not! But I would like to pursue these studies quite thoroughly, since they are of great interest to me, and would like to do my doctoral examination in it also."

Hermann looked at her in amazement. Then, after a while, he said, full of admiration at the seriousness of her intention:

"An examination is, indeed, an excellent means of bringing method and order into every study. For those striving for more depth, however, it is usually an obstacle to choosing the course of study freely, according to their own personality. The value of an exam is mainly an educational one, since it compels us to study even things that are indifferent, even often repugnant to us. If your intention is to train your mind and character rather than to enrich your knowledge, I could only agree with you. However, I believe that you no longer need such training, but only want to expand your intellectual field of vision. Am I right about this?"

"I would like to leave that to your judgment, Doctor! I ask for your advice on that!"

Elisabeth said this with such sincere eagerness that Hermann was quite delighted. And indeed, under the influence of Hermann's words, her intention to study, which had originally been presented only as a white lie, began to change into honest seriousness. When Hermann advised her to leave the question of the exam open for the time being and to begin by listening to certain lectures, she was so enthusiastic about the plan that she could hardly wait for the semester to begin.

"And if I don't understand something or need your advice in any other way, may I always turn to you?" she asked as impartially as possible. A deep blush covered her beautiful face.

"Of course, I am always at your disposal!" Hermann replied with overflowing cordiality.

The Madame Councilor, returning from a visit to the neighborhood, entered the room. She appeared in no way surprised by Hermann's presence and greeted him with courteous friendliness. Enthusiastically, Elisabeth told her about her new plan. Her mother listened with a smile, used to her daughter's sudden and surprising resolutions. Without attaching any further importance to the matter, she asked Hermann if he wouldn't like to stay for lunch. He was only too happy to accept the invitation.

It was not until late in the afternoon that Hermann Kämpfer left the villa in Elisabeth's car. He now believed it was certain, that the girl he loved, loved him again! But would this love be great and strong enough for her to want to belong to him? She was, after all, someone else's bride! Bliss, pain, and doubt wrestled in his heart.

From now on, Hermann and Elisabeth were together almost daily. The opportunities to do so arose casually. The first thing to do was to draw up the work schedule. Together they drove to the university, studied the notices on the bulletin board, and then went through the course catalog together at home. Since Elisabeth's studies included not only the theological, but also the philosophical and natural science faculties, there was a lot to do. When the lectures began at the end of October, almost no day went by without Elisabeth requesting Hermann's academic support. All day long they both looked forward to being together in the evening, and this anticipatory joy gave their daily work momentum and strength. Elisabeth's restlessness was gradually transformed into purposeful calm under Hermann's energetic and clear guidance.

Hermann had postponed his business trip to the provinces as long as possible. But when he had to go, the longing of the two knew no bounds. They exchanged cards or letters daily, and when Elisabeth wrote Hermann one day how much she missed his presence, he could stand it no longer, interrupted his trip and went back to Berlin. Their reunion was a happy one, even though they only greeted each other like good acquaintances. Even without confessing it to each other, both were certain of their mutual love. They found such deep happiness in this unspoken emotion that they were careful not to disturb it with a confession, for such a confession would have to bring up the question that was absolutely unsolvable in the present circumstances.

Between them, the Baron was never mentioned. Since the day Elisabeth had ordered him out of her rooms, he had not been seen again in the Councilor's villa. Elisabeth had told her mother about the incident, and she shared her daughter's indignation. Since then, the two women, by an unspoken agreement, had not mentioned von Werheim.

The true nature of the eager interaction between Hermann and Elisabeth did not remain hidden from the Madame Councilor. First out of maternal weakness, then out of maternal love, she had tolerated this increasingly intimate behavior, then tenderly and considerately encouraged it, because the happiness of her suffering child was more important to her than anything else. Of course, how the matter should end, was something she had lately often considered. She let things take their course, however, with the instinctive feeling that something unalterable was at work here, the necessary course of which could not be stopped by external influence, but could only be delayed.

The Baron's shallow nature, impressed only by tangible things, could not even remotely imagine how deeply he had hurt Elisabeth. He would not have thought it possible, that he could even have lost everything with her. For tactical reasons only, he thought it advisable to avoid the family of the Councilor for a while. He mistook Elisabeth's indignation for a nervous whim. She would ask for him of her own accord and call him one day or, as she often did in the past, drive up in front of the Ministry to pick him up from work. The psychology of women was simple for him, epitomized in the words of Mephisto that "all the woe and misery of women can be cured from one point." He had had no other experience with the female sex, which he enjoyed *ad nauseam*. He knew only broads, no women. And the ladies of his circles were for him only females in the purely zoological sense. For natural reasons, this foreign-blooded son of the desert lacked every organ for German womanhood.

But when several weeks had gone by without anything being heard from Elizabeth, he became suspicious. His friends had occasionally reported to him that she was often seen on horseback or in a carriage with Hermann Kämpfer. But he had not taken it tragically. On the contrary, he saw it as proof of Elisabeth's love, since she obviously wanted to make him jealous. But when such reports increased and his corps brothers even made quite salacious remarks about it, bile rose in his blood. He pondered back and forth how he could bring about an encounter and discussion with Elisabeth.

Then one late afternoon he met the couple on a ride together on the Charlottenburger Chaussee. He had just come from the ministry in the car, which he was driving himself, and was tending to some bothersome official business. The pair of riders presented a splendid picture. They came along on the bridle path beside the causeway in a well composed trot. Elisabeth was laughing and beaming at Hermann's side, who was apparently telling her a funny story. Many a pedestrian stopped and looked at the beautiful couple on the noble animals.

The Baron drove past the riders, not driving too quickly. He saluted. Elisabeth recognized him only when he had already passed. Hermann had not noticed the greeter at all, and Elisabeth avoided calling his attention to him afterwards. But she became very pensive at the sight of the Baron, because the question, which was for her the question of all questions, suddenly appeared before her, demanding an answer.

Hermann noticed the sudden silence of his companion. When they turned onto a side path of the zoo, he brought his horse close to hers, bending over to her anxiously, grasping her hand, and he asked what was wrong. With a tender look she thanked him, and reassured him by putting her horse into a gallop.

The Baron, because he had turned around and gone after the couple, observed this process and suddenly erupted in jealousy. As they galloped away without even noticing him, his discontent turned to rage.

Hermann was not a little surprised to receive a visit the next day from a government assessor, Baron von Oppenheimer, a lieutenant in Guard Corps battalion of the Railway. He came on behalf of Baron von Werheim to ask for clarification as to why he had not reciprocated the Baron's greeting yesterday on the Charlottenburger Chaussee.

Taken aback, Hermann responded that he could not remember having seen Baron von Werheim at all during the last few weeks.

This explanation was not sufficient for Baron von Oppenheimer. He insisted on a written statement of regret on behalf of his client.

When Hermann calmly refused such an imposition, the Baron von Oppenheimer declared "in this case" to deliver a challenge to Hermann from Baron von Werheim for a duel. He asked for the name of an impartial second to determine the conditions.

Hermann had trouble not throwing the insolent man out the door. He controlled himself, however, and calmly refused the request, whereupon Baron von Oppenheimer departed with a deadly serious, but apparently very satisfied expression and a ceremonious bow.

When Hermann informed Elisabeth of the incident, she confessed to him that this encounter with Werheim yesterday had been the cause of her sudden upset. But it had had the good consequence to bring her to a decision. Last night, she had sent Baron von Werheim a registered letter declaring that she considered the engagement with him to be broken.

"Elisabeth!"

Hermann could only say her name. Then he pulled his beloved to his chest and she willingly gave herself to him for the first kiss.

Baron von Werheim was furious when his friend, comrade in blood and spirit, Baron von Oppenheimer, delivered Hermann's refusal. At the same time, however, he breathed a sigh of relief. Then he said, full of contempt: "It was actually to be expected that this lowlife would back down! Cowardly rabble, this bourgeois vermin!"

While he was still speaking this, Elisabeth's registered letter arrived. "Aha!" he said triumphantly, "now she comes!"

"Good fun!" Baron von Oppenheimer agreed with him. "Just don't let go of the reins! Then the most sensitive mare goes soft! One like the other!"

Baron von Oppenheimer kept racehorses. Admittedly, he did not drive them himself, because it was not without danger. But he loved to take his comparisons and images regarding "women" from the sport of racing, if possible. In doing so, he felt very knowledgeable about sports and the subject.

However, when he perceived the face of his brother-at-arms growing longer and longer, still smiling with satisfaction at his well-judged comparison he said, "Well?"

Without a word, Werheim handed him the letter.

Baron von Oppenheimer wrinkled the corners of his mouth expertly, shook his head from side to side, and said only one conected word: "Nebbich!"

After a pause, he then added:

"Now take hold of Witzleben! A nice beetle. There's no trace of Pinke-Pinke, but Mr. Papa is quite a character! She breakfasts often at S. M.! Quite a good tip that! Can be a thing! A big deal!" Thereby he pronounced the word "big" with a distinctive accentuation.

The future Minister of Culture, Baron von Werheim, however, seemed to attach a certain value to Pinke-Pinke after all. He began to become very thoughtful, and as soon as von Oppenheim took his leave, he rang Elisabeth's phone.

He thought she was on the telephone.

"Is that you, Ellichen? Don't give me a hard time, sweetheart!" But there was no answer, only a soft giggle was audible in the receiver. He had been talking to one of the maids. Now he sat down and wrote a penitent and wistfully tedious letter to Elisabeth. He received it back in the mail with the note "Acceptance Refused."

But he did not give up the race yet. He also wrote to the Councilor and the Madame Councilor. From the latter, he received no reply at all, from the former only a very regretful one.

Now he gave the business up for lost, said "well, then no!" and lit a cigarette.

Hermann and Elisabeth now spent weeks of unadulterated happiness. All the while, they had a wonderful, beyond all terms delicious experience.

Without ever having spoken about it, they had both passionately longed for a time when they could belong to each other as husband and wife. Now that the only obstacle standing in the way of their conjugal union had been removed, this ardently desired goal seemed trivial and meaningless to them.

In the meantime, they had settled themselves so completely into a higher, purely spiritual realm, had become so blissfully happy in this purely intellectual give and take, that any change in their present condition seemed to them a threat to their happiness.

To the family of the Councilor of Commerce, they had long been considered engaged. However, they had no desire at all to announce this engagement publicly. They kept away from all social intercourse. Their own world was so rich, and their mutual love grew ever deeper and more profound from day to day, that they felt not the slightest desire for that world of appearances. Hermann had never lacked that world, and Elisabeth now could not even comprehend that she had once been so completely its slave.

The annulment of her engagement to the Baron von Werheim was, of course, vigorously discussed in society, and there was also no lack of blasphemous tongues, which tend to stir up on such occasions. The Baron was shameless enough to make suggestive insinuations, from which one had to infer that the annulment of the engagement had not come from Elisabeth, but from him. He was also not at all afraid to call into question the good reputation of his former bride, without it being possible to catch him at it. Of course, it was Elisabeth's "best friends" who eagerly passed on such gossip and rumors to her. She herself was not inwardly affected by it. But she was worried that Hermann might hear about it. She had not even the slightest fear that he might believe this gossip, or that his love might somehow be touched by it. She feared only the outbreak of his wrath, which would have brought any blasphemer of her honor to a bloody reckoning on the spot. That was also the reason, why she concealed from Hermann that scene with the Baron in her private rooms.

By design, she gradually stopped communicating with these watchful friends. Her studies, which she continued to pursue regularly under Hermann's guidance, gave her the desired pretext.

Hermann's manpower and enthusiasm for work had doubled since Elisabeth had taken part in all his undertakings and plans. The construction of the new factory progressed in leaps and bounds, and by Christmas at the latest, the production of dyed tiles could begin according to the process he had devised and had since patented. Through Elisabeth's love and sympathy, his new technical profession, which at times seemed so dull to him, had now gained content and meaning. Deeply, as at the beginning, he again savored the joy of practical work and activity. The depressing feeling that had often crept over him in the beginning, of having lost so many years uselessly in purely scientific activity, had completely disappeared. For it became more and more apparent how excellent a basis his previous scientific training had been for his new practical occupation. Not only had he acquired extensive knowledge, but he had also learned to distinguish quickly and confidently between the essential and the unessential, and to do everything methodically.

In this he had unusual, but also very essential and immediate help from Elisabeth. When she thought only of him, his work went remarkably smoothly. At first, he thought he was imagining it. Then he assumed it was just a coincidence. In the end, however, he established the fact through flawless methodical experimentation.

This brought him to the problem of remote psychic action (psychokinesis). These observations were perfectly compatible with the known laws of natural science, indeed, they could be subordinated to similar ones from the field of physics without further ado. They had their perfect counterpart in the phenomena of acoustic resonance and electromagnetic influence. Wireless telegraphy provides an almost classical model for them. The vibrations of any system propagate through space in all directions. Another system with the same tuning is able to pick up these vibrations at any place in space. Another such a system is the human brain, in which the powers of the soul converge. It is easy to imagine that every feeling, every thought sets the brain into a particular vibration, which propagate through space quite analogously to electric waves. It is just as conceivable that another brain tuned to the same wavelength is able to pick up these oscillations, completely in accordance with the physical processes mentioned.

Together with Elisabeth he read all the literature on this region of the soul that he could get hold of. He decided, as soon as his time would allow it, to study these phenomena more closely by logical experiments.

In order to be close to Elisabeth at all times, he moved his private apartment from Groß-Lichterfelde to the Grunewald district and set up a comfortable apartment near her Villa. In order to make the best use of his time, he implemented a strict daily schedule.

Together with his beloved he started and finished his day's work. Already early 7 o'clock he sat with her on horseback. After a morning ride of one to one and a half hours, they had breakfast together in the villa. Then Hermann, who in the meantime had been provided with a special car by the Councilor for his business trips, went to Groß-Lichterfelde to work, while Elisabeth went to attend her lectures. At three o'clock they met again for lunch at the villa. After dinner, Hermann worked in his nearby private apartment, and by tea time he was back with his beloved. He now read to the women almost daily, with the exception of the days when he worked through Elisabeth's college notebooks with her.

For the reading hours he had set up a very specific, mixed schedule, which he strictly adhered to. His main focus was on the Gospels and the problem of Jesus, about which he had a considerable private library. He also read the ladies Plato and Dante and introduced them to the main features of Kant's teachings. Then followed selected chapters from Homer and the Nibelungenlied. He introduced them to the austere world of Gottfried Keller and rewarded their perseverance with Theodor Storm and Wilhelm Raabe. Fritz Reuter, his late mother's favorite writer, also came very much into his own.

When the lecture was over, Elisabeth sat down at the piano. With her graceful, well-trained voice, she would sing some song. Then they often went to a good concert with her mother. Only now did Elisabeth gain a true understanding of Bach and Beethoven. They visited the theater less often. The modern sensationalism that dominated the theater life of the capital was repugnant to her deeply collected nature.

On principle, they avoided the opera, since Hermann's nature, which was focused on clear certitude, found this art form to be an unnatural hybrid. For him, music was the highest of all the arts, since it was the direct revelation of our supersensible being. But its spacelessness and timelessness and therefore unlimited expressiveness contradicts the performer's highly limited means of expression through mimicry, which it cannot match in any way. Music breaks down every ray of sensation into a whole spectrum of adjacent color tones, which even the most ingenious performer is incapable of mimetically following. Thus, while the whole spectrum of tones unrolls in front of the spectator's ears, he has to rigidly hold on to the expression of the face, position or movement corresponding to each ray of sensation the whole time or repeat it several times, which results in nothing but unnaturalness, distortion and ridiculousness. One cannot shake the impression that the performer is struggling terribly and still keeps lagging behind the music. In this way, the pure impression of the music on the audience is torn apart and destroyed. It would be just as nonsensical to try to enhance the artistic effect of music with drama as it would be to try to enhance the artistic effect of a marble statue by dressing it in expensive robes or gluing on real hair.

But quite apart from the incongruity of the musical and theatrical means of expression, music is only capable of expressing feelings, never thoughts and actions, which, after all, constitute the core and essence of drama. Opera fails to recognize this elementary fact. The connection of music with the drama must be limited solely to supporting the spoken word or, replacing it where it is no longer sufficient for the reproduction of feelings. Shakespeare is a model for this. With him, music always begins where even his divine power of language is no longer sufficient to lend words to the feeling.

The most expressive and comprehensive of all arts is undoubtedly drama, and the essence of a people and a race is most clearly expressed in it. The deep inwardness of the Teutons is revealed in their attempt to develop the dramatic action from the characters, while the Romans aimed to create effective external situations and entanglements, to which the mostly stereotypical characters are subordinated.

Of the fine arts, Hermann was particularly fond of sculpture. Its unambiguous clarity and simplicity particularly appealed to his nature. He never tired of wandering through museums and exhibitions with Elisabeth. He explained to her that the purpose and goal of this art was the representation of tranquility and sublimity, and that its only object was ideal beauty. He considered the Greeks to be the unsurpassable masters of this art, and he could not be angry enough at certain modern schools that degraded art to the level of distortion.

In a painting Hermann valued mainly the size and importance of the subject, and the masters, the ones he was most fond of, the artists who shaped the immediate effervescent life in a powerful and manifold way. Dürer and Rembrandt were his declared favorites. With joyful pride he told his beloved that the mighty masters of the Italian Renaissance, Michelangelo and Leonardo da Vinci, were also of Germanic blood, and that wherever one looked, it proved again and again that no race in the world could compete with the Teuton in strength of thought and design. A certain instinctual fear of the incomprehensible creative power of the Germans was the sole reason that we have so many enemies in the world. It is only because they cannot understand that we direct our inexhaustible life forces only inward and not outward. They impute to us plans of world conquest and scrutinize our incessant development and growth with such distrust and jealousy, while we are only concerned to preserve the place in the sun necessary for our life and to secure it against hostile onslaughts.

Elisabeth particularly enjoyed it when Hermann would occasionally analyze the essence of different architectural styles for her during tours of the new factory buildings. He derived it from the simple elements of support and load. There, too, he pointed out to her that beauty was always the result of simplicity and practicality. Because the Greek style was composed of the simple functional elements of the supporting column and the load-bearing crossbeam, it was so sublimely simple and beautiful. The Romanesque style developed from the Greek style in that the column rises to become a pillar and the load-bearing crossbeam to become a round arch, and the flat ceiling to the round vault. Correspondingly, the Gothic style emerged from the Romanesque style through the further elevation of the round arch to the pointed arch and the round vault to the pointed vault. Naturally, the columns, pillars and towers also stretched along with these. This completely natural development was caused by advancing technology. Restlessness of style always arises where the simply functional elements are abandoned, and inappropriate arbitrariness takes their place, as in the Baroque and Rococo periods.

Such was the spiritual life that Hermann led with Elisabeth. It was as if Hermann had given her eyes and ears for the first time. The deep inner serenity that saturated and transfigured Elisabeth's entire being also radiated over her mother. Ever since that first reading from the Gospels, an invisible spiritual bond seemed to entwined the three of them. Without being able to explain why, everything they thought and said, did and lived, took on an inner meaning and spiritual value that lifted them high above all earthly and everyday things. This was the immediate effect of the Good News that had risen in their hearts. Often the three of them sat quietly and meaningfully together without speaking a word, for their souls spoke silently to each other. Hermann often held Elisabeth's hand or she leaned her head against his chest, and the mother raised her eyes from her handiwork and let them rest on the happy couple in blessing.

But motherly concerns were stirring in her soul. Abruptly one day, she interrupted the tranquility of this communion with the words: "Don't you finally want to get married, children?

Startled, Hermann and Elisabeth simultaneously let go of their hands. Both of them had long expected and dreaded this question from their mother, without expressing it. And yet the same desire had been stirring in both of them for the last few weeks, first quietly and then more and more powerfully. In her silent hours and dreams, blissful premonitions and children's blue eyes wove themselves, golden blond curls shone into them and sweet little hands seemed to reach for her heart. Then Hermann pulled his beloved closer to him, and she nestled more intimately in his arms. They had not yet expressed with a syllable what trembled in the depths of their souls, and yet each knew what was going on in the other. Then Elizabeth felt the gaze of her beloved man resting on her head, and when she lifted her head and his eyes plunged deep into hers, she quickly lowered her gaze and buried her face against his heart. At the same time, she felt his arms embrace her tighter and his pulses pounding after hers.

Why were they both now terrified at her mother's words?

They couldn't comprehend it or explain it to themselves, but an uneasy sense of unspeakable sorrow crept through their souls.

Hermann had stood up and stepped to the edge of the vine-covered terrace. Red leaves softly and quietly whirled from the trees in the sun-drenched autumnal park, and in the nearby orchard overripe fruit occasionally fell to earth with a dull thud under the kiss of a sunbeam. The whole of nature was saturated with the deepest ripeness and there was a tart sweetness in the clear air.

Elizabeth had folded her hands like she was praying, and looked silently her into her lap. A trace of autumn had caught in the hair on her forehead and, moved by her deep breathing, rippled in the air above her face.

Hermann had turned around and sat down on the marble parapet of the terrace. His gaze embraced his beloved with tender intimacy. When she raised her face and fixed her eyes on him clearly and strongly, he quickly moved towards her and wrapped her in his arms.

Now they knew that together they would bear whatever fate might impose on them. From that moment on, the gloomy and heavy thoughts disappeared and a confidence came over them, which springs from unalterable decisions.

"We shall be publicly engaged at Christmas," said Hermann, "and the wedding shall be at Easter. Is that all right with you, Mamma?"

Without a word in return, the Madame Councilor stood up and kissed Hermann on the forehead. Then she hugged and kissed her daughter.

The Councilor of Commerce was not mentioned. All matters concerning the women were dealt with by the women themselves. His approval was always assured, especially in this case. Although there was no spiritual contact between him and the women, and he rarely met them in person, scarcely even appeared at mealtimes, and led a completely separate life from them, mostly spent traveling, he still seemed to be attached to them with a certain love, especially to his daughter. He expressed this love in his own way. He kept a bank loan open for them in an amount that could satisfy even princely demands. The two women were unable to use up the money at their disposal and this was his pride.

When he was informed by a marriage bureau that the Baron von Werheim was interested in his daughter and was asked to state the amount of the dowry, he first made sure that the Baron was welcome to his daughter. Then he gave double the number of millions that had been mentioned by the office as the minimum sum, since the Baron already had "chances in this amount" elsewhere.

When Elisabeth then broke off the engagement again, this was by no means unwelcome to him, for the Baron had never impressed him. He forgave him least of all for his Jewish descent and the arrogant way in which he nevertheless looked down on Burghamer's Jewishness. Werheim had repeatedly indicated to him that this would in no way make his career easier, since in higher circles there was still a certain prejudice against "former" Jews, despite the fact that even non-baptized Jews were now acceptable today and the *Berliner Tageblatt* already had a quarter of a million subscribers.

In addition, Burghamer was "only bourgeois". He had had more than one "chance" to marry ladies from the oldest "Christian" nobility. If he had nevertheless "reflected" on Elisabeth, then far-sighted points of view had been decisive for this. The general European war, which was hoped for in "their circles" and which would thoroughly clear up the differences in bloodlines and "other prejudices" against the Jews and, above all, would bring Jewish capital to an all-dominating influence in all of Germany, he said was close at hand. However, there was a great danger that Germany would arrive the victor in this world war. This had to be prevented by all means, since otherwise the "future chances" of the Jews in Germany would be over for all times.

So they dropped all personal interests in order to serve the general interest of "their circles". In the coming European war, he, Burghamer, would easily find the opportunity to gain political influence and to double his capital as a result of the connections that his daughter's marriage would open up for him "upwards", especially if he, Werheim, would let his own capital "collaborate" in the process.

What the Baron was able to tell the Councilor was not news to him. He was far better and more accurately informed than the Baron. His investigative organs reached out to every country in the world and he knew that the Anglo-American members of "their circles" had postponed the "run" for a few years, since Europe was not yet ready and, above all, there was still trouble with Russia. First the Balkan war had to be postponed, before that it was Germany's turn. But in this case, he was not the least bit interested in the Baron as a son-in-law. He was not in the least worried about the necessary opportunities for "making money" once the dance had started. A connection with the chatterbox Baron could then at most put fetters on the speed of his undertakings, if not paralyze them altogether. He was therefore very happy to get rid of him as a son-in-law and to get Hermann in his place, from whose abilities he expected completely different successes.

Doubts about Hermann's business acumen only arose when he never touched on the question of the dowry, although it was now certain that he should be his son-in-law. How careless! But he became completely mad at him when one day he brought up this subject and Hermann flatly declared that he would not accept a penny of dowry from him. He considered it a disgrace to degrade marriage into a business. This outrageous bad habit is solely to blame for modern marital misery, since it not only shakes the natural basis of marriage, love, but destroys it completely. This is the point at which the lever for the recovery of German national power must be applied. If it were not possible to get this bad habit under control by legislative means, then every man who made entering into a marriage dependent on a dowry would have to be declared dishonorable. He had no objection to an appropriate dowry within the limits of the circumstances which he himself was able to offer his future wife, but this was not necessary either.

When the Madame Councilor, who was listening to this conversation, shyly objected that there were exceptions, Hermann declared very firmly that under no circumstance could he recognize such exceptions. A man who was unable to maintain a wife and child by his own efforts was not a man at all and should not marry. However, someone who has the shamelessness to let his wife "feed" him is a pitiful bastard.

The Madame now remained silent. Burghamer, however, asked very ironically whether he was sure that Elisabeth will adjust to the more "limited" conditions that he can offer her.

"Why don't you ask her yourself?" he replied.

Elisabeth was called in; she had not thought about this question at all. After a moment's reflection, she explained that Hermann was quite right, and that what he earned was completely sufficient to satisfy her demands.

Shaking his head, the Councilor of Commerce left the room and Hermann gratefully embraced his bride. From that day on, he doubted Hermann's sanity and looked forward to his daughter's future with grave concern.

Quietly, the engagement was celebrated on Christmas Eve in the closest family circle. It was the first Christmas that Elisabeth spent at home since her entry into society, and not in some "Grand Hotel".

Hermann had insisted on preparing the Christmas tree. He used the same ornaments that had adorned the Christmas trees of his childhood. Year after year his father had taken care of it, and every Christmas it did its duty again and again. It was one of the few things that Hermann had saved from the collapse of his parent's home. Since then, he had kept it like a shrine and never dared to look at it for fear that it might break his heart. But when he found a family of his own, then this ornament would awaken to new life. Now he had brought it out for the first time.

Under the burning tree, Hermann put the engagement ring on his bride's finger, calling his parents' blessing on the bond in his heart. A deep blush of shame covered Elisabeth's face, for at that moment she remembered how, a year ago, she had thoughtlessly thrown the paper chain around Hermann. He now gave her back solid gold for her paper superficiality. Quickly she buried her face to the chest of her beloved husband.

The two lovers had agreed not to give each other even the smallest gift on this first Christmas together, as a sign that they wanted to offer themselves completely, one to the other, as a gift for all time and eternity. They were still standing under the glowing Christmas tree, inspired by this single wish and will, when the Councilor of Commerce entered the room.

Without sensing the couple's feelings, he said they still had time for "sweet talk" later, and they should finally come to the table to receive their gifts.

Reluctantly, they followed the request.

An artistically crafted box stood in front of each of their place settings. In hers, Elisabeth found an exceedingly precious set of jewels, complete with the corresponding ear, hair, and finger jewelry, and in his, Hermann found a corresponding set of shirt buttons and cuff links, along with a necktie pin and pinky finger ring. A princely couple could not be more richly endowed.

Elisabeth fell into blazing rapture. She immediately stepped in front of the mirror and put on the jewelry. Hermann, however, was mortally embarrassed. He had suspected and feared such a gift.

"Well?" said the Councilor of Commerce when he noticed Hermann's disapproval. "Not good enough for you, I suppose?"

He took the jewels out of the case and weighed them in the palm of his hand, his eyes sparkling.

"Well, what do you guess?" he then asked, winking, handing it to Hermann.

The latter, however, quietly laid the diamonds on the table beside the box, and only uttered the words, "You are too kind, Mr. Councilor!"

When Elizabeth saw the effect of this gift on her fiancé, she took off the jewelry again and put it back in the case.

"You've gone to outrageous expense, papa!" she said.

"It doesn't matter to me," he replied, "as long as it gives you pleasure."

He pulled her to him and kissed her. She shuddered and put up with it.

Then, bringing salvation to everyone involved, the Madame Councilor entered and asked her children to receive their gifts as well. In the meantime, she had hurriedly set up the gifts under the tree of lights.

Elisabeth reveled in a whole flood of delicious lingerie, lace and fabrics, and Hermann, to his indescribable delight, found a plate full of apples, nuts and baked goods, and to the right and left of it, one covered with colorful sugar curls and gingerbread man, just like he had had in his childhood. Next to it were the recently published first volumes of the Berlin Academy's collected edition of the works of Kant.

Shaking his head, the Councilor observed the childlike, almost exuberant joy that his son-in-law felt at these simple gifts, and with the words "strange fellow, that one," he left the room. But Hermann and the two women, however, lingered under the Christmas tree for a long time, until the Councilor of Commerce asked if they would not finally come to dinner, since he still had business in Berlin this evening and could not wait any longer.

Since that Christmas evening, Hermann could no longer stop thinking about the Councilor. The deep dislike he had felt for him from the moment of their first meeting had completely given way to a fiery desire to win Elisabeth. Now he saw himself at the goal of his desires, his original aversion stirred to a stronger degree. The thought that this Jew was the father in the flesh of his bride, and that his blood would one day flow in the veins of his own children, caused his innermost being to rebel. He tried to reassure himself in vain that Elisabeth's whole being had nothing, absolutely nothing at all in common with her father.

The suspicion, to which he had already clung earlier, that she might not be Burghamer's daughter at all, and that some secret was hovering over her birth, occupied him anew. More than once he was about to ask the Madame Councilor about this, but an understandable shyness kept him from doing so. The small blemish of the lower lip, which Elisabeth inherited as the only trait from her father and which she knew how to conceal with feminine mastery, had not occurred to him until now. He only saw his beloved through the eyes of his love. She could have been ugly and hunchbacked, but he would not have noticed it anyway.

Finally, he tried to reassure himself with the thought that it was the soul that built the body. But his natural science taught him that the soul is also bound by material laws and conditions when it begins to weave a garment for its earthly existence out of the love of two people. Little did he know that we are only the adoptive parents of our children, and that the spiritual beings, depending on their own greater or lesser perfection, attitude and stage of development, choose bodies for incarnation which correspond to their own character. The body is only the instrument on which the soul plays. A highly developed spirit can only find the bodily prerequisites to have an effect in a highly developed organism. A low or bad spirit, on the other hand, chooses a body still closer to the animals in order to indulge its lower urges and lusts.

Thus, the higher races serve predominantly the good and noble, and the lower ones predominantly the lower and lowly spirits for their earthly dwellings. It is not for nothing that we conclude from the outer man to the inner man! But the awareness of these facts slumbered unawakened in Hermann's soul and only expressed itself in the fierce inner reluctance against this marriage in spite of the deep and unselfish love that united him with Elisabeth. The closer the day of the wedding approached, the more insistently and imperiously the inner voice warned him.

Easter and the wedding day approached.

Despite all of Hermann's objections, the Councilor of Commerce insisted on unfolding a feast in the grandest style. Even the spacious villa proved too small to hold the countless guests. The celebration took place in the Hotel Adlon. Hermann thanked his creator when he finally sat in the train compartment with his young wife.

In South Tyrol, he had rented a quiet, secluded cottage to spend the first weeks of their marriage away from all the hustle and bustle. Elisabeth had enthusiastically agreed to this plan. But after only a few days, her nature was transformed. The chaotic blood of her father began to assert its nature. All the fine and subtle senses of her soul seemed to be smothered in its frothy energy. Helplessly, it delivered its bearer over to the unconquered reign of the emotions, and it threatened to burst all the dams of custom and morality. The young woman's sensual desires were so wild and unbridled that Hermann felt downright repulsed by her. All paths to a deeper union of the soul seemed buried in her, and Hermann tried in vain to uncover them again.

The old disquiet and restlessness came over her again. Her longing for the big world became once again indomitable. She wanted to move out of the little country house into the hotel, she wanted to have people, company, cocktails, hustle and bustle, dances, noise, "life" around her.

Hermann was horrified to see Elisabeth's transformation. All his pacifying and reassuring was in vain. In order to put an end to her weeping and wailing, he had to give in to her like it or not.

But even in the hotel, the largest in the small town, she did not last long. It "smelled" to her there too much like "German wool". That was not a "hotel" at all! The menu was provincial German from top to bottom and the head waiter didn't understand a word of English! She wanted Brits and Americans around her, they were the only people who knew how to live! She wanted to go to Monte! She had spent a few weeks there every year with her mother, and Hermann could not refuse her.

Hermann was seething with anger, but he was powerless. If he didn't want a complete rupture on the honeymoon, he had to comply with her wishes. So they traveled to Monte Carlo.

Here, Elizabeth was a well-known and celebrated beauty.

She would not be done with her "visits" and "counter-visits" to introduce her husband to her acquaintances from New York, San Francisco, London, and Paris. Hermann felt like a monstrosity that was shown around at fairs. He endured torture in the process. Balls and parties followed endlessly, and Elisabeth wandered from the arms of one dancer to another, so that Hermann felt as superfluous as possible. Alone, he sat apart and was not able to make any connection with these people, who seemed to be made of completely different stuff than he. And yet he too had once longed for this world! Now he owned this world, but he despised and hated it!

Elisabeth, however, was in her element in this swirling and whirling. She was constantly surrounded by a whole swarm of courtiers and cup-bearers, just like on that Christmas Eve when he saw her for the first time. At that time, he thought he could no longer live without her. And now she was his wife! Was she really? She seemed to belong to everyone but him! A gloomy melancholia descended on him and he saw the future in blackness. The inner voice kept speaking, but he did not hear it and did not want to hear it.

After four weeks, the "season" in "Monte" was over, and now Elisabeth was drawn to Rome and Naples. Hermann was horrified. Since his high school days, it had been his soul's desire to stand on the Capitoline Hill just once in his life, to see the site that was once the heart of the world. But only after thorough preparation did he want to make this trip. It seemed downright sinful to him to go on a whim, like that.

"What is there to prepare for so thoroughly?" said Elisabeth. "I know Rome as well as the Kurfürstendamm, I will guide you!"

And she led him. It was an unparalleled chase. Hermann was glad when, in the middle of it all, Elisabeth suddenly expressed her wish to return to her villa in Bordighera and spend a few more quiet days. By telegraph, the young couple made their preparations, and the same day they set out on their journey.

Elisabeth was tired and demanded to rest. And in fact, Hermann now spent his first quiet hours with his young wife. She suddenly seemed quite her old self again and was content to have him read to her, just as in their courtship. But the peace only lasted a few days. No sooner did she feel somewhat recovered than she was driven on again. When Hermann asked her to stay a little longer anyway, since he liked it here so much, she knew how to make his stay unpleasant. She made oblique references to the Baron von Werheim, to whom she was engaged at that time, which caused Hermann to leave in a huff. But she managed to appease him by expressing her desire to see the winter health resort again, where they had first met.

This wish was not unwelcome to Hermann, since it made the return trip to Germany finally possible. They had been on the move for two months and Hermann had projected the trip to last only three or four weeks at the most.

Hermann felt quite strange as he walked with Elisabeth through the hall of the Grand Hotel, where he had first seen her, and even more so when he stood with her in front of her picture in the villa. One would have thought that a deep feeling of happiness must have now flowed through him, since he was in possession of the girl who had seemed to him so exceedingly desirable and equally unattainable at that time. But on the contrary, a deep dejection now weighed on him and, in that moment, he wished he had never seen Elisabeth.

After an absence of almost three months, the couple returned to Berlin and moved into their new home. Elisabeth, who had lived only in villas all her life, had wanted to move into a floor in a house in the city. At the Reichskanzlerplatz in Charlottenburg they found one in the grand style. The young woman took particular pleasure in wandering through the front suite of nine stately interconnecting rooms, the connecting doors of which always had to stay open. But no sooner had she spent a few days wandering back and forth through the apartment than she felt the desire to go to the sea for a few more weeks.

Since it had become summer in the meantime, Hermann hardly had anything to say against it. But when he told her that he had no time to accompany her, there was the first marital scene. Hermann, however, remained firm. He only made the concession to visit her at least once.

For the first time, the young couple was separated. Elisabeth now wrote such ardent and wistful letters, she knew how to describe the bleakness of their separation so touchingly, and, if Hermann did not visit her immediately, she threatened him with all sorts of stupidities, the execution of which she was completely capable of doing, that he returned to her again after only eight days.

They were together again for a full two weeks, although Hermann only wanted to stay for three days. Then urgent business telegrams called him back to Berlin.

Now the game of Elisabeth's longing started anew, and since Hermann's business actually made it impossible for him to be away from Berlin, Elisabeth also returned to Berlin just a few days later.

Hermann, whose essence was rooted in the spiritual, suffered unspeakably from the purely sensual state to which Elisabeth's love had sunk. But he could not resist the constant cravings of his beautiful young wife, who entangled him with all her feminine devices. When this love life, bordering on debauchery, finally threatened to paralyze his mental powers, he took the next opportunity to go on a lengthy business trip. Only with great effort did he succeed in preventing Elisabeth from accompanying him.

When he returned after a three-week absence, he found her changed. The waves of passion had subsided and seemed to have given way to more intimate emotions. Hermann happily embraced his young wife when she confessed to him what he had already concluded from the change in her nature.

But the strangest whims, bordering on the unnatural and perverse, now had to be satisfied by the young mother-to-be. Sometimes she asked for fruits that were not available in the season, sometimes she ordered this or that food that was difficult to obtain at the moment, only to spurn it with an expression of disgust when it was served. She developed a very passionate affinity for certain overpowering perfumes. One day she bit into a bar of soap whose scent particularly appealed to her. Also on another occasion, she ate some heavily scented orchid blossoms, whose voluptuous forms seemed to especially excite her. At the same time, she demanded to see the most frivolous pictures, to hear the most salacious songs and pieces of music. She insisted that Hermann buy a gramophone so that she could satisfy her strange whims according to these musical needs at any time. For hours this horrible instrument tortured and tormented Hermann's ears.

The desire for her old friends and acquaintances, from whom she had withdrawn completely since they were married, reawakened in her, and before Hermann knew it, his apartment was transformed into an apiary. There was no end to the tea parties and invitations "in the smallest circles."

Considering her condition, Hermann did not contradict any of her wishes and whims. He suffered not so much from the inconveniences and unreasonable demands imposed on him by his wife's covetous and arbitrary nature as from the dawning realization that he must have been fundamentally mistaken in his assessment of Elisabeth. Could the keen desire for higher spiritual things, which she displayed at the time of her acquaintance, perhaps have been only a ruse, caused by the female instinct to please, to arouse interest and sensation?

Constantly he fought down such thoughts. His love for Elisabeth was so immeasurably great that he felt himself a traitor to her when he considered them. But his incorruptible sense of verity forced it on him again and again. Finally he consoled himself with the fact that the great change in Elisabeth's character was only the immediate consequence of her becoming a mother, and that with the birth of the child her old nature would return all by itself.

He became speechless in the truest sense of the word, however, one day when Elisabeth, lost in thought, said to herself, "What could have become of Edgar? He was quite a nice guy after all!"

Almost two years had passed since Elisabeth's rupture with the Baron. In the meantime, she had become Hermann's bride and wife and was soon to be the mother of his child. The Baron had never again been mentioned between them, and now suddenly her former fiancé came back to her mind? Again? Must he not have lived uninterruptedly in her mind, if now, as a mother-to-be, she gave herself over to thoughts of him? Now Hermann recalled that already in Bordighera she had tormented him with apparently harmless memories of the Baron. What was that? And didn't she even call him fondly by his first name? Did she love him in the end and not Hermann, and had she turned away from him and toward Hermann for incomprehensible womanly reason, or perhaps just on a whim? And in all the tender and passionate hours of their young marriage had she embraced in spirit only her former fiancé, who was in fact her love? Hermann threatened to lose his mind at this thought.

But who can describe his horror when one day he found irrefutable proof that she had recently written to the Baron in secret, expressing the wish to see him again!

Carelessly, she had left a letter to the Baron on her desk, which she had torn up several times, on account of a mistake. Initially, she denied having sent a second letter, instead of the torn one. She stuck to this story even when Hermann appealed to her. Only when he showed her the letter himself the following day, which he had meanwhile received from the post office, did she admit it with casual indifference.

Hermann was stunned. So she was not only lying, she was cheating on him too! And worst of all, she seemed totally ignorant of the shamelessness of her behavior!

"What's the big deal?" she said innocently. "Why shouldn't I see again an old acquaintance I once loved?"

Hermann had trouble not chasing her out of the house. If she had not been expecting, God knows he would have. But he restrained himself. He did not want to do anything hasty. To wait and let things develop further, seemed to him, to be the most prudent thing to do.

From now on, however, the devil of suspicion lurked in his blood. Who could guarantee that she had not already deceived him in a completely different way? Yes, was the child she was expecting his child?

Squarely and with almost brutal frankness, he confronted her about this.

With big childlike eyes, she looked at him in utter amazement. Then she said with smiling calmness:

"You're out of your mind!"

This time she spoke the truth. The clarity of her eyes and the certainty of her voice told him that. Even a woman could not disguise herself like that. He pondered and calculated and visualized all the circumstances. He was indeed out of his mind.

Ashamed, he wanted to take her into his arms, but something inside held him back.

Elisabeth, however, seemed like she had suddenly been struck dead. When she threw herself on his chest as if seeking help, he slowly but firmly pushed her away from him, like something alien, even hostile, which he had to keep at bay.

From that hour on the love between the two had ruptured, and both felt that it was fatally so.

Hermann could not stop thinking about Elisabeth's baffling nature. He was not able to find a solution, for he had no idea that it was the fateful mixture of her blood that caused Elizabeth's ambivalence. The Jewish blood of her father drove her to Werheim, the Germanic blood of her mother to Hermann. The former drew her down into the lowest districts of sensuality and selfishness, the latter sought to lift her up into the spiritual regions of love and selflessness. Hermann's influence was able to shroud this ambivalence for a while, but it was never able to compensate for it, since it was a natural necessity. Now, in the primal experience of becoming a mother, it revealed itself without restraint.

Hermann was well aware of the unmistakable contrast between Jewish and Aryan, especially German, nature from the experiences of practical life. He had also encountered this contrast in his religious studies. He was therefore inclined to explain it in religious terms and to confine it to the religious sphere, especially since he found that each race had its own peculiar religion. In doing so, he committed the same mistake that the very best minds still make, in addressing the Jewish question as a religious one and not as a racial one. Nor had it occurred to him to objectively evaluate the fact of this racial difference, to think the idea of race through to its logical conclusion and to draw practical conclusions from it. Brought up in the ideas of the French Revolution, that all men are equal and of equal value, although the simplest observation refutes this false doctrine daily a thousand times over, he had never found opportunity and necessity to think at all about this basic and main question of human and national existence.

Admittedly, he would have resisted marrying a negress or a Japanese woman. But that a Jewess or half-Jewess is racially just as fundamentally different from a German woman as a negress or Japanese woman, that had not yet dawned on him, because it is not as obvious to the senses as that crude difference.

When his child was born to him, Hermann was awakened abruptly from his drowsy ignorance of race.

The closer Elisabeth's difficult hour approached, the more needy she became for assistance and reassurance, and the more fiercely Hermann's struggle raged on. From the moment, when he discovered Elisabeth's incomprehensible attempt to see the Baron again, it had become clear to him how deeply, intimately, and boundlessly he loved her. Again and again, he told himself that in her condition she could not be held responsible for her actions. But he also had to tell himself that her behavior was, after all, rooted in her deepest core and nature, and that its roots would not be removed when she returned to normal health after the child was born. His love had forgiven Elisabeth her misstep long ago. But not even a whole infinity of forgiving, love and kindness would be able to change her natural disposition.

The family doctor, who had been a friend of his since his student days and who was an associate professor at the women's clinic at the university in Berlin, tried in vain to reassure him that pregnancy pathologically changed the nature of some women so fundamentally that even physiologists and psychologists were puzzled. Hermann, who was unbiased and undeterred in his search for deeper connections with scientific urgency, could not be pacified and reassured by such explanations, which were only the admission of learned inadequacy. He was too thorough a natural scientist to be able to disregard such elementary conditions. The thought would not have occurred to him that the mother herself influences the spirit embodied in the maternal fetus, and that conversely, the nature of the embodied spirit must be determined by the nature of her abnormal capriciousness. He saw clearly the abyss into which Elisabeth would have to sink one day, if a miracle didn't close this abyss or her soul didn't grow unimagined wings.

Here now was the point where self-reproaches of the most ruthless kind began in him. Had he not neglected Elisabeth mentally and spiritually in the grossest way since their marriage? Hadn't he himself at first succumbed to the sensual frenzy, instead of opposing it with mental and spiritual energies from the beginning and triggering such energies in his young wife? Where was the knowledge he had gained in life's hard struggles, that the spirit, the first and original, was lord and master of matter and flesh? Truly, he himself was responsible for Elisabeth's decline! He himself had first awakened hers by his sensual lack of self-control and thus driven her to make a mistake! Yes, it was he himself who committed this misstep!

In such a mood he entered the room of his beloved wife one December day at dusk. With pale, tear-stained eyes she rested on her couch and waited with a torn soul for her difficult hour. With the most intimate tenderness he bent over her and kissed her sunken cheeks and her bloodless mouth, which was closed in bitter suffering.

Then, sobbing deeply, she wrapped her arms around his neck and powerlessly sought to rest her head against his chest. She was barely able to stammer his name.

Hermann sank down silently on his knees beside her, laid his head against her bosom, and implored her to forgive him for his unkindness during the last weeks.

"You dear!" she breathed out blissfully and tenderly and ran her pale hand over his forehead and hair.

They lingered wordlessly like this for a long time. A kettle hummed in the chamber of the tiled stove, outside the window snowflakes danced in the gray-blue twilight air. Christmas was just around the corner, and in that hour Holy Christmas entered deeply into the hearts of the loving couple.

A few weeks later, the tree of lights sparkled in Elisabeth's den. Hermann was sitting on the edge of her bed, holding her half-erect sideways in his arms, while they both dreamed the same dream with golden curls, musing in the candlelight.

The birth was expected at the beginning of February. Every conceivable precaution for mother and child had been taken. Hermann himself had taken care of all the arrangements and supervised the execution of the doctor's orders most carefully.

Day and night Hermann did not leave Elisabeth's side. When the contractions began, he held on to his beloved wife's head and hands. The pain she endured he suffered tenfold in his own body. Only at the urgent request of the doctor could he be induced to wait in the adjoining room for the completion of the event.

The birth took place naturally to the complete satisfaction of the doctor. It was a boy. But when Hermann, beaming with happiness, took his son in his arms, whom the nurse handed to him on a pillow, he recoiled in horror.

A dark-skinned, inhuman something, covered in frizzy, pitch-black hair, screeched at him. Deep dark eyes, which seemed to have a bluish tinge, blinked at him from an ancient face under long black eyelashes. A flattened nose gave the head something ape-like in appearance.

Elisabeth, too, was so hysterically frightened when she saw the child that she fainted and sank back into the pillows. When, through the doctor's efforts, she regained consciousness and saw Hermann's horrified eyes above her, she turned her head away to the side, and wept.

Forcefully, the doctor separated Hermann from Elisabeth. His wife needed complete rest now, any excitement could be fatal for her.

"The child just resembles the grandfather," the doctor said as he escorted the badly shaken man into the next room. "A quite familiar phenomenon. It's called atavism."

Silently, with staring eyes, Hermann nodded to himself. Then he asked to be left alone and went to his study. There he sank into dark brooding. "Atavism!" He was familiar with this learned concept from his zoological studies. Finally, he picked up a reference book and read:

> Atavism, reversion, degeneration, the phenomenon that characteristics of earlier generations suddenly reappear in an individual, although they did not appear in his parents. For example, there will be characteristics that are transferred by the daughter to the grandson without being detectable in the daughter. The phenomenon is especially striking when individuals of different races (also human races) come to crossbreed. While the first generation consists of mixed types of both parents, already in the second-generation, single individuals revert to the type of one of the grandparents. (See also the articles on "Heredity" and "Miscegenation").

Greedily Hermann read these entries and the explanations under the other headings. But these meager treatments were not enough for him. The scientist had suddenly awakened in him again. He immediately went to the university library and ordered all the works he could find. Whole batches of books on these problems, which had suddenly become the focus of his interest, piled up in his study over the next weeks and months. He devoured them with a sincere hunger. Every free hour that he could wrest from his profession, he devoted to these studies. Elisabeth and the child had hardly any place in his feelings during this time. They had become a scientific object for him.

The result of these extensive, passionately pursued studies was, in broad outline, the following:

Race is the prevailing physical and mental characteristic of the members of a people, based on common descent. That the individual human races are not the same and of equal value is a fact that is obvious to the senses. A Teuton, a Japanese, a Negro, a Jew, are physically and mentally such different people that every child can distinguish them. The racial value of a people is made tangible in their   geniuses, because they realize the highest core values of a race. Negroes and Botocudo have no geniuses, they are completely incapable of culture, which of course does not deny that they can still learn to read and write, speak several languages, recite the Lord's Prayer and wear tailcoats and patent leather shoes. But any deeper and more active part in a culture and religion imposed on them does not occur, and that alone is the decisive factor here.

The history of states and peoples is the history of their races.[1] Only races that are equally creative are able to inherit from similarly creative cultures. The power of ideas and ideals fails because of the natural endowments of a race. It is not the human race as such that develops, but only it's individual races, and their ability to develop is naturally conditioned and limited from the beginning. No man and no people can escape from its physical conditions of birth and descent. The brain of a Teuton necessarily thinks differently from the brain of a Negro, a Japanese or a Jew, and the emotional and mental life is also necessarily quite different.

The decline and fall of great states and cultures is always the direct consequence of the racial decline of their people, and this in turn is the direct consequence of mixing with inferior and alien blood. Thus Hellas and Rome perished. Both were purely Aryan peoples. Their decline began immediately, however, when Semitic blood, foreign to their kind and inferior to theirs, poured into their lands in growing streams from Asia Minor, Syria, Palestine, and North Africa. The opponents of race theory now claim that it was not racial, but rather social causes that destroyed these giant empires. But they overlook the fact that it was precisely the incorporation of alien elements as slaves, prisoners of war and immigrants that brought about the disastrous social conditions which led to their downfall, and that the downfall was sealed the moment that civil rights were granted to the chaotic foreign rabble. Now there was no stopping on the slippery democratic slope. Proud racial consciousness and with it cultural, national,

---

[1] The Jew Disraeli, who later became English Prime Minister Lord Beaconsfield, to whom England owes its position of world power based on robbery and exploitation, wrote in his novel *Endymion* (1880): "No one is allowed to treat the principle of race indifferently. It is the key to world history; and that is why history is so often confused, because it was written by people who do not know the race question and the dimensions belonging to it. Language and religion do not make a race - blood makes it!"

and state power remained with only a few patrician families who avoided mixture with alien blood; but they were simply engulfed by the ever more powerfully swelling corruption of the blood.

The German folk are a racially pure people, because the components comprising it, the Teutons, Celts, Slavs, and Lithuanians, all belong to the Indo-Germanic or Aryan race. They are closely related peoples by blood, who after a long separation and special development came together again to produced today's German race under predominance of the Teutons. Such long separation and special maturation and later again blending of peoples of one and the same main race, as in the case of the German people, is particularly favorable for the production of high-quality racial characteristics. The implantation of these purely Aryan components in a uniform pre-Aryan substrate, which is particularly evident in the south of Germany, and is expressed externally in the darker tint of the skin, the hair, and the eyes, ensured the formation of the uniform racial character which we today call German. The astonishingly diverse talents of the German people, who achieve unsurpassable feats in every field of human activity, in religion, art and science, as well as in warfare and statecraft, in trade and technology, and whose incredible successes excite the envy of the whole world, find their natural explanation in this favorable mixture of components of one and the same main race.

One race that is physically and spiritually opposed to the German race is the Jewish race. The racial elements composing the Jewish people are, in origin and character, alien to the Germans in blood and soul. While the original homeland of the Indo-Germans, despite continued open debate about selected questions, is undoubtedly to be sought in the north, the Bible places the origin of the Jewish race in Mesopotamia. According to the latest research, East Africa turns out to be the original homeland of the Jews in question. The similarity of some Jews with Negroes is unmistakable. Other researchers place their origin in the countries of the Arabian desert. Further, it is certain that the original Jewish race mixed itself extensively with Northern Egyptian and Syrian-Hittite components. Race researchers agree that in prehistoric times the Indo-European race could not and did not make contact with the Jewish race, so that any blood relationship between the two is excluded.

Nevertheless, the Jews, later in Palestine before they changed over to the inbreeding and pure breeding of their bastard race, also took up a small percentage of Indo-European blood by mixing with the Amorites, so that the most reluctant race elements are bound in them. Tacitus notes that most of the source writers of his time considered the Jews to be Egyptian pariahs, a "race hated by the gods".

In contrast to the German race, one of the outstanding characteristics of the Jewish race is that it does not itself create fruitful and constructive values, but instead shifts the values created by their host peoples in an intermediary manner, thus exploiting their host peoples and making them dependent on them. Already from the Bible, it is clear that the Jews, wherever they came into contact with a people, made it "interest-bearing" for themselves. Also, in its later homeland of Jerusalem, the Jewish people lived only from the exploitation of other peoples. Even imperial Rome had become "interest-bearing" to them. But at that time, Jewish egalitarianism, which later brought about its downfall, had not yet sufficiently affected it, and when the monetary dependence of the Roman masters on the Jerusalem bankers had become unbearable, Rome made short work of it and had the Jewish financial center destroyed by Titus. In Germany today, the Jews, although they make up only one percent of the total population, control not only the money market, but also over ninety percent of the entire German press. Thanks to these two means, their influence in politics, economic life and art is preeminent today, and authentic ethnic German expression is condemned to wither away in these areas.

The abysmal difference between the German and the Jewish race becomes even clearer in the spiritual realm. Jesus, the Aryan founder of the Christian religion, which has become the basis of the German people's feeling and thinking, was crucified by the Jewish people, precisely because his teachings are foreign to their nature and because they violated the historical foundations of Judaism, self-interest, and exploitation. The Jew is incapable of German ideals, German thinking, feeling and will, as expressed in the concepts of God, freedom and immortality, prince and fatherland, duty and loyalty, German joy and strength and greatness, because his race lacks the spiritual organs for them.[2] On the other hand, he is rich in all the qualities which are also the basis of German vices and which the Jew is constantly at work to incite and evoke: greed and selfishness, sensuality and godlessness, unfaithfulness and dishonesty.

The Jews are also aware of their racial contrast to the Germans., Therefore, for purely practical reasons, many also convert to Christianity. But of course, a Jew remains a Jew, just as a Negro remains a Negro, or a

---

[2] See Appendix.

Japanese remains a Japanese, even if he were to be baptized with fire and water a dozen times.[3]

Even by interbreeding with ethnic Germans, the unbridgeable contrast between Jewish and German races cannot be balanced out.[4] In the case of German-Jewish half-breeds, the observation made repeatedly regarding interbreeding between different races is true. They show all the characteristics of the hybrid and accumulate the inferior qualities of their parents and ancestors. These half-breeds are tragic and, as Goethe already pointed out, unfortunate creatures. A German who marries a Jewess, or a German

---

[3] The Jewish writer Artur Landsberger writes in his novel *Millionäre* (Munich 1913): "One can neither exit nor cross over... I have also talked with ethnologists... I have talked about it at length with ethnologists. They share my opinion completely. This pastor, who talked you into this, is either a sheep or a swindler... Imagine a Negro declaring that he was leaving Negroism and entering Germanism! Yes, if you are of the opinion that this Negro, through this leaving and crossing over...has now really become a Teuton - well, then you shall also be right!... One can perceive it as an advantage or disadvantage that one is a Jew— that is merely a matter of taste, for which one is not responsible in the end. But one thing you certainly can't do: you can't change anything about it! And if you let yourself be baptized anew every Sunday evening! It is of no use." (*Deutschvölkische Hochschulschriften* [Ethnic German University Writings] , Issue 3 "Jewish Self-Confessions.")

[4] The Jewish legal philosopher and university professor, Dr. Eduard Gans (died 1839 in Berlin), who was baptized in order to become a professor, openly confessed: "Baptism and interbreeding are of no use at all; even in the hundredth generation we remain Jews as we were three thousand years ago. We do not lose the smell of our race, not even in tenfold interbreeding. And in any cohabitation with any female, our race is dominant: they become like young Jews."

In the anthology "*Vom Judentum!*" [From Judaism] (Kurt Wolff, Leipzig), cited elsewhere, Arnold Zweig writes: "The child of a Jewish mother is a Jew, no matter who the father is—this Talmudic law simply expresses an existing fact that is observed daily in intermarriages of Jewish women."

Houston Stewart Chamberlain, in his essay "Race and Nation" (*Deutschlands Erneuerung*, issue 7, July 1918, Verlag J. F. Lehmann, Munich), states with reference to Darwin: "Cross-breeding erases the distinguishing characteristics of both parent races; what it produces is an actual hybrid, a being whose character is lacking. To this must be added the consideration that the less noble and the sexually stronger race always triumphs. After a few generations, mulattos return to the pure Negro type. The children begotten by Jews with Europeans are hybrids, but invariably they tend towards Judaism. Sometimes this fact remains faintly visible for one, or even two generations; then suddenly, without renewed Semitic admixture, the pure Jew stands before us again as if he had arrived here yesterday from the banks of the Jordan!"

woman who marries a Jew, not only commits a crime against the German people, but also heaps endless mental and physical suffering on his own children and children's children: the sin against the blood takes a terrible revenge on them.

This was the sum of the new studies to which Hermann devoted himself. He found them irrefutably confirmed by his own horrible experience.

Now he fought a mighty battle with his Christian conscience, for this racial doctrine seemed hard and loveless to him. What could the individual people do if they belonged to a higher or lower, a noble or inferior race? But he did not yet know the otherworldly connections that would resolve this contradiction. He did not yet understand that every embodied spirit freely chooses the race, and within this again the individual body in which it will live on earth. Nor did he suspect that mischievous and obstinate spirits choose the lower races in order to better indulge their selfish urges, while nobler spirit beings, more advanced in knowledge, choose the more highly developed human bodies as their earthly dwelling and place of activity. Nor did he realize that the Savior himself relentlessly led the battle against the Jews, and that he knew neither quiet sniveling nor cowardly fear. Hermann had not yet grasped the meaning of Jesus' words: "I have not come to bring peace, but a sword!"

Hermann Kämpfer found this dichotomy unbearable, as well as the shame and disgrace in which he was now condemned to live. He considered whether he should, or even if he must, dispose of himself together with his wife and child. But his religion prevented him from doing so. He was determined to follow to the end the path he had taken through his own fault, contrary to his inner voice, as a warning to his fellow citizens, for the benefit of the German fatherland, and for his own salvation.

Elisabeth suffered inexpressibly from the new estrangement that had developed between her and Hermann since the birth of her child. True, he showed no lack of attentiveness and care, but his behavior bore all too clearly the stamp of chivalrous consideration that lacked any inner warmth.

In her need for love she clung to the child all the more passionately. The horror she had felt at first sight of it had soon given way to the natural instincts of the mother. She nursed it herself. She had been looking forward to this, together with Hermann, long before the child was born. But now she anxiously guarded these sweet hours of maternal happiness from him, and when he once surprised her, she fled with the child into her bedroom, where she locked herself in.

One day, when she was carefully looking at the child while breastfeeding, she was startled. It occurred to her that it resembled the Baron. The longer she looked at it, the more this impression was confirmed. The child's eyes, which originally seemed to be blue, had over the past few weeks become darker and eventually turned black. It came over her like a fever when she realized she had discovered the cause of the striking phenomenon. During the last months before the birth, she had thought of the Baron constantly, without being able to explain it herself! In a kind of obsession, she had even written to him. It was fortunate that Hermann had held back the letter from being forwarded in time. Nevertheless, her thoughts had been drawn back to her former fiancé again and again, as if by magnetic forces. Only since that December day, when Hermann's love enveloped her again, had this compulsion given way. There was no doubt in her mind that she had "yielded" herself in spirit to the Baron, and therefore the child resembled him. She had no idea of the true, purely spiritual cause of these obsessive thoughts, any more than Hermann did, and that the "lapse" she spoke of, was a natural necessity.

The fear now came over her that Hermann might one day make the same discovery. What would happen then? His hot-blooded, impetuous nature would be capable of anything. The most horrible visions tormented her day and night. Anxiously, she made sure that he did not see the child.

On Christmas Eve, they had agreed to give the child their own names, Hermann or Elisabeth, depending on its gender. With a heavy heart, she now looked forward to the day of baptism. When it was imminent, she asked Hermann calmly whether she should maintain the agreed-upon naming.

Hermann had to think about what she meant at first. Then he suddenly said with biting scorn:

"Oh, come on! You can call it Edgar!"

Elisabeth staggered for a chair. Chest heaving, both hands clutching at her heart, she gasped for breath.

Startled, Hermann jumped to her side.

"What's the matter with you?"

"You're foul!" she gasped out without looking at him.

He did not answer and supported her with his arm.

"Can I get you something, a sip of coffee or wine? Or a glass of water?"

"Thank you!" she replied tonelessly.

When Hermann was still struggling to help her, she asked him to leave her alone.

Silently he went to the door. Before opening it, he held the handle in his hand for a while and said:

"Call the child whatever you want. In any case, it won't get my name."

With that, he walked out.

Elisabeth was stunned. Had he already made the same discovery that she had? Straight away, she rang for the children's caretaker.

Hermann had not seen the child in Elisabeth's presence since the day it was born. Now she tried to find out from the attendant by indirect questions, when Hermann had seen the child for the last time. The result was that Hermann looked after the child every day when she herself was resting in her room after the meal. He often looked at it for a long time, but had never picked it up in his arms.

Now she knew enough. Perplexed as to what she should do, she went to see her mother. She let her in on her secret and also did not conceal from her the change that had occurred between her and the husband.

She didn't tell the Madame Councilor anything new. Her mother's eyes had long since perceived everything. She herself suffered unspeakably. After all, it was her own youthful sin that had now come upon her child and her grandchild as an unpardonable guilt.

Contrary to her own observations, she tried unsuccessfully to persuade her daughter that the child did not resemble the Baron. She advised Elisabeth not to return to the chosen name, but to give the child a name that did not occur in Hermann's family. Both women took the calendar in hand and agreed on the name Heinrich.

Hermann also agreed with this, because despite her mother's warning, Elisabeth suggested this name to him the very next day, when she was sitting at lunch in silence with Hermann as usual. He just nodded his head without uttering a word.

Thus, the child was baptized with the name Heinrich. Without any solemnity, the holy act was performed by the pastor of the parish church in the apartment. The family doctor, who was a friend, and the Madame Councilor were the godparents. The Councilor of Commerce was not present. He had entered his son-in-law's apartment for the first time on the occasion of the birth of the child and had not been seen since. Apparently very disappointed to find an unmistakable representative of his own race as heir, instead of a blond nobleman on whom he thought he had every hope of finding, he had left again.

The next day he informed Hermann, in a purely businesslike manner, that he had set up a bank account for his grandchild in Hermann's name, and that he had deposited the sum of three hundred thousand marks in gilt-edged papers as basis. In a purely businesslike manner, Hermann acknowledged this letter, and with that, the kinship needs of both of them were again satisfied for a long time to come. They also rarely met professionally. The Councilor paid almost no attention to the factory, which flourished under Hermann's management. He was exclusively concerned with the licensing of Hermann's patent abroad. He only checked the factory's quarterly balance sheets, and he was so satisfied with them that personal consultation was rarely necessary.

Ever since Elisabeth had learned that Hermann visited the child every day, she did not let him out of her sight as soon as she knew he was present in the house. After dinner, when she was in the habit of resting, she took him into her room. She put the baby carriage right next to her resting place and locked the doors behind her. One day, however, when she had delayed a little, she came to see Hermann pondering over the child.

"What are you doing to him!"

With these words, she pounced on her cub like a lioness.

With a sneer, Hermann left the room.

Elisabeth lay down crying, but she was at least reassured that Hermann's thoughts did not seem to move in a direction she feared.

She had stopped all contact with her friends and acquaintances and received no visitors at all, so that as few people as possible would see the child. She could easily justify this by saying that she was nursing and caring for the child herself. However, when one of her closest friends came to her unannounced and asked to see the child, she could not refuse her request. Whether the good friend had already heard it from others or whether she herself had noticed it, she suddenly burst into an astonished cry:

"My God, how the little one looks like Baron von Werheim! No, what a coincidence!"

Elisabeth was paralyzed and the friend was daring enough to point out her discovery again.

"How funny!" she exclaimed. "Just look! All that's missing is the monocle!"

A few days later, it was generally said in the circles of the Kurfürstendamm that a cuckoo had laid a strange egg in the nest of Dr. Hermann Kämpfer. When the cuckoo in question heard this interesting news, he was deft enough to acknowledge it with a meaningful smile.

The matter also came to the attention of the family doctor, who brought the rumor to the attention of his former school chum and friend Hermann.

In the same hour, the latter went to see the Baron personally. He looked extremely surprised and without being asked, gave a declaration on his honor that he had neither directly nor indirectly caused nor spread this rumor, and as far as his person was concerned, it was devoid of any material support.

"I am convinced of the latter, otherwise you wouldn't be standing here in front of me! And besides, I didn't even ask you about that, you man of honor, you! How dare you even suggest such a thing?"

Since the Baron did not reply, Hermann left him without so much as a glance. The next day he sent his second.

The Baron could not back down, the honorary council of his corps saw to that. Three exchanges of bullets with advance. The duel took place in Grunewald. In the very first exchange of bullets, Hermann shot off his opponent's left ear. The latter roared, threw the weapon away and, whimpering, held onto the dangling ornament with both hands. In view of the Baron's attitude, the referee, with Hermann's consent, dispensed with the second and third exchanges of fire. A few days later, Baron Dr. Edgar v. Werheim, who had in the meantime been promoted to government Councilor, was dismissed from his corps.

Since a humorist could not refrain from tortuously describing this glorious duel in a very well-read newspaper, the matter was brought before the court and both duelists received three months' imprisonment each.

When Hermann returned to his family, little Heinrich was already making his first attempts at walking.

Now began a new time of distress for Elisabeth.

Although Hermann hadn't noticed any resemblance between the little boy and the Baron before, he thought he saw one now. The suspicion took root in him anew that he might have been deceived after all. Since Elisabeth considered it beneath her dignity to give him an answer to his cynical question, he saw her silence as an admission of guilt. Possessed by this fixed idea, he searched for evidence of her wrongdoing. He broke into her desk, ransacked her closets, but to no avail.

One day he came just as the boy was being bathed. He looked at the naked body with scientific interest. There he discovered on the left shoulder of the child a mole of a very definite jagged outline. He himself had the same birthmark in the same place. Tensely he searched the right hip of the child, yes! There was also a very characteristic birthmark, which he himself had.

Now all doubt was removed. He was the father of the child and he had done Elisabeth an unheard-of injustice.

From that hour on, his relationship with mother and child changed. He formally asked Elisabeth for her forgiveness. She accepted his apology indifferently. He had lost her love, that was clear to him. Now his unshakable resolution was to win her back and to become a good father to the child, to raise it conscientiously. At the same time, he was also tempted by the scientific question of whether it was not possible to imprint certain character and mental qualities on a young human child through consistent education, and whether the racial doctrine that blood alone determines mind and character was not just dim scholarly wisdom that did not stand up to experience.

From now on, he spent hours every day working with the child. He played with him and supported him in his attempts to walk and talk. As soon as he was able, he took him for walks, even though he usually had to carry him. He took him to the riding school and put him on a horse. When Christmas came, he decorated the Christmas tree for him and gave him his first toys.

With quiet joy Elisabeth followed this relationship between father and child, which became more intimate every day. Without her noticing it, Hermann's fatherly love threw its rays back into her heart, and when one day he invited her to accompany him on a drive with the boy, she did not say no.

On the child's first birthday, Elisabeth woke up to find a huge bouquet of handsome roses on her bedside table. Since the child's birth the couple had kept their bedrooms separate, Hermann instructed the child's nurse to put the bouquet of roses in place in time without Elisabeth being aware of it. At breakfast, Hermann greeted his wife with a kiss for the first time in years. Delighted, she accepted the tenderness, admittedly without returning it. But she thanked him warmly for the roses. A sleigh ride with the boy concluded the birthday celebration. But when Hermann wanted to kiss Elisabeth again and take her in his arms for goodnight, she resolutely refused. She had forgiven him the suspicion of infidelity and all the suffering he had caused her, but she had not forgotten.

The next three years passed without Hermann succeeding in winning back Elisabeth's love. As often as the boy's birthday came around, the horrible images and events of her first year of marriage were renewed in her soul. Hermann's solicitation was able to disguise them temporarily, but not to cover them up or even erase them permanently. However, when the child fell ill with diphtheria and subsequently with pneumonia a few months after his fourth birthday, the hearts of the spouses were completely reunited during the night watches at his bedside. Their combined love narrowly snatched the child from the jaws of death.

The couple now seemed to have regained the deep love of their marriage. But the black shadow of their unnatural child weighed heavily on them and gnawed at their souls incessantly. And yet only a few weeks ago they had feared for his life together! O tormented strife that entangles us! The most selflessly devoted love, the most honest will to sacrifice and renunciation was not able to redeem it for them.

In vain they resumed their common philosophical and artistic studies; again and again, their thoughts and senses returned to the only dark point in their existence. When they wandered through the museums and galleries as before, every beautiful picture, every magnificent sculpture was only a mockery of the living ugliness that lurked in wait at home. When they went for a walk, drove, or rode a horse, every beautiful person and even more so every beautiful child was a painful experience for them. Wherever they turned their eyes in search of salvation, the black reality was there and stayed there, grinning at them mercilessly. Not even in a theater or concert could they find some relief from it for a few hours. From every seat and chair it taunted them in the flesh, for the theaters and concert halls of the big city seemed to be the sole domain of that sinister race to which they owed the misfortune of their lives.[1]

If they walked through the city, it grinned at them from the shop windows too. It had become fashionable in the last years to give even dress-up dolls and baby dolls the features of this ominous type! If they made an excursion across the country or visited a summer resort or a seaside spa, a castle or a beautiful landscape, wherever they went, every somehow favored spot of the German fatherland seemed to have become the home of this foreign-blooded race. Were there any German people left in the German fatherland?

---

[1] The well-known Jewish writer Dr. Walther Rathenau in his *Impressions* (Leipzig 1902) gives his observations "on Sundays at noon in Berlin on Tiergarten Street or in the evening in the anteroom of a theater" with the following words: "Strange vision! In the midst of German life, a separate, alien tribe of people, brilliant and conspicuously decorated, with a hot-blooded, agile demeanor. An Asiatic horde on the sands of the March! ... not a living member of the people, but a foreign organism in its body."

One winter evening, when Hermann was sitting with his young wife dreaming by the fireplace in the twilight hour, he suddenly pulled her into his arms and whispered in her ear:

"Elisabeth, we must have a second child!"

Scared to death, she freed herself from his arms.

Was he insane? Hadn't he had enough of one misfortune? Had he not given her whole lectures on these questions and made it clear to her that her entire future married life must now be one of renunciation and denial. Had she not submitted to this deprivation for his sake, however much her blood rebelled against it? And now that she had finally succeeded in restraining the impulses of her love and transforming them into spiritual and intellectual values, was she to give up this hard-won condition again in order to face new suffering and new misery? Elisabeth rejected this idea of her husband's with such determination that he didn't dare to return to it for a long time.

But in Hermann's heart the thought germinated and grew, demanding life and crying out for life. The longing of the perfectly healthy man to see himself continued in flesh and blood, the cry of his soul for a child of his own, who would be in his image and likeness, became louder and stronger the more he approached the midday height of his life.

"Look," he said to Elisabeth, "there is one thing I have not considered until now. In a second child the blood of your father does not necessarily have to become effective again! The probability that it will be like our German nature is much greater than the opposite! The blood of your mother and the blood of my parents stands against the blood of your father like three to one! It can only have been a fateful accident that this preponderance of superior German blood did not come into effect with our first child. But even if this ratio were not three to one, but two to two, even then we may still hope, according to the laws of probability, that the hereditary units of our German nature will now also come into their own in our second child.

Elisabeth could not help smiling.

"You are a very clever mathematician," she said, "but haven't you taught me this yourself, and demonstrated it to me by dozens of examples from the past and the present, that, in every union, the hostile blood triumphs, just as in other things in life the base always knows how to displace the noble? Didn't you explain to me yourself and prove to me by examples that ignoble blood, in every case, is so powerful over the noble that a single ignoble creature will certainly spoil the noble upbringing of a whole generation if it comes under it? And didn't you also explain to me why this is so? Haven't you shown me that the structure of the cells of the species of nobler creatures is much more intricate and delicate, and therefore more sensitive, than that of the base ones, and therefore is already changed, or even destroyed, by mere contact with them?"

"That is all true, my darling," Hermann replied. "But the possibility cannot be ruled out in principle that even the noble may one day prove to be just as resilient as the base, especially if, as in this case, it stands in a strength ratio of three to one against the ignoble, meaning it is three times superior to it. You must admit that under these conditions there is not only the possibility, but even the probability, that our German essence will predominate!"

"Even under the most favorable conditions, there can be no question of victory," Elisabeth replied very seriously. "At best, our nature can assert itself alongside the enemy's, but it cannot completely push it back or render it ineffective!"

"Why not?"

"Because it has already poisoned my blood," replied the young woman, deeply saddened. "That's why it will reassert itself in any case, as our first experience has proven!"

"We will now counter this unfortunate experience with one that is all the happier!" exclaimed Hermann enthusiastically. "May we all have hope in it for the reasons I have set forth to you." Tenderly he took his wife in his arms and covered her mouth and neck with heartfelt kisses.

Elisabeth gently escaped from him with the words:

"That you long for a child of your nature, and in his blue eyes you wish to see yourself again…"

"And you, my only, dear, sweet wife," Hermann interrupted her, taking her in his arms anew.

"Let me speak, Hermann! Look, I understand all that well, and it is your right, and should also be fulfilled to you!"

"Elisabeth!"

"Listen, my dear! You shall achieve it, but not through me. I want to separate from you so that you can take another as your wife. I have been thinking about this for a long time, and now I am telling you."

Hermann looked at her in dismay.

"You can't be serious!" he said.

"I'm completely serious," she replied very calmly and firmly, looking him in the eyes.

"Then you don't love me anymore!" Hermann exclaimed.

Elisabeth took her husband's head in both hands.

"I love you so much, you foolish man, that your happiness is more important to me than mine, and that I am able to renounce my love for you for the sake of your happiness. Leave our unhappy boy to me and seek happiness with another woman, which you cannot find through me."

Hermann looked at his wife for a while in astonishment. Then, deeply ashamed, he kissed her hand. He did not dare to take her in his arms, she seemed so big and pure, so completely superhuman to him.

Then he grabbed her hands and said with clear resolve:

"Thank you for this outrageous proof of your love. And now let us speak of this matter no more. I will overcome my longing and we will carry on together with our lives as before. You are both wife and child to me, you are the only one!"

"You will regret it, Hermann, if you don't accept my proposal," Elisabeth said plainly. "I know you better than you know yourself. The fulfillment of your heart's desire is as necessary to your life and prosperity as food and drink, as light and air. I can no longer stand by and watch you harming yourself because of it. Therefore, if you do not want to do without me, I will make another suggestion to you."

"You need not look at me so," continued Elizabeth, smiling, "it's something very simple. Find a healthy girl of your choice somewhere in the country, make her the mother of your child, and bring the child to me, and we will raise it together as if it were ours."

"Elisabeth!" exclaimed Hermann, deeply moved.

"Well?" she asked seriously, barely resisting his kisses.

"You fool!" he answered her, now almost becoming angry.

"But I really mean it," she said clearly and firmly.

"I don't doubt it!"

And when she still looked at him questioningly, he added:

"Can you do that for me?"

Elisabeth buried her face against her husband's chest.

"Well?" he asked in the same tone as she had earlier.

"You dear, you!" she breathed out. Then she looked up to his face and said:

"I want to fulfill for you your soul's desire, may it turn out now as you want!"

"Elisabeth! My wife!"

Elizabeth fought bravely against the demons of her father's blood. More powerfully than ever they sought to assert their control over the soul and senses of the young woman who was to become a mother for the second time. But Hermann's love enveloped and shielded her. She communicated all her feelings and thoughts, wishes and desires to her husband, who enlightened her with deep understanding about cause and effect, so that her spirit remained in complete control of the senses and drives that were hostile to it.

Beethoven's music had a particularly beneficial influence on Elisabeth. The andante and adagio movements of the sonatas and symphonies in particular had a deeply calming effect on her. Divinity itself seemed to descend from eternity, spaceless, timeless, redeeming the wandering, searching, groping human soul from everything that was accidentally earthly and agonizingly worldly. Hermann had to skip the Scherzi and Presti, however, since they had an opposite effect on Elisabeth. Once, when he had played the Scherzo movement of the Ninth Symphony, she suddenly demanded to drink champagne, wished to hear waltz and operetta melodies, and began to dance and twirl around so madly that she could no longer be held and Hermann caught her lifeless in his arms.

Hermann carefully kept everything ugly away from her eyes and was careful that only pure and beautiful images entered her soul. He had tastefully arranged magnificent paintings and sculptures all over the apartment. Wherever she looked, only beautiful things met her eyes. So that she would not see her first child, who was already five years old, in this critical time, he had him removed from the house and placed in an excellent children's home. By careful selection of reading material and entertainment, Hermann ensured that her mind and imagination received only pure, uncorrupted nourishment. He kept strangers away from her, even the servants. He carried out all the servings and small operations himself. He was around her day and night.

During this time, the Councilor of Commerce died suddenly and unexpectedly under circumstances that were soon the talk of the town in Berlin and filled the columns of the tabloid press. Elisabeth took the death very calmly, since she had never had any deeper feelings for her father, to say nothing of childish feelings. But the proximate circumstances of his death were likely to cause her great excitement. And she soon found out about them, even though Hermann had stopped reading the daily newspapers months ago, in order to prevent them from bringing anything ugly or exciting to the expectant mother. It was again her "best friend" who told her everything in detail, even more than she knew. She had used Hermann's absence, caused by the death of the Councilor, to finally get through to Elisabeth.

The Councilor's death was not initially brought to the attention of his family, as he had died outside the home. Nobody noticed his absence. He was in the habit of going into the city and traveling without announcing the destination and duration of his absence.

He died in the arms of three pretty blond girls, for whom he had arranged a shared apartment in the Bavarian Quarter. They did not know who he was, they didn't even know his name, and called him "little Uncle." Since he never carried anything with him that could have revealed his identity when he visited them, the horrified girls had no choice but to enlist the help of the police to dispose of his body. Thus, the corpse came to the inspection house, where it was recognized by an employee of the factory.

Hermann did nothing to prevent the matter from becoming known. It was useless. The newspapers carried column-long reports. Gradually, the following was learned:

The Councilor had set up such "private boarding houses" not only in Berlin, but also in no fewer than five other major German cities, Hamburg, Frankfurt, Breslau, Dresden, and Munich. Illustrated articles appeared in the most well-read weekly journals about the details of their furnishing, and about the ingenious mirror fittings in the bedrooms and bathrooms. Its residents were only blondes.[1] Each of them received, in addition to free housing, food and clothing, a monthly salary, which, depending on the favor in which she stood with her master, increased up to the salary of a Minister. The Councilor of Commerce had the beauties monitored by a whole staff of detectives. The slightest infidelity was inevitably punished by dismissal. He offered a reward equal to her annual salary for anyone who bore him a child. As soon as she gave birth, she was dismissed with a life-long pension for herself and her child, and was replaced by a still virginal comrade. For he was only after untouched blonde virgins, others did not appeal to him. To make these girls into mothers was his devilish delight. It was established that by the time of his death he was paying no less

---

[1] See Appendix.

than 117 such annuities, the oldest of which had been running for over twenty years. The names of all the annuity recipients were recorded in a special will. In a secret compartment in the safe Hermann found a family album with the photographs of all these unfortunate creatures together with their children. The names were written under the individual pictures and corresponded exactly with those in his will. The majority of the unfortunate children were boys. Almost all of them were the spitting image of their sire.

It must be assumed that the Councilor of Commerce did not perpetrate this racial poisoning of the German people merely in order to indulge his carnal appetites, but he was systematically pursuing utterly diabolical goals. This is evident from an exchange of letters which he had conducted with a young fellow Jew. Hermann found this correspondence in his estate. Among them was the following poem:

Ahasver's Merry Wandering Song

Look, I am the rootless one,
not someone wedded to the environment,
not someone drugged by a homesick dream
heart driven into my boots,
for I am a man who has been steeled to suffer.
You drive me from your thresholds,
I am still the most desired!
Your cries of envy bellow,
'cause I drink your springs
and I weigh your values.

Smooth skins of my soul,
salvation, which I suffered in praying;
and yet my booty piles up
and your brides rejoice
to me, the spit of a foreign desert.

Gaping you puff your weed
for a decent digestion,
but I am a clever tester,
and I aggravate your vices
mostly for your own edification.

So I play the games
of my mature wantonness,
strangely, very subtly,
the last one, to you veiled goal
of my Asiatic blood!*

(* This poem was published by the Jew Paul Mayer in issue 5 of the magazine "Aktion", January 1913.)

The lines highlighted by block print were marked by the hand of the
Councilor of Commerce and noted in the margin with a "Bravo! The correspondence showed that he regularly supported the young man with large
sums of money in order to enable him to live carefree dedicated to the
"subtle goals" mentioned in the poem. Furthermore, he gladly agreed to
bear all the costs in case of any consequences for the "brides". But that's
not all! He promised the young man as well as those girls, a certain reward
for each "success", which he could prove with such a blond bride. And the
young friend showed him dozens of such "successes".

Hermann anxiously guarded his horrible discoveries. But incompre-
hensibly, as tends to happen in such cases, they nevertheless became public
knowledge. The sensation they caused was all the greater because shortly
before his death the Councilor had been appointed Privy Councilor of
Commerce for his "undying services to the welfare of the people". (He had
donated several million for churches and other public buildings).

The disastrous effect of this scandal on the young expectant mother
reached its climax when Hermann was called before the examining magis-
trate at the instigation of the public prosecutor's office to determine whether he had known anything about his father-in-law's criminal activities or
had even aided and abetted them.

The court summons was served when Hermann was not at home. As
Elisabeth's wife, she received it in Hermann's absence. In her fear, she
opened the document, fainted and fell down violently in the hallway. The
result was an immediate premature birth.

Before the doctor or Hermann, who were both immediately sum-
moned, could be on the spot, the child was already there. It was alive.
Again, it was black-haired, but this time a beautiful Jewish boy. The mother demanded to see the child. When it was shown to her, she cried out
loudly, and died the moment Hermann entered the room. Shortly thereafter, the child also died.

With silent horror, Hermann stood by the corpse of his wife, unable
to form a thought. Suddenly he got a fright. In her facial features, he dis-

cerned a resemblance to her father. It was the slightly thicker lower lip hanging down in death that gave this impression. For the first time he perceived it. Even her broken eyes now resembled those of the Councilor. Quickly he covered the dead woman's face. And now she was again completely his Elisabeth. In frantic pain he threw himself over the cooling corpse, unable to shed a tear.

The doctor, who had rushed over in the meantime, was able to separate him from the dead woman only with difficulty. He watched impassively as the doctor examined her. He diagnosed the death as the result of a heart attack. She had suffered an internal injury in the fall, and a blood clot had lodged in the ventricle of the heart.

When one of the maids wanted to put the dead child into the arms of the dead mother, Hermann snatched it from her and put it back in the cradle. Then he folded Elisabeth's hands over a small brass cross, which had already served his mother as a death cross, ordered everyone present to leave the room and prayed silently at the bedside of the dead beloved.

Far from her father's grave, far from the grave of her child, Hermann buried Elisabeth's mortal remains.

Now the certainty came over him that the departed woman was not dead, but only stripped of her earthly shell. If our senses were not so coarse, as we wander cradle to grave, we would perceive how the supposedly dead are still around us in bodies of the very finest ethereal material, very surprised at the change that has taken place with them. How they try in vain to make themselves known to us and to get an answer to their questions as to why we are so sad. We would see how foolish and ridiculous they find it that we pay such laborious honors to the remaining husk and behave as if the departed had suffered a misfortune, or was now separated from us. Exactly as before, the presumed dead still live around us until they have adjusted to their new state and realize that now new tasks await them, which they need time, effort, work and experience to become aware of, just as they needed time, effort, work and experience to become clear about their earthly task when they had awakened to their earthly consciousness.

Our earthly life is only a gateway to other finer forms of existence. The hereafter is not a different place, but a different state. The more material and sensual a person was, the more difficult it will be for him to find his way in the new state, to separate from his old surroundings and his old habits. The more internalized and the more spiritual a man was, the more quickly and easily he becomes aware of his new condition. He recognizes his new task and is able to detach himself from his old surroundings and his previous habits in order to devote all the force of his soul to the new task.

But what is this task? To come to an ever clearer, purer and deeper insight into our relationship with God, and thus to find the way back to the divine home, which we had forfeited by abusing our free will. But only selfless love and devotion to our fellow human beings, for whom we should lighten the burden of life and help to find their way back to God, can bring us closer to this goal. That is why love is the highest commandment.

We would also perceive the deep remorse that torments the departed when they survey their earthly life and realize all the unkindnesses they committed and all the missed opportunities to show love and thereby become better, purer, and more perfect themselves. We would see what terrible pain shakes the departed, who, misjudging the earthly purpose of life, led a life of transitoriness, greedy for money and power, rank and fame, failing to become aware of and live out their true destiny. At the sight of these departed we would understand in a stroke the words of Jesus: "For what shall it profit a man, if he shall gain the whole world, and lose his own soul?" We would also perceive the despair of those who softly, weakly, and cowardly avoided the truth and did not find the courage to live their convictions and stand up for them openly. This remorse, this pain, is the purgatory of the departed and this despair their hell!

All of a sudden, they now recognize the divine goal. But in spite of all the agony of longing and deprivation, they are not able to come closer to it. Like Tantalus they reach in vain for the fruits hanging above them, dying of thirst and starvation without being able to die. And in this state, they must remain until a new opportunity offers itself to them to put on the shell of a human body. Then they are confronted anew with the same tasks and temptations, and again and again they have to live a life lived in vain, until they finally come to the realization of the purpose of life on earth, and find the strength to overcome themselves, to live their true purpose in the hereafter despite all the temptations and enticements of this world. What are the eternities we must struggle, against the short span of this earthly life! How pointless it is, to waste whole eternities again and again, for the sake of the fleeting pleasures of these few human years!

But we would also perceive the bliss of those departed who had used their lives according to their higher purpose, who had led lives of selfless love in sacrifice for their neighbors, their people, and their fatherland, who had defended their convictions regardless of their own advantage or disadvantage, who had found the courage to suffer and, if necessary, to die for these convictions. We would recognize that through such a life they gained insight, strength, and the maturity to enter into new forms of life in order to take on new higher tasks, which would bring them closer to the divine goal, until they finally became worthy of it.

But we would also recognize that there is a certain specific race of people in which the stubborn and unteachable spirits, who have turned away from God, prefer to embody themselves again and again in order to lead unsuspecting humanity away from its true destiny by awakening self-ishness and sensual lust. We would recognize that they are the same spirits who were responsible for the apostasy from God ages ago, and have since then done everything to make the return to God difficult or impossible for the spiritual beings who have come to know it. We would not tire of fighting and struggling until this devilish race is rendered harmless to mankind. It will not be possible for the German people to fulfill the task given to them by God, to lead all the peoples of the globe towards internal-ization and spiritualization until they have freed themselves from the influ-ence of this sinister race.

The judicial investigation against Hermann was fruitless. Nevertheless, the blasphemous tongues that connected him with the doings and activities of his father-in-law did not cease. He did not have enough time to take care of it. He had his hands full.

First of all, it was necessary to gain insight into the almost incalculable business estate of the Councilor of Commerce. It turned out that the letters, papers, and books were not at all in the order that one should take for granted in such extensive undertakings. The business correspondence was incomplete and disorganized. Whole parts were missing, and even seemed to have been deliberately destroyed. A number of transactions that were directly related to the stock exchange were only communicated by wire. In many cases, it was not even possible to identify the business partner, since only the telexes of the other side were available and copies of the outgoing correspondence could not be found.

The exchange of letters and telexes spanned the entire globe, but it concerned only brokerage transactions, the buying and selling of grain and coffee, cotton and sugar, hides and skins, ores and diamonds, leather and rubber waste, paper and tin scraps, products and waste of every conceivable kind, design patents and utility patents. The Councilor knew how to profit from every activity performed anywhere by industrious people. Millions of people working by the sweat of their brow in all five continents wriggled on wires that converged in his hands. He sat in his Berlin office like a fat spider, sucking the marrow out of the bodies and souls of all these people through these wire channels.

The gold from which he had amassed his immense fortune had poured in from all over the world. He had pursued it to all countries again and again, in order to force it to return home again doubled and tripled. He didn't allow the capital or the people whose sweat and blood he squeezed, a moment's peace. He was the great pitiless heart that sucked up human blood to turn it into hard cash, whether it sprang from the veins of whites or blacks, yellows or reds, Christians or pagans. Merrily, he walked over the corpses of individuals and families, even of whole peoples, if he could make money out of them.

But he would never have harmed a hair on the head of a fellow comrade of his own race. He needed them and they needed him. They were his agents and the officers who commanded his troops when he fought his battles. And he fought battles, money battles! Once, he bought up in one night the holy bread of God of a whole continent. It was his property! He reveled in the thought that whole peoples had to starve, if it fitted into his calculations!

But the bread of God he played off against copper, and copper again against tin, tin against cotton, cotton against leather, leather against gold, and gold against the souls of men and the souls of men against God! And for these shifts and displacements he needed his racial comrades, those nimble, lanky, and lithe figures with the greedy, unsteady eyes and the silent gait, who, like himself, were fatherless, at home all over the world, and whose military papers bristled with cruciality and indispensability, abounding in heart, lung, liver, kidney, intestine, and stomach ailments. They sat as his scouts and emissaries in all parts of the world, in all news-papers and in all businesses. It was they who provided him with beckons, messages, notes, each worth millions. They controlled the transatlantic cables, the wireless stations, the news sources for the whole globe. If they wanted to, they could unleash a world war overnight, and they would un-leash it as soon as they deemed the time favorable for the "big deal." After all, the destiny of the world is directed by only a few hundred men, all of whom belonged to his race![1]

In all other fields of human activity, too, his racial comrades helped him and conducted his business, in the fields of science and literature, of art and theater, as well as in politics. They are ceaselessly at work to de-stroy those primeval ideals of God, freedom, immortality, prince, and fa-therland, and to put in their place the ideals of false freedom, fatherlessness and godlessness. Since they dominate the world's press, they have an easy time of it. Millions upon millions of copies of these newspapers flutter among mankind every day and hammer these lying ideals into their brains

---

[1] The Jewish private scholar Dr. Walter Rathenau, son of the late director of the Allgemeine Elektrizitätsgesellschaft Berlin, wrote in the *Neue Freie Presse* (Vien-na) on December 25, 1909: "Three hundred men (Jewish banking captains, noted by the author), who all know each other, dominate the economic life of Europe."

The Jew Dr. Moritz Kohn wrote about the all-dominating power of Judaism, according to the *Hammer* of June 1, 1912, No. 239, p. 281): "Without having been absorbed, the Jewish spirit prevails where it was hardly tolerated before. Without us, no potentate in the world today can do the slightest thing, for we control the money market. No word that we do not want comes into the public domain, for we control the press. No thought that we do not like enters the circle of thought of the educated, for we control the stage."

and hearts. By destroying the productive middle classes, by erecting department stores and whorehouses, by the most shameless and filthy advertising, they know how to artificially arouse, nourish, spread, and stimulate unnatural and perverted desires in the masses, just to "make" money, and more and more money.

According to plan, healthy, happy people, are systematically transformed into miserable creatures, sick in body and soul, at odds with themselves and God and the world, desperate creatures, who are now easily stirred up against the existing order. Wherever masses are stirred up under the lying slogan of "freedom and progress," it is members of this race who carry out this agitation. The founder of Social Democracy was a Jew, and Jews are its leaders to this day. They call the arbitrariness and licentiousness which they arouse in the masses "freedom", a freely chosen duty to the Germans, and "progress", the chaos which it is their advantage to bring about. For only in chaos can the wheat of this chaotic race flourish; where order, discipline and custom prevail, it cannot flourish.

And the German workers, deceived and lied to by their Jewish and Judaized leaders, do not even suspect that they are only a means to the end of these "corrupters of the people" to satisfy their own greed for power and money and to establish on their backs the rule of "capital" once and for all.[2]

Hermann gained a frightening insight into these connections from an exchange of letters that one of these "corrupters of the people" had conducted with the Councilor:

> Dear friend and patron!
> I have received the honorable order from our secret committee to ask you once again for the donation of a larger small sum. It concerns 308,000 Marks—a trifle for you—for the purchase of the *Geragemünder Newspaper* and the *City and National Edition* of Eberhausen.
> The newspapers are now both available together for the above amount. After our advertising center has been hanging the bread basket higher and higher on them for years, the desired breakdown has promptly and surely occurred. I myself am in third place with a mortgage of 45,000 Marks. Bills of approximately double the amount are in my hand. When I present, the owner must sell. Quite a simple matter.

---

[2] See Appendix.

Stooge—harmless goy—naturally available. Founding of the LLC already in progress.

Please do not send the remittance to me, but to our "Charitable Fund for Needy Co-religionists", as always.

> With excellent esteem
> Frankfurter M. d. R.

––––––––

Dr. Fritz Frankfurter M. d. R.
Most honored!

I have received your letter of the 12th. But I think you are beginning to go crazy! What are these two cheap papers for? Do you imagine that they can be used to create an artificial bull market or bear market for coffee and cotton? And 308,000 marks? Such a sum is a Bagatelle to you? Have you ever calculated the interest rate, if you set it at only 5½ percent?

> Not to be done!
> Burghamer

––––––––

Esteemed friend and patron!

Your much appreciated letter proves to me that you still know how to joke. May the God of our fathers preserve your divine humor! The famous poet Shakespeare could envy you for it!

Of course, you cannot make these two "International Newspapers" directly serve your noble purposes. However, as you know already, we collect everything into the same barn! And thereby you profit nevertheless most of all! Our great plans can only be realized if we control the press of all countries. The great founder of our Alliance already said that! In France, England, and America, as well as in the other European countries, we have long been in the saddle.

Only in Germany do we still have problems, even though we already have direct or indirect control of over 90 percent of the entire press there. The leading papers in Berlin and the provinces are already entirely in our hands, with only a few exceptions, which the tenacious conservatives and Pan-Germans and a few Catholics still dispute with us. But even among them, we've already succeeded so far that they no longer jostle us too violently at least. Skill goes after the bread! You will seldom have read anything anti-Semitic in most of these timid papers in recent years, and you will even find our people eagerly propagating them. And the part below the line is no less important for us than the political one above the line. Yes, it is precisely here that we can work quite unobtrusively for our cause.

But we are still missing the small provincial papers! We now depend on them above all. The pastors, judges, doctors, senior teachers, the officers of the small and medium-sized garrisons, in short, the representatives of the solid middle class of both denominations, who, along with conservatives and pan-Germans, are the main pillars of throne and altar, must be systematically brought over to us. They are quite happy—to put it another way, and not use the reactionary word, "infected"—they are addicted to quick earnings, to the need for amusements and the increased demands on life and all the little jokes, which we stage-managed with such visible success in the big cities with the help of the press and the theater.

And these capable people are, of course, like all Germans, no less amenable to phrases and catchwords than the already somewhat brighter stuff of the big cities. The German swears by everything printed. So all that matters is that we make everything in the papers that is accessible to him body and mind suitable to give grist to our mills. You should just observe these people in their local pubs! If there is a difference of opinion on political, scientific, or artistic matters, what is written in the newspaper always decides for them. All that matters is that these tame German minds do not notice anything. For this purpose, it is sufficient to make extensive use of the words "German" and "national" and to advocate their repeated demands for salary increases in a bold and dashing manner.

If, furthermore, one tries to tell the German philistine what he wants to hear, to praise everything that can serve as an excuse for his stupid activities, one soon has a winning game. Nothing is easier than to fascinate the German with the words "culture," "freedom of mind and conscience," and so on. He can no more stand the reproach of intolerance and backwardness than he can be forced to do something against his conscience. But everybody rides their own hobbyhorse, and it's only a question of guiding them in such a way that they ride it for us without even realizing it! To dull this all too lively German conscience and to build its convictions on our ideas and premises, that is the skill which we must practice and develop ever more perfectly!

For this purpose, the reactionary concepts of God and immortality, emperor, king, and fatherland, which are the ultimate and real obstacles to the realization of our plans, must be torn out of even the most stubborn Christian minds and replaced by our slogans "world and universal-soul", "freedom and progress", "equality and fraternity", "humanity and humaneness", and so on. The Association of German Freethinkers and the Dissidents' Association alone can accomplish just as little as our well-behaved monists with their scientific Sunday devotions. (I recently attended one such Ostwald service and had trouble remaining serious. These Germans are simply delicious!)

Well, that's not enough. It can only be done through the press. In the feature pages and in the "women's supplement" - a nice word, by the way, isn't it? - we have the best opportunity to infiltrate the Germans little by little with our ideas. Oh, if the good German housewives had only suspected that their "Fashion Review", "German Newspaper for Cleaning und Handicraft", "Home and Hearth", "The German Nursery", "Journal of the German Housewife", and all the innocuous family magazines are staged and financed by us! Apropos! The poem "Ahasver's Merry Wandering Song," recently published in the magazine "Aktion" by that unfortunate Paul Mayer, otherwise one of our most hopeful, was a huge flop! We immediately relieved the careless young man, who here exposed all our cards, from his editor's post. Thank God the "Germans" did not notice anything further!

German beer and the thrice holy morning and evening pint is an immeasurable blessing for us! God keep the Germans thirsty! No matter how hungry they may be as students, the beer finally washes away all their hunger! Once the state examination has been passed successfully and the state nursery has finally been reached, then farewell Dr. Faustus! The scandal sheets, the casino, the bowling club, at best the reading circle, and whoever can afford it, an occasional presentation of "The Robbers," will then satisfy all their intellectual and revolutionary needs. Thanks to this delicious barley juice, we have, so to speak, quite virgin soil in front of us, which is easy to plow and promises a great yield. You can see this in the success of our funny pages. There is hardly a pub or barber in the whole of the Holy German Empire where the satirical "Simplizissimus," the "Comic Pages" and our many illustrated journals are not on display. What our people can achieve by way of ribaldry and suggestion in national and religious matters borders on the miraculous!

But it works, it works! You won't find anything anymore and the circulation figures rise from month to month! Strange people these Germans! A family man, who would chase his daughter out of his house without a second thought because of a misstep, slurps up with pleasure the obscenities we put in front of him and finds nothing but grimaces in the - between us, often all too hideous - "modern art". Even the word "modern"! What a service it has already rendered us!

Actually, we can cover everything that matters to us with it, and men and women of all classes and strata fall for it like flies for sugar! Just think of fashion! Who would dare to go out dressed "unfashionably"! The coup has actually succeeded brilliantly for us! And it is also quite pleasant for us! One does not need to go to the ballet or to the Variété at all! Everything one wishes to see in the cute girls is now available for free on the street and in the very finest society! Splendid! But what am I telling you! You are an expert in that! (By the way, how are you satisfied with the blonde Westphalian I imported for you from Lüdenscheid a few months ago? Fresh as roses! Right?!)

But I've gotten off topic. So can we buy the papers? I assume I've convinced you?

As already mentioned, please send the money to our "charity fund"!

In pleasant expectation of your philanthropic promise.

I remain always your most devoted, in excellent esteem.

Frankfurter, M. d. R.

P.S. I would be happy to visit you personally, in order to explain everything to you in person in more detail! But I know you don't like visitors, hence this long letter.

Dr. Fritz Frankfurter M. d. R.

Most honored!

With kind regards, I confirm your letter of the 14th with your detailed remarks. But don't you have to admit yourself that we are making a tremendous mistake on our side. Far too much publicity for us! Far too much chutzpah! The "Berlin Daily Paper" makes us the biggest Risches [anti-Semites]! "The Frankfurter Newspaper" is much more careful in that regard! This one works much more indirectly! But the Daily Paper makes all Germans out to be Pan-Germans! It is very stupid to think of all Germans as stupid! The conservatives and Pan-Germans are certainly not stupid! They have known for a long time what we want, because the Berlin Daily Paper shouts it too loudly. I fear in the last years we have lost all the good opportunities we have had! Can you please inform me how our things stand? But, do so in writing, if you would, so that I have time to think everything through. I am not averse to doing this with the newspapers, but first I need to see things more clearly.

Yours sincerely

Burghamer.

Mr. Councilor of Commerce Burghamer

Most honored friend and patron!

Basically, you are not wrong. Certainly, the gentlemen from Jerusalem Street are a bit too eager. But don't forget, the Berlin Daily Paper is our central organ, and with its subscriber base of over a quarter of a million, it is the leading German newspaper. It is entitled to take some liberties! Don't forget that it is almost the only and the most widespread German daily newspaper that is also read overseas, and that it's news about German conditions and circumstances abroad are considered authentic. So it is quite good to keep one's mouth a little full. The impression must be created abroad that barbaric conditions prevail in Germany, that the German people languish in slave chains and that they have no greater desire than to abolish the monarchy. Do not think that we underestimate the intelligence and the power of the Conservatives and Pan-Germans!

But precisely because they realize where we want to go and every German who cares about German future should actually be an Pan-German, that is why these people are so dangerous to us, and that is why they must be denigrated by every possible means at home and abroad. Since they are at the same time the unwavering loyalists of the king and emperor, everything must be done to discredit them even at the top.

Also, don't forget that since we have nothing positive to substitute for what we must undermine in order to achieve our goals, we depend on the scolding and yelling and bullying. We would be downright lost if we didn't have Social Democracy, on whose back we are swimming. Of course, we have just as little use for the social-democratic state of the future as for a strong monarchy, as bad luck would only put us into the fire. Basically, we want exactly the opposite of what Social Democracy wants: the absolute domination of international capital, which is already today largely in our hands. The democratization of the Empire is the indispensable prerequisite for this, and with it we are on the most beautiful path. We are making giant strides forward!

The only serious obstacle still lies in the Prussian Parliament. But once we have the right to vote in the Reichstag in Prussia, then parliamentary government in the Reich will come as surely as the child after the wedding, and everything else will then be only a question of time. In this, the government is our strongest ally. The leading gentlemen, insofar as they still belong to the older generation, are truly afraid of us. The accusation of being anti-social or illiberal, of not "keeping up with the times" or of "not understanding the signs of the times" today makes even the most dried-up bureaucrat gush a cold sweat with fear.

And the leading gentlemen of the younger generation have already been inoculated with the bacillus of the opportunistic-egoistic view of life to such an extent that they are hardly any different from us. Old Prussian simplicity and thriftiness can hardly be found among them anymore. They consume money like hay and are therefore absolutely dependent on us, because their manors have long since been mortgaged by us.

Do not get me wrong! There is nothing to be done with "gifts of honor"! Beware! Unfortunately, we are still a long way from reaching that point with them! In France, England and America, these blessed countries of freedom, we are already much further ahead thanks to the parliamentary system! No! But why do we have our daughters! Our biblical ancestors already did the most wonderful business with them. In Germany, people are already so unprejudiced in religious matters that denominational differences hardly play a role in a marriage! Fine! Then we'll just have little Rebecca baptized. Protestant or Catholic or monist, just as you wish.

As is usually the case when we do business, we kill two birds with one stone. On the one hand, those up there become more and more dependent on us, and then at the same time our daughters bring the necessary impact of our blood on Germany.[3] This is the surest way to get rid of anti-Semitism.

Well, you know what I mean! But even in this way, the wonderful adaptability of the Germans to all kinds of foreign things comes in quite handy. The business competition into which they are forced by us, and the resulting continued intercourse with us, has already given rise to a breed of Jewish Christians who leave nothing to be desired in terms of authenticity. That is just what business brings with it. A good businessman today must be a Jew, one way or another, otherwise he's left behind and can't hold his own.

For all these reasons, praise and thanks be to God, we are missing today the politics of the strong hand. Because we are related by marriage, there are so many connections and relationships back and forth that the career of a higher official

---

[3] See Appendix.

now costs such enormous sums, since taking part in all kinds of luxury and glamorous trappings has become such a natural prerequisite that many from our circles, baptized and unbaptized, are up there and consciously or unconsciously influence the whole machine so that it works as we need it.[4]

It will be a great thing when the brakes of the Prussian House of Representatives do not work anymore! I am looking forward to that day! Then we finally will have won the game! Then farewell to the Hohenzollerns and Wittelsbachs and the rest of the German princes! The republic is then only a matter of time! And if only then we will have the United States of Europe! Oh my! The business! Nothing to think about!

Well, unfortunately, we haven't gotten that far yet, and many a drink must still be brewed for the ponderous Germans before their eyes glaze over. Above all, they must not be allowed to catch their breath! The government must be plunged endlessly from one embarrassment to another, how and by what means is all the same. The individual social strata, classes, and professions must be so annoyed at the top that, out of sheer obstinacy, they run to the Socialists or get twisted into the yarn. It's all the same thing to us, because we have them on the leash for a long time. A wonderful anti-government dilemma we have in social legislation! Praise and thanks and reward to its inventor!

And since we always add the costs of the new taxes to the business, without the public noticing anything, so we're killing again several birds with one stone. Up there in the Olympic regions, however, it's a pure club of the harmless. Truly, a lot can happen before they notice anything! Only "him!" I don't trust him. He has damn sharp eyes! But as long as our luminaries have direct telephone contact with him, there is no danger from there.

Unfortunately, the same cannot be said of the younger gentleman. But by the time he has something to say, we will

---

[4] In the great debate on Jews at the session of the Prussian House of Representatives on November 22, 1880, Rep. Bachem quoted from a Reform Jewish paper in Mainz: "German Jewry is now working so vigorously, so immensely, so unchanged on the new culture and science that most of Christendom is consciously or unconsciously guided by the spirit of modern Jewry."

have been in the saddle for a long time! Now is the critical time for us! Unquestionably! But we will make it, if not these ...

The conservatives, namely, and the damned Pan-Germans with their active educational work! They are making us sweat like pigs! You are quite right when you warn us not to take them for fools! We must work against them by all infernal means! Otherwise, they are capable of screwing up our entire butter business at the last hour! The best way is still to watch out if and how and when and where one of them needs money. Our fellow believers from Galicia and Poland, who go about their business from good to good, have already rendered us valuable services. It is a real blessing that a lieutenant of the guard can spend more in one year than ten thousand acres of land can yield.

And then there is this damnable racial doctrine which is now beginning to become fashionable! The impertinent thing is that one is beginning to realize that it is really not a question of religious denomination or anything of that sort, but purely and simply a question of race. Because, let's face it: In no country in the world are people so tolerant towards us Jews as in Germany. We can build as many synagogues as we want. The high and very highest leadership even appear for their initiation. But we don't care about that at all! We want to go somewhere completely different!

So there will still be hard battles with representatives of the race! For this very purpose, we must get complete control of the entire German press, to prevent the matter from becoming popular! The consequences would be unimaginable! The *furor teutonicus* is not to be trifled with! Therefore, believe me, dear friend, every little paper in the Kingdom is important now! We have to plug up every mouse hole, even the smallest, through which anything could penetrate into the people, which does not fit into our concept![5]

Apart from that, of course, it still means getting our people into the leading positions of all professions! We succeed in this from year to year more and more. It is really only the army and the navy are causing difficulties for us. But with

---

[5] See Appendix.

the help of baptism, we are making gratifying progress there as well. Unfortunately, as long as the officer corps chooses their comrades themselves, baptism does not always work. Well, once we have equal suffrage in Prussia and a parliamentary government in the Kingdom, we will make short work of this braid as well. In any case, we already have the upper hand in the spiritual realm. Just look at the list of university professors![6] Not to mention literature, art, and theater! And the numbers, which are not of our blood, must already dance to our tune, if they want to dance at all! And they dance! And quite splendidly! What else would we have our critics for otherwise? And in Berlin, apart from the director of the Royal Theater, there is not a single theater director who is not circumcised! Indeed, wonderful! And our actors and singers! Truly, in the synagogue we are no more among ourselves than in the theater! And then these various Goethe,

---

[6] In 1892, there were already 175 Jews among 1377 university professors = 12%; among 597 private lecturers, already 120 Jews = 20%! In 1905, according to the university calendar, there were 268 Jewish professors and 201 private lecturers, a total of 469 Jews among 3140 university teachers = 15%. The baptized Jews are only partially included and the Jewish teachers of the commercial and other colleges are not included! Taking into account the baptism, the number of Jewish university teachers in individual faculties already increases up to 60%!

No less disastrous is the ratio of Jewish students to German students. According to the "Statistische Korrespondenz" (Statistical Correspondence), in the last years (1907) in the German Reich, 25 out of 10,000 young Protestants attended the university, only 13 out of 10,000 Catholics, but out of 10,000 Jews no less than 160! The Jews thus exceed the average by a factor of eight! Downright frightening is the overcrowding of our Gymnasien and Realschulen with Jewish children. The grammar schools of Berlin had 11,418 pupils in 1887, among them 2346 Jewish = 20%, while the Jewish population of Berlin was only 5%. The French Gymnasium in Berlin was attended by 42% Jews in the same year! In 1904, at the Wilhelms-gymnasium in Berlin, among 487 students, there were 250 Jews = 51.54%! At the Sophiengymnasium, among 568 pupils there were 249 Jews = 43.84%! The French Gymnasium had 102 Jews among 217 pupils = 47.1 %! Of the public higher girls' schools, the Sophienschule had among 679 pupils 298 Jews = 44 %, the Charlottenschule of 710 pupils even 351 = 49 %!!! One has to admire the harmlessness of German parents who send their children to such schools! There is no doubt that at such educational institutions, the fact that a Jew sets the tone and determines the overall spirit of the institution through his loudness, lack of shame, and sexual precociousness! German sense and German morals cannot possibly be at home in such schools!

Kleist, Hebbel, and Kant societies and other cultural societies and writers' associations! It all works great.[7]

The Trade is of course ours! Industry, but unfortunately
only in part. Some are still hanging on to outdated concepts.
But even they will need money at some point. The general
German Teachers' Association has become very valuable to
us, and the middle civil service promises no less favorable
success. The main thing now is to reduce authority and promote self-consciousness. But for this we also need the last
provincial newspapers! So, once again, we can count on you,
most esteemed friend and patron? The matter will pay off!
You can be sure of that!

But now I have rattled on enough! My machine is already
smoking! Because I have to look after the box myself, because of all that! But the main thing is that I have convinced
you! Therefore my best thanks in advance on behalf of our
secret committee.

Your devoted friend and admirer
Frankfurt M. d. R.

Mr. Dr. Fritz Frankfurter M. d. R.
Most honored!

In confirmation of your letter of the 16th, I am ready to
do it. Since, with the acceptance, you will earn around 25
percent yourself, we will agree if we set the 'rotten business'
to around 300,000, which means you still earn 10 to 15 thousand. There is no other way to do it.

A Cashier's check for the Charity fund account is enclosed in the amount mentioned.

Yours sincerely
Burghamer

With bated breath, Hermann had finished reading the correspondence. So it
had already come that far! The German people were being contaminated
and poisoned according to plan! Something had to be done before it was

---

[7] See Appendix.

too late! The only thing that could and had to be happen at all was to inform the government and the people about the nature, purpose, aim and
plan of this race. Hermann immediately sent a copy of the correspondence
to the Emperor, the Imperial Chancellor, to all the Princes of the Federation, their governments and to individual members of the Reichstag.

In the meantime, he continued to arrange the estate.

Only in the last fifteen years had the Councilor of Commerce also
dealt with the exploitation of patents. The inventors were settled once and
for all with low lump sums. Only a few had a share in the permanent earnings, while he earned millions with them. The Councilor himself did not
use the patents for manufacturing purposes; he only granted the right to
manufacture in the form of licenses. It was not important to him to do
something useful, to "make" money was his only ambition! Money, money, money! How he put it together didn't matter to him. The only value-
creating enterprise in which he had ever participated was the factory run by
Hermann, and that was exclusively Hermann's work.

Two hundred and sixty-four million marks alone were in the cash
accounts that the Councilor had with the banks. But strange! Only a small
fraction of this sum, a little over ten million, was placed in German banks.
The entire immense remainder of over a quarter of a billion was invested in
English and American banks, but mostly in Swiss and Swedish banks. Truly, the Councilor was well prepared for the coming world war! He had
placed the lion's share in neutral countries, and in the presumably hostile
ones he had left only so much to be able to make his war profits there, too,
through the mediation of his fellow racial comrades living abroad. From
neutral countries he could send his reserves to friend and foe depending on
the course of events!

The Councilor of Commerce had bequeathed no less than 50 million
marks to the 'Alliance Israélite Universelle'. The will contained the note
that it had already been informed of this inheritance and had been author-
ized by him to withdraw the sum from his Paris bank immediately upon
learning of his death. The rest of the huge fortune was inherited in equal
shares by the Madame Councilor and Elisabeth. Since Elisabeth had died
in the meantime, Hermann had now become heir to a fortune of over 100
million marks that was allotted to her. He didn't doubt for a minute that he
shouldn't keep this accumulated money for himself. All he was thinking
about was what charitable purpose it could best be used for, and he soon
figured that out too.

From the answers that he received to his petitions, Hermann saw the
incomprehension with which the ruling circles faced the danger by Jews

that threatened Germany's entire future. The emperor's civil cabinet replied that the document was "not suitable for submission to the highest authorities. The replies of the cabinets of the other federal princes were similar, as far as they took any notice of it at all. Only the Bavarian government explained that she was well aware of these "evils", but that unfortunately, according to the "state of affairs", a remedy could not be found. The German Chancellor did not comment at all. The future of the German people seemed to be of no concern to him. The members of the German Reichstag thanked him for the valuable material, but warned Hermann to be on his guard. Anyone who dared to take action against Jewry was not only putting his life and fortune at risk, but also his honest name, since this race would stop at nothing to make its opponents harmless.

Hermann had no regard for himself or for others, when it came to acting in accordance with his convictions. Danger could only irritate him, but could not hold him back. He therefore quickly came to the decision to use the entire fortune inherited from the Councilor, after deducting the compulsory portion allotted to his son, to fight against Judaism. He had the rock-solid confidence that the German people would of their own accord find the ways and means to rid themselves of this enemy, once they had recognized him in all his terrible and insidious nature. He therefore donated a quarter of his inheritance, amounting to about 12 million marks, to a scientific society for the purpose of founding an institute for racial research and racial hygiene. He stipulated explicitly that all employees of this foundation, from scholars and civil servants down to the last servant, must be ethnic Germans and not Jews. Any resident of Germany whose ancestors still had adherents of the Mosaic faith in their grandfather's lineage should be described as a Jew, as a member of a race alien to Germany, and not as a believer in any "religion".

A second quarter was transferred to an ethnic German association with the purpose of continuously enlightening the German people by word and writing about the nature and essence of Judaism and its ultimate conscious and unconscious goals. The remainder, amounting to more than 25 million marks, was used for the founding of ethnic German newspaper enterprises with the special aim of breaking the Jewish monopoly on newspaper advertising, on which the main power of the Jewish press was based.

In this way, Hermann Kämpfer sought to atone for the crimes his father-in-law had committed against the German people, but at the same time he was atoning for his own sin against the blood, of which he had become guilty through his marriage, half consciously, half unconsciously.

Never before had Hermann found the hustle and bustle of Greater Berlin so unbearable as since the death of Elisabeth. Because he lived on the out-skirts of the city at Reichskanzlerplatz in Charlottenburg and his factory was in Lichterfelde, he rarely came into contact with Berlin proper. He only entered the inner city when he had business there or had to go to one of the train stations to start a journey. Now, however, the arrangement of the estate and the settlement of inheritance and foundation matters took him to Berlin almost daily and forced him to spend hours and days there.

In doing so, he noticed that he was still overcome by that mixture of fear, despair, and inexpressible sadness that threatened to suffocate him when he first entered the metropolis from the Potsdam train station seven years ago. It was not the feeling of abandonment and helplessness that tends to overwhelm visitors from the provinces when they are exposed to the big city for the first time. This suffocating feeling was a different, more ominous kind. He had not been able to get rid of it since he had settled in Berlin, had married and had attained position and prestige.

Once, when he accompanied Elisabeth on a shopping trip to a de-partment store, this desolate feeling had overpowered him. These people scurrying about, shackled only by the most miserable interests of the mo-ment, reduced to the barest necessities, they seemed to have lost the last remnant of their divine dignity. They buzzed around like bluebottles. It was as if maggots and worms swarmed around him. Nameless pity and insurmountable disgust choked him. At that time, he had grabbed Elisabeth by the arm and pulled her out of the seething turmoil onto the street and into the car. When she questioned him in bewilderment, he silently waved her off. He ordered the driver to go out into the Grunewald as quickly as possible. There he stopped and spent some time in the fresh air, breathing for liberation. But the royal Prussian pines, set up and aligned like a regi-ment of guards, sandwich papers and scraps of newsprint lying around everywhere, the sparsely growing grass rising up out of the sandy March, did not give him the mood and strength to banish the horrible impressions.

He went home, hastily packed his suitcase with the most necessary things and proceeded to travel with Elisabeth for a few days to the Thurin-gian Forest. Only there in the mountains, under the rustling trees, between the murmuring brooks, on the heights and slopes, in grass and flowers, among the simple, natural, hardworking people, did the nightmare leave him and he find himself again.

Similar feelings, of which he was not yet able to give an account, had already seized him in his childhood when he entered a fair or was taken to a public amusement. Once, when, despite his reluctance, his father had put him on a merry-go-round with his siblings, he jumped off in the middle of the ride. Although he was bloodied in the fall, his enraged father, who interpreted his behavior as defiance, gave him a beating on the spot, to the great amusement of the crowd. Then Hermann had run away into the forest and had thrown himself crying into the grass. When he returned home in the evening, he calmly looked forward to further punishment, which, however, did not come at his mother's request. Since that time, he could no longer hear the loud, blaring carousel organs from afar. The same dark melancholy had later crept into his heart when he entered a pub for the first time as a student. For the same reason, as long as he was still unmarried, he had eaten his lunch or dinner in inns only on the direst occasions. If he could not eat at home with his landlady, he would buy something to eat at home or in the open air.

The noise, the commotion and tumult of the big city was unbearable to him. The eternal rattling and ringing of the streetcar! The thunder of the elevated and subway trains! The hissing and pounding, ear- and brain-piercing screeching of the tram brakes! The whirring and whizzing, tooting and trumpeting of the automobiles! The shouting of the criers and newspaper vendors! And between all this, these eternally rushing, running, stumbling, chasing people! What are they chasing? Money, money, only money! And from money to pleasure, and from pleasure to greed, and from greed again to pleasure and greed and finally into the grave and into the gray nothingness! That's what they think! What an awakening this will be for them one day! But they have no time for reflection and thinking! They must hurry and rush, run and chase, in order not to be late, not to be left behind, because the other is otherwise always already there and has already occupied his place!

When do these people actually sleep? Or when do they just rest? At night? That's when life and the swarming and surging begins! And Lucifer's torches shine in addition! Fireworks flare up, fountains of colored light, whole clusters and sheaves of blazing, dazzling rays shoot up incessantly from every street and square into the black-blue night sky. Lightning, not followed by thunder, repeatedly rips apart the same front of the house at the same spot, over and over, six times a minute; each time they set fire to a giant hat bearing the inscription "Tipp-topp!" Six times a minute, three hundred and sixty times an hour, two thousand one hundred and sixty times in six hours, "Tipp-topp!" Rockets shoot up and light an inscription "The new method! Success! Wealth! Guarantee!" Flaming snakes and fire wheels spin ceaselessly around a cigarette and necktie poster.

On the gable of a department store, a sun, now red, now green, now violet, spins madly, spitting colored fire onto the roofs, houses, streets and squares below. A light arrow continues to jump back and forth between the double gables of a rival business. From one side, it points to the giant flame inscription: "Laundry sale! "Only tomorrow!" A gigantic illuminated frame stretched over several roofs, on the border of which a flaming snake continuously runs around shimmering in all colors of the rainbow, changes the inscription every five seconds: "Mayer's fat powder is unrivaled!", "Haarofärbin hair dye rejuvenates you by 20 years!", "Smart mothers feed with breast milk substitutes!", "Latest Parisian models just arrived", "Central Theater! For the 486th time, 'The Cinema Queen!'", "Palace Variety new programs daily!", "National Cinema! On the heights of life or the false countess!" etc. etc. It's like a satanic brain is constantly formulating new madness and insanity.

And above it all shined the eternal stars! Don't these people of the asphalt come to their senses when their eyes touch the sky? Were they still human at all? Hermann had once flown over Berlin on a balloon ride. From the balloon, this Berlin looked like a large honeycomb, and involuntarily the thought came to his mind that people built their cities out of instincts very similar to those of the animals. And truly, these people were also nothing more than animals, which lived only from physical drives and for such drives! This crawling and scrambling swarm was not aware that they possessed a divine spirit, coming from eternity and returning into eternity.

Hermann had always fled from this soulless city life to Elisabeth. Now he did it again. His thoughts stayed with her inaudibly, and when he came home tired and weary, it was as if she were around him just as before. The feeling of her living presence was so strong that, as before, he invited her to sit with him on the sofa at the twilight hour and chat with him a little. Then he took her in his arms, laid her delicate head against his chest, and dreamed with her by the fireside into the twilight of the winter night. He would also lay his head against her delicate neck or in her lap, and it was as if she were stroking his forehead and eye with her precious hand as she used to do, or running her delicate fingers through his hair.

No, the beloved woman was not dead! Now more than ever she was most intimately united with him, only she was detached from all sensual heaviness and material conditionality of earthly existence. Truly, his happiness in love and marriage would have been perfect only now, if the bodily presence of the unnatural child had not repeatedly embittered and destroyed it.

But now he had to atone for the grave sin he had committed all his life against the holy blood of his race. Not even the unselfish love from which his marriage with Elisabeth had sprung absolved him from this sin. His race had the right to demand from him renunciation of this marriage, and he had the duty to fulfill this demand. Only now, when this love had become an incorporeal union of souls, did he suspect the conditions under which he alone should have been allowed to enter into a union with Elisabeth. Their common task should have been to overcome the physical urges and to preserve that purely spiritual form of their love which had constituted the whole bliss of their marriage. Only now did Hermann understand the anxious premonitions that crept over him at that time, when, contrary to his inner voice, he went from engagement to marriage, under the compulsion of custom and morals.

Thus Hermann lived with his departed lover. Lately, however, he made a realization that seemed inexplicable to him. He often caught himself thinking not of Elisabeth, but of Röschen Brunner. As ridiculous as this seemed to him, and as much as he tried to overcome these thoughts, they returned again and again to the girl and that last night in May, when he grabbed her to himself in intoxication and passion, and she gave him spontaneously and without resistance the sweet blossom of her young body.

How long ago was that? About eight years! What could have become of her? Suddenly a hot thought shot through his mind: what if that passionate night had not remained without consequences? But then the girl would have written to him! She had written to him, but her first letters contained nothing of the sort. He had not answered them at all, and when two more letters arrived later at short intervals, he had first hesitated whether he should send them back unopened, since these relations could not lead to anything, since his heart belonged to Elisabeth. But then he had come to his senses, he did not want to cause such pain to the girl and so he had put the letters aside, unopened. They must still be lying in a certain drawer of his desk, and now suddenly the impulse came over him to read them. He immediately found the letters where he suspected.

Hastily he tore open the first. It was as he had suspected. In unhappy, unspeakably sad, but not at all reproachful words, she told him that she felt she was carrying a child. She understood perfectly that he could not marry her, since she was of lowly birth, but she hoped that he would not abandon her now in her distress, even though he had not answered her earlier letters. In order to spare her old father the shame, and since he would chase her out of the house, she wanted to look for a position far away from home in a foreign city, where there was a clinic for such girls as she had now become, and where she would ask then to be admitted in order to give birth to the child.

But she did not have enough money to travel, she wanted to go to Leipzig. The train ride there would cost 11.80 marks, and then she would need some money for her first living expenses until she found a job, all in all she would need 25 marks. She asked him to send her this sum, since she knew of no one else she could ask. She said that she would pay him back the money in pennies and nickels as soon as she had earned that much. In the end, she assured him of her burning, inextinguishable love, and that she was actually quite happy now, despite everything, to have a child, which she had wanted since she was a little girl, when she was still playing with dolls. If it were a boy, she would have it christened Hermann, and if a girl, Hermoine.

When Hermann read this letter, he felt like a dishonorable lowlife, even like a criminal. Tentatively he opened the second letter, written about nine months of a year later. She began by saying that she had never really wanted to write him again, since he could never have loved her, otherwise he would have lent her the money she wanted. But she still loved him and for that reason could not marry another, although she had often had the opportunity to do so, because she could never forget him, especially now that she had such a sweet child by him. She said she never wanted to bother him again with letters in the future, especially since, as she had heard, he had become such a great and distinguished gentleman, and he was going to marry soon. But she would like to see his bride once. She had heard that she was a millionaire and very beautiful. But he need not worry that she will demand something from him again. She earned enough for herself and her child and had even saved something. She wanted to write to him today for the very last time that the child was a boy and already two months old. At birth he weighed almost nine pounds and was big and strong and healthy and already resembled his father. He had the same blue eyes, the same soft blond hair and the same fine white skin. Even his nose was beginning to become sharp and straight, just like his. The end of the letter read literally:

"Now I say goodbye to you for the last time, my dear darling. Even if you have forgotten me, I will never forget you.

I love you so true and hot,
until red roses turn white,
until white roses turn red,
I love you to death."

Your Rosele

It is not possible to describe the feelings that surged through Hermann's soul when he read these letters. After awakening from a kind of stupor, he immediately wrote to old Brunner to learn the girl's present whereabouts. After three days the letter came back with the note "Addressee deceased". The same post office, however, brought a second sealed registered letter in chancery format. It bore the heading "Leipzig Municipal Hospital. It contained an official letter from the hospital administration and a second sealed letter bearing Hermann's address, written by a woman's hand unknown to him. The official cover letter read:

"Dear Sir!
Yesterday afternoon at five o'clock, in the municipal hospital here, the unmarried Rosalinde Brunner, born in Heidelberg, 26 years old, for seven years a maid in the employ of the local city councilor Mr. Teichmüller, died of pneumonia. She left the stipulation that the following letter should be sent to you immediately after her death. By fulfilling the last will and testament of the deceased, we hereby sign

Respectfully,
Hospital Administration."

Moved, Hermann opened the enclosed sealed letter. It was written by Röschen herself with a trembling hand. The lines stood crookedly across the page, individual words fell out completely, as is the case when one writes in an uncomfortable position in bed. The letter read as follows:

"My dear Hermann!
I now have to die because I caught a bad cold when I was washing up the stairs. That's a shame, because I would have loved to have lived on. But nothing can be done now. I think of you all the time and still want to say goodbye to you and ask you to take care of our little boy. That won't matter to you now that you are a millionaire and your wife has died, as

my friend wrote me. Our little boy is already big now and goes to school. He has a very good head, which he got from you. He also resembles you completely. He is with my aunt Mrs. Barbara Bürgle in Neckargemünd, Eberbacherstrasse No. 21. I would have loved to look at you and our child once again. But it is not possible. Don't be angry with me if I write to you again today, but it is definitely the very last time.

A friend of mine, who is working in Berlin for a company very close to where you live, wrote me that you now also have a boy. But he looks like a Jewish boy. I had to laugh right away, because you have never suffered the Jew. Your dear wife has now already died, my comrade wrote to me. That really hurt me quite a bit for you. Is it true that she died of her second child? But now I must close, because my eyes are flickering again. Goodbye to you now, my dear sweet darling, for the very last time and take care of our little boy! It is becoming quite easy for me now that I have written to you. I include you in my dying prayers and I will pray to the dear Mother of God that she will always protect you and our little boy.

Yours faithfully, Rosele."

Hermann was deeply shaken. Now he could understand why he had thought of the girl constantly during the last days. Her thoughts had called his, and it drove him in her dying hour to seek out her letters and read them. Immediately he got on the train, and already a few days later he had his blond boy, his spitting image from head to toe, with him in Berlin.

The good craftsmen, who cared for the boy, could not be persuaded to accept any compensation. Rosel had always paid her board money punctually. She had even left her child a savings bank book in which 635 marks had been deposited. Faithfully, as Rosel had said in her last letter, the foster parents delivered the book to Hermann. Since they could not be persuaded to accept any gift, Hermann donated a few thousand marks to the local poor fund. From Neckargemünd, Hermann had gone with his boy to Leipzig to Rosel's grave. He had brought for her a giant wreath of snowdrops, mayflowers, and violets, with which she had once decorated his desk every spring. Then he ordered her a tombstone of snow-white marble with the golden inscription, "Love never ceases."

The unexpected fulfillment of his soul's desire to have a child in his own image filled Hermann with a happiness he had never known. From the bottom of his heart, he thanked Providence, which so visibly guided his life. Now he had a new task, which was worth living for. Now it was necessary to educate this child, to prepare a man out of him, a man who should be useful to the fatherland. The hard experiences of his life, the serious mistakes that had been made by his parents and school in his own upbringing, were not to be in vain now. He himself would guide the education of his true child and watch day and night over his life, development and growth, but this blessing should now also benefit his unfortunate ersatz child, that was his decision. Since Elisabeth's death he had neglected him completely. His fatherly love should now also belong to him again and he should become a person for whom his soul is more important than all the apparent happiness in the world.

Heinrich was six and Hermann seven years old. From Easter onward, Heinrich attended the pre-school of the local grammar school. But the father gave up on this plan. From now on, he decided to teach both boys and prepare them together for the sixth year of the humanistic grammar school. The deftly organized factory ran almost by itself, so he could spare the time.

Although Hermann was a natural scientist, he held on to the humanistic education that he himself had enjoyed. It gave the spirit a breadth and depth that a one-sided technical education could never produce. In the widespread effort to give children unilateral practical vocational training as early as possible, Hermann identified one of the main causes of the barren materialism that had been circling the globe for several decades and has alienated mankind from its divine destiny. Germany, called to the spiritual leadership of all mankind, has all the more the duty to constitute the professional education of its sons on a spiritual foundation. This is at the same time most suitable for a practical profession, for it is simply not true and merely one of those numerous uncritical slogans that a classical education educates impractical paper scholars! Our greatest practitioners of life, generals, statesmen, natural scientists, chemists, technicians were humanists! Just go through the whole line of men, headed by Moltke, Bismarck, Alexander von Humboldt, Justus von Liebig, Werner von Siemens!

Above all, it is important to make a whole person and character out of a child. Such a child will find his way in the practical world all by himself and through his comprehensive education he will always be superior to those who are only practically educated. However, classical studies should not be the main purpose of the Gymnasium, but should only be the background and standard for the German style, German life and German greatness. It is not necessary for the student to be able to write entire essays in the classical languages or to read the classics without the aid of good translations. That is, in fact, dead paper scholarship. Instead, one should get to know a far greater number of the classics and each one of them far more thoroughly than is possible with the method hitherto used. German history and German language instruction must also be the main focus of the humanistic Gymnasium as well. Physical education should be no less important than intellectual education—in the original sense of the word "Gymnasium"—without exaggeration, of course.

This is how Hermann wanted to educate the two boys and he resolved, if necessary, to set up a private school himself that would be run according to these principles. Above all, however, it was important now to free little Hermann from the stain of his illegitimate birth. He immediately took the steps required by law to give him his own name. After this was done, he began the consequent instruction. He had set up a special schoolroom for this purpose.

Little Hermann quickly got used to his father and the new situation. The fact that his mother had told him a lot about his "little father", as Hermann had gathered from the child's reports, was a major factor in this. But the father's heart was stabbed when he learned from him stories that he had often received gifts from his mother, which he, the father, had supposedly sent to her for the boy. When the boy asked why his father did not live with them, as he did "with his other child," his mother had always answered that his father did not have time for that, because he always had to be in Berlin to earn a lot of money so that he, the little boy, could one day become a rich, distinguished gentleman.

But if he was always good and hardworking, and always brought home good grades, then as soon as he was 10 years old, he would be allowed to visit his father in Berlin, in order to ask him if he could go to "high school", so that he could also become a "studied" gentleman like his father. Hermann was put into no small embarrassment by the boy's question as to why Heinrich had always been allowed to stay in Berlin with his father, while he had had to stay with his aunt for so long in Neckargemünd. Finally, Hermann came up with the flimsy excuse that there wasn't room for two boys at his aunt's in Neckargemünd. When the boy all the more made the logical objection that he could have lived in Berlin, his father cut him off by taking him to himself, hugging and kissing him so hard that he lost his breath.

Although little Hermann had already attended elementary school for three quarters of a year, his father decided to teach both boys together at the same level and to start the lessons with both of them from the beginning. This may have contributed from the outset to Hermann's feeling of superiority over his younger half-brother. He treated him with almost condescending good nature, which amused his father. However, this good-naturedness soon turned into jealousy, even downright hostility, when Heinrich not only soon caught up with his older brother, but even showed himself superior to him in some subjects. This was especially the case in arithmetic. Heinrich had long since been able to solve simple adding and subtracting problems in his head, while Hermann still had to laboriously compile the results on the calculator.

It had happened once that the little Teuton, in a rage over this, threw the entire calculating machine over the heap, so that his father, who was, however, quietly pleased about this outburst of temper, had to punish him seriously. Hermann was by no means less talented in arithmetic than Heinrich. It was only a certain dreaminess and not staying on task that made it difficult for him. In the middle of a task, if his eye happened to glance at the window, he could get caught spellbound by a passing cloud. On such an occasion, he once asked quite abruptly whether "cloud animals could really bite" and "what they eat and where they sleep". But if the father then energetically engaged him, the arithmetic went excellently. Such fantasies, however, did not distracted the younger boy's mind, any more than that of a juggler who stares at his balls and throws them around with dexterity without letting them fall to the ground. Yes, it seemed that with the younger one all the impressions he received from the outside world first passed through a kind of number-sieve, in whose narrow mesh everything got caught that was number and measure, dullest soberness and usefulness.

For the first Christmas that Hermann spent with his two children, he had prepared a particularly beautiful Christmas tree. While little Hermann, his cheeks flushed, gazed into all the radiance as if into an unearthly world, Heinrich had first critically examined his gifts, then looked at the Christmas tree very calmly and attentively made the observation: "There are 56 lights."

Hermann was a great believer in visual instruction. He had acquired dozens of those large, beautiful panels that show children the various fields of human activity and commercial industry, a farm, a blacksmith's shop, a cobbler's shop, etc. Here the different dispositions of the two children became characteristically revealed. The father often took the two boys on excursions so that they could actually get to know the circumstances and objects that these visual images represented.

One day they visited a farm. On this occasion, Hermann, who as the son of a farmer and was interested in such things, had also inquired about the current prices of cattle, without it being his intention to instruct the boys about this as well. When the boys were supposed to recount in the next lesson what they had heard and seen on their last excursion, the only thing Heinrich remembered was that a milk cow cost 350 marks and a calf 60 to 75 marks. When his father finally asked him to tell what he had seen with his own eyes, he had nothing to say except that a cow was bigger than a calf, a calf bigger than a sheep, a sheep bigger than a chicken, that the cows only gave milk and no coffee, and that the fresh milk tasted awful. Little Hermann, on the other hand, described a vivid picture of farming activities, as far as he had gotten to know them that day from his own experience. In addition, he had so much to say about farmhands and maids, animals and equipment, that it was obvious with what unselfish interest the boy looked at people and things, while Heinrich looked at them only from the point of view of utility.

The different imaginative powers of the two boys, especially in a creative sense, came to the fore when it came to retelling fairy tales and stories. It became apparent that both boys had excellent memories. While little Hermann very easily lost the thread of the chronological order and added all sorts of details of his own imagination to his retelling, even expanding minor facts of the narrative into completely new stories, Heinrich always delivered a highly sober report, whose strict objectivity surpassed the original narrative even in that it now offered a single, straightforward line, stripped of all decorative tendrils. But when it came to inventing stories himself, Heinrich failed completely. At best, he told, with meager changes, what he had already heard.

The big difference in talent and character of the two boys was also revealed in their play. Hermann built entire houses, cathedrals, and fortresses with the stone construction kit without any models, Heinrich, on the other hand, could only be persuaded by his father's special instructions to try his hand at such building activities. Even the humblest construction was not possible without a template. He did not get beyond a simple yoke, consisting of a support and a crossbeam. He preferred to lay the stones together in monotonous, endless, meandering bands, or to form simple symmetrical shapes like stars or squares, or even completely meaningless flourishes without any articulated structure.

While Hermann arranged his lead soldiers into tactical formations, fought entire battles with them and shot them to pieces with his pea cannon, Heinrich amused himself by lining up the soldiers side by side, like pipe organs according to their size, with no distinction between the branches of arms, and on a small scale to determine how many smaller warriors went on a larger one or on the different stones of the construction box.

The large rocking horse, which belonged to both boys together, had soon become so exclusively Hermann's property that the father purchased a somewhat smaller one for Heinrich. Now "races" were organized by Hermann. Despite the fact that he hit his brother's horse fiercely with his whip, it did not really want to get going. He himself rode his horse with such impetuosity that one day it overturned, and it was a miracle the bold rider didn't break his neck or legs.

Every day and basically in any weather, the father took the two boys for a walk in the nearby Grunewald Park. On Sundays, they took longer day trips into the wider surroundings of Berlin, to the Havel lakes, to Potsdam, to Rheinsberg, to the Spreewald. Hermann showed a pronounced sympathy for nature. He collected insects, plants, and stones, caught newts and slow-moving worms, even grass snakes, and never tired of researching and asking questions. Heinrich, on the other hand, always stayed with his father and preferred to be led by the hand. Hermann boldly crossed over small ditches, even when he once jumped too short and had to crawl to the shore like a wet poodle. Heinrich would not have been able to cross a narrow footbridge or a small stream at any price if his father had not carried him or at least held him by both arms and guided him. But even that did not happen without a fearful outburst. While Hermann could not get enough running, jumping, and climbing, Heinrich, whose badly built feet made it difficult for him to walk, soon got tired and had to be carried by his father.

He showed an almost comical fear of geese. It's true that Hermann was also scared at first of these chattering animals when they came at his legs with their hissing necks. But when his father laughed at him because of his fear, he remained the next time, he stood bravely and with a stick he had picked up along the way, he cut the neck of the onrushing bird in half. He was dismayed to see the dead animal wriggling in the dust. The horrible certainty forced itself on him that he had killed a living creature of God, that he had shed blood. Ashamed and pale as a corpse, the boy awaited his punishment from his father. Hermann perceived what was happening in his child's mind and only punished him lightly for wantonly teasing the animals. He considered it a practical demonstration of what can happen if one lets oneself be carried away by foolish and hasty actions. Besides, he paid with a grin for the Sunday roast, which the young hero now had to carry home in his little backpack as punishment. Heinrich, however, cried out loudly when he saw the blood trickling over the snow-white feathers. However, when he was satisfied that there was no danger to his own life, he looked at the dying animal with such heartless curiosity that he was seriously rebuked by his father.

Heinrich also had tremendous respect for the locomotive. When the train pulled into the station hall, he would always cower fearfully behind his father. Hermann, on the other hand, couldn't get his nose close enough to the train. It gave him great pleasure to stand in the "wind" that the train was blowing. When he was energetically pulled back by his father, he said: "It can't run me down dead, because he has to stay on the rails!" He couldn't get enough of the locomotive. The father had to regularly miss the first light rail train on the way home with the children to give the boy an opportunity to see the engine up close. His dearest wish was to be allowed to ride on a locomotive one day. He wanted to be an engineer, that was clear! But Heinrich asked whether the man at the front of the machine also had to have a ticket, or whether he could ride along "for free".

The father insisted on teaching the two boys athletics at an early age. Twice a week he did light gymnastics and calisthenics with them. Above all, they had to learn how to swim. He gave them these lessons himself. The swimming lessons were always a celebration for the blond boy. The black-haired one, however, was so afraid of water that he had to be dragged in by force. When he didn't want to overcome his fear, his father made short work of it. He tied him to the swimming line and, despite his screams and wriggling, threw him over the railing of the pool into the water. And while Hermann was soon jumping, swimming, and diving like a frog, Heinrich never learned to swim.

After two years, both boys were ready to register for the Sexta. Each passed the entrance examination without any difficulty, but Heinrich did considerably better than Hermann, even though he was more than a year younger. He was better than him in arithmetic. He could not be baffled or upset by anything unless there was direct danger to his life, while Hermann's attention was easily diverted in the new environment.

The school was a reformed Gymnasium. The curriculum was entirely in keeping with his father's ideals. The Christian religious instruction met with his approval, in particular. It was based on the fact that the foundation of the Old Testament was not Jewish but really Aryan spiritual material, that this was only taken over by the Jewish writers of the Bible on their detour via Babylon and remodeled, even falsified, according to Jewish special purposes. The learning material offered to the children was freed from all Jewish manipulations and distortions. In the higher classes, these Jewish elements and falsifications were discussed in more detail, their meaning, e.g. the story of Esau and Jacob, was put into perspective and the unmistakable contrast of the Jewish and Gentile prophets was pointed out.

The fundamentally different aptitudes and faculties of impression of the two boys now came into full fruition at school and in their dealings with their comrades. It turned out more and more that it was completely useless to try to develop them in a certain direction or to suppress or even transform their innate racial characteristics. The proverb of Horace, "*Naturam expellas furca, tamen usque recurret*" ("You may throw nature out with a pitchfork, she'll return nonetheless!") was confirmed. It is the foundation of all spiritual being and becoming in this world.

While Heinrich quite soon made friends with Hinz und Kunz among his schoolmates and was a jack of all trades, Hermann showed himself to be very selective in the choice of his friends. He had become "blood brothers" with one boy who was blond like himself. This was Ludwig Hege, a native of Oldenburg, whose father was a mechanical engineer in the Vorsig Locomotive Factory. Ludwig Hege had said that he had often ridden on the locomotive in the factory and that Hermann would be allowed to do so if he visited him. This possibility had undoubtedly contributed significantly to the formation of this blood bond, because Hermann had originally chosen another, equally blond boy for this dignity. It was Wend von Pfeil, a native of Pomerania, the son of a general staff officer. Wend was already able to ride properly, which impressed Hermann enormously. And that he was not just bragging about his horsemanship, Hermann was soon able to see with his own eyes.

One Sunday, when he went for a walk with his father in the Grunewald, Wend rode up on his pony accompanied by his father. From that hour on, the little Teuton fought a mighty mental battle as to whether he should not have become blood brothers with Wend rather than with Ludwig. Finally he took his father into his confidence. As always, he knew what to do, and recommended that Hermann form a blood alliance with both Ludwig and Wend. Blissfully happy with this solution, he could hardly wait to meet Wend at school the following day. He responded enthusiastically to the proposal, and Ludwig was also happy to agree.

So this three-man alliance was concluded and sealed in blood that very morning during the long ten o'clock break behind the gymnasium. The boys exposed their left forearms by pulling up their sleeves, and without batting an eye, each of them carved a small wound with a pocket knife. A few drops of the oozing blood were transferred from one wound to the other by means of the blade of a pocket knife and mixed there with the blood of the friends. The unwritten rule of this blood covenant culminated in an oath to help and protect each other and to remain faithful to each other "until death". This blood bond put the three boys in tremendous respect among their comrades, and as a result, connections like this spouted up like mushrooms among the boys. The blood alliances joined together to form clans, feuded with each other and fought real battles.

Heinrich, however, could not be induced to join such an alliance. While his comrades fought their snowball fights or beat their bodies blue with their wooden swords, he sat at home and voluntarily did arithmetic problems. Thus he soon got a reputation for being a nerd. He attracted the boundless contempt of the blood brothers, but this did not affect him. The success of this nerdiness was that he became first in his class and was allowed to keep the class book. This gave him the further advantage of being allowed to stay upstairs in the classroom during breaks, while the others were horsing around in the school yard.

The father had promised the two boys that they could learn to ride if they got very good report cards at Easter. He had to make this condition more stringent, since there was no question that they would both reach the goal. Hermann was fifth among 36 pupils and Heinrich was first. While the latter was by no means enthusiastic about the prospect opened up by his father, Hermann could hardly contain his joy. So far, he learned easily, but had not become exceedingly diligent.

Now, however, it had become a matter of honor for him to show what he could do. He cracked the books and brought home first place in his class at Easter, much to the delight of his father, while Heinrich moved over to second. Already on the first day of vacation, the riding lessons began. The father himself gave the two boys instructions at a neighboring riding school. As much as Heinrich resisted, he had to get up on the unsaddled horse. Immediately, he fell down on the other side. But in spite of all his whining, he had to get up again and again. His father, however, took great pleasure in Hermann's courage and agility. His pride was enormous when he was able to ride out with the boy for the first time; they now often rode together with Wend von Pfeil and his father to the Grunewald Park. His father soon gave up taking Heinrich on these rides. His restlessness, timidity and fear on the open road was such that he wreaked havoc. As a reward for his brilliant autumn report, in which he again beat his brother Heinrich, Hermann received his own riding horse. The boy's happiness could not be described.

So far, Hermann had asked his father in vain to be allowed to visit Ludwig Hege in order to ride with him on the locomotive. In the meantime, the father had obtained permission to visit Vorsig's machine factory with his two boys. Ludwig's father offered to give them a tour of the plant himself. This was an event of the first order for little Hermann. When he was still with his foster parents in Neckargemünd, where he saw the trains pass by every day, he had racked his brains in vain about how locomotives "come into the world". His foster father had answered that they were made in large factories. But he could not imagine that. He thought these snorting monsters were living creatures. Eventually, he had formed the idea that "bad men had to eat fire as punishment," which turned them into locomotives. But now he saw that his foster father had been right after all.

They were there just in time to see the superstructure of a machine being placed on enormous wheels. Hermann thought that it could probably turn on now right away. But then his father let him in on the secret of the locomotive's life. He learned that its soul was artificially generated from water and fire. The movement of the wheels through the action of steam on the piston in the cylinder and the return of the piston through the supply of steam to the other side of the piston by means of the slide control, all this excited him so much that he recorded it again and again at home. Heinrich, on the other hand, showed not the slightest interest in this miracle. He anxiously pressed himself against his father amid the roar and pounding of the giant engine, he could not wait for the time when they would leave the factory again.

Today, however, Hermann's most ardent wish to ride on a locomotive was to come true. For him, that was the highlight of the whole visit! When they re-entered the factory grounds, where a shunting machine was moving wagons, he approached Ludwig. He conveyed his wish to his father, who laughingly had the machine stopped and invited the three boys to climb aboard with him. Heinrich resisted with kicking and screaming, so his father stayed behind with him. With a beating heart, Hermann climbed the iron steps. His breath caught with joyful excitement when Ludwig's father asked him to open the regulator himself to start the machine. The slider went so heavily that he had to brace himself with his chest against the lever to move it.

But now the machine picked up and made its first deep puff! What a feeling! He would not have traded places with any prince at that moment! And now it breathed and ran faster and faster! At the same time, it rose and fell and made slinging movements that made Hermann sway back and forth. He had not imagined it like that. It was a jolting and stumbling, wobbling and shaking that you lost hearing and sight! If you even stepped on the connection between the machine and the tender, the ground seemed to disappear from under your feet. Now the stoker tore open the furnace! It was quite impossible to look into the embers, which took your breath away.

Then some workers ran across the tracks and the engineer blew the steam whistle to give the warning signal. Wow, how that rang so close in your ears! And when you looked through the small front windows to the right and left along the boiler on the track, it looked as if the engine was eating the rail track into itself. Now Ludwig's father had the engine stopped, the regulator was closed, the stoker applied the brake, the driver put the steering wheel around, and they returned to their point of departure. How the air from the tender blew in your face, so that your breath stopped when you opened your mouth!

With oily hands and a few splashes of soot on his face, Hermann left the machine proud and highly satisfied. He greeted his father, who was waiting with the anxious Heinrich, with jubilation. From that day on, he decided to become a machine engineer instead of a locomotive engineer, since he makes the locomotives and is allowed to drive on all the locomotives, and all the locomotive engineers must obey him.

It is a significant and as yet unexplained fact that each season has its own children's games, which are by no means conditioned by it. Thus, the boys' sport of shooting marbles and making spinning tops that dance with whips can be practiced on any dry day of the year. However, the time when marbles are shot is the first spring alone, while spinning tops are common only in autumn. Winning at the game of marbles is based on the skill of using the slightly larger game ball to shoot the marbles placed in a square by the other players out of it. The game is an excellent exercise in making the eye and hand accurate.

Since Heinrich, despite all his efforts, got nowhere in this art of shooting, but was eagerly anxious to increase his possession of marbles, he now tried to "shoot" the thing in another way, and he succeeded admirably. He devised a kind of lottery game, in which he would, without any risk to himself, very quickly become a very rich man in marbles. He made eleven lots from small pieces of paper numbered consecutively. Each ticket cost one marble. When the eleven tickets were sold, the drawing took place. The winner received ten marbles. In this way, Heinrich won a marble every time he played. So he made a profit of ten percent each time. Since this could be repeated every five minutes, he soon had effortlessly filled all his pockets with marbles.

But when another classmate took it upon himself to spoil his business by opening a rival enterprise, he raised a great hue and cry and turned to his brother for protection. He was chivalrous and foolish enough to forbid the competitor to continue the business and to lend this prohibition tangible emphasis on the grounds that his brother Heinrich was the inventor of this idea and therefore alone was allowed to exploit it. But this appealed to Heinrich's arrogance, and this was to be his undoing. He soon started to issue up to twenty lots instead of eleven, so that he was now working with a profit of no less than one hundred percent, depending on the number of lots he sold each time. In this way, Heinrich had deprived the majority of his classmates of all their jam. This led to a conspiracy of the aggrieved parties, and since among them were Hermann's two "blood brothers," the former declared himself unable to take Heinrich's side. However, he had agreed with them to remain neutral, so that he had nothing to fear for himself.

Now the conspirators gave Heinrich the ultimatum to pay back by the next morning all the marbles he had cheated his comrades out of, otherwise he would be roughed up miserably. (One can see that these boys showed a very healthy response to solving the Jewish question). Because of this Heinrich reported sick the next day, complaining of severe stomach pains. His brother Hermann showed him full contempt for this pathetic evasion, but would not have "ratted" on him to his father for any price. Eventually, however, the day came when the capable little businessman had to go back to school. His hope that his comrades would have forgotten about the matter in the meantime suffered a miserable shipwreck. It fell to Wend von Pfeil to fix poor Heinrich, and he did it so completely and thoroughly with his Pomeranian fists that Heinrich was once again unable to attend school for a long time, but this time not because of stomach pains, but because of other pains he felt in all his ribs and bones.

A detailed physical examination by the family doctor revealed the new cause of the illness, and so the story came out. The father, far from defending the sorrowful child, declared that he had been justly served, that he should take note of it, and that in the future he should only do real business with his fellow men. Then he ordered him to return all the marbles to his comrades. With a bleeding heart, the little merchant delivered his treasure of marbles to Wend v. Pfeil, who distributed them to the rest.

One is mistaken, however, if one believes that this experience left a lasting impression on Heinrich or was able to curb his greed. He continued to exercise it in other ways. Since the boys attended the Gymnasium, they received a weekly allowance of 50 pfennigs. They were required to save half of it, and from the other half they had to cover the small school needs of pencils, pens, erasers and the like. What they did not use from the second half, they were allowed to use for themselves. The father had set up a small housekeeping book for each of them, and they had to keep a record of every income and expense. Each week, the father checked the book and the cash register. It turned out that Hermann's bookkeeping and cash management left a lot to be desired, and he never saved a penny beyond the prescribed half. He spent the money on decals, cap gun primers and the like.

Heinrich, on the other hand, kept the book and cash register in good order, apart from the greasy condition they were always in. He was always very frugal with his money and made considerable savings over and above the obligatory half. He did not allow himself even the most modest expenditure, and of the small articles of daily use for the school, only the most necessary. However, when his father once unexpectedly took stock of the money in his coffers, there was an additional amount of fifteen pfennigs over and above what was on the books.

At first Heinrich claimed that he had found the money, but when cornered he confessed that he had found a pencil and eraser and sold them to his comrades. Further investigation revealed that he had stolen the eraser and pencil. Now he received a good beating from his father and had to return the pencil, eraser and money immediately; his pocket money was withdrawn for four weeks; if he needed any purchase, his father would get it for him himself. In contrast to Heinrich, Hermann, even if he had something to answer for, was simply incapable of telling an untruth; indeed, he admitted every offense when questioned with a certain defiance and cold-bloodedly awaited his punishment.

Fourteen days after this incident, Heinrich was surprised by his father as he counted a matchbox full of individual pennies. When his father asked him where he got the money, he said that his classmates had given it to him. Hermann was unable to give any further information about this, since he had already been absent from school for several days due to a sprained foot. Wend and Ludwig, however, who visited Hermann, found out that Heinrich had licked the shoes of all 36 of his classmates to the great amusement of the class, for a fee of one pfennig each! It was quite impossible to make the boy understand the dishonorable nature of this behavior; he lacked any organ for it.

The older Heinrich became, the more bad experiences his father and teachers had with him. When he was barely twelve years old, he was expelled from school because he had attempted a sexual assault on a porter's child.[1]

Since no school would accept the boy anymore, the desperate father had no choice but to take him back into the house. He now gave him a tutor who was not allowed to leave him unsupervised for a minute. He had to take the boy outdoors often and made him work out physically. Swimming lessons were resumed, but again without any success. The father bought a small piece of garden, which Heinrich and Hermann, who were now twelve and thirteen years old, had to cultivate together. But Heinrich undertook this activity only with reluctance, while Hermann found great joy in it. The interest in this occupation did not grow in the younger one even when the father showed the children how to graft buds and propagate seedlings.

On one of the many excursions that the father made crisscrossing the country to teach the boys how to find their way by map and compass, they had come across a wild rose bush. On this bush, the father transplanted various noble rose species onto it. When, in the coming summer, the wild bush was adorned with roses of different colors, this delicious wonder of nature made no impression on the boy, who was incapable of noble emotions. Young Hermann, however, could not wait until he himself had tried

---

[1] This incident occurred in the nineties at a Gymnasium in Reichsland. I also experienced the story of the Marmel lottery described on page 230, when I was a fifth-year student with a Jewish classmate whose name I can cite.

his hand at this art and had succeeded in it. All attempts by the father to awaken selfless pure interests in the younger boy were in vain.

  One day the following happened. During a boat trip, which both boys made with the educator on the Wannsee, Heinrich fell into the water. Without thinking, his brother jumped after him fully clothed. Heinrich, however, in his fear of death, hindered the rescuer in such a way that both sank. In vain the educator also jumped into the water, but he could not catch them both, and they disappeared without a trace into the depths. It was not until several hours later that the bodies of the two boys were successfully fished out of the lake.

It took months before Hermann awoke from the stupor into which he was thrown by the sudden death of his only son, for he had lost only the one, since he loved only this one. Again, as before, he read Plato and Kant. But these enlightened thinkers offered only nourishment to his mind, they did not nourish his heart, which ached for relief from the pain. He reached for the poets and opened Aeschylus. There he found the passage:

> "Yours is wisdom, Zeus, and you decree
> that we mortals also taste wisdom
> through suffering, through deep suffering, for that makes wise.
> Dead hope, that has given us the deepest insight.
> Whoever is torn apart by pain, knows about men,
> knows about gods. Like in the rainy season
> the gray waters drip incessantly,
> so sorrow rushes into our anxious nights,
> constantly dripping on the heart and infusing it
> with wisdom. From gods on high
> it springs down, and we become wise
> even against our will."

Hermann listened. He read the passage a second and third time, he read the whole *Oresteia*, and put the book down, pondering. The poetry had shaken him, but it had not brought him salvation, but it had awakened the memory of another book that also spoke of suffering and overcoming it.

For the first time in many years, Hermann picked up the Gospel again. His happiness at being a father, which had come to him so unexpectedly, had numbed him to the Word of God. Happiness makes us deaf and blind to the higher purposes for which we walk on earth; only suffering is able to open our eyes and ears to them and keep them open. That was the realization he had come to now.

Suddenly, the meaning of the suffering that God had sent him became clear to him. His only son was taken from him in order to open his eyes anew for what is the only important thing in this life, to find the way back to the father! His only beloved blond boy was already ripe for this return, and therefore he was already allowed to take off this human shell, but he was not yet ready! For him it meant to endure and to fight on and to fulfill the demands of the day, until his time had come as well! And he was given enormous strength to endure and persevere: the Good News, the Word of God, which he held here in his hands, and which he had carelessly passed by for years.

His unfortunate second son, however, had been called away by God's mercy in order to save him from further serious error and sin in this life that he had chosen for himself. For we ourselves choose with free will the parents and the conditions under which we want to spend our physical life for the fulfillment of the tasks which are set by God for our purification and for our inner advancement, or which we set for ourselves out of our own knowledge when we have already progressed further. It may well happen that the tasks and temptations we set ourselves to overcome are too great and too difficult, since we were not up to them, so that God's grace and goodness must intervene to redeem us from life and give us new opportunities for new tasks. Stubborn spirits choose a life full of hedonism and selfishness, and it is that chaotic race which is especially drawn to these incarnations. It is rare that a good spirit dwells in a body of this race!

But if it is once the case, he is always recognizable by the fact that he keeps himself apart from the selfish activities of his fellow comrades. The Gospels, especially the Gospel of John, gave Hermann innumerable indications of these connections. An unprecedented trust in God's guidance filled him and gave him unimagined power and strength to complete his path in life and suffering. The example of Christ shone before him, great and glorious and transfiguring his suffering!

It is as if the deceased were helping their loved ones so that they too would soon be able to follow them back to their father's home. Shortly after the boys' deaths, the Madame Councilor also died. Although her blood did not flow in the veins of young Hermann, the child had become deeply attached to her. She had become a mother to him, just as she had been a housewife to his father in his last years. On Hermann's advice, she had already bequeathed her entire fortune to her numerous poor relatives during her lifetime. Hermann only inherited from her the ownership of the second half of the factory, of which he was now the sole owner and master.

But this technical-commercial profession had not satisfied him for a long time. Since the factory was well-organized and no longer demanded any creative activity from him, he had lost all inner interest in it. He had entrusted the management to a competent and reliable director, to whom he gave a high share of the net profits. He himself was only in charge of the supervision. He devoted a large part of his activities to the Racial Research

Institute, to which he had been appointed to take care of by the society to which he had donated the money for its foundation. Again and again, he had the same dismal experience that the addiction to acquisition, enjoyment and luxury had already undermined the racial instincts of the Germans to such an extent that they showed almost no understanding of and interest in this question on which the happiness and prosperity, existence or non-existence of Germany's future depended. They already seemed irredeemably addicted to the vague internationalism which annihilates every peculiar life. The internal enemies, who, out of a hunger for money and power, were constantly working to destroy the German manner and essence, had an easy game with them and, as it seemed, had already won. Truly, only a war could bring the Germans to the realization that they had to lead a life of their own and in their own unique manner for the benefit of all humanity.

This work alone could not exhaust Hermann's productive power. Already some years before the death of the boys he had resumed his chemical research activities and set up his own scientific laboratory. With the intention of continuing his work where he had left off, he contacted his former colleague Dr. Siegfried Salomon, to whom he had given all his scientific material at that time. The latter had long since become a professor, and in fact, as it now turned out, he owed his appointment solely to Hermann's work. It had indeed proved to point the way in a new direction. Those beautiful crystalline suns, which Hermann had recognized as containing barium, were really, as he later suspected, the barium compound of the simple protein body, whose synthetic representation he had had finally succeeded in synthesizing. The private lecturer Dr. Siegfried Salomon had published this discovery under his own name, without even mentioning the true discoverer. When Hermann questioned him about this, he explained that he had transferred the material to him at that time for free use as his own property. That was certainly true. Dr. Siegfried Salomon, however, lacked any understanding of the duty of honor not to conceal the name of the discoverer.

When this fact had become known to him, Hermann made nothing further of the matter, but had quietly continued his own work. Now that he had come to new sensational results, he felt compelled to publish the facts as they had occurred with the alleged Solomon discovery.

A storm of indignation went through the daily press, but not against the current Professor Dr. Siegfried Salomon, but against the "dilettante" Dr. Hermann Kämpfer. As always, the meager German press had no deeper interest in such a case, since it focused exclusively on politics. They did not even notice that their all-Jewish opponents had only achieved such powerful political influence because they knew how to dominate the entire German intellectual life, science, literature, art and theater. The clamor in the press, however, was only just beginning, when a university that still preserved as much German independence as possible, offered Hermann a professorship.

Now a veritable hounding began against him. It was claimed that he was forced to give up his academic career because his talent had not been sufficient. That was the only reason why he had handed over his material to Dr. Siegfried Salomon. The latter had first worked out the core of the idea, since Kämpfer himself had not been able to do so. He himself was, as his later successes showed, "quite a good technician", but not an independent "scientific thinker". The work that he now published was based solely on the "epoch-making discovery" of Professor Dr. Siegfried Salomon.

But it was not only his talent, also his character that they tried to degrade; indeed, the aim was to destroy him spiritually once and for all. They reproached him that the "religious intolerance" he had displayed by founding the Racial Research Institute had not prevented him from marrying a millionairess, whose father ironically belonged to the "denomination" he had reviled. It was very striking that he had been practicing this "religious intolerance" only since his father-in-law had died and he had managed to get possession of his entire fortune. It was also very significant that the only rightful heir to this huge fortune had recently died in such a strange way. They were not afraid to bring up the earlier scandalous stories of his father-in-law and to connect him with them. There were many suggestive hints that Hermann must have been involved somehow, otherwise no judicial investigation would have been initiated against him. This was already evident from the fact that he had meanwhile adopted as his own the child of one of those unfortunate creatures who had served the lusts of the Councilor of Commerce. The fact that his examination was broken off at that time could only be explained by the fact that justified doubts about his "mental health" had arisen. This was probably also the reason why the public prosecutor's office had decided not to investigate him in the conspicuous death of the rightful heir of the Councilor's property.

Hermann was powerless in the face of these efforts to destroy his honor. No sooner had he won one libel and slander suit than he was forced to fight a second, a third and fourth. He found himself entangled in a battle with a hydra that grew several new heads for every one he cut off. Yes, this monster was mostly invisible and elusive. It sprayed its poison from countless secret cracks and crevices, that could not be attacked. Several of his lawsuits were dismissed because they were allegedly not sufficiently sub-stantiated. But if the opponent was caught and convicted after all, the pun-ishment was extremely mild. Everywhere in the German judiciary, the members of this foreign-blooded race formed one big conspiratorial socie-ty against the German nature and character and was ready to destroy by any means necessary anyone who dared to expose its nature.[1]

The result of this activity was that Hermann's appointment was not confirmed by the government. The arms of this mafia already reached up to the highest levels of government.

But it was not only Hermann's honor that was sought to be destroyed, the axe was also laid to his economic existence. By invisible hands his fac-tory was deprived of orders and the revenues decreased from month to month. The managing director, a Swabian, was faced with a conundrum. He doubled his efforts, but in vain. One day he had to suggest to Hermann to close the factory, since the business was no longer profitable. Hermann did so with an easy heart, for he had saved enough to be able to live inde-pendently.

One day, distant relatives of the Councilor of Commerce made claims to the estate of the deceased Heinrich. They derived their demands from some alleged agreement that the Councilor was said to have assured them in front of witnesses in the event that he left no direct descendants or that they died under age. Hermann had placed the compulsory portion due to Heinrich with various banks; he himself did not even benefit from the in-terest. Without even examining the claims of the treasure hunters, he hand-ed over Heinrich's entire fortune to them, since he did not want to burden

---

[1] The Jew Conrad Alberti-Sittenfeld writes in his repeatedly mentioned essay "Judentum und Antisemitismus" ("Gesellschaft" 1889): "One of the most danger-ous, specifically Jewish characteristics is the brutal, almost barbaric intolerance.... A worse tyranny can never be practiced than is practiced by the Jewish clique ... Whoever dares to oppose the Jewish clique, the latter inevitably tries to trample him down with vicious brutality. And there is still a great difference between the intolerance of the Teuton and the Jew. The former fights the opponent in open, honest battles; above all, he calls again the spirit into its place against the spirit.

"The Jew, however, tries to destroy his opponent in the spiritual field mostly by depriving him of the material basis, by undermining his civil existence, or by concealing the existence and the aspirations of his opponent from the world as much as possible, by trying to lie to it, by simply denying those who think differ-ently. The basest of all forms of combat, dead silence, is specifically Jewish. As an opponent in the social struggle, the Jew prefers to use the lowest means, because he knows that the Germanic Christian would rather give up the struggle than follow him into the realm of vulgarity."

himself with the trouble of a lawsuit, the favorable or unfavorable outcome of which was of no concern to him. This imprudent act gave the inheritance chasers the courage to lay claim to Hermann's own fortune as well, on the grounds that "it had been formed from the fortune of the Councilor of Commerce." Now Hermann became furious. However, it was of no use; he lost the lawsuit and his entire fortune. The voluntary surrender of Heinrich's assets was considered by the court as proof of the legitimacy of the claims made by his opponents. The money that Hermann had donated for the foundation of the Racial Research Institute and the ethnic German newspaper concern was also reclaimed by the opponents on the basis of the preliminary decision of the trial.

Within a few years, Hermann was a beggar on the street, worn down in body and soul. In order to eke out an existence, he first took an assistant's job at a chemical testing laboratory for foodstuffs and luxury items with a monthly salary of 150 marks.

The abrupt change that had taken place in Hermann's economic circumstances had no influence on his inner state. He got along just as well on 150 marks a month as on 1500, or 15,000. The only thing that hurt him was that under his new circumstances he could no longer keep a riding horse and was again forced to make do with a rough apartment, since a quiet room in Berlin could not be rented for little money. But then luck came to his rescue. In the Tiergarten district, he found a lonely, modestly furnished attic in a good house, which satisfied his demands for peace and quiet; he did not attach any importance to anything else. It offered enough space for his small library. This consisted of the New Testament and the works of Plato, Kant, Aeschylus, Shakespeare, Kleist, Schiller, and Goethe. With these spirits he lived and weaved in the eternal and infinite, what did he care about the perpetual daily grind of yesterday! Solitude had always been his refuge, where he felt at home.

But it was a deprivation of a different kind that he suffered from painfully in the long run; he lived without any love. In the whole world he had not a single person with whom he was united in love, and his longing for a wife and child was so great in him, beyond all measure, that he, the strong, hard-living man, often cried to himself like a child. As much as he was rooted in the spiritual realm and was still emotionally connected to Elisabeth, he stood as a full-fledged human being and man in the fullness of his years with both feet on this earth, which also demanded its due. And his cruel longing for love was able to attract the soul he now needed in his heart, he met the woman who was to bring him this fulfillment, and with her new unspeakable suffering. He could not and did not want to understand the signs of fate, which God had given him through his previous love and marriage, that it was the task of his tenure this time on earth to overcome the gross pleasures of love in order to become pure and mature and strong for a higher type of love, which sees its purpose and goal only in the spiritual.

While jumping off a streetcar he slipped, broke his foot, and had to spend several painful weeks in a hospital. There he was cared for by a nurse who at first sight was a delight to his eyes: a well-built, blue-eyed blond, a full-blooded woman of about thirty. "She ought to give you children!" was his first thought. She, too, became his at first sight, but she didn't reveal it to him immediately. When he left the clinic after six weeks and asked her for her hand in marriage, she gravely looked him in the eyes and rejected his proposal flatly.

Hermann had not expected that, because his feelings again told him that she loved him. When he asked her whether she was not free, she said no with a pensive smile. At parting he asked her if he shouldn't see her again. That would probably be best for both of them, she replied, and warmly shook his hand in farewell.

Deeply depressed, Hermann sought distraction in his work and studies. But his thoughts kept returning to the girl. Did she have a reason not to marry? Was she perhaps ill? A ridiculous question! This healthy creature! Or did she have a tragic love she could not forget? Did she even have a past? A sharp bolt of jealousy and pain shot through his heart and mind. It was unthinkable to him. She was the daughter of a civil servant from Mecklenburg. But even if she had a past! She did not have to account for it to him! He loved her, and that was all that mattered for him, and again she loved him, he read it in her eyes and heard it in her voice. And even if she brought an illegitimate child into the marriage, what would that change about his love? And it would, no doubt, be a blond child! He would love it and educate it like his own! He was thrilled at the thought. It would be a proof of his love for her! Quickly he sat down and wrote the following letter:

> "Dear Nurse Johanna!
>
> You didn't tell me the reason that led you to reject my proposal. There can be no reason to maintain your refusal except that your heart belongs to another or that you don't love me in return. You have denied the first yourself, and my feelings disprove the second. Therefore, I ask you again for your hand. It will be easy for me to get myself a position and an income again that is worthy of you and ensures you a carefree existence.
>
> An unconditional promise is awaiting you.
>
> Yours, Dr. Hermann Kämpfer."

He sent this letter to the post office at the same time as he sent a second letter in which he applied for an advertised position as a senior chemist at a Berlin Sanatogen factory. The very next day, he received a request by pneumatic tube from the factory to present himself, and that same day an employment contract was signed. However, the following day, Johanna again sent a negative reply. She urged him to forget about her, since she was determined to remain unmarried. She wished him, in his ensuing life, well-being and the fulfillment of the happiness she was unable to offer him.

Hermann was not a man to let himself be diverted from a goal, once it had been set in his mind, unless the inaccessibility of this goal was shown with clear reasons. The letter again contained no such reasons.

He knew Johanna was off-duty at three o'clock in the afternoon on a certain day of the week, and that she was accustomed to walking from the train station at the Zoological Garden to the Grunewald Park at that hour to get some fresh air. He was waiting for her at the station entrance. She didn't seem surprised at all when she saw him. He asked for her forgiveness for his importunity and for permission to accompany her. She granted him this request.

When they were finally alone outside, he begged her to explain the reasons for her repeated rejection of his proposal. She just shook her head thoughtfully. But he did not relent, and swore that he would desire her as his wife even if she had committed a crime.

"What permits you to speak to me like that?!" she fumed.

"My love!" was Hermann's simple, irresistible answer.

He grabbed her hand.

"Johanna! Answer me one question: would it be possible for you to love me?"

Without thinking, she replied "Yes!" "But I'm not allowed to" she added then somewhat meekly.

"Why can't you? Let me tell you why you think you can't! You are a mother!"

She flinched and tried to snatch her hand away from him, which he held tightly. Then she looked him directly in the eyes again and asked:

"How did you know?"

"I suspected so!"

She looked at him puzzlingly. After a pause, she continued:

"I'm not a mother, but I was. My child died a few hours after birth, and that was a good thing. It would have been horrible."

"Is that your reason now for rejecting my proposal?"

"Yes!"

"Johanna! I'm begging you, become my wife!"

She stopped. "You still desire me as your wife?"

"I love you, Johanna!"

"And you won't ask me about my past?"

"You don't owe me an account of your past, I don't even want to know about it. Whatever it was, I'm sure it was only done out of love! I don't want your past, Johanna, I want your future, and above all your love!"

He pulled her passionately to his chest and kissed her on the mouth. Carried away by the greatness of his fervid love, she yielded to him.

Half a year later, Johanna was Hermann's wife.

The marriage was not happy though. The love that brought the couple together was based on passion, and passion never leads to bliss. Although Hermann did not stir up his wife's past life with a single syllable, and she thanked him for it with self-sacrificing love and devotion and came to live only for him, the shadow of her past always pressed between them and settled like an oppressive nightmare on Hermann's soul. Perhaps it would have waned, if she had been able to plumb the depths of his feelings or to follow his flights of thought. But her sensual, earthy nature was only able to penetrate skin-deep into his being. Thus her love remained stuck in the lower regions of sensuality and she did not know the deeper happiness of spiritual understanding. Hermann felt lonelier than ever.

Her husband's deep dissatisfaction did not escape Johanna, but in keeping with her own nature, she sought the cause in externals, and through externals she strove to eliminate it. She was an excellent house-wife and knew how to deliver external comfort, but she did not understand that this was not enough to make a man like Hermann happy. She fulfilled every wish she could see in his eyes; she cooked his favorite meals, served him herself, provided him with every comfort, and tried to cheer him up with her coarse cheerfulness. All this, however, only served to increase Hermann's irritability, because nothing is more tormenting for finer na-tures than the eager affection of an inadequate understanding. It could even make him furious when she surprised him with gifts, with which he wanted nothing to do. His open and ruthlessly honest nature was unable to feign joy where he felt none, or to hide his embarrassing feelings. Displeasure and disappointment increased daily on both sides.

More intimate feelings, however, stirred in Hermann for his wife, when he learned he could again anticipate the joys of fatherhood. All of Johanna's ancestors were, like his own, blond northern Germans. So once again, he cherished the fulfillment of his life's desire to have a child in his own likeness.

But to the horror of the mother and father, the most incomprehensi-ble, most monstrous thing happened, she gave birth to a thoroughly Jew-ish-looking child, with frizzy black hair, darkish skin, and shady eyes. Hermann roared like a dead bull, when he saw it.

"Whore!" he shouted at his wife.

As if struck by lightning, she collapsed in physical distress under this devastating word.

And now he imperiously demanded an account of her past. She confessed that about ten years earlier she had been seduced by a baptized Jewish officer, who had promised her marriage, and then subsequently abandoned her. In order to save her parents from the disgrace, she had kept silent. Under the pretext of wanting to become a nurse, she left her parents' home to give birth to the child. As he already knew, it died immediately after birth. It was impossible for her to understand why this child, Hermann's child, also looked like her first child.

But the mystery was solved when Hermann learned the following: In animal husbandry, the prevailing wisdom affirms that a noble-bred female will become forever unfit for noble offspring, if she has been inseminated by a male of inferior heritage. By such a maternity, the whole organism of the noble-bred female creature is poisoned and changed towards the inferior race, so that it is only capable of giving birth to ignoble offspring, even in case of fertilization by a noble-born male. The more highly developed a living being is, the more insistently this law of heredity appears, and its highest and most momentous effect is naturally achieved in man.

Now measure the damage done year in and year out to the German race by Jewish youths, who seduce thousands and thousands of German girls every year!

Hermann imperiously demanded that his wife tell him the name and the regiment of this Jewish officer. She did so in horror. That same night, Hermann drove to the garrison near Berlin.

In the meantime, the lieutenant had become a captain. When Hermann now demanded satisfaction from him, he explained that he could do nothing for him, and insisted he leave his apartment immediately.

Hermann did not move from the spot and repeated his demand. Then the Jew threatened to have his servant throw him out, if he did not leave at once.

No longer in command of his senses, Hermann drew his automatic pistol and shot down the villain.

Untroubled in the aftermath, he drove back to Berlin, determined to turn himself in to the police there. When he returned his apartment to make final arrangements, he found his wife dead. She had killed herself and the child with morphine. The syringe was still stabbed in the area of her heart.

The courtroom could not hold the crowd, tickets had to be issued. Luminaries of science were invited as expert witnesses and the Jewish press had been shouting "Crucify him!" for months.

Pale and serious, Hermann sat in the dock. He had refused to take a defense attorney. Finally, however, he had been forced to do so for technical reasons. But he stubbornly refused to give the defense counsel any explanation of the crime and his motives. He would present everything that was necessary himself. He rejected one of the judges named Ehrlicher and three jurors named Mannheimer, Jeiteles, and Rosenfeld as biased.

In court he stuck to his statement made in the preliminary investigation that he had shot the captain on purpose and that he had gone to the garrison with this intention. His testimony was contradicted by the testimony of the houseboy of the dead man, who had overheard the exchange of words in the next room. He testified that the shot was fired only after the captain had twice refused to give the defendant satisfaction and had threatened to have him thrown out, if he did not remove himself at once. The prosecutor Dr. Katzenstein tried to refute the testimony of the boy by saying that the witness had been so perplexed that he had not even rushed to his master's aid, he had not arrested the defendant after the crime, and had not even attempted to call others for this purpose.

When asked by the chairman of the jury whether he regretted what he had done, Hermann answered with a firm "No".

In his indictment, the public prosecutor particularly emphasized that Hermann had been in full possession of his mental capacities before and during the crime, just as he was now still. This was confirmed by the opinions of the experts who had appeared here, and who had each observed him for months with regard to his state of mind: Professors Dr. Maximus Hirschhorn, Privy Councilor Professor Dr. Maximilian Markuse and His Excellency, the Privy Councilor Professor Dr. Sally von Cohn. Fritz Mantheu, the chief expert responsible for all scientific and non-scientific questions, had also expressed the same sentiment himself only last night in the largest and most widespread of all German newspapers.

"But," continued the prosecutor, "in addition to the expert opinions of these luminaries of German science, we also have the admission of the accused that he carried out this horrible act of blood with premeditation and deliberation. Even if we must doubt other statements by the accused, he undoubtedly tells the truth on this one point! The prosecutor also explained that he was untruthful when he claimed that he habitually carried the pocket pistol with him on all his journeys, for he himself admitted that before setting out for the scene of the crime he checked the pistol and was convinced that it was in good working order! We are dealing here with a dangerous man, who murdered, out of the sheer religious hatred, the former member of a state religion, which, although not Christian, is recognized as having equal rights with the Christian religion.

"The accused attacked a Royal Prussian officer, who had a bright future ahead of him, in broad daylight in his own apartment and shot him down out of religious fanaticism! What other plausible motive could the accused have had for such an atrocious deed? Perhaps the illusion that the family honor of the accused had been violated by the murdered man? Oh, gentlemen, thank God we live in a more reasonable age nowadays! Today, we live in an age of humanity, humaneness, and human love! And therefore this brutal act of a highly educated man is doubly despicable and criminal! Consider for a moment, gentlemen of the jury, what benefit the defendant's family honor, allegedly violated by the murdered man, now has from this bloody deed! Has this murder eliminated the misstep of the accused's wife, which was committed more than ten years ago and which was quite understandable and forgivable? And what personal damage did the defendant suffer from the misstep of his wife? Was she not an excellent, loving wife to him despite this failure? Or did the defendant suffer personal damage from the fact that the child his wife bore him was not blond, as he had hoped, but black-haired? Gentlemen! What backward, reactionary, antediluvian prejudices speak from this narrow-minded view of the defendant!

"And, gentlemen, what guarantees do you have that in the present case the woman's earlier intercourse with the murdered man is really to blame for the child's appearance? A much simpler and more natural explanation seems to me to be closer! I do not want to offend the deceased wife of the accused! But since she had already shown a certain preference for dark-haired men in the past..."

"Shut up, you vile dog!" Hermann, beside himself, interrupted the prosecutor.

"I must beg very much," said the latter calmly, "that I not be interrupted in my speech by the accused."

"You mustn't make any interjections," admonished the Chairman to Hermann sympathetically. "Above all, you must not insult the State's Attorney, although your agitation is understandable to me. You will be given the floor for an unrestricted defense. For the rest, I would ask the public prosecutor not to further elaborate on the idea he has just suggested. I believe the jury has understood what the prosecutor wanted to say."

The jurors' faces were filled with outrage at the scurrilous undertone of the prosecutor, eagerly they nodded in agreement with the presiding judge.

"It may well be," continued the prosecutor calmly, "that these laws of race, of which the racial experts spoke, are valid in the breeding of animals, but what does that prove for humans? There is no doubt that man has evolved from the animal kingdom and that the same biological laws apply to him as to the other living creatures. But that this should also be the case also with regard to race, seems to me highly doubtful! Race, in general! What does it mean? A human being is a human being, no matter what denomination he belongs to! I consider this whole question of race to be a hoax, and in the present case, it does not play the slightest role in the justification of the accused.

"As for the opinion that the accused was incited to commit his crime by the murdered man, who refused to give him satisfaction for the youthful escapade he had committed more than ten years earlier with the wife of the accused, notably, with the full consent of the wife, such an opinion is completely incomprehensible to me. If I demand of someone, and he refuses the demand, then according to the generally accepted code of honor, the matter is nevertheless done. With this demand, the defendant had completely fulfilled his duty of honor and should actually be glad that the matter went off so smoothly. Shooting down the enemy thereupon is excessive and undue, gentlemen! And as for the refusal of the murdered man, I find it quite understandable. Who among us wants to recall all the girls we pulled a fast one on in our youth! And, hand on heart, gentlemen of the jury! In youth, every one of us had our tramps! Young people just want to let off steam! If all of us present here could expect to be beaten down for some juvenile mischief in broad daylight in our own homes after more than ten years, then, gentlemen, all coziness would cease! Very few of us would still be alive then.

"We Germans are known all over the world as the people of poets and thinkers, and that is why we understand the weaknesses of our fellow human beings! The accused did not show such understanding, he disregarded the simplest laws of humanity and, driven by reactionary prejudices, he shot down a defenseless man! We Germans are an open, honest people! The accused, however, acted dishonestly and insidiously, and therefore un-German, by gunning down an unsuspecting person in broad day-light! Such a nefarious, insidious, un-German atrocity demands the heavi-est punishment!"

After these and similar remarks, the prosecutor concluded his speech with the following words:

"The German people, gentlemen of the jury, expect from your hard and heavy duty that you will find the accused guilty of having intentionally and deliberately killed the Royal Prussian Captain Paul Kornacker on Sep-tember 1 of last year!"

Murmurs of dissatisfaction filled the auditorium after this speech.

Now the defense attorney was given the floor.

He first objected indignantly to the prosecutor's method of dragging the honor of the defendant's deceased wife into the mud even after the fact and of glossing over the dishonorable deed of the Jewish officer. The audi-ence agreed with him so loudly that the chairman had to threaten to clear the auditorium.

Then the defense attorney addressed the efforts of the prosecutor to devalue the testimony of the servant and to present Hermann's deed as having been carried out with intent and deliberation. The support for this opinion by the defendant himself proved just the opposite, because he was convinced that the defendant intended to obtain a death sentence against himself, so that an end would be put to his lamentable, failed life, which his Christian faith forbade him to bring about by his own hands. Then he described this life and explained how it had been systematically destroyed by the Jews. Jewish greed and Jewish usury had already driven the father of the accused to despair and death. Through Jewish dishonesty the de-fendant had been deprived of his scientific successes and his fortune. Only Jewish lechery and unscrupulousness were to blame for the shocking trag-edies of his two marriages.

And then one should be surprised, when a man who has been perse-cuted and tormented by the Jews, and who has been deprived of all his life's work and life's hopes, at the moment when all these Jewish crimes are crowded together before his soul, when the desecrator of his wife and his family honor refuses him satisfaction and threatens to throw him out of the door, should one be surprised if the accused, exasperated to the point of blood at that moment, let himself be carried away by an act which he would never have committed if he had thought it over calmly? For a dis-honorable scoundrel, as the man who was shot proved to be, and as the testimonies about his other transgressions against German girls unani-mously state, is not worth a shot of powder!

"The defendant," the defense attorney concluded, "has been so terribly distressed and antagonized by the endless ill-treatment inflicted on him and his family that he could at most be convicted of manslaughter, and accordingly, punished by imprisonment only if he had possessed his free will at the moment of the act! But he undoubtedly did not have it! In spite of the expert opinions of the gentlemen, I, and with me without question every unbiased person, stand on the position that the accused committed the deed in a state which excluded his free determination of will, and that consequently all questions of guilt are to be answered in the negative, and he must be acquitted!"

Loud applause and bravos followed the nearly two hours of statements by the defense counsel, so that the chairman now seriously threatened to clear the hall.

At long last, Hermann was given the final word. He began:

"The views which the public prosecutor developed earlier are an apt proof that he, just like all his racial comrades..."

"How dare you take me for a Jew!" cried the public prosecutor in the most sensitive manner.

Hermann: "I don't understand the prosecutor's excitement, I didn't even say the word 'Jew'!"

Chairman: "I must draw the attention of the prosecutor to the fact that the defendant now has the floor! I expect the defendant to exercise moderation and to speak only to the point!"

Hermann: "Earlier, the Chairman assured me of unrestricted freedom of speech. What I have to say is absolutely part of the matter. It is important for me to make the reasons for my actions perfectly clear, and that includes answering the public prosecutor's questions. May I do that?"

Chairman: "You have the right to defend yourself in any direction. But that must not tempt you to put forward things here that go beyond the scope of your defense!"

Defense counsel: "I urge you not to restrict my client's freedom of speech! I draw attention to the fact that I would see in this grounds for a mistrial!"

Chairman: "Your client has complete freedom of speech, of course. But that must not prevent me from admonishing him to speak only to the point! The defendant now has the floor and I urge everyone not to make any comments!"

The defense attorney beckoned Hermann not to be intimidated, and Hermann, who had remained quite calm, continued:

"I say that the remarks of the public prosecutor are excellent proof that he, like all Jews, for reasons which are necessary by nature, lack any organ for German concepts of honor. Besides…"

"I urgently request the Chairman to forbid the defendant from speaking about me personally here! I am a Christian, just like the defendant, and I absolutely refuse to accept any remarks about my sense of honor!"

Chairman: "I again admonish the defendant to refrain from any remark not pertaining to the matter!"

In perfect silence, Hermann continued:

"For the rest, I quite agree with what the prosecutor said. He is indeed right. If all his racial comrades had to pay with their life for the sins they commit by making German girls unfit to bear German children, then there would probably be no Jews left in the German fatherland! Just take a look at the pitiable creatures on whom these countless Jewish store clerks and grocery boys, these military guards, traveling salesmen, married and unmarried bosses and under-bosses practice their arts of seduction! Check out the restaurants and entertainment venues, cinemas, and theaters after closing time!! It is the unsuspecting German girls, unaware of the consequences of their actions, who, having succumbed to the temptations of the big city, are sport to be seduced by men of foreign blood and robbed of the ability to bear German children to German men! It just makes your wrists twitch when you see a German girl on the arm of such a Jew boy! Both of them should be smashed!

"Have you ever seen a Jew lure a member of his own race in order to satisfy his extramarital desires? They don't excite his desires! It must be German girls! If possible blond German girls! If you read the popular Jewish literature on child-rearing, you will find this confirmed! It is the blondness of our girls that they're after! The crime that they commit day in and day out against German blood and German national strength is outrageous! We have a little over half a million Jews in Germany, and this half million is enough to racially corrupt the German people in a hundred years, so that it is no longer possible to speak of a German race! It is long overdue that laws are finally created which put a stop to the racial corruption of the German people by Jewish blood! Marriages between Germans and Jews should be forbidden by law![1] Any Jew who dares to defile a German girl should be punished by imprisonment!

---

[1] When Goethe learned at that time of the law permitting marriage between Christians and Jews, he was quite beside himself. The chancellor F. v. Müller reported about this on September 23, 1823: "I had hardly entered Goethe's room at around 6 o'clock, first to announce Professor Umbreit for tomorrow, when the old gentle-

"No less disastrous than this racial contamination is the spiritual contamination by the Jews, which the German people is increasingly experiencing from decade to decade." And now Hermann described for an hour and a half the poisonous and corrosive influences which the Jews, through their financial power, through the press, literature and theater, through the judiciary and the teacher's unions, exert indirectly and directly on German feeling and thinking, on German manners and views, on German trade and change, how they unceasingly seek to confuse and dilute our original, primordial German concepts of God and religion, of freedom and immortality, of loyalty and devotion to prince and fatherland, and to replace them by revolutionary and international false ideals. Change must be created here from the ground up through law and justice if German spirit and German essence are not to disappear from the face of the earth in the foreseeable future.

He culminated these statements with the demand: "No Jew may be a teacher of a German boy or girl anymore![2] No Jew may have the chair of a German university or college! No Jew, whether baptized or unbaptized, may sit in judgment over a German! O unbearable shame, that this is possible at all in the German fatherland! Immigrated Asiatics sit in judgment on born Germans! With indignant pride every German should reject every Jewish judge, whether baptized or not! Only a German may and can judge a German! No Jew may ever again hold a public office again! No Jew may acquire real estate in Germany![3] The Jews are alien to us by blood and spirit and must be regarded as aliens and treated as aliens according to special laws, if we are not to be destroyed by them!" Hermann justified his demands on the basis of overwhelming statistical material. Then he continued:

"The claims of the prosecutor that I committed my crime out of religious intolerance, out of denominational hatred, is nothing more than the old Jewish trick of obscuring the core of the issue at stake here! Religious

---

man poured out his passionate anger about our new Jewish law, which permits marriage between the two religious groups. He foresaw the worst and most glaring consequences of this, claiming that if the General Superintendent had character, he should rather resign his position than marry a Jewess in church in the name of the Holy Trinity. All moral sentiments in the families, which rested on the religious sentiments, would be undermined by such a scandalous law. Besides, he only wanted to see how one could prevent a Jewess from becoming the Grand Mistress of the Court. Foreign countries must absolutely believe in bribery in order to find the adoption of this law comprehensible; who knows whether the almighty Rothschild was not behind it." (Biedermann, *Goethe's Conversations*, Vol. 3.)

[2] See Appendix.

[3] See Appendix.

intolerance! Where in the whole world is there a country where such freedom of mind and conscience prevails as in Germany? Who in the German fatherland hinders anyone in his confession and in the practice of his religion? Who in our country begrudges the Jews their religion? In which country are there so many synagogues as in Germany?

"No, gentlemen! Here we are dealing with something quite different! As soon as someone dares to criticize the Jews in any way, or even to defend himself against Jewish patronage, oppression and exploitation, there is immediately a great clamor in the Jewish camp about "religious intolerance"! In this way the general public, who are not enlightened about such things, is diverted from the core of the matter and deceived into thinking that these are religious and denominational questions, and not purely social, biological and racial questions, on which the prosperity and ruin of the German people depends! And the timidity, fear and cowardice before everything that is Jewish and Jewish-related is so great among us in Germany that even in our national circles all these questions are touched upon only with the greatest hesitancy, and one does not dare at all to speak the word Jew aloud or to call the things that are involved here by their proper names! Such is the tremendous power of Jewry already today in the German fatherland! Truly, our ancestors knew well why they locked this people up in the Jewish quarter!

"But today it's the other way around! Today we Germans sit in our own homeland in the German quarter! For a German who still dares to feel German and to think German and to give expression to his German sentiments and thoughts is out of the question! And no government protects him! Because our government protects and supports these deceivers and corrupters of the people and forbids the mouth of every German who dares to speak against them! All our great German leading intellects, Geiler, Luther, Herder, Frederick the Great, Kant, Fichte, Schiller, Goethe, Richard Wagner, Treitschke, Mommsen, Menzel, Bismarck, never tired of drawing attention to the dangers threatening us by the Jews and of fighting against them! But we systematically breed and raise this dangerous race and uncritically hand over our nation to it!

"Now, in order to draw the attention of the general public, which is methodically kept in ignorance about these things, that is why I did what I did. It was my well-calculated and well-thought-out intention, by means of a very unusual, sensational act, to direct my fellow people to these questions, which decide the being or non-being of our German future! Because there is no other way! If I had tried, by means of newspaper articles, books, and lectures, to make the public aware of these questions, it would have been in vain! The essays, books and lectures would not have been printed or discussed, but would have been suppressed and hushed up, for the Jews are in possession of almost the entire German press and not a word is printed in this press that would be capable of lifting the veil over these things! Even petitions to the high authorities and princes are of no use, as I will prove to you in a moment, because the power of these foreign-blooded people already reaches into the very highest circles!"

Now Hermann read out the correspondence of Dr. Fritz Frankfurter, Member of the Reichstag, with the Councilor of Commerce Burghamer, and told of his futile attempts to bring it to the attention of the Emperor and the other princes of the federation. He then concluded his remarks with the following words:

"If the German people does not succeed in shaking off this Jewish vampire, whom it unsuspectingly suckles with the blood of its heart, and in rendering him harmless - and this is already possible by simple legal measures - then it will perish in the foreseeable future. In order to cry out this warning from this place, from my heart to the whole world, for that reason and that reason alone, I did what I did. I have consciously sacrificed my life for my fatherland and I hope that I haven't done it in vain! I hope that my death will be the signal to rage against this inner enemy, which threatens the future of Germany more terribly than any external enemy, because it cannot be defeated with the sword in hand!

"To give the full truth, I will also confess to you that this was not yet my intention when I left my apartment that night. At first, I was only concerned with bringing the defiler of my family honor to chivalrous account. But when the thought occurred to me on the way, gun in hand, that he could possibly refuse me satisfaction, it was my rock-solid resolve in this case to shoot him down, not out of revenge, but solely for the purpose that I have just explained to you. So I repeat truthfully, I carried out my act with intent and deliberation. You are bound by the law, gentlemen of the jury, and the law punishes the willful and deliberate killing of a human being with death!"

Hermann's speech made a tremendous impression on the judge, jury, and listeners. It was not a defense speech; it was a terrible double accusation. The dreadful truth of Hermann's life shocked everyone. Even when he pronounced the death sentence on himself, of which there could hardly be any doubt, many a woman could be seen holding her handkerchief to her eyes.

Breathless tension prevailed when the jurors reappeared in the courtroom after two hours of deliberation to announce their verdict. They negated all questions of guilt and agreed with the opinion of the defense counsel that the defendant had committed the deed without intent or deliberation in the highest state of affect and in a state of mind that precluded the free determination of his will before and during the crime. The verdict was accordingly acquittal. Hermann was immediately set free. He left the court amidst cheers and commotion.

His speech, however, was reproduced without abridgment only sparsely by the national press. In more than 90% of all the German newspapers it appeared only in excerpts and with accompanying commentary to the effect that this strange acquittal had obviously only taken place because the jurors, despite the contrary opinions of the experts, had become convinced that they were dealing with an insane man. Nevertheless, the public prosecutor lodged an appealed against the verdict.

Hermann accepted the verdict in silence and shock. At last he believed that he had recognized the purpose and goal of the unbearable suffering God had imposed on him. This suffering should harden and steel him, so that he would find the strength to sacrifice his life for the fatherland, to give the German people the impetus to free themselves from the powers of darkness! He regarded himself as an instrument of God, willingly laying down his life for this higher task. And now he was mistaken about this, too.

Astonished, he opened a batch of letters that the post office brought him the next day. They were congratulatory letters on his acquittal from people completely unknown to him. They praised him for his manly behavior and welcomed in him the leader they had long hoped for to finally take up the fight against the deceivers and poisoners of the people. From mail to mail, the letters piled up. Whole baskets full were brought to his house. He was unable to read them all or even answer them.

Now a new awareness dawned on him. What if he was called not to die for his task, but to live? How, if this was the meaning of his life's suffering, would he find the strength and greatness to renounce wife and child and earthly happiness in order to put all his poetry and thinking, his will and action into the service of this higher life-task, which required all the strength of a whole man? Couldn't he somehow serve the fatherland more effectively, than by climbing the scaffold now in order to be free at a stroke from the fetters of life and suffering? That would certainly be easier than taking up the struggle for life anew!

Yes, did he not have to admit to himself that the desire to end all the agony of life was the mainspring of his decision to commit the act which the law punished with death? That such considerations had a part in determining his actions was something he realized with a shock when the defense attorney struck out against this idea in his closing speech. He had blushed with shame, and he blushed again at that moment. Had he not thereby incurred the same guilt as the suicide, who ends his life out of cowardice? For a sinful desire, which we do not battle and overcome, counts before God like an executed deed! How merciful this God had been again, that He had saved him from this disguised suicide, and now gave him the opportunity to recognize this sin in time and to make amends!

No! The time, when he could leave this earthly life, had not yet come for him! He still had before him one task to serve, a lofty, glorious task!

Bringing spirit victory over matter and leading all mankind in their struggle towards their divine destiny was the goal that God set when he created the Teutons. Since then, all good spirits who have come to recognize the sinful abuse of their free will, who have the honest desire to find their way back to their Father's house through suffering and purification, have embodied themselves in them. And in the Jewish race, those powers of hell have embodied themselves since time immemorial which cause the apostasy from God and are constantly at work with their Satanic arts to block the return of struggling souls to their Father's house. The peace among nations, for which humanity struggles and longs, can and will come all by itself, only when humanity has again become aware of its divine destiny and has recognized the meaning and purpose of this earthly life, which is only that of finding the way back to the Father's house.

Helping to awaken this realization in his fellow Germans and cheering them on to fight against those infernal powers was the unambiguous task which God had assigned to him, and which he was the humble instrument of. Putting his fate in God's hands, he was now determined to live this task to his last breath!

Wonderful and inscrutable are the ways of God, and He does all things gloriously. If we have a pure and deep desire and ask God for it, he will grant it to us, when we are ready for its fulfillment.

Thus, our friend's fervent wish to be allowed to "shuffle off this mortal coil" would soon come to pass. A few weeks after his acquittal, the World War broke out. As a reserve officer in a Prussian infantry regiment, he was dismissed with a simple farewell from the rank of officers soon after his deed, but he was highly honored, personally, by his comrades. He now enlisted with his old regiment as a war volunteer. In the very first battles he distinguished himself before the enemy in such a way that he was again appointed an officer. Decorated with both iron crosses, he fell on Christmas Eve during the first year of the war, while on a daring patrol operation. The bullet hit him right in the heart after piercing the image of his little boy.

And so his wish to die for the Holy Fatherland was fulfilled after all.

End.

APPENDIX
Extended Notes

Chap. 16, Note 3: In his excellent book, *Der falsche Gott, Beweismaterial gegen Jahwe* [*The False God, Evidence against Yahweh*], Theodor Fritsch makes the following sensational statements about the unmistakable contrast between the Jewish God of the Old Testament and our Christian God, and the unbridgeable moral contrast between Jewish and Christian religious thinking and feeling, striving and aspiring, which can only be given here in excerpts, and which, if they stand up to scientific scrutiny, are of the most momentous importance for Old Testament criticism:

"Through Luther's translation of the Bible, some characteristic features of the old scriptures have been lost to us. In order to emphasize more clearly the image of the one-god doctrine, Luther has always translated the alternating names of the gods of the original scripture - Elohim, Yahweh, El-Elion, El-Shaddai, Adonai, Zebaoth etc. - are always replaced by "God the Lord". Thus, an apparent monotheism arose even where it did not exist. Incidentally, however, the image of the essence of these different gods was blurred.

"More important to us are El-Elion and El-Shaddai, which Luther left standing a few times, but also translated mostly with "God the Lord". Our theologians used to interpret El-Shaddai as the "highest God" and El-Elion as the "very highest", an interpretation for which there are no serious linguistic foundations whatsoever. It is just an embarrassing interpretation.

"El-Elion and El-Shaddai were gods of the Canaanite Peoples before the Jews came into the area. It would make no sense to see these two divine names as beings of equal value; what reason had the Canaanites to think of two gods of the same kind, one of which was only one step higher than the other: a "highest" and a "very highest"? It is much more probable that - similar to other old religions - these Canaanite gods also embodied opposites: a good and an evil spirit."

Prof. Adolf Wahrmund, teacher at the Oriental Academy in Vienna, in his *Law of Nomadism and the Present Rule of the Jews* has first opened up to us the deeper spiritual being of the Hebrews as descendants of the desert nomads and desert robbers. He has already hinted at the connections discussed here by saying in the book mentioned:

"An even deeper, even more natural model of the archetypal turns of fate of the nomadic life than the enemy raids, is to be looked for in the frequently recurring, all-destroying desert storm, the mighty destroyer, who leaves behind desolate emptiness and barren nothingness. He is personified by Typhon or Seth of the Egyptians, the Shaddai (i.e. the mighty and terrible one) of Abraham and Balaam. He therefore rides on the wings of the wind and descends in thunder and lightning. The storm wind is his breath, steam rises from his nostrils and devouring fire from his mouth. The desert nomads are his true sons, for they too, like their god, can only destroy. - According to some ancients, Typhon was the father of Judeos and Hierosolymus, and the Gnostics have called the Jewish God a Typhonian being."

According to the Egyptian view, Seth is the evil spirit, "the god to whom everything corruptible can be traced". Sched and Schedim are also found in Assyrian inscriptions as evil demons.

All of this seems to indicate to me that in Shaddai we are dealing with the "evil spirit" feared as an enemy by the Canaanites, the spirit of darkness. The devil is called Sheitan in Turkish. A station on the Rustschuk-Barna line is called the Scheitan-Schuk - the Devil Hole. In light of this, it is strange that Abraham, when he made his entry into Canaan, did not make his covenant with El-Elion, but surprisingly with El-Shaddai - and only with him. So that there is no doubt, the passage from the original text is reproduced here.

Thus, 17th chapter of Genesis begins:

1. וַיְהִי אַבְרָם בֶּן־תִּשְׁעִים שָׁנָה וְתֵשַׁע
שָׁנִים נִרְאָ יְהֹוָה אֶל־אַבְרָם וַיֹּאמֶר אֵלָיו
אֲנִי־אֵל שַׁדַּי הִתְהַלֵּךְ לְפָנַי וֶהְיֵה תָמִים:

2. וְאֶתְּנָה בְרִיתִי בֵּינִי וּבֵינֶךָ וְאַרְבֶּה
אוֹתְךָ בִּמְאֹד מְאֹד:

In faithful translation, that is:

"And Abram was a man of 99 years. Then Yahweh appeared to Abram and said: I am El-Shaddai, walk before me, and be obedient (devoted to me), and I will make a covenant between me and you, and will make you very great."

And in Genesis 17:7 it says further: "And I will establish my covenant between me and you and your descendants and their descendants as an everlasting covenant, so that I may be your God and the God your descendants after you."

Since El-Elion, the God of light, truth and goodness, is nowhere mentioned in this covenant, I can conclude nothing else out of it, with the best will in the world, than that Abram made his covenant with the "evil spirit". He pledged - to speak in medieval terms - his soul to the devil. That explains everything!

It is not difficult to see that the name Yahweh was only later substituted for Shaddai, that the original God of the Jews was El-Shaddai, and that the covenant with this God extended only to Abram and his descendants, not to other nations.

It should hardly have required scholarly investigations to recognize from descriptions of the oldest Jewish history that Yahweh is not a being of goodness and truth. All the facts described in the preceding paragraphs confirm it: Yahweh is El-Shaddai, the evil spirit, the spirit of deceit, who has nothing in common with our Christian God. We must emphatically object to the transposition of the two. Shouldn't the fact that the name Yahweh-Jehovah does not appear anymore in the New Testament be enough to make us aware of the difference between the gods?

Neither Christ nor his disciples know the name Yahweh-Jehovah. On the cross, Christ calls: *"Eli Eli, lama sabachthani"* ["My God, my God, why hast thou forsaken me?" (Matthew 27:46; compare to Mark 15:34)]. And the surrounding Jewish people, raised in Jewish views, were astonished at this exclamation, which they did not understand. Some thought that he was calling the prophet Elijah. In any case, it is clear that Christ called his God by a name unknown to the Jews and the rabble of Jerusalem. And the name sounded similar to Elijah to them. Should he not perhaps have called: "El-Elion, why did you leave me?"

Following these indications by Fritsch, I find in Eisenmenger's translation of the Talmud, *Das entdeckte Judentum* (Königsberg, 1711), second part, p. 432 and 433, the following remarkable passages, the examination of which I urgently recommend to the scholars:

> But the so-called good, holy and righteous devils are called Schedin Jehudain, i.e. Jewish devils, because they study the law of Moses like the Jews, go to the synagogue and perform their prayers. — Joseph is not called Scheda without cause, for a Sched, i.e. a devil, taught him. They (namely the Jewish devils) are like the angels whom the devils serve, because they are Jews and marked with the sign of Shaddai (understood here as circumcision)!

The conceptual connection between Sched, devils, and Shaddai, the mark of God, with whom Abraham made his covenant, seems to be evident here!

Now, an expert theologian, to whom I submitted these facts, still emphasized the passage at Exodus 6:2-3, and writes: "What Luther translated with "Lord" is just "Yahweh" in Hebrew. What Luther translated as "almighty God", is "El- Shaddai". So this passage really reads: "Elohim spoke with Moses and said to him: I am Yahweh. I appeared to Abraham, Isaac and Jacob as El-Shaddai(!) But my name Yahweh was not revealed to them." The theologian further pointed out to me that this passage belongs to the last part of the 5 books of Moses. It comes from the so-called Book of Consolation, which was probably written by Ezra around 450 BC. One must reckon with the possibility that this conflation of El-Shaddai with Yahweh is only a later combination by the priests! By the way, Genesis 2:6 looks back to Genesis 1:17, where the revelation to Abraham actually reads: "I am El-Shaddai"! [i.e. "I am the devil!"]

Hence, it is entirely possible that Abraham actually made his covenant with the evil spirit! The deeds of the original Jewish God and his patriarchal protégés provide extensive testimony to this in the Old Testament! Everything that is conceivable in terms of fraud and deceit, desecration, murder, and manslaughter, is carried out there by order of "God"! It was only later that a Jewish priest falsified the matter and replaced the devil's name with that of God! That this Old Testament Jewish God at least had a double face, completely in accordance with the ambiguity and hypocrisy of Jewish moral doctrine, that he appears sometimes as the principle of good and sometimes evil, that is undoubtedly clear from the Old Testament. It is also conceivable that his originally good principle, which he possessed as the ancestral god of the pre-Jewish Aryan native population of Canaan, was turned into its opposite by the character of the immigrating Jews. The Savior seems to have held this view. When the Jews invoke the God of Abraham as their father in contrast to the God taught by the Savior, the Savior denies that the Jews have the benevolent God of Abraham as their father and hurls the devastating words in their faces:

> You are of your father, the devil, and according to your father's pleasure you will do. He, the very same one, is a murderer from the beginning, and does not exist in the truth; for the truth is not in him. When he speaks a lie, he speaks of his own: for he is a liar, and the father of the same (John 8:44).

It seems to me there is a problem here that would be an important task for critical theology to clear up.

Chap. 16, Note 11: The explanation in this chapter about the origin of Jesus and the connection between religion and race should be supplemented by the following remarks by Theodor Fritsch in his book *Der falsche Gott*, which has been mentioned several times:

> This one consideration, the requirement of circumcision, should suffice to illustrate the contrast between Yahweh and the Christian God. Since the Christians do not practice circumcision, they prove that they have nothing to do with Yahweh and his covenant. But as uncircumcised, they are an abomination to Yahweh and have to recognize him as an enemy, who seeks to deliver to them the threat: "Everything that is not circumcised from the foreskin of his flesh, that shall be cut off his soul." It is incomprehensible how Christian theologians of all times could overlook this fact and consider Yahweh to be the God of Christianity as well.

Thus says Theodor Fritsch. Every unbiased person must admit that circumcision is in itself something so unnatural and disgusting that the God who prescribed it and the people who accepted it cannot possibly lay claim to pure and uncorrupted sensibilities. The ancient source writers report that the Jews were pariahs expelled from the cultural lands. It is very possible that these outcasts formed an alliance against culture and custom and chose circumcision as a secret sign of the alliance. The fact that circumcision, according to Herodotus, was also common among other peoples of antiquity [*Histories*, Bk 2, 104], does not change the mental assessment of a people, who elevated it to a religious mark, and does not eliminate from the world the unbridgeable moral gap between Jewish and Christian feeling and thinking. [Ed.: This is a remarkable statement, but vastly overrated. To realize that Jesus and the Founders were all Jews is to finally illuminate the last great mystery of Western civilization.]

Chap. 16, Note 14: Even today's Jews have in their sure racial instinct a distinct feeling that the Israelite prophets are not of their tribe. Although they still prefer to give themselves Old Testament names, it never occurs to any Jew to call himself Jeremiah, Isaiah, Ezekiel, Hosea, Joel, Amos, Abodja, Zephanja, Micha, Haggai, Malachi or Nahum. Even to our ear, these names differ considerably from the genuinely Jewish ones. The passages in the prophetic books later inserted by the Jews or reworked in a Jewish tone are unmistakable. The reader can get clarification about these connections from the chapter "On the History of the Origin of the Old Testament" in Theodor Fritsch's book *Der falsche Gott*, and in a small work by an unnamed author, "Juda und Israel als weltgeschichtliche Doppelgänger" (Judah and Israel as World-Historical Doppelgänger), Berlin, Verlag W. Giese, but above all, from the Old Testament writings themselves, if he reads them impartially and calmly.

The fundamental work by Friedrich Delitzsch "Die große Täuschung, kritische Betrachtungen zu den alttestamentlichen Berichten über Israels Eindringen in Kanaan, die Gottesoffenbarung vom Sinai und die Wirksamkeit der Propheten" [The Great Deception: Critical Reflections on the Old Testament, Reports on Israel's Invasion of Canaan, the Revelation of God from Sinai, and the Efficacy of the Prophets] (1920) sheds a clear light on the history of the conquest of Canaan and the untruthful historical tradition, unscrupulous displacements and falsifications by the Jewish writers of the Bible and the need to examine and fundamentally redesign the Old Testament beliefs that have been handed down to us.

The ingenious means with which the Jews continue their tactics of falsification and concealment even today can be seen from the writing *The Great Deception of the People and the World by the International Association 'Serious Bible Researchers'*, by August Fetz.

Chap. 16, Note 16: The Jew Klötzel writes in Issue No. 2 of the journal *Janus* (1912) under the heading "Das große Hassen" (The Great Hate), among other things: "Just as we Jews know that every gentile, somewhere in a corner of his heart, he is and must be an anti- Semite, so every Jew, at the deepest core of his being, is a hater of everything non-Jewish…. Nothing is more alive in me than the conviction that if there is anything that unites all the Jews of the world, it is this great sublime hatred."
Semi Abraham, in the work, "Von Juden zum Christen" ["From Jews to Christians"] (1912), says: "This is, after all, how Jewish children are brought up; hatred of anything Christian is instilled in them from their earliest childhood."

As is well known, Goethe had already said of the Jew that "he feels no love."

The *Shulchan-Aruch*, the contemporary rule book of the Jewish religion, commands that Jews pray the Shepthoch prayer (Orach chajim 480, Haga) on the eve of Pesach (the evening before Easter). It reads:

Pour out your wrath on the goyim who do not know you, and on the kingdoms that do not call on your name: for they have devoured Jacob, and laid waste to his dwelling place.

Pour out your rancor upon them, and let the embers of your fury reach them!

Pursue them in anger and extinguish them from under God's heaven.

[Ed.: This seems to be an incorrect citation to the *Schulchan Aruch*. But the equivalent passage can be found (twice) directly in the OT—Psalms 79:6 and Jeremiah 10:25.]

Chap. 16, Note 20: The reader will find an extensive collection of passages from the Talmud, which not only allow lying and deceit, theft, embezzlement, and damages of all kinds, even assassination of a Christian, and even, under certain circumstances, mandate it, in Theodor Fritsch's much-recommended book, *Der falsche Gott*. I must content myself here with reproducing some from the newer code of the Jewish religion, the *Shulchan-Aruch*.

Choschen ha-mischpat 848, 2 Haga:

מעות עכו"ם כגון לחמעותו בחשבון או להפקיע הלואתו מותר
וכלבד שלא יודע לו דליכא חילול השם ויש אומרין דאסור להטעותו
אלא אם טעה מעצמו שרי:

"It is permitted, through the error of an *Akum, for* example, to cheat him in arithmetic or not pay him what is owed to him; but only on the condition that he does not become aware of it, lest the Name be profaned. Some say it is forbidden to deceive him; but that one is only permitted to benefit, if he has made a mistake of his own accord."

Choschen ha-mischpat 283,1 Haga:

ישראל שהיה חייב לעכו"ם ומת אם אין עכו"ם יורעין מת איש
חייב לפרוע ליורשיו:

"Say there is Jew, who owes something to an Akum, if the Akum dies and no other Akum knows anything about it, the Jew is not obligated to repay his heirs."

Choschen ha-mischpat 266,1:

אבידת העכו"ם מותרת מותרת שנא' אבידת אחיך והמחזירה תרי זה
עובר עבירה מפני שהוא מחזיק ידי עוברי עבירה ואם החזירה
לקדש את השם כדי שיפארו את ישראל וידעו שהם בעלי אמונה
תרי זה משובח:

"An object lost by the Akum may be kept, for it is said, 'Your brother's lost thing' must be returned; indeed, whoever returns it (to the Akum) commits a great sin. But if he returns it in order to sanctify the Name, so that the Jews may be praised, and it is avowed that they are honest people, it is praiseworthy."

Choschen ha-mischpat 156,5 Haga:

אדם שיש לו עכו"ם מערופיא יש מקומות שדנין שאסור לאחרים
ליך להיותו ולעסוק עם חעכו"ם ההוא ויש מקומות שאין דנין ויש
מתירין לישראל אחר ליך להעכו"ם ההוא לחלוות לו ולעסוק עמו
ולשחותיה ליה ולאפוקי מיניה דנכסי עכו"ם הם כהפקר וכל הקודם
זוכה ויש אומרין:

"If a Jew has a 'good customer', who is an Akum, there are places where it is judged that others are forbidden to compete with him and do business with that Akum; and there are places where it is not (so) judged, and some allow another Jew to go to that Akum, lend to him, do business with him, cheat him, and take (his money) from him, for the Akum's money is like ownerless property, and anyone who comes first takes possession of it. - Some forbid it (for one Jew to compete with another)."

Choschen ha-mischpat 183,7 Haga:

מי שהיה עושה סחורה עם העכו"ם ובא חבירו וסייעו והטעה
העכו"ם במדה או במשקל או במנין חולקין הריוח בין שעשה עמו
בשכר או בחנם:

"If someone does business with the Akum, and another Jew comes along and helps him, and cheats the Akum in measure, weight or number, they share in the profit, whether he helped him for money or for free."

Choschen ha-mischpat 28, 3:

אם עכו"ם תובע לישראל ויש ישראל יודע עדות לעכו"ם נגד
ישראל ואין עד אלא הוא והעכו"ם תובעו שיעיד לו במקום שדיני
העכו"ם · לחייב ממון ע"פ עד אחד אסור להעיד לו ואם העיד
משמתין אותו:

"If an Akum has a claim on a Jew, and there is a Jew there who can testify for the Akum against the Jew, without any witness besides him, and the Akum calls him to testify for him, it is forbidden to testify for him in a place where it is the law of the Akum that money can be demanded on the testimony of a witness; and if he has testified, he shall be excommunicated."

Jore de'a 239, 1 Haga:

יהודי שגנב לעכו"ם וחייבוהו לישבע במעמד שאר היהודים
ויודעים שנשבע לשקר יכופוהו שיתפשר עם העכו"ם ולא ישבע
לשקר אפילו אם היה אנוס על השבועה הואיל ויש חילול השם
בשבועתו ואם היה אנוס וליכא חילול השם בדבר מבטל השבועה
בלבו הואיל והוא אנוס בשבועה כדלעיל סי' רל"ב:

Hierzu Kommentar באר הגולה:

עיין שם סעיף י"ד בהנה דבמקום דבמקום שיש עונש מיתה מקרי
שבועות אונס ולא חילק אם יש חילול השם בדבר ובאונס ממון
כתב והוא דליכא חילול השם בדבר:

"If a Jew has stolen from an Akum, and in the presence of other Jews he is compelled to swear an oath, and they know that he will swear falsely, they shall compel him to compare himself to the Akum and not to swear falsely, even if he were compelled to swear because the Name would be desecrated by his oath. But if he is forced (to swear), and there is no desecration of the Name in the matter, he shall declare the oath invalid in his heart, because he has been forced to swear (as was already said above in §232)."

"See there (section 14 in the Haga): Where capital punishment is threatened, it is called an oath of necessity, and no distinction is made whether or not there is any desecration of the Name; but in the case of fines, he writes, he may swear falsely only when there is no fear of desecration of the Name."

Choschen ha-mischpat 388, 10:

מותר להרוג המוסר בכל מקום אפילו בזמן הזה ומותר להורגו
קודם שימסור אלא כשאמר היריני מוסר פלוני בגופו או בממונו
אפילו ממון קל התיר עצמו למיתה ומתרין בו ואומרים לו אל
תמסור אם העיז פניו ואמר לא כי אלא אמסרנו מצוה להורגו וכל
הקודם להורגו זכה ׃

"Everywhere, even today, it is lawful for one to kill the traitor; yes, it is permissible to kill him even before he denounces, but only if he says: "I will denounce such and such a person', (so that he) suffers damage to his body or his money, even if it is only a little money, then the traitor has given himself up to death, and one warns him and says to him: 'Do not denounce!' But if he defies them and says: 'No, I will report it,' then it is a good deed to strike him dead, and anyone who strikes him dead first has merit (for it)."

Choschen ha-mischpat 388, 15:

מי שמוחזק ששלשה פעמים מסר ישראל או ממונם ביד עכ׳׳ן
מבקשים עצה ותחבולה לבערו מהעולם ׃

"If someone is found to have betrayed a Jew or his money to an Akum three times, ways and means are sought to get rid him."

Choschen ha-mischpat 388, 16:

הוצאות שעשו לבער מסור כל הדרים בעיר חייבים לפרוע בהם
אפילו אותם שפורעים מס במקום אחר ׃

"All the inhabitants of a place are obliged to contribute to the expenses incurred in getting rid of a traitor, even those who pay their taxes elsewhere." (Emendations of the above Hebrew texts were supplied by Dr. Erich Bischoff, scholar of Oriental literature in Leipzig.)

The above examples, as well as those listed under notes 8, 9 and 10, paragraph 2, are taken from an original translation prepared for a court report by the sworn court expert and private lecturer for Semitic languages at the Academy in Münster and later professor of the Hebrew language, Dr. Jakob Ecker. The judicial report had been requested in the well-known "Judenspiegel Trial", which came to trial on December 10, 1883 before the Criminal Chamber of the District Court in Münster. It is noteworthy that the verdict was acquittal, despite the fact that the Jewish seminary teacher Treu was consulted as an expert! In 1884, Dr. Jakob Ecker also published this expert opinion in print under the title "Der Judenspiegel im Lichte der Wahrheit" ("Mirror of the Jews in the Light of Truth") in the publishing house of the Bonifacius Press in Paderborn. It can be obtained at the price of M. 1.80 through the book trade. The report contains more than a hundred similar passages from books of Jewish religious law, mainly from the *Shul-chan Aruch*, in the original Hebrew text and in German translation. In the preface the reader will also find more details about the Judenspiegel trial.

The accuracy of Dr. Jakob Eckert's translation has now been corroborated by a new expert opinion. On February 14, 1895, a trial was held before the First Criminal Chamber of the Regional Court in Breslau against the distributor of a leaflet which reproduced a number of passages from Dr. Eckert's "Judenspiegel" with Hebrew and German text. The court expert was the private lecturer Dr. Georg Beer. He testified under oath "that he had found all the Hebrew passages in an edition of the *Shulchan Aruch* taken from the Breslau City Library, and that the German text standing next to the Hebrew text represents a translation of the Hebrew words that is entirely in keeping with the meaning, even if it is sometimes free." In answer to the question whether the commandment to kill, which occurs several times in the passages cited, could be applied not only to apostate Jews but also to other people, Dr. Beer testified "that the commandment to kill expressed in those sentences, as is evident from the whole meaning of the passage, also refers to Christians." In answer to the pointed question of the prosecutor whether the Hebrew expression did not admit of a more lenient translation, such as "worthy of death" or the like, the expert stated "that these sentences contain a quite strict commandment to kill." So, there can be no doubt that these laws are translated correctly.

It should be expressly noted that there are also passages in Jewish religious books that disapprove of usury, fraud, theft, and manslaughter when they are practiced on non-Jews. Already Eisenmenger says in his work, "Das entdeckte Judentum" [*Judaism Discovered*] (1711): "It is quite common among the rabbis that two opposite teachings are found among them." It is therefore entirely at the discretion of the Jew to follow one or the other, according to his own advantage. If one wants to nail him down to an immoral passage, he quickly fetches another that proves the opposite and assures and convinces us that the Talmud is the book of the deepest wisdom and morality and that the Jews are the most harmless and virtuous people in the world. Theodor Fritsch remarks ("The False God"): "In truth, the Talmud is a puzzle box with a double bottom, in which one can make good and bad appear and disappear at will, as required."

On January 13, 1921, the "Zentralverein deutscher Staatsbürger jüdischen Glaubens" (Central Association of German Citizens of the Jewish Faith) held a closed lecture evening at the Philharmonic in Berlin, to which numerous invitations had been sent personally to elementary school teachers, academics, clergymen, etc. Dr. Paul Fiebig (Lic. theol., Leipzig), who has gained a reputation for his work on the Mishna and Talmud, spoke on the subject: "Are there secret Jewish laws?" In the subtitle it was announced that the attacks which Theodor Fritsch and I had made against Jewish religious writings were to be repudiated and that the baselessness of our assertions was to be demonstrated. Neither Fritsch nor I received an invitation. However, I had been made aware of the lecture by friends of mine, they provided me with one of their tickets, and so I was able to speak up quickly in my own defense. This was made very easy for me. The lecturer summarized his remarks in the classic words: "You see, ladies and gentlemen, here (in Jewish religious law) everything and nothing is valid at the same time! So I only had to thank the speaker for his excellent lecture to the German people, and to ask the board, whose uninvited guest I was, to recruit Lic. theol. Dr. Fiebig as an itinerant speaker, so that his wisdom would also benefit the other local groups of the Central Association, because the speaker's remarks coincided exactly with what Fritsch and I maintain about the Jewish religious laws.

In view of the monstrosities of certain Jewish religious regulations directed against Christians and state laws, one usually assumes that these Jewish religious precepts are no longer valid today. But this is not so, although the Jews naturally assure us the opposite. The *Shulchan-Aruch* (in German "Zugerichtete Tafel" or "Gedeckter Tisch" [Set Table]) was written only around the middle of the 16th century! (The first edition was published by Rabbi Joseph Caro in Venice in 1565.) It consists of a methodical summary of the laws of all previous Jewish religious books, Talmud, Mishna, etc. The purpose of this summary, according to the preface, is to give a general overview of the Jewish religion. The purpose of this summary, according to the preface, is: "so that the law of the Lord may become familiar to every Jew". The preface goes on to say: "Even the young pupils should constantly study it (the Shulchan Aruch) and learn it by heart, so that the practical laws become familiar to them from early youth and they do not forget them in old age." Furthermore, "that through this book the earth may be filled with the knowledge of God, small as well as great, pupils as well as wise, world-famous as well as humble scholars." The sentence of the preface is very significant: "I gave the book the title "Set Table", because those who study it will find all kinds of exquisitely prepared and selected delicacies dished up in it"!

Dr. Rahmer, Rabbi in Magdeburg, writes in Pierer's Konversationslexikon, Vol. 16 (1879): "The *Shulchan Aruch* is regarded by the Israelite communities as the authoritative guideline for religious practice." Heinrich Ellenberger in his "Historical Handbook" (Budapest 1883) states "that after its publication the *Shulchan Aruch* was recognized by all rabbis as the only valid code of law and was spread everywhere since the invention of the printing press". He further writes, "For three centuries, the *Shulchan Aruch* has been the only theological code of law for the Jews and our catechism".[1]

A Jewish general synod, which met in Hungary in 1866, decided: "to declare to Christians that it renounces the *Shulchan Aruch*; in reality, however, every Jew must follow the *Shulchan Aruch* at all times! This resolution was signed by 94 rabbis, 182 lawyers (including 16 judges!), 45 doctors and 11,672 other Jews. It was printed in Lemberg in 1873 together with the signatures under the title "Leb haibri".

Not only the *Shulchan Aruch*, but the older Talmud is still binding for Jews. This is evident from the fact that wherever Jews live in large numbers there are Talmud Torah schools. Dr Jakob Fromer, formerly the librarian of the Berlin Jewish community, has vividly described in his book "Das Wesen des Judentums" [The Essence of Judaism] how he was brought up entirely in the spirit of the Talmud in his Galician homeland, and how at a young age did not get to know any other literature at all than the rabbinical-talmudic. The Jews coming to us from Russia and Austria, who make up a considerable percentage of our Jews, are undoubtedly steeped with Talmudic spirit. But even our devout German Jews are also regularly taught the Talmud in the Talmud congregations which exist in all the larger German cities. The authoritative Jewish year-book "Archives israélites," published in Paris, writes (1865, p. 25): "As far as the Talmud is con-

---

[1] Ed.: For an excellent short study and analysis of the *Shulchan Aruch*, see the book by Erich Bischoff, *The Book of the Shulchan Aruch* (2023).

cerned, we confess its unconditional superiority over the Law of Moses."
In the Marburg trial against the teacher Fenner in April 1888, the forensic
expert, the famous Kant scholar Professor Cohen affirmed under oath that
the Talmud is still to be regarded as the source of Jewish morality. In the
trial against the editor of the Hanoverian Post, J. Rethwisch, which was
tried before the Regional Court in Hanover on November 23, 1894, Rabbi
Dr. Gronemann, who was called as an expert witness, affirmed: "The Talmud is the authoritative source of law for the Jews and is still in full force."
According to a report in Hirsch Hildesheim's "Jüdische Presse" of January
31, 1913, Dr. Mannheimer, state rabbi in Oldenburg, in a lecture called
"the Talmud the lifeblood of Judaism and the home, the banner and school
of Jewry and the training of its intellectual faculties."

But even modern, free-thinking-atheistic Judaism, as it is embodied in
the "Berliner Tageblatt" and the "Frankfurter Zeitung", cannot get out of
its Talmudic skin, because the Jews did not become what they are only
through the Talmud and the *Shulchan Aruch*, but these Jewish law codes
are conversely a very characteristic product of the Jews, who for many
thousand years always were, are and will remain what they are! Race characteristics are ineradicable! Talmud and *Shulchan Aruch* remained in full
force in the Jewish blood, even then if they were overruled by legal means.

It is well known that Jews keep their religious laws strictly secret, and
that they do it with good reason, according to the above examples, is very
understandable. Besides, the Talmud itself strictly commands them to do
so. In Sanhedrin 59a, and Chagiga 13a, it is taught that a gentile who studies the Talmud and a Jew who teaches a gentile the Talmud deserve death.
In the Shaare theshuba it is written that a Jew who translates something
from the Talmud or the rabbinic writings and makes it accessible to non-
Jews is to be considered a traitor and must be secretly eliminated! With
what conceivable means of bribery and threats the Jews actually prevented
the translation and publication of their religious books, and how those involved often died in a very mysterious ways, one may read in the introduction to Prof. August Rohling's work "The Talmud Jew". The Jews have
also managed to prevent the translation and publication of Jewish religious
books by the state, which have been repeatedly demanded.

In order to understand by what machinations rabbis of today try to
disguise or deny the ambiguity and unambiguity of certain Jewish religious
precepts, one should read the author's pamphlet "Lichtstrahlen aus dem
Talmud" (Rays of Light from the Talmud), the open letters to the state
rabbi of Saxony-Weimar-Eisenach, Dr. Wiesen, and the public appeal to

the rabbis Dr. Bruno Lange in Essen and Dr. Rosenack in Bremen, as well as to all rabbis of Germany.

Despite my public request to disprove this document, which contains the sharpest attacks, not only on individual rabbis mentioned by name but on all rabbis in Germany, a refutation has not taken place to the present day, one and a half years after its publication. The history of this work had given me cause for filing a lawsuit against Rabbi Dr. Wiesen, which ended with his conviction in the first instance. When, in the main hearing on December 17, 1919, at the district court in Eisenach, I asked the rabbi to disprove my writing with his refutation, he answered to general amusement: "I will be careful!

Jewish religious regulations themselves now furnish the evidence that Jews do not profess a religion that is morally equal to the Christian faith, on an equal footing with it, and compatible with the welfare and security of the Christian citizenry and with the laws of the German state. The Jews do not form a harmless religious community, but rather a religious community which is inimical to the Christian German state in the midst of the German state. According to the judgment of outstanding minds like Kant, Schopenhauer, etc., and according to the admissions of outstanding Jews like Heinrich Heine, Moses Mendelssohn, etc., the Jewish religion is not at all a religion in the literal sense of the word, but is purely a constitution of state laws, which regulates the relations of the members of this Jewish state among themselves and to the members of other peoples. Kant writes in his essay "Religion within the limits of mere reason": "The Jewish faith, according to its original establishment, is the epitome of merely statutory laws, on which a state constitution was founded; for whatever moral additions were attached to it, either already at that time or subsequently, do not belong to Judaism as such. The latter is actually not a religion at all, but merely an association of a multitude of people who, since they belonged to a special tribe, formed themselves into a community under merely political laws, thus not into a church.

The fact that this constitution of state is based on theocracy, that is, on the name of God, who here is worshipped merely as a worldly ruler who makes no claim at all on the conscience, does not make it a constitution of religion." And Schopenhauer in "Parerga und Paralipomena": "Accordingly, it is an error if the Jews are regarded merely as a religious sect; but if, in order to promote this error, Judaism is called a "Jewish denomination" by an expression borrowed from the Christian church, then this is a fundamentally false expression, calculated to mislead, which should not be permitted at all. Rather, "Jewish nation" is the correct one."

The noble Jew Moses Mendelssohn, whose authority no one can doubt, expressly confesses in his work "Salvation of the Jews": "Judaism is not revealed religion, but revealed legislation." And the less noble Jew Heinrich Heine, in his "Travel Pictures," calls the Jewish religion a "so-called positive religion," and in his "Confessions" he writes: "The deeds of the Jews and their customs are completely unknown to the world. One believes one knows the Jews because one has seen their beards, but one has observed nothing but their beards. For the rest, they are still, as in the Middle Ages, a wandering mystery."

Every German who loves his people and fatherland must therefore see to it that the unsuspecting German people are enlightened about these conditions! And the demand must be raised with all determination to create laws that protect the Christian citizens of the German state and the interests of the German state against the immoral, criminal, and dangerous laws of the Jewish state, which hides behind the Jewish religious community. The demand must be made again and again that the law books of the Jewish religion from the Talmud to the *Shulchan Aruch* and all the commentaries and interpretations belonging to them be translated by the state from Hebrew into German without any gaps and be made accessible to the public!

There is no German translation of the *Shulchan Aruch* by impartial non-Jewish scholars, although the Jews and certain Christian theologians writing on behalf of the Jews claim the contrary. The translations published by the Jews themselves or by gentiles on behalf of the Jews are incomplete, inaccurate and misleading and therefore scientifically completely worthless. The same is true of the German and Latin translations of the Talmud. We Germans have the right to know precisely the regulations of a religion which has been recognized by the state as having equal rights with our Christian religion!

Furthermore, it must be demanded with all decisiveness and resolution that the state law, which brought the Jewish "religion" equal rights with ours, be subjected to a thorough re-examination, since the legislators of that time did not know and could not have known the instructions of the Jewish religion directed against Christians and the German state law and institutions, for only in recent times has it been possible to bring them to light!

Chap. 16, Note 21: In the *Jüdische Rundschau* of November 21, 1913, it is reported: "During a trial before the regional court in Lemberg, a Jewish lawyer, Dr. Alexander Klaften, representing allegedly aggrieved peasants against Jews, who were accused of perjury, declared that the Jewish religion and Jewish solidarity permit perjury when it is a question of saving a Jew." Consider the consequences of the fact that 11 1/2% of the judges in Berlin's district courts are Jewish! At District Court 3 in Berlin, eleven of 16 commercial judges are Jews! (Statistics from 1906 according to Theodor Fritsch, *Handbuch der Judenfrage*, 26th ed., p. 324. The statistics do not take into account the baptized Jews! Since then, the number of Jewish judges and public prosecutors has increased quite significantly!) The number of Jewish lawyers today is already enormous. According to official data of the Minister von Schönstedt, there were 526 Jews among 851 lawyers in Berlin in 1901! That is about 62%!! In the same year, among 176 notaries, 65 were Jews!!! That is 37%!! Again, the statistics do not take into account baptized Jews! These circumstances make it understandable that our courts show a conspicuous tendency to take Jewish views into account. The Jewish technical expert and chief appraiser in commercial, scientific, literary, and moral matters is a well-known phenomenon in court.

The Kolnidre prayer has the following wording:

כל נדרי ואסרי ושבעי וחרמי וקונמי וקונסי וכנויי ושבועות
דנדרנא ודאשתבענא ודאחרימנא ודאסרנא על נפשתנא מיום
כפורים זה עד יום כפורים הבא עלינו לטובה בכלהון איחרטנא
בהון כלהון יהון שרן שביקין שביתין בטלין ומבטלין לא שרירין
ולא קיימין נדרנא לא נדרי ואסרנא לא אסרי ושבועתנא לא
שבועות :

"All vows, renunciations, bans, confiscations, castigations and pledges under any name, also all oaths, that we have vowed, sworn, banned and renounced on ourselves- from this Day of Atonement until the next Day of Atonement, which may come for our benefit—we hereby repent them all; let them all be dissolved, voided, unbound, annulled and destroyed, without obligation and without continuance. Let our vows not be vows; let what we have said not be renunciations, and what we have sworn, not be oaths."

(The original Hebrew text and German translation are taken from Theodor Fritsch's *Der falsche Gott*, 4th ed. 1916. Proofreading by Dr. Erich Bischoff, scholar of Oriental Literature in Leipzig).

The Kolnidre prayer has recently been set to music by Max Bruch and is occasionally sung in Hebrew at public concerts. The Jews then present understandably burst into roaring applause afterwards, which the Christian audience, in their ignorance, usually follows.

Chap. 16, Note 23: Heinrich Heine (regarding his Jewish identity, see the works of his racial comrades Karpeles, Jungmann and Plotke) writes in his diary shortly after his baptism:

> "And you have crawled to the cross,
> to the cross that you despise,
> that only a few weeks ago
> you thought to tread in the dust."

In the letter in which he informs his friend Moser of his conversion, he writes: "I want to become Japanese. There is nothing they hate so much as the cross. I want to become Japanese."

To another friend Heine said: "I make no secret of my Judaism, to which I have not returned, since I never left it."

In "Travel Pictures" he writes: "But there came a people out of Egypt, and besides the skin diseases and the stolen gold and silver dishes, they also brought a so-called positive religion with them ... That mummy of the people, who walks over the earth, wrapped in its diaper of old letters, a hardened piece of world history, a ghost that trades in alterations and old trousers for its sustenance.... It is by these long noses, a kind of uniform, that the God-King Jehovah recognizes his old bodyguards, even when they have deserted."

Prof. Dr. Heinrich Graetz (with his real name Hirsch) writes in his "Geschichte der Juden" [History of the Jews] (Leipzig 1870) Vol. 11, p. 368, about Börne and Heine: "They have both outwardly renounced Judaism, but only like fighters who seize the enemy's armor and flag in order to destroy him all the more surely. Both have expressed with a clarity that leaves nothing to be desired how much they cared for the religion of the cross."

In Paris, in 1864, the "Archives israélites" writes: "The seal of the Israelite is impressed upon us by birth, and this seal we can never lose, never take it off; even the Israelite who denies his religion, who is baptized, does not cease to be an Israelite, and all the duties of an Israelite are incumbent upon him continually."

E. M. Oettinger writes in his "Offenen Billet-Doux an den berühmten Hepp-Hepp-Schreier und Judenfresser Herrn Richard Wagner"[Open Love Letter to the famous Hep-Hep Crier and Jew-hater Richard Wagner],

Dresden 1869 p. 5: "Above all, the writer of these lines must say in advance that he, a Jew by birth, became a Catholic Christian only in order to have the right to remain a Jew without danger.

In the "Allgemeine Zeitung des Judentums" 1898, No. 36, Moritz Scherbel writes about a Jewish doctor who had been baptized and said to him: "By the way, if a geschmadter (baptized) Jew tells you that he has geschmadt out of conviction, he is lying."

The Protestant preacher Wallfisch declared in 1894 in a lecture "Unparteiisches über die Judenfrage" [Impartiality regarding the Jewish Question] (see Deutsche Wacht, 16. 3. 1894): "I am a Jew and remain so, indeed, now that I have come to know the Christian faith, I have only become a true Israelite."

The pastor Dr. Moritz Schwalb confessed in his farewell sermon in March 1894: "He always felt himself genuinely to be a Jew racially, and had tried in vain to build a bridge between Judaism and Christianity. He confessed that at heart he had always remained a follower of Jewish teachings."

Emin Pasha (his real name is Dr. Schnitzer) declared to Julius Edward Cohen ("Allgemeine Zeitung des Judentums 1895): "You know that I am a Jewish renegade: despite my conversion to Christianity and later to Islam, I have never ceased to remain faithful to the religion in which I was born and brought up." (The above passages are taken from the "Deutschvölkische Hoch- schulschriften," issue 3, "Jüdische Selbstbekenntnisse" [Jewish Self-confessions].)

Chap. 22, Note 2: In the anthology "Vom Judentum" [On Judaism], issue by the well-known Leipziger Jewish publisher Kurt Wolff, Hans Cohn writes: "Today we are Jews, Jews by descent, by history, determined in our thinking and feeling by the factors of blood."

In a Zionist meeting in 1913, a Jewish student ("Im deutschen Reich" [In the German Empire] 1913, p. 211) declared: "I am not a German, I am a Jew, of the nation of Jews, I am not a German, because I do not grasp their kind - there are no Jews at all who have ever deeply felt or can feel a German folk song!" At the meeting of the "Central Association of German Citizens of the Jewish Faith" of May 17, 1913, Dr. Arthur Brünn said (according to the report of the journal "Im deutschen Reich," July/August 1913): "Then I will briefly define my position on this, that we may very well be good German patriots, good German citizens, and not only citizens, but to a certain extent imbued with a strong German cultural feeling, but that we cannot have German national feeling." Furthermore: "By Jewish national consciousness I understand the living consciousness of a common descent, the feeling of a togetherness of the Jews of all countries and the firm will of a common future."

The Jew Stefan Großmann, feuilleton editor of the "Vossischen Zeitung", conveys the views of the Viennese zionist students in the magazine "März", June 1908, p. 496 ff.: "We are of course Jews, that is our nation, the German ... ah, that is only mentioned because of the language and because of the areas in which we are responsible. What is German about us, they say, is only on the outside, what is Jewish is on the inside. And this is not only the way the Jewish finches talk, no, this is the way recognized, serious, famous people talk, people who like to pretend they are European, especially the so-called Young Viennese poets, Mr. Richard Beer-Hofmann, Mr. Felix Salten, the late Theodor Herzl. Almost all the Young Viennese poets are Germans of the Jewish nation."

Dr. Leopold Kohn, rabbi in Vienna, said in a speech he gave in 1919 at the Jewish school in Pressburg: "The Jew will never be able to assimilate; he will never adopt the customs and traditions of other peoples. The Jew remains a Jew under all circumstances; any assimilation is only a purely external one!" (Eberle, Großmacht der Presse [Great Power of the Press]).

The Viennese *Jüdisches Volksblatt* declared in January 1903: "We Jews, as a result of our race, as a result of our oriental descent, as a result of that bottomless ethnological, ideational and cultural gulf, which separates us from the Aryan tribe and principally from the Germanic people, are not in a position to make even the slightest claim to German customs and German usage, and, in a word, have nothing whatsoever to do with the Germanic people."

Chap. 25, Note 1: The Jewess Anselma Heine writes about the Jewish writer Jacobowski in the "Literarisches Echo", issue 3, 1912/13, published by the Jewish publishing house Egon Fleischel and Co., Berlin: "It was a vengeful delight for him to gain power over women, and he was never more derisively labeled the plebeian, than when he boasted of having subjugated the fine wives of the blond nobles with brutal force."

The Jew Conrad Alberti-Sittenfeld writes in a note of his essay "Judentum und Antisemitismus" (Society 1889) about "sexual intercourse, especially the behavior of rich Jewish boys towards poor girls, nurses, etc.": "This reaches an unbelievable level of cynical crudeness, to which I have never seen Christian young people sink. Most of them still retain a last vestige of shame toward women, which our stock market jobbers lack to a fraction."

The "Israelitische Wochenschrift" of November 10, 1899 reports: "Galician Jews unquestionably participate to a large extent in the disgraceful selling and negotiating of white slave women. Almost every trial that has been conducted in this dark field in recent times proves this."

In the illustrated monthly for Jewry, "Ost und West" [East and West], August 1913, the Jewess Bertha Pappenheim states in an essay on the trafficking in girls: "that with us Jews, girls are a commodity of international exchange, and a colossal number of dealers and traffickers, middlemen and agents are Jews and Jewesses." She adds that even Western European and American Jews "do almost nothing to combat the traffic in girls."

Chap. 26, Note 2: The Viennese *Jüdisches Volksblatt* wrote after the *Staatsbürger Zeitung* of August 3, 1899:

"The Jews have not yet brought blessings to any party to which they have unconditionally and wholeheartedly adhered.... Let us promote the Social Democrats as best we can, but let us be careful in doing so, lest the broad masses realize that the Social Democrats are only a Jewish protection force, and lest there be any occasion for opponents to call the party in question slaves of the Jews."

In the paper "Aus dem Sittenverfall des Judentums" [On the Moral Decay of Judaism], edited by Mendelsohn (Berlin 1878), the following passages can be found according to Otto Glagau ("Kulturkämpfer" [Culture Warrior] of December 15, 1884): "The Jew is a highly ingenious thinking and acting character, who has spread over the universe and is gathering fortunes with all possible manipulations, be it directly or indirectly.... He has been able to appropriate the largest industrial enterprises, palaces, capitals, etc., etc., by means of frequently dishonorable actions, and he has succeeded in nesting himself more and more firmly among us. For this purpose, he also appropriates literary undertakings, newspapers, etc., in order to win the press for himself and his way of acting. From all this, it is certainly evident that the whole of civilized society is not only suffering from the pressure of Jewry, but is gradually losing its property, sense of justice and social decency ...."

The Jew Conrad Alberti-Sittenfeld writes in his essay "Judentum und Antisemitismus" [Judaism and Anti-Semitism] (Gesellschaft [Society], 1889, S. 1718): "Judaism has a harmful effect in political terms as an element that is both ultra-reactionary and ultra-radical at the same time. For these two qualities are found in wonderful mixture in Judaism. With fanatical tenacity, it clings to the most rotten, senseless institutions and views, and at the same time with the same fanaticism it builds barricades, throws bombs and dynamite shells where it can ... By thus embracing two extremes, Judaism becomes the natural enemy and impediment of gradual organic development, which alone is the nurse of healthy decency in all things. No one can deny that Judaism participates outstandingly in the mire and corruption of all conditions. A characteristic trait of the Jews is the persistent endeavor to produce values without the expenditure of labor, that is, since this is an impossibility: the swindle, the corruption, the endeavor to create false value through stock exchange maneuvers, using the press and similar methods."

The rabbi A. M. Levin says in his writing "Vertrauliche Mitteilungen eines Patrioten"[Confidential Communications of a Patriot] (Berlin 1856): "No one is so dangerous to the state and throne in its apostasy as the Jew. The year 1848 gives evidence of this ... The talents which the Jew possesses as a democrat for agitation are a rarity among Christians, and even if the Jews are fewer in number, they are nevertheless very dangerous to the state."

Theodor Mommsen, whom the Jews so eagerly defend, writes in his *Römischen Geschichte* [*Roman History*]: "Even in the ancient world, Judaism was the most effective ferment of cosmopolitanism and national decomposition."

Chap. 26, Note 3: Houston Stewart Chamberlain, in his essay "Race and Nation", discusses this question, which is so fateful for the German national power: "When actual Judaism (as distinguished from the broader culture of Israel) was founded - namely after the return from the Babylonian captivity - one sin was emphasized as the most serious of all sins, as "the sin against God" (Nehemiah 13:27): "if your sons take foreign wives". This law still applies today, as it did 2500 years ago.

"But it is a completely different thing to permeate the foreign nations with Jewish blood; this has always been pursued with systematic thoroughness. For already, the old law regards the marriage of the Jewish daughter with a gentile, though not desirable, as a lesser sin; and by marrying its daughters to princes and nobility, today's international Jewish plutocracy acquires access and influence precisely in those authoritative places which would otherwise remain closed to it, without its own pure Jewish tribe being polluted by a single drop of goyim blood, or - to use the language of the Bible – "that the holy seed be made common with foreign nations" (Ezra 9:2).

"Of all the large Jewish families of today, there is not a single one which has mixed blood in its male tribe. Even the few owners of large banking houses who have been baptized (for reasons unknown to me), such as Erlanger, Oppenheim, etc., remain purely Jewish. And so that you don't think that I am talking into the blue, I ask you to take a reliable book, e.g. the Jewish Year Book, and look up the chapter about the Jewish nobility of England. You will see that to this day, not a single male scion of these families - not even a younger son - has married outside of pure Jewry, and that of the daughters only a small percentage have had to sacrifice themselves to the holy cause into the arms of gentiles - but then with wise selection of the highest court circles. Here, where the facts are clearly laid out and documented, you can get to know the behavior of Jewry with regard to the intermingling with us gentiles.

"Of course, there are Jewish men in bourgeois circles who marry non-Jewish women, but the number is infinitesimal, and I have already been able to observe in several such cases with what sure sense of race these Jews, who ostentatiously entered into "mixed marriages" chose their Christian wives from families that were strongly interspersed with Jewish blood. We Europeans pay no attention to such things; however, from the cradle to the grave, the Jew never loses sight of the interests of his race."

Dr. Bernhard Cohn says in the "Jüdisch-politische Zeitfragen" [Jewish Political Questions of the Time] (Berlin 1899): "When we see that the affinities of the noble houses with Jewish families, no matter how rich, are increasing, we must regard this, in spite of our liberal views, as the beginning of a moral decline of the nobility." - About the Jewish families of Christian denomination, it then goes on to say: "A social circle of German citizens of Jewish descent and Christian denominations is thus forming, as it were, and the nemesis of compelling logic is making the religiously assimilated regress to the real national Jew. For their attachment to the Jewish community, the actuality of which, according to what has been said, is not to be doubted, no longer has a religious, but a real national basis."

Chap. 26, Note 5: It is very interesting that the justification and necessity of anti-Semitism is admitted by individual Jews themselves. Thus the Jewish writer Dr. Elias Jacob (Fromer) writes in the "Zukunft" [Future] of June 18, 1904, about anti-semitism to his tribal comrades: "You answer that this condition was artificially caused by some person or current and must therefore cease with the disappearance of this person or current. But how do you explain that this hatred - open or hidden - is still prevalent today almost in all countries where you are present in considerable numbers?

And how do you explain the undeniable fact that at all times and everywhere you have come into contact with other peoples, this hatred has always lived under the most diverse names, pretexts and forms? ...

"Have you never noticed the similarity between the language of a horse mackerel, a Lutheran and Haman? Do you really think that all this was only artificially made? ... Or is the purpose of your mission fulfilled when you push yourselves against every new movement and destroy it by your participation and cooperation? Liberalism, in the middle of the 19th century, was a vigorous sapling that might have borne much good fruit. Then you approached without being called, clinging to it like chains, with your needs, your longing for emancipation and bourgeois equality, until it collapsed under your weight. And do you think that social democracy, the stock exchange, and the newspaper business will fare better under your participation?"

In the "Zukunft" of July 23, 1904, its editor, the Jew Maximilian Harden (Isidor Witkowski) wrote: "Jacob's essay has aroused a howl of rage in Jewry that I had not expected, despite some experience. Is it permissible to speak ruthlessly about every other religion, every race and class, and only against Israel not to dare a critical word? That would be a marvelous demand; all the more marvelous because it seems to be made by people who daily clamor for tolerance."

According to Glagau ("Kulturkämpfer", February 1884), Saul's "New Epistle to the Hebrews" (Pressburg and Leipzig 1884) contains the following: "As a Jew and as a human being, I cannot be anything other than an anti-Semite.... If anti-Semitism had not stirred, within a short time all state offices would have been occupied by us Jews, we alone would have taken all the teaching pulpits, art and science would have passed completely into our hands.... With what right do we force our way into the municipal councils, into the administration of the local institutes, into the chamber of commerce, the school board and the like, if we do not have the slightest feeling for the general interests of the place, for the fame of the same and for its future, because we pack up at the first economic situation and move on, and take with us what we have sucked out of the place through long years of usury and other practices ...

"We Jews regard humanity's most cherished, inalienable possessions as mere commodities. If a business turns out to be more profitable run as a "religious cooperative", we declare ourselves to be a religious cooperative; if again the business grows better as a "nation", we are a nation. However, we also trade in foreign nationalities, the give and take after political fluctuations. If, in the polyglot countries of Hungary and Bohemia, Germanism is valid, we are committed Germans; if the Magyars and Czechs come back on top, we are quickly Magyar and Czech chauvinists again ... Anti-Semitism represents the reawakened idealism."

At a meeting of the Jewish student body in Berlin called by Zionists in July 1901, the student Rosenthal, among others, declared: "Anti-Semitism is in the innermost soul of the German people. I cannot blame it, if it wants to keep itself pure."

Student Cohn said, "It is true we have a power more fearsome than any other. Look around you: Who is the audience in the theaters? Jews! Who runs the press? Jews! Who influences German art in the strongest way? Jews! Then one can truly understand that anti-Semitism is growing, and one must not resent it."

The Jewish writer Otto Weininger says in his well-known work "Geschlecht und Charakter" [*Sex and Character*] (1903): "The fact that outstanding people were almost always anti-Semites (Tacitus, Pascal, Voltaire, Herder, Goethe, Kant, Jean Paul, Schoenhauer, Grillparzer, Wagner) is due to the fact that they, who have so much more in them than other people, also understand Judaism better than they do.... The genuine Jew lacks that inner nobility which results in self-dignity and respect for the other self. There is no Jewish nobility; and this is all the more remarkable, since among the Jews inbreeding has existed for thousands of years ... The real Jew has no ego and therefore also has no intrinsic value ... The Jew is always more lustful, hornier than the Aryan man ... The Jew is born to blur boundaries. He is the antithesis of the aristocrat ... The Jew is a born communist."

The "Kreuzzeitung" [Cross Newspaper, No. 429] published in September 12, 1912, a letter from the Jewish side, containing the following passage: "The measure of self-criticism on the Jewish side has always been quite moderate, criticism from the other side is also very unpopular, and one simply helps oneself by calling the other an anti-Semite, but oneself a martyr. If one had used only a small fraction of the temperament in one's own house, which one continuously sends on the warpath against the state, the crown, and institutions in the Jewish press, then the unbelievable suffrage within the Jewish communities - in truth the most miserable in the world - would have fallen long ago, then one would make the preacher Kohn the center of a campaign, not Jatho and Traub, then one would not take the liberty of judging the Christian churches with a disgustingly low level of taste.

"The position one has attained in the legal profession, in the press, in finance, in the theater does not give one the right to behave as if one, alone and against innumerable enemies, represented all that one likes to call freedom and justice. One can and must demand that everyone who owes his education to a culture which neither he nor his fathers helped to build, behave loyally, or else take upon himself the very sharp opposition about which he continually complains."

A very relevant counterpart to this outspoken Jewish confession is the no less outspoken one by the Jewish writer Klötzel. He writes in issue 2 of the journal "Janus" (Munich) 1912/13: "Nobody can shake the fact that a strong Jewry is a danger to everything non-Jewish. All attempts of certain Jewish circles to prove the contrary must be called as cowardly as they are strange. But it must seem even stranger when gentiles in all seriousness demand of us Jews to renounce the exercise of our natural hatred, when they demand restraint, modesty, humility from us." (Deutschsoziale Blätter, No. 89, November 6, 1912.)

Chap. 26, Note 7: The Jewish writer Moritz Goldstein, in the March 1912 issue of "Kunstwart" (F. Avenarius, Munich) under the heading "German-Jewish Parnassus", writes: "Jews are suddenly standing at all posts from which they are not forcibly kept away; ... more and more it seems as if German cultural life should pass into Jewish hands ... We Jews administer the spiritual possessions of a people who deny us the right and the tenacity to do so .... No one seriously doubts the power that the Jews possess in the press. Criticism in particular, at least in the capitals and their influential newspapers, is on the verge of becoming a Jewish monopoly. Equally well known is the predominance of Jewish element in the theater; almost all Berlin theater directors are Jews, as are a large part, perhaps the largest part, of the actors as well, and the fact that without Jewish audiences, theater and concert life in Germany would be virtually impossible, is repeatedly praised or lamented.

"A completely new phenomenon is that even German literary studies seem to be on the point of passing into Jewish hands, and it is, depending on one's point of view, comical or tragic to survey the members of the "Germanic" seminaries of our universities. (I myself have been one of them.) Many a guardian of German art knows to his anger how many Jews there are finally among the "German poets".... We no longer preach a "Mosaic confession," but believe in a Jewish people with innate, indelible characteristics."

Houston Stewart Chamberlain, in his "Goethe" (F. Bruckmann AG Publisher, Munich), shows what became of German literary studies in the hands of Jews. Referring to Goethe's remark, "It only takes a beggar Jew to mock a God on the cross," Chamberlain explains on p. 689 the following: "By the way, this very sentence has had an instructive fate; for both of Goethe's grandsons, following the flow of time, believed they could do no better than entrust the correspondence between their grandfather and Knebel, in which it appears, to the Jewish scholar Guhrauer for publication; Guhrauer, who in his preface allows himself the usual Hebrew impertinences about Goethe's longtime, reliable friends, Riemer and Chancellor von Müller, and who assures us - of which we have no doubt - that he has the "original writings" in mind, simply deletes the entire paragraph containing that important saying! He also deletes the name of the Jew mentioned in Knebel's previous letter! But this case is not yet closed; for when the Weimar edition of the letter to Knebel of January 12, 1814 came out, it found it incompatible with its principles to follow the example of Professor Guhrauer, who had penetrated our Christian culture so much against Goethe's will; it restored the text intact—as everywhere, no doubt, here too— thus revealing the forgery; but it, which in the admirable "apparatus" at the end of each volume records every smallest deviation from earlier texts (e.g. in the letters to Schiller and to Zelter) with the most meticulous accuracy, conceals the gap in Guhrauer's edition here and makes the false assertion due to its concealment: Printed: Correspondence 2, 125."

Chamberlain also points to another literary falsification by Guhrauer and remarks: "in this case, however, the Weimar edition calls attention to Guhrauer's omission, which it does not do where Jews are affected by it!" Then he continues:

"Externally, this episode doesn't really fit into the text of my book, but it should serve as an example of what beleaguers us now and falsifies our culture in the large and small, until one day the real German - in thinking, feeling, creating, being - like the Sumero-Akkadian in ancient Babylon, being smothered, shattered, buried under a mountain of desert sand by Syro-Semitic ignorance and aridity of heart and poverty of spirit, will serve only as an archaeological curiosity for mixed-race scholars in complicated excavations and reconstruction attempts. Goethe, as humane, as generous as he was, as ready as he was to praise the skill of individual Jews, and especially so exuberant in his appreciation of the books (the writers of the Bible.) - not written by them, but transmitted to us through them - judged here, as in other matters, with unswerving objectivity."

The Jewish novelist Conrad Alberti-Sittenfeld writes in his essay "Judaism and Anti-Semitism" ("Gesellschaft" 1889): "Unfortunately, it cannot be denied that modern art, especially the theater, has only been corrupted by Jews. In general, for the Jews, art is only an object on which to exercise their wit, and the common danger of this peculiarity consists in

the fact that they impose this insipid wit on the world with the greatest audacity as genuine criticism."

The Jewish writer Dr. Elias Jacob (Fromer) wrote in the "Zukunft" of
October 28, 1911, in his essay "The Jews in the Economy": "The Jews
(considered as a whole) have never possessed the ability to bring forth a
great idea and to develop it systematically. This is evident when one considers the focus of their intellectual activity, their literature. There is no
book to be found in which a new, presuppositionless idea is worked out
according to a fixed disposition. Everything is commentary."

Chap. 32, Note 2: In his monumental work *Goethe* (F. Bruckmann AG
Publisher, Munich), Houston Stewart Chamberlain writes on p. 688 and ff.:
"This affirmation of Christianity (by Goethe) even includes a negation of
the un-Christian or anti-Christian, which is to be emphasized with all clarity and energy. In the same place where we read the words: "We hold fast
to this religion (the Christian one)," there is a momentous sentence which I
would like to see brought under the eyes of every single German in the
whole world: "In this sense" - namely in the education of all children to
Christianity - "we do not tolerate a Jew among us; for how should we grant
him the share in the highest culture, whose origin and tradition he denies?"

These words first prove how inseparably culture and religion belong
together for Goethe. An unreligious culture is nonsense for him, a *contra-
dictio in adjecto*; such a culture does not deserve the name culture. Moreover, he concludes from this - "perhaps pedantically but nevertheless logi-
cally", as he himself puts it - that a culture, since it rests on a religion,
should not grant any share in its life to those people who reject this religion
and historically belong to a completely different one. Religion must and
will always be the soul of a culture; either it is one religion or it is the other; if we hand over our Christian culture to the enemies of Christianity, we
ourselves lay the axe to our culture. At this point Goethe has the teachers
in mind first of all: no teacher on any level may be a Jew.

But he goes further and even forbids the Jews from any "share" in our
culture. Even his League of Emigrants "beware them", since they "know
how to outwit those who are at rest and to transgress those who are fellow
emigrants". So we must not only tolerate no Jewish professor at our universities, but no Jewish artist, poet, natural scientist, politician, officer,
judge, civil servant, man of letters, journalist, according to Goethe's conviction, among us; may the Jews work on their own culture; that would be
beneficial; we should not grant them a "share" in our culture, which de-
serves the title of a "highest" because of its religious soul. The number

does not do it; not a single one must be granted entrance into our sanctuary. "It only takes a beggar Jew to mock a God on the cross," remarked Goethe.

In the united Diet in 1847 Bismarck said: "I am not an enemy of the Jews, and if they should be my enemies, I forgive them. I might even love them under certain circumstances. I also grant them all rights, except that of holding an office of authority in a Christian state. The realization of the Christian doctrine is the purpose of the state; I cannot believe, however, that with the help of the Jews we should get any closer to this goal than we have hitherto…. If I think of a Jew as a representative of the holy majesty of the king, whom I should obey, then I must confess that that I should feel deeply weighed down and bowed down, that the joy and upright sense of honor with which I now endeavor to fulfill my duty to the state would desert me…. It seems to me a strong conclusion that because someone cannot become a civil servant, he must become a usurer!"

Chap. 32, Note 3: In his essay "Race and Nation" in the July 1918 issue of the monthly magazine *Deutschlands Erneuerung* [Germany's Renewal], Houston Stewart Chamberlain writes:

"Only since 1723, i.e. more than half a millennium after the foundation of the English Empire and only after a permanent consolidation of land ownership, did the English people allow the Jews to own land. Who knows whether today's England - the world power - would have ever come into being under different conditions? I do not believe it. For in the early Middle Ages the Jews were very numerous in England; and if you read the economist Cunningham's work, *The Growth of English Industry and Commerce during the Early and Middle Ages* (3rd edition, 1896, p. 199 ff.), you will see that these Jews, to whom every trade and every craft was open until the year 1290, and against whom no prejudice yet prevailed, were exclusively engaged in money usury and other improper business practices. The government's many attempts to persuade the Jews to take up decent trades failed. (p. 203.) And so Cunningham compares the Jewish colony of that time to "a sponge that sucked up the entire wealth of the nascent nation". Exactly the same thing happened to the French nobility at that time; almost all their property was pledged to the Jews in the 13th century (see Andre Reville: *Les Paysans au moyen âge* 1896, p. 3).

"Now what did these countries appreciate before they were completely denationalized in the early stages of their existence as a state? Only the clause which excluded the Jew from land ownership. Without this measure, the entire countries of England and France - apart from the state domains -

would have been Jewish property from the 13th century onwards, and the families that have made English history since then would have had to eke out an existence as servants of the usurers!

"But that one measure was not enough to stop the corrosive influence of the large Jewish colony in England, and so the English, who had always been practical, decided to take a more thorough approach: they removed all Jews from the country. From 1290 to 1657 there were no Jews in England - that is, during the whole consolidation of the nation, from the great Edward the first (the first true national king and founder of the actual Parliament) until after the death of the great line of rulers beginning with Henry VIII, culminating in Elizabeth and ending with Cromwell and his far-sighted overseas policy. This fact has remained of lasting influence to the present day. For while there had been 16,000 Jews in England at the time of the expulsion (see Green: *History of the English People*, book 3, chap. 4), which, according to the most reliable estimates of the population at the time, was at least 1%, but probably around 2% of the population, in pre-sent-day England (according to the *Jewish Year Book* for 1898) there are not quite 0.25% Jews. In the meantime, the English people had become stronger in every direction, and so the Jew could never gain a foothold to the same extent as before, even though all doors and gates were open to him."

One does not need to be a blind Jew-hater to recognize from several thousand years of history that the Jew has everywhere and always been a destructive element. Both his good and his bad qualities work to either destroy what he touches or to appropriate it to the detriment of others. The Jews possess many qualities worthy of respect; but every insightful and knowing man must admitted that they are devoid of every political instinct, of any tact at all. That is why that great, wise man who has been friendly towards the Jews from his youth - Goethe - was allowed to make the asser-tion: "Tolerance towards the Jews threatens the bourgeois constitution" (*Dichtung und Wahrheit* [Poetry and Truth], 13th book). Their whole char-acter urges the Jews to grasp the present intensely and only the present; politics, on the other hand, is the understanding of the future. And while politics is always occupied with reducing the friction between what is and what will be, carefully preventing today from being impoverished and bled to death by the higher demands of tomorrow, but at the same time ensuring that the inheritance of future generations should not be consumed by the present. The Jew has no understanding for either of these tasks. Even the "noble Jew" is therefore of no use to a young, nascent nation; even he can only harm it ...

Shall I still draw the conclusions from what has been said? No, right? It isn't necessary. Down with all persecutions of the Jews! Down with all absurd, medieval superstitions! Down with all social contempt and personal hatred! Grant the Jews the same inviolable protection that you grant to all strangers; grant them, moreover, as old inmates of the country, even more extensive privileges; admit them (since you can no longer prevent it) into commercial and industrial competition. — but keep a close eye on them! However, do not grant them any political rights and no right to the ownership of property. And see to it that the Jews do not become the masters of public opinion through the newspapers, and not the masters of hearts and minds through the domination of the book market and the schools. The former Berlin representative of the Times (a Jew) published a book about Germany a few years ago in which he triumphantly announced: "There is no more German literature, but only Jewish literature in the German language. Protective laws would be desirable here, but even more important is the active defense against Jewish influence through the conscious recognition of its danger to the public." Not that I want to suspect the motives of the Jew, I do it just as little in the spiritual as in the commercial field; the Jew has the right to be as he is; the tenacity with which he holds on to his peculiarity is admirable and worthy of imitation; but for our spirit and for our mind, his spiritual influence is a corrosive poison.

The Jewish weekly "Volk und Land" [People and Country] in the 2nd issue of January 9, 1919, published an essay by John Fraser "Die amerikanischen Juden und ihr Berufsleben" ("The American Jews and their Professional Life"), which gives a vivid picture of the unheard-of position of power that Judaism already occupies in America. It states:

"American Jews provide the mass of the population not only with clothing but also with housing. The "Real Estate Yearbook" contains a complete list of all land owners in New York. This book is a continuous index of Jewish names. Smith, Robinson, O'Brien, and Murphy are represented only sporadically, but the names Cohn, Levy, Kahn, and Rosenthal fill entire series of pages.... A considerable number of today's millionaire Jewish landowners were peddlers only a few years ago. ... There is no doubt that in a few years Jews will own by far the greater part of Manhattan Island, the most expensive piece of real estate in the whole world.

"In New York, half the students at Columbia University and three-quarters at New York University are Jewish. These young people are already flooding the civil authorities and crowding out their American and Irish competitors.

"The medical and laboratory professions, in which New York employs an entire army, are almost entirely filled with them. They also form a large majority in the engineering profession. In the lower courts they hold most of the positions which the whole city has to give ...

"The large department stores as we know them today owe their origin to Jewish minds; the names Straus, Altman, Bloomindale, Siegel, Grenhut tell of the department stores of the large cities, the majority of which developed only in the last generation from the smallest beginnings.

"Jews also dominate the whiskey and liquor business in the United States. Eighty percent of the organized merchants in this industry are Jews. In the distillery and wholesale trade Jews also account for 60 percent here.

"In the intermediary trade, they have control of California's wine production.

"It is similar with the tobacco industry. Jews visit the tobacco- producing states, buy up almost the entire quantum of leaf tobacco, so that the big tobacco companies have to buy the raw product from them....

"The American railroad system between the Mississippi River and the coast of the Pacific Ocean, and south from the Missouri to the Mexican border, is now largely in Jewish hands, with the company Kuhn, Loeb u. Co. playing the largest role....

"In the United States, the places of amusement are also almost exclusively in Jewish hands; at least 90 per cent of the opera houses, theaters, cinematographs, etc., are operated by Jews; they devote themselves to this business not as actors who have advanced to theater directors, but because they see great opportunities for earning money in it. There are half a dozen large theater companies whose owners are all millionaires. One of these companies, Schubert, has nearly 20 theaters in New York and is involved in at least 80 others. The great majority of Jews in the American theater business have only pecuniary interest and make no pretense of promoting the art."

The Jews are about to take over the world! It's high time that the cultural peoples of the whole world finally open their eyes to this fact!

For us Germans, the Jewish question is the question of all questions, because its solution is the precondition of a German renewal and a new German ascent! But as long as German feeling, thinking and will are inhibited and held down by the Jewish, there can be no thought of German rebirth! And certainly not under the sign of the Republic! If this form of government is to be a blessing to the German fatherland, then ways and means must be found to break the predominance of Jewry in Germany! For the recovery of the German people, artificially made ill and impoverished by the Jews, nothing more is required than that in Germany the German should become his own master again and independent of the Jew! We demand for ourselves only the right of self-determination within our own border posts!

What would the Jews say if Germans interfered in the affairs of the Jewish communities or even claimed leadership in them? Or if a German had the ambition to become prime minister in the new Jewish state of Palestine? And we don't want to enforce our right to self-determination against the Jew by force, but by legislative means through a referendum! That is the solution to the Jewish question that we are striving for! And for this nothing more is necessary than enlightenment about the nature of Judaism and its disastrous influence on our entire economic and cultural life, and the union of the enlightened into a firm organization! Enlightenment, enlightenment, untiring enlightenment in word and writing, from man to man, from woman to woman, from house to house, that is the only thing necessary to save us from enslavement and impoverishment by Judaism! Everything else comes by itself through legal channels by the will of the people.

Whoever wants to contribute to breaking the overwhelming power of Jewry in Germany and thereby lead our unfortunate fatherland towards recovery and resurrection from misery and night, shame and disgrace, should join one of the associations which make it their task to fight against the predominance of Jewry in speech and writing by legal means. The two most important are: The "*Deutschvölkischer Schutz- und Trutzbund*" [The German National Protection and Defense League], and the "*Deutschbund*" [German Union], Gotha. The membership lists are not published.

The aforementioned associations represent the following demands:

1. A German law against Jewish immigration.
2. Creation of a Foreign Law for the Jews.
3. Promotion of all efforts to establish a home for the Jews in their homeland, Palestine.
4. Combating the malign Jewish influence on our spiritual, moral, and economic life.
5. Translation of the Jewish religious scriptures and examination of their content by the state.
6. Promotion of all efforts to raise the racial, mental, and economic health of the German people.

FURTHER READING

Overview of Writings on the Jewish Question

Anyone interested in gaining insight into the racial question, especially into the fateful contrast in nature between Germans and Jews - and this duty is incumbent on every German who loves his fatherland - should read, above all, Chamberlain's *"Die Grundlagen des 19. Jahrhunderts"* [*The Foundations of the 19th Century*] (a new popular edition of this classic work, the 12th edition, has been published by F. Bruckmann, Munich.).

Next to this book, I [Artur Dinter] recommend Gobineau's *"Versuch über die Ungleichheit der Menschenrassen"* [*Essay on the Inequality of the Human Races*] in the excellent German translation by Ludwig Schemann. (Fr. Frommanns Verlag, Stuttgart, 3rd edition, 4 volumes.) This work, published in the fifties of the last century, for the first time dealt with the question of race as a question of the destiny of peoples. In some individual scientific questions it has been overtaken by the latest research, but the basic doctrine, carried out with incomparable genius, that the cultures of all peoples and times are of Aryan (Indo-Germanic) origin, and that the Germanic race is the noblest and leading cultural race of the world and the actual culture-generating element of the non-German cultural peoples of the present day, will be and remain the irrefutable result of racial scientific research. Gobineau's work ends in the gloomy prophecy that the racial decline and with it the downfall of the Germanic peoples is unstoppable as a result of the Semitization of the European peoples, which has already progressed too far. However, contemporary scientific anthropology does not share this view. We have it entirely in our hands, through purposeful racial hygiene, to keep our German people at the very respectable height of their present racial strength, especially through protection from further blood supply alien to their kind, and thus to guarantee them a still completely unimagined future.

Ludwig Moltmann has offered a political theory based on racial science in his seminal work *"Political Anthropology"*. (Publisher Eugen Diederichs, Jena.) Here, for the first time, a racial-scientific system of practical politics is set up. The development of family rights, the social history of the estates and professions, the political development of the peoples, the origin and development of political parties and theories are racially justified with the strictest scientific reasoning. No statesman or politician should fail to study this thorough work.

The "*Politisch-anthropologische Monatsschrift für praktische Politik, für politische Bildung und Erziehung auf biologischer Grundlage*" [*The Political-Anthropological Monthly for Practical Politics, for Political Education and Upbringing on a Biological Basis*], founded by Ludwig Woltmann and edited by Dr. Schmidt-Gibichenfels (21st volume, Politische anthropologischer Verlag, Hamburg 1, Ferdinand-Str. 5) continues Woltmann's work.

The following writings acquaint the reader with the essence of the "Jewish religion":

"*Der Talmudjude*" by Professor Dr. August Rohling, new edition by Carl Paasch (Deutschvölkische Verlagsanstalt, Hamburg).

"*Der Judenspiegel im Lichte der Wahrheit, eine wissenschaft- liche Untersuchung*" [*Mirror of the Jews in Light of the Truth, A Scientific Investigation*] by Dr. Jakob Ecker (Verlag der Bonifaciusdruckerei, Paderborn). This strictly scientific work contains over two hundred passages of Jewish religious law in the original Hebrew with German translations.

"*Blicke ins Talmudische Judentum, nach den Forschungen von Dr. Konrad Martin, Bischof von Paderborn, dem christlichen Volke enthüllt.*" [*Glimpses into Talmudic Judaism, according to the research of Dr. Konrad Martin, Bishop of Paderborn, revealed to the Christian people*]. (Verlag der Bonifaciusdruckerei, Paderborn.) "In the booklet various teachings of the Talmud are illuminated and their dangerousness and harmfulness for social life are shown."

"*Unmoral im Talmud*" [*Immorality in the Talmud*] by Alfred Rosenberg (Deutscher Volksverlag, Munich), offers his excellent methodical survey of the teachings of the Talmud which are incompatible with our German, Christian feeling and thinking.

"*Biblischer Antisemitismus*" [*Biblical Anti-Semitism*] by Pastor Karl Gererke (Deutscher Volksverlag, Munich.), reflects the world-historical guilt of the Jewish people in the anti-Semitic book of Jonah in the Old Testament.

"*Baldur und Bibel*" [*Baldur and Bible*] with 36 illustrations by Fr. Döllinger (Verlag Lorenz Spindler, Nürnberg.), brings new revelations about the Bible and the pre-Jewish, Aryan culture of biblical Canaan. (Cf. note 4).

The untruthful historical tradition, unscrupulous displacements and falsifications, and the need to examine and authorize from scratch the Old Testament beliefs handed down to us, are revealed in the sensational work by Prof. Dr. Friedrich Delitzsch, *"Die große Täuschung"* [*The Great Deception*] (Deutsche Verlagsanstalt, Stuttgart and Berlin 1920.).

The ingenious means with which the Jews continue their biblical falsification and concealment tactics today is illustrated in the book *"Der große Volks- und Weltbetrug durch die internationale Vereinigung 'Ernster Bibelforscher'"* [*"The Great Deception of the People and the World by the International Association 'Serious Bible Researchers'"*] by August Fetz (Deutschvölkische Verlagsanstalt, Arthur Götting, Hamburg.).

This clarifies for the reader the obfuscation of the original teaching of Christ by the Jewish spirit of the Old Testament and the resulting Jewish distortion and clericalization of the Christian church, as well as the necessity and the possibility of restoring the teaching of the Savior in its original purity, in the classic work of its kind, *"Der deutsche Heiland"* [*The German Redeemer*], (New Edition, "Anticlericus") by Friedrich Andersen, senior pastor in Schleswig. (Munich, Deutscher Volksverlag, Dr. Ernst Boepple, 1921.) This book also shows that Jesus did not complete the Old Testament, but destroyed it. The New Testament is not the consummation of the Old Testament, but rather the Talmud is. The doctrine of the Savior as divine revelation and the Christian religion as the only heroic world religion, is put into the brightest light by Andersen. Catholics, Protestants and other Christians will be deeply edified reading this book, because it does not depend on one or the other confessions, but only on the fact that we are Christians, deeply imbued with the divinity of the Savior and his teachings, as they are expressed non-dogmatically in the Gospels, but especially purely in the Gospel of John.

A quick but deep insight into the core of the Jewish question is offered by Theodor Fritsch's *"Beweismaterial gegen Jahwe"* [*Evidence against Yahweh*] (Hammerverlag, Leipzig, Königstraße 17, 7th ed.) and Roderich-Stoltheim's concise book *"Das Rätsel des jüdichen Erfolgs"* [*The Riddle of Jewish Success*].[1] (Hammerverlag, Leipzig.) A wealth of historical, sociological, literary, and statistical material on all questions connected with the Jewish problem is given in the excellent *"Handbuch der Judenfrage"* [*Handbook on the Jewish Question*] by Theodor Fritsch (Sleipner-Verlag, Hamburg 36, Neue ABC-Strasse 8, 28th edition).

Extraordinarily instructive is Hammer-Schrift No. 19, *"Jüdische Selbstbekenntnisse"* [*Jewish Self-confessions*] compiled by Ernst Kämpfer and the first booklet of the Deutschvölkische Hochschulschriften

---

[1] Fritsch's *Riddle* has been released in a new English edition in 2023, by Clemens & Blair publishing.

"Judentum und deutsche Literatur" [Judaism and German Literature] by Adolf Bartels (Commissionsverlag Volkstümliche Bücherei, Berlin).

An excellent literary history written from the point of view of the racial question is: *"Die deutsche Dichtung der Gegenwart"* [*The German Poetry of the Present*] by Adolf Bartels. (Leipzig, Verlag H. Hässel, 9th ed.)

The following journals, which are consciously German in character, report on the incessant destruction, pursued by pan-Judaism, of German feeling, thinking and aspirations in the fields of literature and the theater, art and politics:

"Der Türmer" [The Tower Keeper], publisher: J. E. Freiherr von Grotthuß (Verlag Greiner und Pfeiffer, Stuttgart), quarterly (6 issues).

"Deutschlands Erneuerung, Monatsschrift für das deutsche Volk [Germany's Renewal, Monthly Magazine for the German People], edited by Privy Councilor G. v. Below, H. St. Chamberlain, H. Claß, Professor R. Geyer-Wien, Privy Councilor M. v. Gruber, Privy Councilor Prof. Dr. Dietr. Schäfer, Dr. G. W. Schiele, Minister President v. Schwerin, Privy Councilor R. Seeberg. Editor Dr. Erich Kühn. (Published by J. F. Lehmann, Munich.) Quarterly.

The weekly magazines "Deutschvölkische Blätter" (36th Vol., Hamburg 1, Ferdinandstrasse 5) and the "Hammer, A non-Partisan Journal for National Life," keep the reader informed about all political, social and literary questions connected with the Jewish problem. (21st volume. Monthly 2 numbers, quarterly. Editor Theodor Fritsch, Publisher and Editor's Office Leipzig, Königstrasse 17.). In addition, "Auf Vorposten" [At the Outpost], a monthly journal of the "Verband gegen Überhebung des Judentums" [Union against Jewish Presumptions] published by Müller von Hausen, provides information about this area. (Quarterly. Publisher: Auf Vorposten, Charlottenburg 4.)

The nature of the all-Jewish press is aptly portrayed in the work of August Eigenbrod: "Berliner Tageblatt und Frankfurter Zeitung in ihrem Verhalten zu den nationalen Fragen 1887- 1914" [Berliner Tageblatt and Frankfurter Zeitung in their Attitude to National Questions 1887-1914] (Verlag A. Albrecht, Berlin-Schöneberg). — "Die Hammerschrift" [The Hammer Writings] No. 28 "Der jüdische Zeitungspolyp" [The Jewish Newspaper Polyp] by Theodor Fritsch the Younger (Hammerverlag, Königstr. 17.), provides an - admittedly still very incomplete - directory of the Jewish and Jewish-influenced newspapers and magazines in Germany.

An indispensable reference work is the "Semi-Kürschner", a Literary Dictionary of Writers, Poets, Bankers, Moneymen, Doctors, Actors, Artists, Musicians, Officers, Lawyers, Revolutionaries, Suffragettes, Social Democrats, etc., of the Jewish race and tribe, who from 1813-1913 were active or known in Germany, with the participation of ethnic associations, scholars, artists, clergymen, politicians, lawyers, agrarians, craftsmen, industrialists, merchants, men and women from Germany and abroad, published by Philipp Stauff.

No less important and significant is the "Semi-Gotha", historical- and genealogical pocketbook of the entire nobility of Jewish origin (1200 pages, 2nd edition, Kyffhäuser Verlag, Zechner & Co., Munich 23).

Whoever wants to learn about practical racial hygiene and its biological preconditions, should read the quite excellent and substantial book *"Der völkische Gehalt der Rassenhygiene"* [*The Folk Content of Racial Hygiene*] by Dr. F. Siebert (Verlag J. F. Lehmann, Munich.).

In an unsurpassable way, the work of Wilhelm Meister covers *"Judas Schuldbuch"* [*Judas' Book of Debts*] (Deutscher Volksverlag, Munich), the immense guilt of Jewry for our moral and political collapse and for all the of the hardship and disgrace and shame through which our unfortunate people and fatherland must pass through today. This excellent work is warmly recommended to the reader. It draws, as it were, the sum of the cultural and political questions raised in my contemporary novel and puts it to the test for the most tragic example that world history has ever experienced.

The two sensational works *"Weltfreimaurertum, Weltrevolution, Weltrepublik"* [*World Freemasonry, World Revolution, World Republic*], a study of the origin and ultimate aims of the World War by National Councilor Dr. Fr. Wichtl, (J. F. Lehmanns Verlag, Munich) and *"Die Geheimnisse der Weisen von Zion"* [*The Secrets of the Wise Men of Zion*], edited by Gottfried zur Beek (3rd ed. Verlag "Auf Vorposten", Charlottenburg). The book reveals the Jewish leadership of world Freemasonry and the systematic incitement of the world war by international Jewry for the ultimate purpose of destroying all the Christian monarchies of the world and Christianity, and of establishing Jewish world domination under the mask of individual national republics.[2]

"Die Judenfrage im Ausland" [*The Jewish Question Abroad*] is the title of a series of books published by the Deutschvölkische Verlagsanstalt (A. Götting), Hamburg. The first book in the series, "Die Judenfrage in England" [The Jewish Question in England] by G. E. Winzer, has been published and gives the reader a vivid picture of the anti-Semitism that is beginning to stir in England.

---

[2] Under the usual title *Protocols of the Elders of Zion*, this book has also been released in a new English edition in 2023, by Clemens & Blair.

Editor: These, of course, are all older, mostly German works, which were the main sources of information for Dinter. There naturally have been many relevant books published in the 100 years since then. Among the more recent are these three that I have written or edited:

- *Classic Essays on the Jewish Question: 1850 to 1945* (T. Dalton, ed.), 2022, Clemens & Blair.
- *The Steep Climb: Essays on the Jewish Question* (by T. Dalton), 2023, Clemens & Blair.
- *Eternal Strangers: Critical Views of Jews and Judaism through the Ages* (by T. Dalton), 2020, Castle Hill.

Then we have the two mentioned above in notes:

- *Protocols of the Elders of Zion: The Definitive English Edition* (T. Dalton, ed.), 2023, Clemens & Blair.
- *The Riddle of the Jews' Success* (by T. Fritsch), 2023, Clemens & Blair. (original from 1922)

Finally, I must mention the two National Socialist classics: *Mein Kampf* by Adolf Hitler, and *The Myth of the 20th Century* by Alfred Rosenberg. Both have been released in new translations by Clemens & Blair.